Dodendal

Valley of Dreams

A Novel

Jim Holmgren

Dodendal, Valley of Dreams
Jim Holmgren

Copyright © 2013 by Jim Holmgren
All Rights Reserved

Cover photo: Brandon Holmgren

This book was self-published by the author Jim Holmgren. No part of this book may be reproduced in any form by any means without the express permission of the author. This includes reprints, excerpts, photocopying, recording, or any future means of reproducing text.

Published in the United States.
ISBN 978-0-9898251-0-8

Also available as an eBook:
ISBN 978-0-9898251-1-5

This is a work of fiction. All the characters and events portrayed in this novel are fictitious.

Version 1.0
Printed by CreateSpace, a DBA of On-Demand Publishing, LLC

ISBN-13: 9780989825108
ISBN-10: 0989825108
Library of Congress Control Number: 2013915358
James Holmgren, Wappingers Falls, NY

*Dedicated to my wife, Alste,
to my children,
and to my extended family*

Forward

Music is an important theme in this book. It has a significant influence, and at points a profound impact, on the main characters. If you enjoy music and have access to any of the following pieces, you might enjoy listening to them when you encounter them in the chapters.

Chp 1	Jay Ungar, "Ashokan Farewell"
Chp 3	George F. Handel, *Water Music*, *Music for the Royal Fireworks*
Chp 5	Ludwig van Beethoven, "Moonlight Sonata – Adagio", "Fuer Elise" Claude Debussy, "Claire de Lune" Robert Schumann, "Traeumerei" Franz Liszt, "Liebestraum"
Chp 17	JS Bach, "Prelude & Fugue in G Major ('the Great') BMV 541"
Chp 22	Bruce Springsteen, "If I Should Fall Behind", *Live in Dublin* album
Chp 29	Duke Ellington, "Take the A Train"

Chp 36	Richard Wagner , "Liebestod" from his opera *Tristan und Isolde* Arvo Paert, "Spiegel im Spiegel"
Chp 38	JS Bach, "Prelude & Fugue in G Major ('the Great') BMV 541" Dave Brubeck, *Time Out* album, "Take the A Train" from his *Berlin, 1966* album
Chp 39	JS Bach, "Prelude & Fugue in G Major ('the Great') BMV 541"
Epilogue	Maurice Ravel, "Une barque sur l'ocean" Gabriel Faure, "Barcarolle No. 4 in A-Flat, Op. 44" Richard Rodney Bennett, "Barcarolle" Charles Tomlinson Griffes, "Barcarolle, Op. 6, No. 1" Franz Schubert, "Auf dem Wasser zu Singen" Sergei Rachmaninoff, *Vespers*

Part 1
VALLEY OF THE DEAD

Shortly after the summer holidays, maybe even while the last grains of beach sand were trickling out of our hair, our friend was either missing or was not, and nobody was willing to query the meaning of that casually tossed "vanished without trace," and I again failed to utter, swallowed the word *why*.

Guenter Grass, *Peeling the Onion*

Chapter 1
FRIDAY, JULY 3

Ian looked over his shoulder again. His squinting eyes blocked the afternoon sun and kept the sting of his sweat at bay. As before, he didn't see anyone who looked suspicious. But the modern-day bogey man was good at blending in with others.

He tried to smile at his concern. But he couldn't. He knew that the sweat wasn't just from the heat of the sun. It was also the tangible proof of his fear. He tasted it in the salty sweat on his lips.

Ian reached back and nervously stroked his shoulder bag. It was that one item among the others in his bag that made him nervous. If it hadn't been there, he wouldn't be on edge now. But it was.

He shook his head to rid himself of his nagging fear and continued on toward his apartment. It was the end of the week and he was looking forward to the upcoming Tricentennial celebrations. He tried to concentrate on that.

Ian passed others absorbed in their transponded music, news, lessons or whatever was being 'sponded into their heads. He preferred to tune his 'sponder out – to the extent it would be considered acceptable and therefore not attract attention. He liked being tuned out – to hear the noises of the walkways and streets – to be able to think things through.

He also liked studying others as he walked along – guessing what they were tuned into. Were they blissfully listening to a Bach partita, being angered by current events, pondering lessons on Corporate duties? But after a few minutes of being amused by so many oblivious figures floating along, a thinker like himself would invariably catch his eye. For a split second they would stare at each other – but then break off and continue on their separate ways.

Hoping to divert his mind from his shoulder bag, Ian tuned in to Bach's "Goldberg Variations". Of all the music Ian enjoyed listening to, Bach was his favorite. He was always swept up by the majestic beauty of the music – and by its sheer driving power. It always moved toward a logical conclusion – one that was inevitable. He could get completely lost in the music, or use its force to drive his thinking along. This latter effect was probably the reason many said it was best not to listen to Bach too much – that it could make one a person of interest.

Ian glanced nervously over his shoulder again.

The same was said about other classical music as well. So it was best to mix in other musical genres, and then mix in news, lessons and so on. "Keep under the radar." Supposedly listening to a lesson on corporate benevolence funding could buy five hours of Bach. But who knew for sure? Snooping on the general population would take huge amounts of resources, so Ian couldn't believe The Corporation would be that inefficient. But they certainly would have Organic Intelligence models targeting people, especially persons of interest. So it was best to play it safe – which was exactly what The Corporation wanted everyone to do.

Ian continued walking past the narrow gardens toward his apartment building, or "dom" (domicile, or domestic unit). When The Great Corporate Restructuring began in the mid-2050's, Poughkeepsie was designated a Corporate City. The decision was made to concentrate new living quarters in the city in what had become known as Midtown – that area between Old Town and what had been Vassar College. Fortunately, The Corporation had decided to keep many of the Old Town buildings on Main and Market Streets and much of the area down toward the Hudson River, and use them for recreational boutique shopping and entertainment. Regular shopping was done virtually without the need for "brick and mortar" stores.

The Corporation had also located the regional upper-form school in the facilities of the former Vassar College, which was where Ian taught historical awareness. This was a subject unique to the upper-form schools, since The Corporation had determined that the middle and lower forms didn't need to understand history beyond rudimentary levels. Ian was thankful that The Corporation hadn't torn down this historical site, but had restored many of its buildings to their former beauty with modern functions.

Ian reached his dom. He paused and casually studied the people who were now passing him by. Most were lost in their 'sponds. One or two looked at him as if to ask "what?" Normal reactions. But one never knew. Ian figured corpos must be well trained in following marks without attracting attention. The important thing was none of the people behind him appeared to be under twenty-five – the age range of cadets, the corpo-wannabes. Since they worked as volunteers, they were the ones who supposedly did routine following and observing.

Ian walked up to his dom – a large, tall, glass rectangle, similar to the many other doms in the district, but with enough difference to make it identifiable, if not interesting. There were small, pleasant gardens laced among the many buildings where one could sit on benches and enjoy a variety of hearty plants, weather permitting. There were no streets in the dom district, in fact there were few functioning streets in Poughkeepsie. After all, people could walk where ever they needed to go, and were encouraged to do so for health reasons. Or they could take a tram for longer distances. Other than for recreation there was no need to leave Poughkeepsie, as The Corporation emphasized.

The front door recognized Ian and opened for him. The front hall always had a numbing effect on him. Probably because it looked like the front halls of all the other doms. DomFab Corporation had made some modifications in each dom to make them appear different. For example, laying out some of the doms in reverse order to the others. But Ian only found this confusing. His dom's superintendent tried to spruce up its looks. Last week he had changed the lobby wallplay to a holoplay showing the signing of the Declaration of Independence. But for some reason it wasn't running right now. In the end the doms were all the same.

When the elevator opened, a man he recognized from one of the other floors stared at him blankly, nodded in recognition and walked out. Ian sighed and stepped in.

He took the elevator up to his apartment on the 8th floor. His door recognized him, opened, and closed after he walked in. Through his front glass wall he spotted the Hudson River in between the many other doms. Black clouds were building over the Shawangunks. They'd be in for a brutal storm. Of course, he would barely feel it, sealed away in the vault-like security of his dom.

Ian usually had a three-dimensional woodland theme with a running stream on the other walls. But there was nothing in play now. It must have been another glitch in the building wallplay system. Without a theme playing, his walls were a Spartan off-white. Ian dispensed a fruit drink and ordered up a shad dinner with mashed matoke and seaweed salad from the dispenser. He then 'sponded in to some Civil-War-era songs recorded by an instrumental folk group from early in the century.

As he sipped his drink and waited the few moments for his supper to appear, Ian glanced around his apartment. Listening to the "Battle Cry of Freedom", he noticed that his bust of Bach seemed out of place. Did it just look that way because the wallplay wasn't running? Did he just imagine it because of what was in his shoulder bag? He walked over and looked at it closely. There were no indications that it had been moved or touched. With his dom's air-filtration system there were never any foreign elements like dust in his apartment, so there would be no tell-tale indications that it had been disturbed. But it still seemed slightly out of place. Was his nagging fear of the corpos making him see things that weren't there?

Should he hide what was in his shoulder bag? No. These apartments were built with virtually no places to hide things. It was best to "hide things in the open" so they wouldn't attract attention. Having "nothing to hide" was the best defense. Yes, he'd do that before he went out later on.

The chime sounded for his dinner, so he pulled his meal out of the dispenser and put it on his table. The shad was a treat – processed directly from the Hudson at a small, local plant owned by the DelikatEssen Corporation. But the matoke and seaweed were nondescript.

When he had almost finished eating, the hauntingly beautiful melody of "Ashokan Farewell" began. Ian's gaze out of his front glass wall drifted toward the northwest's Catskill Mountains – to where the tiny hamlet of Ashokan had been. In the sad strains of the music he imagined a lone man from the hamlet slowly walking down a dusty, dirt road, turning and waving goodbye to his wife, children and aged parents as he headed toward the killing fields in America's great tragedy. He would never return. Either he would die on a far-away battle field, or a different man, scarred by the horrific slaughter, would come back.

When one peeled back the layers of history, the Lincolns and Davises, the Grants and Lees, it all came down to this single, lone man walking down that rutted, dirt road toward a future fraught with risk, and death, doing what he had to do – no, making the decision to do what he had to do. To Ian, this was history – individual, personal. That's why he was so passionate about the subject he taught.

Finishing his meal, Ian cleared his table and started rereading the corrected compositions his students had written. The assignment was to research and write about a topic of their choice related to American history and to tie it into the current Incorporated States of America.

Even though his students were from the top of society, they had difficulty with writing and even with reading. The world had been increasingly moving away from the written word, but with the initiation of mandatory transponder implants in 2062, most learning became much more auditory/oral and symbolic/scenic in nature. In lower-form schools, reading and writing beyond a rudimentary level had largely disappeared.

During a typical historical awareness session, students would discuss what they were exploring, what 'spondsources they were using. They would then 'spondcompose their presentations – largely verbal with visual objects and symbol-enforcers. In the end, Ian and the other students would 'spond into their presentations, or they would be presented in wallplay or holoplay format. Finally, they would discuss their work.

Students could call up books using their transponders, but for this exercise Ian required that they use hard-copy books from the school library where available. And instead of 'spondtranslating their thoughts into written form, he required that they check out one of the school's few remaining pads and type out their compositions. They then had to transmit their compositions to his pad. He read, corrected and commented on their compositions and transmitted them back to the students to rewrite/improve their work.

What he had now was their corrected work in printed form which he would read again and hand back to them with comments. This was, of course, an excruciating exercise that the students complained about at length. But Ian felt it was important from an historical perspective for young people to understand what laboriously plodding work people used to have to go through to compose their ideas. It would have been like a teacher in the early part of the century requiring students to sit down and hand-write a letter and send it through the mail. Unfortunately, this was one exercise Ian could no longer do, since students were no longer taught to write by hand and the postal service had disappeared long ago.

Ian hoped that this "slowed-down" process would put his students in a more contemplative mood, in which they would put more thought into their work than they usually did in their 'spondpresentations. After all, they were the leaders of tomorrow; a small, elite group of young people that The Corporation wanted to be able to think, though at the same time toe The Corporate line. It was a fine line to keep in focus. Or as Ian liked to believe, if a teacher was doing his job right, he was dancing on the razor's edge every day.

Chapter 2

After finishing a number of compositions, Ian decided he'd start off discussions in class with Linda Xiaobo's "The Rise of The Corporation". He put the last composition down and looked out his glass wall. The storm had blown through, the sky had cleared and the sun was moving lower across the Hudson. He hoped there wouldn't be too much damage done outside of Poughkeepsie. The doms had been built to withstand today's violent weather and older dwellings in Poughkeepsie could be repaired.

But during the Great Restructuring, The Corporation codified a trend already in process. It determined that it was too uneconomical to maintain and repair structures outside of the limits of designated Corporate Cities and Corporate Villages, so home and business owners outside the limits were left to fend for themselves.

After each violent storm there would be a trickle of "refugees" coming to Poughkeepsie. Ian felt sorry for them, but like any other dwellers in a Corporate City, he was concerned about the pressure they put on rental fees and home prices. DomFab wouldn't build more doms till they were sure they could fill them immediately, thus maximizing profits. So most of these migrants were forced to take up residence in the older houses in the city.

As the sun slowly became a brilliant, orange ball dipping toward the distant Shawangunks, Ian made himself ready to head out to the Walkway over the Hudson to observe this evening's Corporate fireworks. Modern light shows were much more impressive. But given the important historical milestone of the Tricentennial, The Corporation decided to go with the popular, old-fashioned fireworks.

Since the sun was going down, he wouldn't need to put on his UV-resistant, self-cooling clothing. What a pleasure to wear his old-fashioned chinos, t-shirt and sandals! As he walked out of his bedroom, Ian stopped and looked at his holomirror. He saw a 38-year-old man looking back at him. Light-brown hair with strands of gray. Hazel eyes. Ian figured he was not unattractive. Most women he had dated said he had a kind look. An intelligent, professorial look. None of that sounded very sexy to Ian. Women weren't lined up to meet him.

His 1.9 meters of height helped hide his 90 kilos. Turning the holomirror to the side view he reminded himself to straighten up and suck in his growing gut. Getting pudgy in his comfortable, middle-aged existence, he chuckled.

But when he looked into the eyes of the man in front of him, he found it difficult to hold the gaze. He saw disappointment. He didn't understand. Why disappointment? He felt fortunate every day to be teaching his favorite subject to students who were there to learn. And he knew he was lucky to have his apartment and rewarding interests that fortunately didn't strain his budget. He should feel happy, fulfilled. Well, maybe it was just the nature of the beast not to be satisfied with what he had. Ian shrugged and moved on.

It would still be brutally hot outside, so he grabbed his water pack as he headed to his door. Ian took one last glance back at his shoulder bag which he had casually flung onto his table to get that "nothing to hide" look. Satisfied, he walked out his door and headed to the elevator.

When the elevator door opened, Ian was greeted by Bill Wiley who lived up on the 10th floor. Bill was a bit shorter than Ian and had a broader build. He always had a warm smile that matched his easy-going nature – the kind of person who was easy to like.

Like most people, Ian didn't often communicate with the others who lived in his dom, let alone know their names. Most people had their 'sponders tuned in as they moved along. It was considered poor manners to interrupt them, beyond a polite nod. But Bill was outgoing, and since Ian was often tuned out, they usually struck up a conversation when they met.

"Hey, Ian, how's it going?" Bill smiled. "Is your wallplay on the blink too?"

"Yeah. Any word on when they'll be up?" Ian asked. Bill always seemed to know what was going on in the dom. Others just waited patiently for things to get fixed.

"The super says by later this evening, but don't hold your breath. You know how it is with PleaseCo. But what can you do when they're the only game in town? The Corporation should put the wallplay contract out to bid, but PleaseCo seems to have a lock. Probably some sweet deal between them and The Corp."

Ian nodded. Most people had that view of PleaseCo Entertainment Corporation.

When the front door to the dom opened, they were hit by a blast of hot air.

"Still hot, but cooling down," Bill commented. "The storm helped. There's almost a freshness in the air," Bill commented as he sniffed. "Look at all the debris lying around."

"I was going through some of my students' work so really didn't notice. Yeah, a strong one. Are you going to the Walkway for the fireworks?"

"Yeah. You too?"

Ian nodded.

"Mind if I tag along?"

"No. Glad for the company. Caitlin coming?"

"I'm meeting her there. She had to work late. Trying to increase her credits through overtime."

At Market Street, they were met by tuned-in people streaming northward toward the Walkway. They walked by the Civil-War-era Bardavon Opera House and saw that the old black-and-white, silent movie *Modern Times* would be presented with accompaniment by the Wurlitzer theater pipe organ, just as it would have been done in the early 1900's.

"You might get into the showing during the fireworks, but you wouldn't stand a chance afterwards," Bill remarked as he glanced up at the marquee. "PleaseCo is charging an arm and a leg then too. That place is a gold mine. I go there once in a while when Caitlin drags me in – kinda fun in a retro way. But you can always get a 3D version of any movie on the wallplay – so why come down here for it?"

"I like those old 2D movies at the Bardavon, especially the silent ones with the organ accompanying them," Ian said. "It's like stepping back in time to a simple era, when the world was just getting into technology and was excited by it. The best are the live presentations – especially the plays and the symphony orchestra performances. I try to imagine what people were like before 3D wallplays and transponders. This was their grand entertainment. Everything was so real, so tangible."

"You and your history!" Bill laughed, but added quietly, "Do you wish you had lived back then instead of now?"

Ian looked around. No one had settled into their pace nearby. "No, I guess not. I don't think life was a picnic for anyone at any time. But somehow their lives seemed to be more meaningful – more responsible – more independent."

After walking for a stretch in silence, Ian stopped Bill at the corner of Market and Main Streets. "Do you know the historical significance of this corner?"

Bill looked around and up and down the two streets, and finally said, "Mario's? I like their food. And Market and Main. Old, original, streets?"

"You're right. This was the 'epicenter' of Poughkeepsie at the time of the War for Independence. After the war in 1788, the US constitution ratification convention for New York met at the old courthouse that was located just across the street. After much debate, New York luminaries, like Alexander Hamilton and John Jay, finally ratified the Constitution of the United States, making New York the eleventh state to join the union."

"I never knew that," Bill said, staring across the street.

"There's an old historical brass plaque across the street. Not too many people would notice it."

"Thanks for the history lesson, perfesser."

Ian laughed at Bill's light-hearted admonition.

As they neared the end of Market Street, the majestic Walkway over the Hudson came fully into view. It was a great iron structure that reached 70 meters above the water and spanned the Hudson and low-lying land for a length of two kilometers.

Looking cautiously around, Ian continued, "One more history lesson for this evening. The Walkway was originally a railroad bridge built in the 1800's.

But after years of disuse in the late 1900's, a group of people took the initiative to transform it into a pedestrian walkway for all to enjoy. And the actual transformation was accomplished during the Great Recession. This could never happen today. First, who would take the initiative? And without an immediate, quantifiable payback, The Corporation would never help fund it."

"But how about The Corporation restoring Old Town?"

Ian paused, glanced around and continued in a quieter, confidential voice, "Did you know that The Corporation's one-quarter owner of PleaseCo? PleaseCo began buying up businesses in Old Town before the details of the Great Restructuring were announced. When they were announced and all the malls outside of Poughkeepsie were left out in the cold and eventually closed, Old Town pretty much became the only place to physically shop and go out for entertainment. I'm sure The Corporation's business case projected a large payback over the years, which it has certainly done. Just look at the Bardavon.

"And, by the way, the Bardavon had been scheduled to be knocked down in 1976. But visionary people saved it and restored it over years, not The Corporation. That's true of many of the other buildings in Old Town as well."

"I hear you," Bill said as he moved along, staring at the ground.

Damn, there I go again being the "perfesser", Ian thought as they moved along in silence. He realized he was going beyond just an historical description of what they were seeing. What was he trying to prove to Bill?

Finally, he said in a lighter voice, "Listen, I've been blathering on like an old 'perfesser'. Let's talk about something more important. How are your and Caitlin's plans coming along?"

Bill looked over at him and smiled, "We're both trying to build up credits for when we meet with the Life Changes official for approval. Caitlin has the better job so her overtime earns more credits. Her being a woman earns more 'intangible points' too. We're going for double approval, to get married and to have a baby."

"Great! But isn't it pretty difficult to get a double approval?"

"If we can get recommendations from both of our managers, we'll have a pretty good shot. Anyways, nothing ventured, nothing gained."

"That's for sure. Will you just have the mandatory Corporation wedding, or also a religious one after that?"

"Caitlin wants to have a Buddhist wedding too. You know, The Corporation wedding is pretty dry. You show up at the Bureau of Life Changes, pledge allegiance to The Corporation, say 'I do', and, boom, you're married. Caitlin thinks it's not very meaningful, and neither do I. Caitlin's Buddhist, so we'll have a Buddhist ceremony."

Bill looked uncomfortably at Ian. "My mother's a Congregationalist and would like to see us have a mixed Buddhist/Congregationalist ceremony. But Caitlin and her mother said no. I'm not the sharpest tool in the shed, but I do know enough not to cross the bride and future mother-in-law when it comes to wedding decisions. I told Mom no. She was disappointed, but understands."

"Smart man. They say all the groom has to do is show up and say, 'I do', and after that learn to say, 'Yes dear'." They both laughed. "If you get the double permit, will you hold off having your baby?"

"Caitlin wants to have it right away, and tell the official that too, so we can hopefully get a two-bedroom dom apartment. Plus, she's been saving up her eggs at the egg bank and has selected a good candidate, so she's ready to go. As soon as we get married, we'll work on lining up womb space at CaringMother. They have a good reputation for quality and good upper-band, tri-year nursery facilities, so Caitlin says that's the way to go." Then frowning he added, "Of course, they're the only wombcare facility in Poughkeepsie, so there's really no other choice."

"Have you two thought about waiting a little while after you get married before you have your baby? This will be your first experience of living together, and that could take some adjustment. This is your one shot to have a baby, so you want to be sure it's as great an experience as possible."

Bill took a long sip of water and finally responded, "I've thought about that too, but Caitlin said no, so we'll go for the baby right away."

"Preference for a boy or girl?"

Bill shrugged, "I'm OK with either, but Caitlin really wants a girl, so we'll go with a girl."

"Sounds great. I wish you two all the best."

They were approaching the Walkway, so they started taking in the elevated scene under the darkening sky as they walked along in silence. Ian reflected on their discussion. He noticed that Bill had deferred to Caitlin's views on all their important decisions so far. He wasn't surprised. Society had emphasized forging women's rights and independence for so long that men had increasingly taken a passive "back seat" in couples' decision making, as well as in most areas of modern life.

Ian was concerned about this same passive attitude that he saw in many of the boys in his classes – after all, they, along with the girls, would be the leaders of tomorrow. He had approached his school director about starting a special program to encourage males to become more assertive, or even having select all-male classes so they could find their own stride without being intimidated by girls in class. But she had turned him down. So Ian kept pushing and encouraging the boys in class as well as in his office when they stopped by.

When they reached the walk that lead up to the entrance to the Walkway, Bill said, "This is where Caitlin's going to meet me." Indicating a holokiosk. "She just 'sponded me that she'll be here in a minute."

When Ian stopped, he turned and caught the eye of a man who immediately looked away. Had he seen the man earlier as they were walking along talking? Ian wondered.

After a few minutes, Caitlin jogged up, breathing heavily. Her energetic personality always seemed ready to burst out of her petite size. Bill's large frame seemed to engulf her as he gave her a warm hug. And just as her size and temperament contrasted with Bill's, her dark hair and dark-hazel eyes contrasted with his sandy hair and gray eyes.

"We had a lot of work to do before we left!" Caitlin continued with a broad smile. "Well, my manager said she'd give a good recommendation to the Life Bureau – for the marriage AND the baby!"

Bill gave Caitlin another hug. Ian heartily congratulated them both.

"Now *you're* going to have to lock in your manager's approval. I'm sure that now that I have mine you should be able to get yours," Caitlin said.

"For sure! I'll revisit it with her on Tuesday. We're going to have to celebrate after the fireworks! Let's leave a little early so we can try to get into a restaurant before the crowds move in. Join us, Ian?" Bill asked.

"Thanks, but no. You don't need a third wheel," Ian responded.

"You sure? We'd like to have you along," Caitlin said, studying his face.

"I'm sure. Us old bachelors are used to being alone, and even come to enjoy it. Have a great time tonight. I'll enjoy the fireworks on my own. Congratulations again."

"Well, OK. We'll be seeing you soon," Bill said.

"Sure, keep me posted as things progress."

"Will do."

Ian watched them move off into the crowd. He had to admire Caitlin. She knew what she wanted and was going after it. But, like many men, Bill seemed to be just going along for the ride. This put more pressure on Caitlin to succeed. She must be at least a band 7 or 8 with a potential of being a 9, which would lock her in for marriage and a baby. But Bill was probably only a 5 or 6, and if he didn't actively pursue approval, he wouldn't get it. Then where would he be with Caitlin? Well, Ian wasn't going to solve their problems. As they disappeared into the night, Ian noticed they were hugging as they talked excitedly. He was happy for them.

Ian had become a "confirmed" bachelor over the years. He wasn't happy about it. But he was becoming comfortable with his station in life. He had dated a number of women, but he could never get comfortable enough to move beyond casual dating and the occasional fling. Most of the women only seemed to want to talk about themselves, their work and career potential. When he lost interest in them, they usually didn't take it well. And that's when things got complicated – sometimes threatening. He eventually figured it was easier not to date at all. *I guess I've become one of those passive males I'm concerned about*, Ian thought, letting out an audible sigh.

As he headed toward the entrance to the Walkway, Ian noticed commotion ahead. When he got closer, he stopped and stared in disbelief. He felt that same fear from after school growing in his heart as it reached up and choked him. He flashed back to his shoulder bag lying on his table at home.

Moving on, Ian tried to assess the situation.

Chapter 3

"Spencer, what are you doing? Come down from there!" Ian said perplexed as he looked up at one of his best students. Spencer Galloway was standing on a bench, smiling down at him, swaying back and forth.

"Hey, Ian, juz havin' my zay on'a ztate a'the ztate!" Spencer slurred out.

"You know this kid, mister?" an annoyed policeman asked Ian.

"Yes, he's one of my students, officer." Ian responded.

"Well, I'm just about to take him in for disturbing the peace. He's up there ranting on about how life's so unfair and it's The Corporation's fault."

Ian had heard what Spencer was saying to the growing crowd as he approached and had immediately scanned the faces to see if any had shown intense interest in what he was saying. Most were just laughing at him or milling around. But a few had the serious looks of corpos. He took a nervous look around and then responded, "I know his parents. I'll 'spond them immediately. Look officer, he's just a kid. I'll take responsibility and see that he gets home. Spence, get down here!" Ian reached up, grabbed Spencer's arm and dragged him down to a sitting position on the bench.

"Well ya better get him outa here quick. He was sayin' alota bad stuff about The Corporation. He could get himself in real trouble." The policeman then turned to the crowd and yelled, "OK folks, the show's over. Break it up."

"Thank you, officer. I'll see that he gets home safely," Ian said gratefully. While 'sponding Ian's mothers, he looked around and saw several more of his students walking toward him.

"Are you guys with Spencer? What's going on?"

"Some of us from the dorms decided to take you up on the offer for extra credit for coming to see the fireworks. Spencer and Juan came over from their homes and met us on campus. They had obviously been drinking," Allison reported.

"Any sniffing?" Ian asked concerned.

"I don't think so. I don't think they're into that," Allison said looking at Spencer as he looked up and smiled at her.

"Allison, yer zo butiful. Will'u marry me?"

"Has anyone else been drinking or sniffing?" Ian asked as he scanned the other faces.

"Yeah, Juan. He's passed out on that other bench back there," Jonathan said.

Ian looked back and thought he saw a figure lying on the bench in the faint light left over from the sunset.

"OK, Spencer's mothers are coming with a taxi in a few minutes. Let's try to move them back to a bench closer to the street. I'll 'spond Juan's parents."

As he stood up to concentrate on his 'spond, Ian scanned the few remaining faces left over from the crowd. His heart skipped a beat when he saw a young man staring intently at the whole scene. Ian bet he was a corpo. Maybe a cadet. It wasn't smart to engage corpos. Best to ignore them. But Ian was afraid for Spencer. He wasn't going to let that corpo hang around spying on them. He surprised himself as he boldly marched toward the man, ready to interrogate him. To his relief, the man turned and walked off toward the Walkway and soon disappeared into the streaming crowd.

Shaking from his unexpected bravery, Ian walked back to the others and coaxed Spencer into standing up.

"Can you walk without falling over?"

"Zhure, if Allizon holdzona me." Spencer said grinning at Allison.

"Jonathan, you hold on to Spencer. I'll get Juan," Ian said as he saw the relief on Allison's face.

When they had Spencer and Juan sitting slouched over on a bench by the street, Ian took a deep breath and asked the others, "OK, give me the story."

"Like Allison said, the five of us from the dorms were talking after class about going to the Walkway to watch the fireworks," Julie answered. "We thought it'd be fun and a good way to earn some extra credit. Spencer and Juan overheard us and kinda invited themselves to go along. But when they met us at the front gate a while ago, they were obviously drunk. We told them they should go home and sleep it off. But they tagged along, joking and giggling. You know, being pains in the butt."

"We tried to ignore them, hoping they'd turn back," Randal commented, "but they kept up with us, being noisy and obnoxious. I've never seen either of them act like this. I was surprised."

"I waz z'prized," Juan piped in trying to imitate Randal's deep, sober voice.

Ian looked at him and then at Spencer, who was passed out now.

"And then what happened?" he asked.

"We got up to where you found us," Allison joined in. "Suddenly Spencer jumped up on the bench and started telling all the people walking along that they didn't know what freedom and independence was, that they were just leading the controlled, thoughtless lives that The Corporation wanted them to."

"We tried to get Spencer to get off the bench but he ignored us, so we stepped back into the shadows," Rochelle jumped in. "We were embarrassed, but didn't want to leave the two of them alone. Luckily, most people seemed to assume that they were just a couple drunk kids and ignored them and continued walking. Or they stopped for a few minutes, listened, laughed and walked on."

"How long was this going on before the cop got there?" Ian asked concerned.

"Not long. He got there and then you showed up shortly after that," Allison said. "Ian, I'm really glad you got there when you did. That cop was really getting mad. I was afraid for Spencer."

Ian looked down at the two boys and nodded. Smiling faintly he said, "Well, all's well that ends well."

"William Shakespeare," Julie said automatically.

They all laughed.

"Look, thanks for caring for your classmates and sticking around. I'm proud of you. Have any of you been drinking or sniffing?"

They all shook their heads no.

"And you're all OK?" Ian asked looking at each of them as they nodded.

"Then take off and have fun. Be careful and stick together! 'Spond me if you run into trouble. I'll wait here for their parents – they'll be here soon. Ya done good!"

"Extra credit?"

"Oh, yeah!"

As the five of them walked off talking animatedly amongst themselves, Ian watched them and considered what had happened here. They were from executive families. From the Millbrook and Rhinebeck executive patents. One from Manhattan. So they were living in the dorms at the school. They had been born into lives of privilege, destined to attend an upper-form school. Eventually they'd be executives in corporations somewhere. They were good kids, but they had never known adversity.

Then he looked down at Spencer and Juan. Both were from upper-band families. They were attending upper-form school because of their exceptional abilities. But they were "outsiders" who didn't belong in an upper-form school, as many executive parents would complain. They tried to fit in, but there were always the subtle comments from the others that they didn't belong there. Ian didn't allow that kind of talk in his class room, but he knew it went on outside class. He could imagine them "inviting themselves along" and the others reluctantly acquiescing.

And Spencer. Ian was almost shocked. But knowing young adolescents, he was never shocked. What had gotten into him? He was a highly intelligent, gifted kid. But he tended to hold back in class. Kind of shy. So jumping up on a bench and haranguing?

Then he heard a laugh from the group of disappearing kids and could see in the light of the lamp they were passing under that they were all circled around Allison. Hmmm. She was very popular at school. Very good looking. Already a beauty. But also an outstanding personality. Friendly with everyone.

He recalled the awkward crush he had had on Madeline Garrison when he was a little older than these two. She was gorgeous – an unattainable goddess from his view. But he loved her because she acknowledged his existence, in spite of her being popular with the "in crowd". He, a socially awkward kid who dreamed about getting more of her attention. But in the end he appreciated being occasionally on the periphery of her circle, catching her warm glances, her friendly words. He sometimes thought of Pluto being in the outer reaches of the solar system. Cold, dark. But those few faint rays of the sun were proof that all was well.

Yes, he wasn't that old. He understood Spencer's and Juan's actions. He looked down at them and felt a tug at his heart. He could imagine their parents lecturing them tonight for their foolish actions. But then, after they dropped into their beds to sleep off their drunkenness, he could see their mothers taking one last look into their bedrooms to be sure they were OK. Seeing their sleeping babies, but also understanding what their budding adults had done.

Just before their parents showed up, Ian thought about how he had gone on with his life after school. He hadn't kept in touch with Madeline – not that she would have wanted to. No, he had a warm feeling in his heart, knowing that she was out there somewhere. Knowing this, he knew that all was well.

When he was in his late twenties he met an old friend who told Ian that Madeline had unexpectedly died of a brain aneurism. At that point a perfect world that existed somewhere at the center of his being disappeared. Its sun was extinguished. He sadly accepted what he had really known all along. He lived in a world that was not perfect.

He wished better for these two sleeping boys. He wished for them to find their constant suns, but ones whom they dared to approach – ones they could hold.

Ian looked up toward the Walkway. Sitting on their remote bench he felt detached from the swirling life on the Walkway. But as he turned his head toward the sprinkled lights in the night skies of Poughkeepsie, he felt a contentment sitting with his boys. Protecting them.

As Ian walked along, he kept a constant eye out for the young man he suspected of being a corpo. His stomach was in knots again, wondering what he would do if he saw him. Best to do nothing, or maybe just stare at him as if to say, "Yeah, I've got your number too." His hope was that the incident with

Spencer had been so brief that the corpo hadn't triangulated their identification. He convinced himself that if he had been a cadet, he wouldn't have the resources to triangulate at all.

Ian was in a conflicted state of nervous anticipation and relief. Nervously scanning faces, yet relieved when each face was not the man's.

Entering the Walkway, he could see PleaseCo sight-seeing boats out on the river with reveling customers who could pay their exorbitant fees. Ian tuned in Handel's *Water Music*, which had originally been composed for the king of England in the early 1700's. The king would listen to the *Water Music* as he floated down the Thames on his barge waiting for the fireworks to begin, at which time he would be serenaded by Handel's *Music for the Royal Fireworks*. Ian chuckled about the appropriateness of his selection. He would switch over to the *Fireworks Music* once the show began.

Weaving his way through the hoards of people making merry, Ian was relieved that he hadn't seen the young man again. Eventually, he settled into a spot with a good vantage point. When twilight turned to true night and the fireworks were ready to begin, Ian observed people closing into couples and groups separate from him, obviously enjoying each others' company. At first he felt alone, but gradually he got swept up in the spirit of Tricentennial celebrations.

And somewhere in the back of his mind he felt that he wasn't alone out there far above the Hudson.

Chapter 4

Like everyone else on the Walkway, Ian was enjoying the fireworks. At each burst of light and boom he joined into the "oohs and ahs!" It was fun. He guessed that not too many people were really thinking of the meaning of the Tricentennial. The Corporation only transponded vague references to the War of Independence and the causes and thoughts leading up to it. The typical transponded commentary was to build up the accomplishments of The Corporation and how it had saved the American people from the brink of disaster, thus enabling this perfect evening and free fireworks brought to them by The Corporation.

He was sure people weren't tuned in to The Corporation's 'sponds, but in to their favorite music to accompany the fireworks. Ian liked to guess what kind of music they were listening to as he glanced around. Though The Corporation did control and censor music that was transponded, it was surprisingly liberal in what it did allow to get through. Basically, only music that had anti-Corporate messages was not allowed.

He guessed that his fellow classical music lovers were the ones not moving a lot, but seemed to be transfixed on the fireworks. The Elvis cult types were obvious. The men wore DA (duck's ass) hairdos like the King, and were dancing with typically middle-aged women, more into the dancing and music than into the fireworks. He could also tell the ones who were tuned into techno music. They were in their 20's, here as individuals, or "individuals in groups", stomping around in a trance.

Ian wasn't sure when he first noticed a woman who had also obviously noticed him. As he looked around at the revelers, guessing their music preferences, he occasionally caught glimpses of her in the periodic flashes of light from the fireworks. What caught his attention was that she always appeared to be looking in his direction. She never glanced away. If she had, he would have been suspicious of her as a possible corpo. Ian was careful not to stare back but carefully studied her and her situation. In the flashes of light she appeared to be attractive, and alone. Her being alone was not out of the ordinary, since people often attended events alone, women as much as men. Like himself she seemed to be a stationary, independent entity in this sea of ongoing movement.

He decided to walk past her and further up the Walkway. After he had come to a stop and started looking around at the crowds again, he saw that her gaze continued to be in his direction. She was obviously looking at him and didn't mind him knowing it. What should he do? He decided to fix his gaze briefly on her and smile. Anything beyond that could be considered aggressive behavior. She would have to take the initiative if she was interested. Ian continued to look at her for an acceptable seven or eight seconds, then turned around, leaned on the rail and watched the fireworks.

After a few minutes, a husky but unmistakably feminine voice said, "I wonder what the people were like who were watching fireworks during the Bicentennial celebrations."

The woman's hands were holding the rail very close to his. This made him feel vaguely uncomfortable as he turned to look at her. What struck him was her beaming, confident smile as she gazed up at the fireworks. So, she was enjoying the fireworks and just happened to be standing next to him, not hitting on him? This put him at ease. She had pale skin, dark hair, and a shapely build – just on the petite side.

Her question was one that he had asked himself this evening as well. It wasn't small talk so he didn't want to give a small-talk response. But it could invite criticism of their present-day Corporate world. She didn't seem to be a corpo. Corpos didn't have beaming smiles. Of course, as soon as you thought you had their dark personalities nailed down, they would surprise you. Best to be careful.

He smiled and said, "I think very much like us. Humans don't change that fast. Maybe they watched their fireworks wondering what the Centennial people had been like."

She chuckled, putting him more at ease.

"Though," he added reflectively, "I think they probably thought more about what they were celebrating – since they were closer in time to 1776."

"A very thoughtful, studied response." She turned and looked up at him, continuing to smile radiantly. "I couldn't help but notice that you seemed to study people on the Walkway more than you watched the fireworks."

Man, she really didn't believe in chitchat, and was certainly open about having her eye on him. Where was feminine coyness? The world hadn't changed that much. "Just out of curiosity, how long were you watching me?"

"Oh, from about the time you took notice of me."

Ah, there it was! Ian couldn't help but laugh. She was refreshingly honest. So he told her how he watched people and guessed what music they were tuned into. As he talked she gazed up at him, listening attentively. She had light eyes, probably pale blue.

"So, what do you think I was listening to?" She asked.

"Hmmm, you're a hard one. Straight-forward but complicated, reflective. I'd say classical. Not Mozart – too obviously beautiful. Something more powerful, hard-driving – Beethoven."

She laughed, "Way off. Actually I was listening to Diana Krall, easy-going jazz from early in the century."

"Well, there go my powers of observation! But your voice does remind me of hers, low and husky, but definitely feminine. What do you think I was listening to?"

"Hmmm. Since you brought up classical music and seem to have an understanding of it, and you're obviously the observant, analytical type, I'd say Bach."

"Wow, you win the stuffed bunny! Actually, Bach *is* my favorite, though I was listening to Handel's water and fireworks music. You were close." Ian couldn't help staring at her. "By the way, my name is Ian Vanderkill," he said bowing. He would not ask her hers; it would be too forward.

"I'm Siobhan Carlson." She said also bowing.

"Spelled the modern, phonetic way, S-h-a-v-o-n?"

"No, the old, Celtic spelling."

"Beautiful name. Do you have an Irish background?

"Yes, on my mother's side. But mostly my parents liked the name. There was a warrior queen named Siobhan in Ireland in the pre-English days. But there's no solid proof she existed. Like King Arthur. My father's side was Swedish-German, therefore the last name."

"An interesting and attractive combination," Ian said, realizing he was flirting but he couldn't help himself. He was attracted to her. *God, that radiant smile!*

The fireworks were building up to the grand finale, so they both started watching again, joining the quaint, if not downright corny, "oohs and ahs" of the crowd and laughing after each one.

When the finale was over they joined the crowd heading back to Poughkeepsie. "Old", Old Town, nearest the river, had many small, personal restaurants, cafes, bistros, bars, and snort'n'sniffs. As they walked along chatting about the fireworks and music, Ian felt that if he was going to get to know Siobhan better he would have to take the initiative. Alcohol and other "enhancers" would be out of the question, and a restaurant could carry too many connotations, so he asked her, "I was going to stop at Anna's Konditorei on the way home for a coffee and kuchen. Would you like to join me?"

"Sure, I'd like that."

At Anna's they only waited for a few minutes for a small, intimate table for two tucked into the windowed corner. In the privacy of their corner, Ian studied Siobhan's light blue eyes and raven-black hair. Her skin appeared even more pale in contrast. She was a classic Celtic beauty. The name Siobhan suited her well.

They ordered a "kaennchen" of kona coffee, marzipan torte for Siobhan, and for Ian, his weakness, Scharzwaelder Kirschtorte. After the waiter walked away, they smiled awkwardly at each other. This was not a typical first evening.

Typically the two would have been introduced to each other by mutual friends, or they would have met through a Corporation-certified transponder matching service. In either case, Siobhan would have used a Corporation-certified service like Manhunt to see if Ian had ever been accused of, let alone tried and convicted of, a sexual infraction. Manhunt would also contain comments from other women who had dated Ian. They would also grade him on various parameters like courtesy, likeability, dependability, and overall. Manhunt was open to women only, free of charge. Ian's mother had told him that he was rated well in the courtesy and likeability categories, but consistently low in the commitment and dependability categories.

"What's the frown about?" Siobhan asked. "A credit for your thoughts."

"Siobhan, I'd like to get to know you better. But when you check me out on Manhunt, you'll find out I'm not even rated average."

"Oh, I think I already know you better than what Manhunt could tell me. Plus, don't you know that women are always looking for a challenge, looking at the raw materials and figuring out how they can change them for the better?"

They both laughed, but then Ian added reflectively, "But then the disappointment sets in when they realize that men are a lot harder to change than they thought."

"Well, I'm not too concerned," Siobhan smiled warmly.

Ian studied her face. Her strong jaw and somewhat wide mouth kept her from being a conventional beauty. But those irregularities added to her personality, as did her beautiful eyes that had an edge of sadness. They spoke of life experience. The women he had gotten to know were mostly not out of their twenties yet. He guessed Siobhan to be in her early to mid thirties.

What he saw in Siobhan's face was a quiet, optimistic certainty that he had first seen in her on the Walkway. That, coupled with her thoughtful comments and responses, led him to feel she embodied a certain feminine grace.

Their order arrived, jolting Ian out of his thoughts. He poured their coffee and glanced at her somewhat guiltily, but then smiled. Ian was careful not to ask too many personal questions, but Siobhan appeared to be quite open. Her family home in New Hamburg down the Hudson had been flooded and finally destroyed by the rising waters of the ocean and storm surges.

"So I became a 'coastal refugee' like so many others. Since I worked in Poughkeepsie and it's on high ground, I looked for housing here. I found an old house in the southern part of the city. I love the old place, but it wasn't built to withstand the violent weather we have today. I'm afraid it's just a matter of time till it'll be torn beyond repair by the weather. I hope to get into a dom before that happens. I was thankful today's storm didn't do any damage to it," Siobhan added pensively.

"I live in one of those doms," Ian said. "I have to admit I feel totally secure when the storms hit. But it's like being locked into a vault – such an artificial existence. I love the personalities of those old homes."

"If you're looking for authenticity, I'll be glad to change places with you," Siobhan said teasingly.

"I wouldn't want to deprive you of such a real-life, though maybe terrifying, experience!" Ian countered as they both laughed.

While talking, Ian noticed people vacating Anna's quickly. He tuned in to the weather alert. A follow-on storm was building up in the Catskill Mountains, and would hit Poughkeepsie in forty-three minutes. Since the bill was by default half charged to each of them based on the entry scan, Ian and Siobhan were free to go. Each 'sponded a tip and the waiter thanked them on their wait out.

"It'll only take me about twenty minutes to walk home. But I'm guessing it'll take you a while longer. Will you be alright?" His first faux pas of the evening – such a sexist question. The neo-feminist sayings of "helping is domination" and "dependence is submission" flashed through his mind and he felt himself reddening. "Look, I'm sorry I said that. It was a knee-jerk reaction."

"It's OK. And yes, I'll be fine. If I can't make it, I'll duck into a tram booth and wait for the storm to blow over."

As they walked out into the cooling night, Ian decided to go for broke. "Siobhan, I've got a reservation on the Henry Hudson paddlewheel tomorrow at 10am to head down to Bear Mountain. Would you like to go?"

"Do you think they'll still have an opening?"

"They might." Pausing, he continued, "'Spond it tonight and let me know if you can make it. I have an open address."

"OK, if they have an opening, I'd like to go. Well, Ian From-the-Creek, I'm glad we hooked up tonight. Hope to see you tomorrow."

Ian's gaze followed her solitary form disappearing into the night. She already seemed like a dream as the dimness of the walk lights pulled her from his world. He was heading to his modern dom, and she into a past that would soon be blown away.

Ian was attracted to Siobhan. They had had an enjoyable evening together. He was pleased that she seemed interested in him and was not focused on herself. In fact, she had said very little about herself. He knew he had a weakness for women with her physical appearance, but his attraction went beyond that. There was a certain mystery and humanity to her that had burrowed its way into his thoughts – that excited him but also disturbed him.

And why did he feel this need to protect her? And from what? From whom? He had almost offered to make a reservation for her. He'd have to be careful – he didn't want to lose her before he even had a chance to get to know her.

Ian revisited his evening with Siobhan on the way home. He remembered every word, every nuance in their conversations. Every smile, every glance. Was she really interested in him? He hoped so.

But when he walked into his apartment, the sight of his shoulder bag lying on the table, immediately changed his thoughts to the incident with his students at the Walkway. A cold shudder raced through his body as he picked it up and pulled out that one item that had caused his fears earlier in the day. He sat down and began to reread Spencer's composition, "The Declaration of Independence". Spencer showed deep thinking well beyond his years. Independent thinking that Ian encouraged in his students, and was so gratified when he saw it.

But he was afraid Spencer may have stepped over the line in what he said about The Corporation. If this paper were to fall into the wrong hands, Spencer could be in serious trouble. He didn't want to think about what would happen if a corpo got ahold of it. And that episode at the Walkway? Somehow he'd have to pull Spencer back over the line to safety without dampening his spirit.

He thought back to that young man who was so intently observing Spencer at the Walkway. He was sure he hadn't seen him again this evening. But if he were a corpo he knew Ian had "made" him. If so, wouldn't he have passed Ian on to someone else?

Siobhan? Suddenly he was thinking about her in the light of suspicion that was so natural in today's world. She had certainly been studying him. And she had approached him. Why had she picked him up? Had her quiet grace really been the calculated maneuverings of a corpo? Had he been such a blind fool that he hadn't seen it?

As these dark thoughts were cycling through his head, he received a 'spond from Siobhan. She was looking forward to seeing him at 10 at the paddlewheel. It ended with a 'spond vision of her smiling at him. He halted the vision and studied it. The same smile he had seen so many times tonight. A deeply human, natural smile that had enchanted him before and did so again.

No, she was no corpo. He couldn't believe it. But there *was* something about her that he wasn't reading right. There was something, or someone, that flitted across the periphery just beyond his view. Something that he wasn't seeing because of his attraction to her.

Ian got into bed and lay for a long time, his mind racing with all that had happened today. He finally dropped off into a restless, dreamless sleep.

Chapter 5

The Hudson River Valley has always been enchanted – some say haunted. Washington Irving gave witness to this in "The Legend of Sleepy Hollow", "Rip Van Winkle" and other stories. "[Sleepy Hollow] is a little valley, or rather lap of land among high hills, which is one of the quietest places in the whole world. A small brook glides through it, with just a murmur enough to lull one to repose, and the occasional whistle of a quail, or tapping of a woodpecker, is almost the only sound that ever breaks in upon the uniform tranquility ... A drowsy, dreamy influence seems to hang over the land, and to pervade the very atmosphere."

Up the river from Sleepy Hollow lie the Hudson Highlands – a stretch of the Hudson that the Native Americans avoided. The steep, rocky mountains made farming and hunting difficult and the narrow, constricted flow of the Hudson in the Highlands made navigation treacherous. But the early Dutch settlers also came to understand from the Native Americans that the Highlands were haunted. Over time, the Dutch came to believe that the highlands were protected at the north end by the brooding Storm King Mountain. At the south end they were jealously guarded by de Heer van Dunderberg and his ghostly minions.

The Lord of Dunderberg had his ways of making himself known. Indeed then, as now, it was common to see clouds build up on the western side of the Hudson through the Highlands, as if held back by an invisible hand, while the sky on the eastern side remained a cloudless blue. The clouds would build into churning black towers, finally releasing torrents of rain and angry bolts of lightning and thunder, seeming to center over the majestic Dunderberg, or Thunder Mountain. Then suddenly the clouds would jump across the Hudson and race across the eastern Highlands releasing the rest of their pent-up fury. At the same time the wild winds would race up the canyons of the Hudson in the Highlands causing such an echoing howl, that one would repent of having ever doubted de Heer.

When the Dutch settlers of Nieuw Nederlandt began moving up the Hudson looking for new lands to settle beyond Nieuw Amsterdam and the lower Hudson Valley, they found a small, elevated, but inhabitable valley at the northern base of Dunderberg. Since it was uninhabited, several families moved in, cleared back many of the trees, and began farming the rocky soil. As they eventually discovered, the Native Americans along the river avoided this valley because it was haunted. Using the Native Americans' descriptions of the valley, the new settlers named the valley Dooddal, Dead Valley, or alternatively Dodendal, Valley of the Dead.

The Dodendalers lived a peaceful, secluded, agrarian existence in their quiet little valley for the next hundred years. But many changes were taking place in the world outside their dreamy valley. The British took over Nieuw Amsterdam and Nieuw Nederlandt and renamed them New York, and Englishmen started moving up the river and settling next to the earlier Dutch settlers.

In 1777, less than a year after the War of Independence began, a contingent of 2000 British troops landed at the southern base of Dunderberg, moved north through the gap between Dunderberg and the Timp, and arrived in Dodendal. Legend has it that when they asked the inhabitants what the name of their hamlet was, Dodendal, or Dooddal, sounded like doodle to their English ears, so they started taunting the villagers by singing "Yankee Doodle" over and over. After they took provisions from the villagers, the soldiers continued north to attack Forts Montgomery and Clinton. Some old documents indicate that the soldiers had brutalized the villagers and laid waste to some of their buildings. Perhaps as a badge of pride for their suffering, the inhabitants renamed their hamlet and valley Doodletown after independence.

Over the next hundred-fifty years, growth and activity was the hallmark of New York, The Empire State. The Hudson became a great, flowing highway to the Midwest after the Erie Canal was built. And wave upon wave of immigrant populations landed at the lower end of the Hudson on Ellis Island and from there poured forth up the river and out to the Midwest and beyond. But Doodletown, hidden and constrained in its valley high above the Hudson and surrounded by Dunderberg, the Timp, West Mountain and Bear Mountain, continued on as it always had. The souls who lived in this quiet valley continued to farm, fish, and hunt, but also they ventured forth to the outside world to bring in extra income.

In the early 1900's, influential New Yorkers realized that it was important to begin setting aside land for recreation in the increasingly crowded Hudson Valley. As a result large portions of the highlands were bought up and a hundred-kilometer string of state parks were established. When Bear Mountain State Park was founded and began to expand outward, the Doodletowners eventually found themselves surrounded by it. One by one, they sold their property to the state and left; typically taking as much building material from their homes as possible.

By 1976, the Bicentennial, all of the valley had been purchased by the state, and after three hundred years Doodletown was reverting back to its natural state. As with much of the parklands in the highlands, one could now wander through the mountains and valleys and by the streams and ponds, pondering the life of the people who had lived here and were now gone; with only the disappearing stone walls, stone building foundations and occasional graveyard to indicate that they had ever been there. Doodletown was again the Valley of the Dead.

Saturday, July 4

Ian arrived at the Poughkeepsie dock at 9:45. The *Henry Hudson*, a replica of the old Mississippi sternwheelers, was already being boarded. The morning was already hot, but not unbearably so, and the forecast called for a partly sunny day with no inclement weather, so they should have a good time. Like the others boarding the boat, Ian was wearing his self-cooling, UV-protectant clothing as a precaution, and had his cooled water pack slung over his shoulder. Though it wasn't supposed to get over 40 degrees Celsius today, even that could be threatening if it got too humid or one were in direct sunlight too long.

Ian glanced up the street and saw Siobhan hurrying toward the boat. Ian chuckled. Siobhan's protectant clothing was not exactly the sexiest get up, especially the floppy, wide-brimmed hat. But he was glad she was prepared for adverse weather.

"Sorry I'm late. I just couldn't get going this morning."

Ian noticed that she did seem a bit frazzled, but that she had a short chuckle when she took in his outfit.

"No problem. Glad you made it and that you didn't get caught in that storm last night."

They walked up the gangway. The scancheck gave them the green light to go on board, and they proceeded to the upper deck stern. The bow was already packed on all three levels. Their position would give them good views of both sides of the river without being too crowded. The steam whistle blew and the long, massive connecting rods to the paddle wheel began their powerful back-and-forth movement, sending the wheel into an urgent, splashing spin. They both stood mesmerized for a few minutes looking at the moving paddle wheel, caught up in the spell of this historic anachronism.

"Did you sleep well?" Ian asked. "We were up pretty late."

"Yes, but it wasn't really restful. Maybe a nagging fear of my house falling down around my head! How about you?"

"After reading several students' compositions, I dropped right off. It'll do it to you," he smiled. That would have been a lead in to her asking about his work as a teacher, and from there into questions from him about her work, but she didn't bite. "Have you been to Bear Mountain before?"

"Yes, a few times."

"Ever been to Doodletown?"

"No. I remember seeing signs pointing down a path, but I never did go there. Just the usual – swimming, picnicking, cable car to the top of Bear Mountain."

"Do you feel up to a couple klicks' hike up to Doodletown?"

"Sure, what's there?"

"Well, it's an interesting old ghost town. You can still see the old stone walls and find some of the house foundations if you look closely. And a spooky, old cemetery."

"A bit morbid! Do you always go on first dates up there?" Siobhan laughed.

"No. But that's where my name-sake family originated in America almost 400 years ago. You could say this is our Quadracentennial."

"Oh, I get the family tour?"

"Not much left, but I can give you some perspective and tell you some family stories. I noticed last night that you knew what my last name meant, so you obviously are somewhat familiar with the original Dutch settlers."

"Yeah, I guess that comes with being born and raised in the Hudson Valley."

"Years ago I met people from Holland. They had no idea that a 'kill' was a creek in Old Dutch. The one finally mentioned a couple place names in the Netherlands with 'kill' in it, and pointed out that they were situated on creeks or rivers. So they believed me."

At about that time the captain announced that they were passing the old Fishkill Landing on the left.

"And of course there was the animal rights organization from Washington in the 1990's that also had no idea what 'kill' meant and started a campaign to get the village of Fishkill to change their name to Fishlove – to promote positive feelings in children for animals," Ian said.

"Oh Yes. Odd that they never brought up the Catskill Mountains, the Beaver Kill or the Landsman Kill!" Siobhan added.

They both rolled their eyes and laughed at that well-known local recounting.

The paddle wheel soon cruised past the remains of Bannerman's castle on Pollepel Island. They were entering the Hudson Highlands, guarded by Storm King Mountain on the right. On the left was Mount Beacon, which got its name from the fire signals lit on its top during the War of Independence to warn the people of the valley that the British were coming. The Hudson flowed along squeezed by verdant, rocky mountains on either side.

They eventually floated by West Point, which had been a critical, narrow, sharp bend in the river where the American army had stretched a massive chain across the river to block the British ships from proceeding further up the river. After the war, a national military academy was built there to train army officers. But when The Corporation took over the government, it was identified as a monumental waste of taxpayers' money and was shut down. When the armed services were outsourced to the defense contractors' consortium, they found ways to train their officers in a much more efficient manner.

After they had passed the swirl and suck of World's End, the gothic Bear Mountain Bridge came into view, stretching between the mountains on either side of the river like an elegant silver necklace. Then cruising under the bridge, they landed at the Bear Mountain dock and the passengers disembarked.

Ian and Siobhan walked up hill with the crowd till they saw the blue-and-yellow historical marker that briefly detailed Doodletown's historic encounter with the British during the War of Independence, though it didn't indicate that the barely-noticeable trail behind the sign eventually led to what was left of Doodletown.

On the trail they noticed that there was no one ahead of them, or behind. There was an almost immediate hush as the noise of the crowds behind them quickly receded. In its place was the droning buzz of cicadas. Even though the dense underbrush and trees along the way prevented the heat of the sun from coming through, they also prevented any breeze from reaching the two.

The atmosphere they were entering was different from what they had just left. It wasn't oppressive, but it did have a denser, richer feel to it, almost as if there were more air to breathe. There was a smell of damp, rotting leaves – an autumnal smell that causes one to slow down and reflect on the passing of life.

When they found the old road, now reduced to a gravelly path coming up from the river by Iona Island, they took a sip of their cool water before proceeding up into the Valley of the Dead. They almost immediately saw steps leading up to nowhere through the old stone wall on the right. Siobhan marveled at the towering trees with vines hanging down. Ian grabbed a long vine, yanked to test it, and then ran and swung out over the downhill path. He made a long, slow-motion arc through the air and slowly came gliding back to his take-off point.

Siobhan laughed, "I've got to try that!"

Like Ian, she too made a slow-motion arc into the air, whooping and laughing, and came slowly gliding back. Ian instinctively caught her by the waist as she zoomed in. This was the first time he had touched her, and he felt conflicted.

He liked what he felt but was concerned about her reaction to the contact. But she smiled at him, showing complete trust in him. As if she had known him for a long time and wasn't concerned about being so isolated with him.

"Wow, that was so much fun! But I didn't think I'd ever land again. Motion just seems to be so slow here!"

"It's that the vine is so long," Ian explained. "It must be twenty meters to the top of it!"

After they each tried it again, they laughed and then continued their walk up the path.

They soon came around a sharp bend and encountered two mature whitetail deer. Siobhan gasped, but the deer just looked at them, slowly turned and walked off into the deep woods.

"That's the closest I've ever come to a deer."

"Yeah, all the animals are tame up here. They probably see so few humans and the ones they do are typically calm and quiet – lost in their own thoughts. Maybe they just see us as being no threat."

They continued walking up the road till they came to a pond on the left and could see a cemetery on the other side. There was a man sitting on a large rock near the cemetery, gazing into the waters of the pond. Ian waved, but the gazer didn't respond.

They soon came upon a woman sitting on a portable chair next the pond, gazing off toward Dunderberg and the few hints of the Hudson far below. They were only a few meters from her and in her peripheral vision when Ian and Siobhan both gave a short wave and said "Hi". She didn't respond. Siobhan looked up at Ian with a confused look as they continued in silence.

When they were out of ear shot, Siobhan said quietly, "Ian, that was spooky. What's going on?"

"This is an incredibly peaceful and quiet valley, being surrounded by mountains and park lands. So as you've probably noticed there are no human sounds coming into the valley. And because of the mountains and the river, and the steep access, it really is cut off. You'll rarely see many people here.

"But I also have to tell you that the original immigrants settled here because it was uninhabited. The Native Americans wouldn't come to this valley because they said it was haunted. The Dutch settlers named it *Dooddal* or *Dodendal*, which is Old Dutch for Valley of the Dead. *Dodendal* eventually became anglicized into Doodletown."

After a pause Ian continued, "I've hiked many places in the Hudson Valley, especially the parks in the Hudson Highlands, and have seen many peaceful, haunted reminders of worlds now gone. But I have to agree with the Native Americans that there seems to be a special haunted quality here. It latches on to you and draws you into a sort of timelessness – where you're open to seeing what's gone before – and maybe what can be."

Ian looked into Siobhan's eyes and saw some concern mixed with disbelief.

"Are you saying those people were ghosts?" She asked kiddingly.

Ian smiled and said, "No. Listen, let's continue up the path along the creek and just go with the flow so to speak. I like tuning into some flowing piano music." At this point they tuned in and synced up on Beethoven's "Moonlight Sonata's Adagio" and "Fuer Elise", Debussy's "Claire de Lune", Schumann's "Traeumerei", Liszt's "Liebestraum", and selected pieces from Satie's "Gymnopedies" and "Gnossiennes", Bach's "Goldberg Variations" and Chopin's "Nocturnes".

They started walking up the path again. After leaving the pond, the woods closed in and the way became dark and hidden. The stream at their side wafted a cool breeze up at them. They could see the occasional, casual movement of small animals on the ground and gliding hawk up through the ancient trees. The old stone wall on the right hinted at the world that had been here and had now all but vanished. The music enhanced the tranquil, ethereal feel of their surroundings, causing them to slow down to a comfortable, pondering pace.

After some time of strolling along, Siobhan finally sat down on a large rock and sat gazing into the stream. Her graceful pose and longing look reminded Ian of the famous statue of the little mermaid on the shore of the harbor in Copenhagen. He could see that she was now leaving him and entering a different world. He left her alone and wandered off toward a glen to look for raspberries.

When Ian returned, he sat down next to Siobhan. She hadn't changed her pose but now she was crying.

"Siobhan, are you OK?"

"It's so beautiful. So calm – so peaceful. But scary. I feel like I'm dreaming my life away. I could easily stay here and listen to music flowing on with the brook – forever."

Then looking around and finally up at Ian again, she added in a confused voice, "And I could have sworn I heard children laughing, but there aren't any kids up here."

Ian wanted to cradle her face in his hands, to put his arms around her, but he couldn't.

Slowly Ian began, "Sometimes when I come up here and become totally relaxed, I can hear them too. And sometimes I believe I can see my ancestor, Jan van de Kill, looking down at me from where his place had been further up the creek.

"Whenever I come up here with a dog from Rent-a-Pet, it'll always pause and try to walk up the steps through the stone walls along the path. It'll stand with its front paws on the first step and look upward toward where the house had been, whine, and turn toward me asking me with its eyes why we aren't going up to visit. When I do humor them, they run up the steps, circle around where the foundations would have been, and finally giving up, gaze up at me with a confused look as if to ask where the people have gone to."

Ian continued on in a thoughtful voice, "I think there are places that are especially open to other worlds beyond our understanding. And this valley is one of them. Maybe there's a strong residue left by the people who'd lived here. Maybe it's another dimension – or a relaxing of the restrictive dimension of time. I don't know. But I've sensed it and the dogs sure have."

After drying her tears and recovering somewhat from her reverie, Siobhan looked quizingly into Ian's eyes and said, "Ian, why do you come here?"

"Well, I have no idea where my family came from in Holland, but I do know this is where I'm from in America. It's my roots. I loved my grandfather, and some of my fondest memories from my youth were when he'd bring me here, tell me stories about the old Dutch settlers, and we'd go hunting for foundations, tombstones, bottles, and farm equipment."

Following a short silence, Siobhan said, "I think there's more to it."

Ian felt he could trust her. "Well, at first I came here to recapture fond memories of my youth. But then I started slipping more and more into the reverie of the place. As you said, it was kind of scary at first. I'd be like those people at the pond, or like you a few minutes ago, lost in the peace and beauty and not able to easily pull myself out of it. But when I did, I'd be refreshed and able to go back to my daily life with a clear head, ready to face life again. Life as it is. It's ironic that when I leave this Valley of the Dead, I feel more alive than I do when I'm among the living."

Siobhan looked around her and said, "I know what you mean about this valley. I'm feeling refreshed – a little light-headed." Siobhan looked back at him, and her expectant silence encouraged him to go on.

"History has always been my passion. I know where this county has been and can see where it is and where it's heading. I know The Corporation saved us from collapse and chaos. We were so grateful when The Corporation took over. But I think we gave up too much when it did.

"Now we're defined by our jobs. Our lives are 'T-accounts' with ever-changing debits and credits. Since our band, earnings and job potential define everything we'll receive and achieve, all our thinking revolves around our jobs and positions within The Corporate scheme of things. Birth, marriage, even death are driven by the needs of The Corporation. And in between we scurry around trying to keep under the corpos' radar. I know that's heresy, but I know things aren't right.

"So I come up here and I feel like I'm communing with my past – my grandfather – my ancestors. I sense that those who've passed on are encouraging me to return to the world and be a positive force. And that's what I do, trying to make my students aware of the world they live in; its past, present and its future. Encouraging their humanity to come out in them."

They both gazed down the path and didn't say anything for a while.

Finally Siobhan spoke up, hesitatingly at first, "Ian, I think you've been honest with me. It's time for me to be open with you. I've appreciated your not asking me more about myself, including about my work. There's a lot I can't tell you at this point, and a lot that I don't want to. But I'm going to tell you something that you must never tell anyone unless I permit it. Tell me that I can trust you."

Ian was at first taken aback, but he looked into her eyes and could see that she was completely serious.

"OK. But if I don't like what I'm hearing, I'll tell you not to go on."

"Fair enough."

Chapter 6

"Ian, I'm involved with a group of people, who, like you, are trying to be a positive force in our world. We're also aware of the greatness of our country's past and want to steer it toward a better future. We aren't an organization. Even the word group is strong. We're individuals who are linked by similar values. Our activities are based on the needs and opportunities we identify.

"I'm going to tell you about an initiative I've identified and am developing on my own. I've discussed it with others but only at a theoretical level. This minimizes exposure to others if something goes wrong. "

"Ian, you're a critical key to the success of this initiative. I've learned a great deal about you over the past several months. I've learned enough to know that you're a good person and that I can trust you."

Siobhan studied Ian's face. He was looking at her intently with a wide-eyed expression as if he couldn't believe what he was hearing.

His face took on a sad, deflated look and he said, "I'm an idiot. I should have known when you approached me on the Walkway that it was more than animal magnetism. You weren't the type of woman who picks up men at random. My vanity stopped me from being suspicious. I wish you had simply said that you had a business proposition."

"And you would have walked away. Or reported me to the corpos. I had to get to know you enough to trust you. And now I do. I have to say that I looked forward to meeting you because I did find you attractive."

"That's nice to know."

"Ian, I didn't pick you up. I approached you and we struck up a conversation. And after that things developed naturally. I felt that I was getting to know you for myself, not for the task. Ian, I like you. I'm sorry there were ulterior motives involved. I really hope we can continue to develop our relationship."

"To what end? Because you like me or to use me?"

Siobhan looked down and said, "I know this complicates things. But none of us in our group feels used. No one is forced to do anything. We all feel we're doing positive things because we want to."

She looked up and their eyes met again. "Do you want me to continue?"

Ian nodded.

"I work for the Management Assessment Division of the EvalProm Corporation. Our division contracts out to other corporations as well as The Corporation, to run their management assessment programs. We have a lock on that market niche. Our programs identify which employees have what potential. The corporations use our work to slot employees into appropriate development streams: staff, manager, director, executive. Those identified as executive material are then groomed by the corporations, that is, they are given the work experiences that will enable them to become executives.

"Our work is important because once an employee is slotted, the die is cast. Their future is locked into place. It's harsh, but it meets the needs of each corporation. By the way, this isn't a new innovation since The Corporation took over. Corporations have been doing some version of this for a long time, though in the past it had only been one element in advancement."

"Yeah, I've heard of EvalProm and their work."

"When The Corporation came to power, management assessment became codified. Now all corporations follow the same procedures which makes things very efficient, though inflexible. Of course, the employees that are being evaluated during our programs know that their future is being determined, so they're under great stress. I've always tried to put the participants at ease and have maintained a positive tone in doing their evaluation reports, no matter what the outcome.

"Potential executive material candidates are elated. Those who bomb out realize their future is bleak. Very few people know this, but a large portion of those who do poorly in the assessment check into a Euthanesta sleep palace. God Ian, these are young people in their twenties! They should have other options."

"That's awful! I never knew, though I shouldn't be surprised," Ian commented.

Siobhan continued, "Seven years ago, The Corporation asked us to set up a pilot program to assess children going into their first year in the upper form schools. We modeled a lot of it after the management assessment programs. But we didn't want to stress out the kids, so we structured it around a fall camp where the kids have fun while being assessed. And we told The Corporation that our assessment should only be used as a first predictor – that it was too early to put kids into executive/non-executive tracks. Many kids, especially boys, are late bloomers, so slotting this early would be uneconomical. They accepted this. Big 'C' and small 'c' corporation executives have kids in the upper form schools, so they don't want to see their kids' chances being cut short."

Ian was attentive and nodded in agreement.

"Well, we created a fun fall camp. Kids go horseback riding, swimming, rappelling, zip-lining. But we also created many opportunities to assess their abilities. For example, taking the kids through the basics of a play, like Shakespeare's *Taming of the Shrew*, then letting them work out the production themselves. We then observe the kids, seeing who shows leadership by naturally taking charge, how well each interacts with the others, who shows initiative by taking the more difficult parts and quickly learning their lines, and who's able to relate to what's going on. We provide a stage and props like Elizabethan clothing to make it more real and fun.

"Then after the production we discuss the play with the kids to get an idea of how well they can adapt to a different language and culture and understand the important ideas in the play. We assess how well the kids empathize with the other sex. Can the girls get beyond their knee-jerk comments about sexism in discussing Petruchio? Can the boys understand Kate's frustrations of living in a male-dominated world? We get an incredible amount of insight into each child's personality, capabilities and potentials. And, of course, we do plain old, non-fun testing, like for IQ. The kids are so used to testing, that they're not surprised.

"The pilot program was such a success, that The Corporation asked us to start implementing it throughout the Upper New York and New England Division for all children entering the first year of upper-form school. We've done this. Now we're in the process of rolling it out to other divisions.

"Since I was involved with the pilot and really like kids, I was asked to stay on with the NY/NE Division program – running the camps and identifying areas where we can improve the program. The kids do have fun and I think it's a good non-stressful means of making an in-depth assessment of kids' potentials without slotting them more than has already been done. I feel much better about doing this work than the management assessment programs."

Ian nodded. "I'm aware of this. It sounds like a positive means of doing assessments, as long as it isn't used to cubby-hole kids. It is too early to start putting kids in the upper form on certain tracks. But how do I fit in?"

"OK, like I said before, you must promise never to tell anyone what I'm about to tell you unless I give you permission."

"I promise."

"Last fall one of your students, Spencer Galloway, attended one of our camps," Siobhan continued. "He did extremely well on the standard testing, like IQ. When we turned the students loose on *The Taming of the Shrew*, he hung back at first, and didn't take the lead in discussing how the play should be acted out or in assigning parts. It was as if he expected the adults to step in and take over, as many kids tend to. When the students conducted audition readings, Spencer performed his parts flawlessly and was assigned the lead male role."

"I'm not surprised. He's a very bright kid."

"With this he started blossoming. As the production progressed, he became the natural director, explaining the subtle meaning and humor, helping the other students learn their lines and better understand what was going on. Spencer helped the cast understand the particulars and the universal truths that make Shakespeare's plays so timeless. Because of Spencer, his group put on the best presentation of that play we evaluators had ever seen.

"This was a trend we began seeing in Spencer with each activity he became involved in. In each, Spencer tended to hang back, but then took the lead – not in an arrogant manner, but in a helpful one that was appreciated by the other students. Largely due to him, all his rotating groups in each activity outperformed the others.

"We rotated observers on different activities, and then I took their assessments and collated them. Everyone was extremely impressed with Spencer, but it wasn't till I took all the assessment inputs and test results and fed them into several of our predictor models that I realized that Spencer has the highest potential of anyone I've seen in the seven years I've been involved in this program. Our predictor models were modeled after great leaders like the ISA's founding father, Kenneth Rechner, to help us scale performance. In short, Ian, Spencer has the potential to become the Chief Executive Officer of the Incorporated States of America." Siobhan paused for a moment.

Ian stared at her in awe and said, "Whew. I've only had Spencer since January. I realized he was an extremely bright, capable kid, but he does seem to hold back, letting me take the traditional lead as the teacher."

"Well, he has the *potential* to become the CEO of the ISA. That's where you come in. I wanted to make sure you're aware of his outstanding potential and that you'll do everything in your power to help develop it over the next 18 months that you have him as a student – and hopefully beyond that as a friend."

"Sure I will. I do what I can for all my students."

"But maybe let go of the traditional teacher roll sometimes? Maybe let Spencer and the others step up to lead more?"

"OK, point well taken."

"Spencer does have some areas that he needs help in. First, he's a male, so will tend to accept his more passive place in society. Second, his mothers are gay. I believe he hasn't had a consistent, strong male role model."

"Well, I'll do what I can on that front, but what is a good, male role model and is it something he should aspire to?" Ian asked, throwing his hands up. "Shouldn't he be aspiring to a more female one? I'm not sure I'd be the best model if there were a good one."

"That may be the most difficult thing to figure out. He is a male, and has to come to terms with it in a positive way if he'll ever have a chance to reach his potential."

At this point Siobhan paused and with a concerned look on her face she continued, "And Ian, this is very important. Spencer's what we call a 'wild card'. I suspected this and it was confirmed by our predictor models. This is a common element in many natural leaders. It's an element of unpredictability in their natures. It can take them and those who follow them to greater heights or to greater depths.

"Some in the highest levels of The Corporation would understand this as an essential element of change in the otherwise stagnant, codified, straight-jacket structure of The Corporation. They know that the inability to change means extinction.

"But there are others at all levels who'd feel threatened by a wild card," Siobhan continued. "They'd fear his ability to change the world, and they'd seek to destroy him. A wild card will not toe The Corporate line. If he chooses not to be a total rebel, he'll be smart enough to know his limits as he works his way up the ladder in which ever direction he goes. But within these limits he'll always push to create change.

"Think of the wild card as Nietzsche's *Uebermensch*, an individual who has moved beyond the accepted way of viewing things, an individual who identifies needed change and has the ability to create that change. Or think of the wild card as a lemming who can see that the others are heading off a cliff *and* can figure out a way to divert them from disaster.

"Ian, I need you to help direct Spencer toward those greater heights while developing his humanity, his empathy and compassion for his fellow beings. Developing a sense of compassion is especially difficult for most upper-form kids – coming from lives of privilege as most of them do. Maybe one benefit Spencer has is that neither of his mothers are directors, let alone executives. They're both upper bands – one's an 8 and the other's a 9."

After a pause, Siobhan added, "You know, Ian, Spencer could become a St. Thomas Aquinas, or a Benito Mussolini; a Dietrich Bonhoeffer or an Adolf Hitler. I think he's a good kid, but he's at an impressionable and vulnerable age. He needs all the good influence he can get.

"And finally, you need to always guard his back against anyone who would harm him or seek to destroy him."

"What? He's only a kid!" Ian countered though he knew she was right.

"Ian, you know the corpos! Look, as soon as I had an inkling of Spencer's potential, I ran the programs myself and have carefully guarded the findings.

Per our agreement with The Corporation, we give them a brief, high-level assessment of each student and the groups in general so as not to slot them into specific categories. It's uneconomical for them to be 'checking the checkers', so they're content with that.

"But there are those in The Corporation who would go to extraordinary measures if they knew I was holding a wild card – including disappearing him, me, his mothers and anyone else who knew. It's important to keep him 'flying under the radar' so he can survive and eventually make a difference. But at the same time we need to help him develop all of his talents."

"Have you told his mothers?" Ian asked.

"No. The fewer who know, the better. I did tell them that Spencer is a very bright young person with great potential. They appreciated the feedback and I let it go at that. Right now they're doing a fine job with him without knowing more."

"So who knows the detail of what you just told me? Who knows about Spencer?"

"You and me."

Ian looked down the path in thought and then back at Siobhan.

"And you were lying in wait for me last night?"

"Yes. I was waiting to see if you'd show up. I had good reason to believe you would. So I waited near the entrance to the Walkway. I was still undecided about making contact with you. I was really conflicted. But then I saw Spencer making a scene so I made my way toward where he was. When I heard what he was saying about The Corporation, my blood froze.

"I was ready to intervene when I saw you approaching from the other way. I held back and watched. His actions convinced me that I couldn't wait any longer to contact you. And yours made me feel that I could trust you – you obviously cared about him and the other students.

"And I followed you back down the walk toward the street – so I could help out if necessary," Siobhan went on, looking intently into Ian's eyes. "I watched from the shadows as the other students left and you sat alone between the two boys. I saw you spread your arms out along the back of the bench and look down at them. Just the way you looked at them, I knew you'd do whatever necessary to help them – to protect them."

The two of them sat in silence when Siobhan finished speaking. Finally, she continued, "Ian, I hope you'll help me – help Spencer. I'm sorry I had to get you involved. Things could get dangerous. But it's too important not to take action."

Ian looked into her eyes and said, "Yes, I'll help. I'd do it for any of my students."

As the two of them headed back toward the Bear Mountain boat dock, Ian reflected on how his comfortable life had been overturned in such a short time. Meeting a woman he was attracted to, only to learn what was really behind that meeting. He was trying to sort out how he felt about her now. And Spencer? Now Ian's concern for him had taken on a whole new light. He knew he wouldn't sleep well tonight.

Siobhan tried to take Ian's hand. At first he instinctively pulled back, but then he looked down at her and tentatively took her hand. As the shadows grew longer in the Valley of the Dead, they walked hand-in-hand down the dusty path, knowing that they would have to be able to trust each other if they were going to help Spencer – and survive.

Chapter 7

After he reread Spencer's composition, Ian tried to read some of the other students' pieces, but he couldn't concentrate on them. He tuned in some soothing music by the turn-of-the-century Irish singer Enya and tuned in a 3D beach scene on the wallplay. But his thoughts were elsewhere.

He thought about his day with Siobhan. Despite learning the truth about their "chance" meeting, he was still drawn to her. She was fun, intelligent and attractive. And her commitment to Spencer revealed a fearless strength he had to admire.

He was still internalizing everything she had told him today. It was as if he had stepped through a looking glass into a strange, though imaginable, world.

Ian sometimes thought he had a passion for history because it was safe. It was past, distant, non-threatening. When he read personal accounts of men who had fought in the Civil War, he wondered if he would have had the strength and conviction to walk down that dusty road toward a world of unspeakable horrors. In his deepest thoughts he feared he would not. At these times he would brush aside those doubts and move on to other historical subjects.

Then, within a matter of minutes today, he became involved in a world that was at the very least potentially conspiring against The Corporation. Ian had thought about this world. He knew it was out there. And he had glimpsed his involvement with it on his way home from school yesterday, thinking about Spencer's composition.

But Spencer wasn't some rabid terrorist. And Ian was just a teacher legitimately trying to expand his students' awareness of their world! Of course, if he were investigated, his activities would be judged by a corpo and those people weren't exactly the freest of thinkers.

His knowledge now of Spencer's possibilities made his situation especially critical. Spencer was definitely highly intelligent and capable, and a deep thinker. But Ian could see that Spencer was a wild card too, and needed guidance. His criticism of The Corporation could land him in serious trouble.

Ian lay for a long time on his couch trying to enjoy the scene and Enya, but his mind raced on. He finally dropped off into a restless sleep.

He dreamed he was coming home from school, frequently glancing over his shoulder. He was sure there was something back there, and it scared him. But what, or who, it was he didn't know. All he knew was that he had to get away from it. So he scurried on toward his dom.

But the faster he tried to go, the slower he went. The harder he tried, the weaker his muscles seemed to become. Was it the heat? Fear? He glanced around at the doms and realized he didn't recognize any of them. Or more accurately, they all looked the same and he couldn't make out any distinguishing characteristics that would tell him how close he was to his dom.

As he hurried along he noticed that the bright, hot sun light was no longer beating down on him. Was he in the shade of the doms? He looked around and was surprised at how large and luxuriant the narrow dom gardens had become. They seemed to be responsible for the shade. The trees and bushes were now towering over him – their branches reaching down. He instinctively moved away from them and skittered along the safety of a dom wall, glancing from the way forward to the threatening plants and back again.

Just when he was fully concentrating on keeping away from the plant life, he heard a faint laugh behind him. It was an evil, sarcastic laugh as if to say, "You can't get away from me, little mouse!" Ian tried desperately to turn around and see his pursuer, but he couldn't. A powerful force was holding his head in a forward position. So he redoubled his efforts to move forward and away from the evil behind him.

But now he saw vegetation on both sides of him. The assurance of the dom wall was no longer there. So he looked ahead, keeping a cautious eye on the plants as they seemed to move in toward him. His pursuer's laugh grew louder. He was gaining ground.

The vegetation became increasingly dense, until he found himself fighting through it. He could see a clearing up ahead, faint at first, but increasingly clear as he moved toward it.

Ian finally emerged close to the pond in the Valley of the Dead. He was hot and sweaty and gasping for air from the exertion. As he moved closer to the pond, the sky clouded over, or maybe the sun was going down. He looked across the pond at the cemetery and saw a number of figures. He didn't know any of them at first. They were all staring at him and his adversary. He felt that his only chance for safety was to reach the other side. As he walked into the pond he began recognizing people he knew. He saw his grandfather standing near Jan van de Kill. Then he saw Spencer and Juan.

And finally he saw Siobhan. As he waded deeper into the water, he reached his hand up toward her. But she turned back toward the tombstones, in the gloom of the trees. When she turned back to look at him, he saw that sadness he had seen in her eyes before. He wanted to ask her what was wrong as he slowly waded deeper, but he couldn't talk.

Suddenly, he felt hands on his shoulders pushing him down into the water. He looked up at the others and could see that they all felt sorry for him but could do nothing to help him. As the assailant's hands exerted more force, an evil, hissing voice said, "They can't help you – they're all dead!"

Ian was under water, terrified. He desperately needed to breathe. He struggled to get away from the iron grip, but it was useless. He prepared to drown in the murk of the pond.

But as he relinquished his struggle he thought of Siobhan and Spencer and the others standing on the bank. He thought about what they meant to him. Siobhan and Spencer were now depending on him. He thought of the courage Jan and his family must have had to come to this new world – to struggle against all odds for their lives; for their future. Slowly he could feel his fear turning to anger. And then a sense of determination came over him and he yelled, "No they're not!"

With a primal, violent twist he freed himself from the grip and swam upward through the murky water till he burst gasping into the air.

He was back in his apartment and on the floor in front of his couch.

(Note: Linda Xiaobo's and Spencer Galloway's compositions are optional reading. They can be found in the appendices.)

Part 2
BROKEN DREAMS

We all at some time journey through realms of darkness. It is what we learn from those experiences that shapes our souls.

    Rumi al-Ghazzali, *Reflections*

Chapter 8
SUNDAY, JULY 5

"... and just as our founding mothers and fathers fought the tyrant king of Great Britain for independence so that they could practice their Christian religion in peace, The Corporation has brought us an unparalleled period of peace since saving us from chaos and war over a quarter of a century ago. Let there be no doubt that Jesus, the Prince of Peace, would have been the greatest supporter of The Corporation. Always keep that in mind when you gaze upon our Corporate Church flag with the cross safely imbedded within the protective confines of the Corporate triangle."

It wasn't the words of Reverend Johnson that brought Michael Chan back to the service, but the supporting 3D images flashing by that showed scenes from the Middle East Wars and the Second Mexican War, ending with a family playing in a field with woods and mountains in the background. That was the effective part.

Nice touch. He looked around and saw everyone shaking their heads in affirmation.

"But remember there are those who seek to destroy us because they hate our freedom and Christian religion." At this point holoplay images of mideastern types wearing turbans and running forward with various weapons flashed forward toward the congregation. Everyone instinctively pulled back, gasping.

Again, well done, Michael thought as he looked around again, smiling.

"They're training abroad, studying our weaknesses and looking for the perfect time to interject their terrorists into our country, or worse yet, to recruit and brainwash followers from our midst. So be diligent. Look for those who find fault with our religion," Again a shady looking mideastern type with glaring eyes. "And those who find fault with our government." Now flashes of every-day Americans. "Never take your freedom and peace for granted. Guard them every day against those who would take them away from you. They are in our midst. Be aware. Be diligent." After a slight pause, "Let us pray." The field scene returned, but in place of the family playing was The Corporate triangle with the cross in the middle.

Michael bowed his head, smiling. Julianna gave him a poke. His wife knew what he was thinking. Analyzing the effects of speeches and holoplays had been his work for the past several years.

To advance his career in the Corporate Bureau of Investigation, Michael had taken a stint in the CBI's Department of Public Education, Washington Division. He'd put together transponder programs and wall- and holoplays, mostly of the cautionary type, with titles such as, "They Lurk Among Us" or more directly, "How to Identify and Report a Potential Terrorist". The reverend had used some department terrorist footage. Michael was glad to be back in the detective division now, being promoted to chief inspector, in charge of younger, less experienced, agents.

Finally, the benediction was spoken and the congregation sang the recessional hymn, "Onward Christian Soldiers", as the minister and then the choir walked down the aisle to the back of the church. While he and Julianna were waiting their turn to get into the isle, Michael glanced up at the gold cross on the field of white, bordered by a gold triangle, and wondered what the real Jesus had been like. Would he really have been an avid supporter of The Corporation? He didn't think so. Michael saw that it was their turn to move, and with one last glimpse at the cross, he turned into the isle.

As with most social events, this special Tricentennial service had been held in the evening to avoid the brutal heat of the day. As they walked outside the church it was almost pleasant. The sun was setting, and even though it was still hot, the humidity was low so they could visit a bit.

One of his old colleagues from the CBI, Sean Fitzpatrick, waived to him and yelled, "Hi Charlie!" Michael cringed. When he had originally made detective grade, some of his colleagues had started calling him Charlie after the famous, but stereotypical, Charlie Chan, the detective from the popular movies of the 1940s and 50s which still had a cult following. Since it had been his Chinese-background colleagues who had started this, he couldn't say much.

Julianna had always insisted that his mischievous personality and charming looks reminded her much more of Jackie Chan, the popular kick-boxer movie star from the turn of the century. This always fed his vanity and brought out his boyish "Jackie" smile. Michael hoped "Charlie" wouldn't be brought up again in his new position. After all, he wanted to maintain the respect of his colleagues and subordinates.

The two walked toward each other and bowed. As they started talking, their wives stepped aside to begin their own conversation.

"Hey Sean, starting to attend church here?"

"Yeah, Maria thought it might be good for my career. We had always gone to the Catholic Church but one of the guys recommended that we try it. We like the services and people. I didn't know you were a member too. I hadn't seen you at the services we attended."

"I've been pretty busy transitioning from my old to new job."

"I heard you had returned from the education stint, and gotten a promotion! Good going Michael!" Sean said with real enthusiasm, but Michael detected that subtle glance of pity in his eyes.

"Thanks Sean. Yeah, chief inspector – though you made that grade, what, eight years ago?"

"Yeah. You should have then, too. Damn office politics!"

"You did a stint in Chicago, right? And now, assistant director of the Mid-Hudson Valley Interview Center. Wow!"

"It was a good promotion but I miss the detective work. Maybe someday I can head back in that direction again."

"It'd be good to work with you again." After an awkward pause, Michael said, "Well, take care; and now that we're both attending the same church, let's keep in touch."

"Sure. Good seeing you Michael – and Julianna." The two couples bowed and went their separate ways.

Julianna looked at Michael, "It still hurts, doesn't it?"

"Yeah."

"You did what you thought was right, and you did finally get the promotion. You've got to move beyond the past and keep a positive outlook."

"I will." He took her hand and she squeezed it. It had hurt her too, but she had been his unquestioning support through everything.

As they walked back to their dom in the cooling evening air, Michael reflected on his "error in judgment" nine years ago that had cost him the career advancements he should have been making.

He was obviously brooding over that time, so Julianna said, "Michael, you investigated that train wreck and determined it was faulty construction on NorEast's part, not terrorists. I'm proud of you for standing firm on your findings."

"Yeah, I just wish my boss had been too before he reassigned me to another case and put Sean on the wreck."

Julianna stopped, turned Michael toward her and said, "Michael, he was just after the politically convenient resolution. The execution of those young Muslim men Sean went after will be a stain on both their souls. You're better than that."

"Yeah. You're right," Michael responded and started walking again, averting his eyes to the front.

That incident had taught him to act more quickly and harshly. He still believed that the young men had been innocent and that he had done the right thing at the time. But that was nine years ago – and he had paid dearly. Now he had finally gotten his promotion to chief inspector and would be tested in his new position. He wondered how he would have handled this case if it had come up now.

Michael and Julianna were finishing their late-evening snack when he received a 'spond from the Poughkeepsie bureau chief that there had been an incident at the LEPGen Technologies research and development laboratory on South Road which required his immediate involvement. He 'sponded his two protégées, Lenora Davis and Tony Ragusini, to meet him at the corner of Market and Montgomery.

This could be his first big case since his promotion, so he was excited, but felt a certain dread as he thought about what it could be. Per CBI protocol, he wouldn't be able tell Julianna anything about it till he concluded it – or was reassigned. Over the years he had instinctively told her less and less about each case as he finished it.

As he approached the door to go out, Julianna took his hand and he turned toward her. She said, "I love you." But her eyes spoke of the fear she felt when he went out on a new case. He would be largely gone, physically, but even more so mentally, till the case was done. Would he come back to her unchanged, or would there be that small, additional change as with each case?

"I'll be fine. I'm sure it'll be routine. Probably just have to wipe some exec's ass," he laughed as he kissed her. "Don't wait up for me."

Michael walked through the door but glanced back one last time and again said, "I'll be fine." But he knew his words sounded unconvincing.

Chapter 9

Michael drove his car out of his dom garage and onto the street. As a CBI investigator who needed total mobility, he was one of the fortunate few who had a car at his disposal. But this required that his dom have a garage and access to a street, which had restricted where he could live.

The problem in having a car wasn't so much the cost of purchasing and maintaining one, it was more the tolls. Early in the century financially-strapped governments saw privatizing roadways as a way to earn extra money while eliminating an expense. Eventually, most expressways and highways became privately-owned toll roads.

When The Corporation took over, all remaining roads and even streets were privatized and became toll roads. Car-ID chips made scanning for fees easy. But tolls became an expense increasingly difficult to justify for individuals. After The Great Corporate Restructuring and its emphasis on healthy lifestyles through walking, at least within Corporate limits, driving became unnecessary. It was a luxury of the few, or for those whom The Corporation was willing to pay for, like Michael.

Michael drove a CBI-supplied Consort Firestorm, a four-seat, pathetically-underpowered, ridiculously-named, but importantly-energy-efficient model with electric power. As fewer and fewer people had cars, the remaining car companies formed a consortium, aptly called the Consort Corporation, to produce and sell 'lectrobiles and 'lectrocycles. Receiving an exclusive-supplier contract from The Corporation, eliminated the threat of competition from the few remaining foreign car corporations.

The toll companies were also forced to consolidate. In the northeast they were bought up by NorEast Transpo Corporation. With fewer cars to pay tolls, many roads outside Corporation limits were simply abandoned. NorEast had also wanted to abandon many streets within Corporation limits, but The Corporation reluctantly paid a subsidy for those streets it deemed strategically important.

Michael pulled up to the corner of Market and Montgomery at the southern edge of the pedestrian-only dom district. While he waited for Lenora and Tony, he gazed across the street at the Soldier's Fountain, a memorial to those who fought and died in the Civil War. This had always been one of Michael's favorite spots in Poughkeepsie. The large, spraying fountain had always intrigued Michael. It was so impractical, that he figured it *had* to be a true work of art.

It reminded Michael of a picture he had seen of a huge fountain in far-off Savannah, Georgia. And here Poughkeepsie had one just like it! Well, OK, smaller and maybe only similar. But how exceptional! Especially in contrast to the totally rational and practical doms. He always wondered why The Corporation not only had not demolished it, but actually kept it up and running with no obvious financial gain. After all, given its location, it wasn't an income-producing tourist attraction like the Walkway over the Hudson. It's only function could be to offer beauty for beauty's sake, and to be an historical reminder to the people of Poughkeepsie.

Michael sometimes wondered whether the fountain was a crack in the dike. He had seen other cracks in the dike. But his attraction to this one always left him with mixed feelings. It attracted him but was also a threat. His job was to run around putting his fingers in the dike, to fix the cracks. But he sometimes wondered whether despite his and other agent's efforts, that dike would someday burst and the flood waters would wash him and everything away.

"Hi Michael, what's up?" Lenora asked when she opened the front door and hopped in.

"I got an urgent 'spond from Connie. I'll brief you when Tony gets here and we get under way." Then after a pause Michael asked, "How was your date with Randolph last night?"

Lenora rolled her eyes. "He was a perfect gentleman till we got to the party, but after a few snorts he started ogling other women. I put up with it for a while, but when he started paying more attention to other women than to me, I insisted on leaving.

"Outside, he started apologizing and giving me that 'you're the only one for me, babe' line, which only made me angrier, because I knew what he was after. I told him I could have him up on sexual indiscretions charges. Well, he just laughed! I couldn't believe it. I was so mad I could imagine myself flashing my holobadge at him and actually taking him in."

"Whoa," Tony said as he settled into the back seat. "Intense!"

"I know. It was silly. He knew I wouldn't do it. So I just stormed off to my dom. He tried to follow but finally gave up. Sometimes I think the neo-fems were right. Men are totally useless! They *are* the problem and *definitely not* part of the solution."

"Present company excluded?" Tony asked in a fake, pleading voice.

Lenora eyed Tony and Michael skeptically and said, "That remains to be seen!"

"Ouch!" They both instinctively said.

Looking Lenora up and down and making his best "Jackie Chan" smile, Michael said, "Well, I've got visual proof right in front of me that Randolph ain't too bright if he treated you that way." Lenora gave him a light swat but laughed as they pulled away and headed down South Road.

Like Michael, both Lenora and Tony had started with local police departments, had shown exceptional abilities and were recommended to apply to the CBI. After being accepted and successfully completing their CBI training, they were assigned to the Poughkeepsie Bureau. Having completed short rotations in different areas, they were then assigned to Michael. Although they were both in their mid 20's, Michael amusedly viewed them as a couple of snot-nosed kids just learning the ropes. They reminded him of himself when he had first started working for the Bureau – overly eager to prove themselves and make names for themselves.

"OK kids, start peddlin'!" Michael joked as his car slowly accelerated in spite of his foot pushing the accelerator to the floor.

"Hey, this is a lot better than those whimpy 'lectrocycles the Bureau gave us to use!" Tony exclaimed.

"Don't worry, keep your noses clean and to the grindstone and in twenty years you'll be whizzing along in style like me!" Michael joked.

Lenora was an attractive black woman, very sharp and intelligent. She would do very well moving up in the CBI – she would certainly be mentored along the way – or in whatever direction she decided to go in. He hoped Tony would have good opportunities open to him as well.

"So what's the scoop boss?" Tony asked.

Michael turned serious. "All I was told was that there had been an 'incident' at the LEPGen R&D facility and to meet with an Emma Treadwell, one of the directors there.

"Best not to conjecture what it could be – keep an open mind till we get there. But when the bureau chief tells you to go to a highly restricted R&D facility and only vaguely tells you to investigate an 'incident', it's probably a big deal. This could be your first big case." Michael didn't mention that this could also be his first big one in his new position.

As they drove through the darkness, the moonlight and occasional light exposed the derelict strip malls on either side of the old Route 9. Michael had seen wallplays of how crowded Route 9 had been in the old days with high-powered gasoline-powered cars full of people going shopping. He could vaguely recall it from when he was young – or did he just imagine that? Michael had always wondered why people didn't just 'spond what they needed, or shopped "on line" before transponders.

The LEPGen Technologies R&D facility reminded Michael of a prison as they pulled in. There was a high, chain-link fence with razor-wire topping all the way around. Behind the fence was a stretch of older, monolithic, interconnected buildings. And beyond that the Hudson River, and the steep, wooded cliffs on the opposite side.

They pulled up to the front gate with its flood lights glaring down on them. A serious-looking guard came over and studied them. They had obviously been scanned, because he immediately directed them to the main building entrance. They drove up to the entrance of the reception area and parked. There appeared to be very few other parking spots and cars. Most employees here would take the South Road tram to get to work.

The reception area also reminded Michael of a prison. Stark walls and utilitarian furniture. The holo-receptionist told them to take a seat and that Dr. Treadwell would be right out. Michael looked around. There was the ubiquitous wallplay portrait of LEPGen's most famous son, Kenneth Rechner, who had been CEO of LEPGen Technologies, and then moved on to become the first CEO of the Incorporated States of America. There were also wallplay portraits of the current LEPGen CEO as well as one of the current head director of this R&D facility. Michael assumed that the smattering of displayed objects had been developed here.

A middle-aged, Chinese-looking woman came out and introduced herself as Emma Treadwell. Treadwell was certainly not a Chinese name, and women had long ago stopped taking their husbands' names when they got married. So where did that name come from? Dr. Treadwell was a harshly attractive woman, in the way a fanatical female triathlete would have that hard, determined look and build, but yet her svelte body and face could still have their feminine charm.

As she bowed to each of them while Michael introduced himself and the others, he reflected that it had been the Chinese who had introduced the custom of bowing. Shaking hands had started going out of style during the great 'flu pandemic of 2023. But it became even less accepted when neo-feminists identified it as a way men intimidated women with their greater physical strength. They insisted it was a form of fondling women. So the "Chinese bow" eventually became the norm. It wasn't just a nod, which would be seen as smug or cavalier. The "Chinese bow" was like an exaggerated nod with a slight bow at the waist to indicate that one really did acknowledge the other person's presence.

"Now, you do understand that as soon as you walk through these doors into the facility, your scan will indicate that you understand, and will comply with, the LEPGen Technologies R&D facility non-disclosure agreement. That disclosing anything you see in this facility without my express permission will make you liable for criminal prosecution."

Lenora and Tony gave Michael an unsure look, but he said, "Yes, we do."

"Please follow me."

The large, front doors to the facility opened automatically and Treadwell lead them through a maze of hallways toward the back of the facility. As they walked along, she explained what some of the areas were developing. One area's project was to develop a super-booster for electric motors that would give the small electric motors in many vehicles an added kick in acceleration, with little added loss of stored power. Michael and Tony smiled at each other and did a thumbs-up.

They finally came to a door that stated, Authorized Personnel Only. Treadwell stepped up to the special retinal/facial scan. When she was cleared, the large, solid door opened and they passed into a large open hall with smaller corridors and hallways leading off from it.

"We'll go to my office so I can give you some preliminary information." They went down a narrow hallway with a number of doors and into Treadwell's office. Though windowless and harshly lighted, it was relatively spacious and she had added touches to make it personal. She had hung several pictures of natural scenes and hanging plants. *Hmmm – outdoorsy type,* thought Michael. There were pictures of young-to-teenage children on the shelves behind her desk, but also a number of pictures of the same dog – a German short hair. *No partner pictures,* Michael observed silently, *so obviously the dog is her partner/child, outdoors companion. The kids are probably friends'/relatives'. Also, using pictures rather than wallplays, she's obviously the no-nonsense, solid, but rather old-fashioned type.* Michael always had to smile when he did his quick estimates of others based on their "stuff." He usually nailed them right away. Maybe he *should* change his name to Charlie – hehe.

"Please take a seat around my conference table. Detective Chan, do I detect a smile?"

"German short hair. Excellent outdoors, hunting dog. Do you do any hunting?"

"Oh no. I like to go for hikes out in the woods and mountains. Brute is a perfect dog for that."

Michael noticed in the one picture that Brute was a neutered male. *Hmmm. Large, male outdoors dog. She named him Brute, but cut his balls off.*

Perfect male companion. She probably sleeps with him, Michael thought, but then mentally slapped his face for being so sexist and judgmental. OK, so that was part of the fun of his job. Good thing transponders couldn't read your thoughts. Yet.

"I want to explain a few things before we go to the lab where the problem is cropping up. How familiar are you with how your transponders are made and operate?"

The three indicated that they had only rudimentary knowledge.

"OK let me give you some technical background with some history thrown in. It's important that you have a good, basic understanding of transponder development to put what you're about to see in perspective.

"The original transponders back in the 20's were merely glorified cell phones that people had carried in their pockets and purses and then ridiculously hung remote earpieces over their ears. They became so ubiquitous, that our engineers decided to develop a model that could fit into your ear and be activated by your voice. You could still hear the "outside world" pretty well, though this didn't seem to be an important concern to most marketing test groups. This "inner ear" model became wildly popular and sales financed further investments in R&D for us. The next steps were to keep miniaturizing them and then to implant them so they would be totally out of the way and free up both ears again when not in use. The implanting was the difficult part.

"But finally in the early 30's, after years of development, testing and getting government approval, we came out with the original implant, the 'Sponder Model 1c. Though crude by today's standards, it *was* a miniature implant, and could be turned on and off by brain waves, though calling and selective receiving still had to be activated by voice commands. This was an amazing achievement and those 'sponders were very well made. Some older people still use them today. They prefer them even though they are very limited and crude by today's standards – and, of course, they're totally non-morphing.

"I don't know what models you have, but they're probably in the CZs. So you, like most people, can make and receive calls, carry on conversations, receive and listen to broadcasts, search out information and actively utilize that information – all by just using your brain. I'm sure you also have the visual feature that allows you to seek out information about stationary objects, like when you look at a restaurant and call up their menu, prices and ratings, all based on GPS location.

"The way we've accomplished all this has been by developing morphing technology, which was started in the 40's. I'm sure you've heard of this but, like most people, aren't well versed in it – as long as it works you're fine. Morphing is electro-organic based technology. Since the 50's all transponder implants have used this to an ever-increasing level of sophistication.

Very simply put, the implants put into people are basically electronic instruments with an inert organic component that activates once implanted. This component grows and creates a net over your brain that interacts with your sensory functions. Even the most sophisticated models today are basically an outgrowth of that original, crude Model 1c's brainwave-activated on/off switch. Any questions at this point?"

"I've 'sponded a blogger program that said that scientists are developing 'sponders so you can read other people's minds – like your boyfriend's to see if he really, uh, you know, loves you," Lenora ventured, though she was somewhat embarrassed when she saw Michael's and Tony's bemused responses. "Of course, I was monitoring that blogger in an official capacity for the CBI. It was really a smogger, you know, blowing smoke up people's rear ends, that I was investigating."

Treadwell smiled and continued, "Agent Davis, you bring up a good point that really leads into why I brought you out here. We are the main site that does research and development on 'sponders. I can't tell you everything we do here; basically we explore every avenue for potential. We could explore using 'sponders to read peoples' minds (I'm not saying we do or don't). But in a case like that we'd have to think seriously about the potential impact to society. I wouldn't want to unleash a horde of women chasing after their boyfriends and husbands with carving knives." She watched Michael and Tony squirm, though she noticed only Tony instinctively covered his crotch with his hands. "If we did develop that capacity, it'd probably only be limited to use by police when investigating criminals."

After a few moments of no further questions, Treadwell continued, "OK, I'm going to take you into one of our main labs, where we've been experiencing the problem. This will be where things are highly confidential. Again, you don't tell anyone what you've seen without my express permission. You know the dire consequences if you do. Follow me." She opened the door and led them down a long corridor to another large, solid door with another retinal/facial scanning device.

Chapter 10

Dr. Treadwell opened the door and led them into a large cavernous hall with a number of smaller, glass-paneled rooms located at different junctures, as well as what appeared to be walk-in coolers or freezers and other temperature-controlled rooms along the walls. "Welcome to what we humorously call the 'inner sanctum'. But this place is no joke. No one just drifts in here. As you saw, all entry is strictly controlled – everyone is thoroughly scanned when they enter and leave. We keep records of all this activity forever. I'm going to show you some things that you may find disturbing. Just remember that everything we do here is to advance science. In the long run it is for the good of all people."

I've heard that canned speech before, thought Michael.

"Our preliminary work is always done with Organic Intelligence models. But then we move on to rats and then on up the chain to primates; chimpanzees. But at some point it's necessary to work on humans. This is the lab where we get to the human stage of our work. We like to use volunteer prisoners for these experiments, or donated bodies. But our current work has to do with implanting organic growth in the very early stages of life, including before birth – from conception to nine months gestation.

"What you'll see in here are living fetuses at various stages of development, with different experiments being done to them. Before you get upset, these are all fetuses that normally would have been terminated because of various defects."

As they walked along they peered into the rooms with row upon row of fetuses in what appeared to be standard glass artificial wombs. Michael's tendency was to think warmly of the fetuses as developing human beings. He had to remind himself that these were defective fetuses that would have been terminated anyway, and at least here they were being useful.

"Where do the fetuses come from?" Michael asked.

Treadwell lifted an eyebrow. "What's your need to know?"

"Dr. Treadwell, I'm assuming a crime was committed here. Crimes don't happen in the vacuum of laboratories. They're always tied to the outside world. Crimes are messy screw ups caused by humans at large, not tidy little experiments that take place in controlled environments. If you want us to help, you'll have to be open kimono with us."

"Open kimono, Detective Chan? I don't like the graphics of that expression."

"Oh, sorry; totally open with us, answer all our questions. Just as you have your 'inner sanctum', we cops have our 'open kimono'. A cop expression, no sexual innuendoes intended."

"Well – OK – the fetuses come from CaringMother Corporation. We usually get them from the CaringMother facility here in Poughkeepsie. That minimizes transportation risk and cost."

"OK, thank you. That could be important knowledge later on."

She then led them to a room where there were little, breathing bodies laid out in rows. "This is where we do our post-birth testing. Again, these are fetuses that were charted to be terminated. We just let them develop to the post-womb level. Up to the level of two-year-olds. Our work has to do with injecting totally organic transponders into the very young. We need to know if they'll work on humans as they do on chimpanzees, as well as at which stages it's viable and optimal.

"If we can make this work, then we can save untold billions in the expense of surgically implanting transponders into everyone as we currently do. There's always a risk with the current surgical procedure. Just think of the lives this would save over the current implant method. And if this organic procedure is successful, it could open up a multitude of possibilities.

"Imagine if we could develop this organic procedure to the point where we could simply inject lower-band fetuses with genetic material containing the necessary information that would allow them to function in their work life. Just think of the billions that could be saved in educational expenses! Of course, much of this is a long way down the road."

Michael wasn't going to waste his breath asking her if all this were legal, let alone ethical. Basically, anything that increased the profit of corporations, and in turn The Corporation, was legal. Especially if the golden child LEPGen Technologies was doing it.

"And this leads us to our problem. Statistically, we're experiencing an abysmally low success rate on our experiments. Oh, we know that in the long run our new approach will succeed. But in the mean time we're really struggling."

"So you think there's some sabotage going on?"

"Exactly. It seems that whatever we do, whatever adjustments we make, statistically we're not making the progress we should be. When we run our OI models, the answer keeps coming up sabotage. Unfortunately, the models are no help in figuring it out. They follow statistical trends. It's conjecture. This has been going on for about half a year now. So we thought we had better call in the CBI for help."

Yeah, to cover your asses and cast the blame elsewhere, thought Michael.

"How do you know it's not just something that's not currently doable given today's technology?" Michael asked.

"Well, all of our OI models indicate it should work, and we had a great deal of success on the chimpanzees before we started on human fetuses. So we should be seeing progress. We just can't put our finger on what's causing the failure. A lot of speculation, but nothing solid. It's very complicated."

"So would you say it's an inside job?"

"It has to be. We even went back to installing old-fashioned security cameras. Nothing."

"What have your security people come up with?"

"They've run the analyses of the scans and found nothing abnormal. And they've checked and rechecked the camera recordings, and nothing. Look, they're just outsourced rent-a-cops. Good at basic security, but not detective work. That's why we've finally decided we need your expertise."

"Going back to CaringMother, could someone be causing the problem at their end?" Lenora interjected.

"Good question, Agent Davis," Treadwell said. "They supply us with a report on each fetus – what their defects are. We do have a quality control person who is present when they make their deliveries and he does the inspections when the shipments arrive here. But we don't have any control over what happens at CaringMother before they arrive here."

"Yes, *very* good Lenora," Michael said as he flashed a smile at Lenora, as if to say, *That's why we need open kimono.* He turned back to Treadwell and asked, "Any problems with the quality of the fetuses you received?"

"No. They've always checked out. No quality problems."

"Do you have any internal suspects?"

"No. Everyone who works here was thoroughly checked out before they started on the project, and we have periodic rechecks. But nothing."

"Are there any motives you can think of? You know, disgruntled employee, industrial spy? Terrorist?" Michael asked.

"They're all possibilities."

"Who are your main competitors, in case there are industrial spies?" Tony asked.

"On this front, it's really NuTense."

"How about the quality control person?" Tony continued.

"Could be, but no more so than anyone else. He receives the fetuses, checks the paperwork, does a prelim quality check, and ensures that all artificial wombs are active."

Michael paused and took a long look around the room. Finally he said, "OK, I'm going to need a list of everyone that works in this area and your key contact at CaringMother. Can we 'spond into your people's records from the outside?"

"No, only from a secure room here."

"We'll need access to those records from our office downtown. Our being here now could raise suspicions so I don't want to do preliminary investigative work from here."

"OK, you'll have access by morning."

"Who knows about this problem?"

"Everyone who works in the lab. But only the location general manager and head of security know that I've called you in. We had a meeting today and decided this was best. We figured late Sunday evening would attract the least attention."

Michael nodded his head in agreement. "As soon as we start investigating on site, whoever is behind this, if it is sabotage, will become very cautious. You might start seeing success with the project. But we still have to get to the root of the problem – whether experimental short comings, technology just not doable, or sabotage. And if sabotage, who the perp is.

"If you need to let someone else know, please check with me first. If the word somehow got out to unofficial 'oggers, they'd have a field day with this and then we'd be under intense pressure to come up with a quick answer. Believe me, I've been through these cluster - , uh, goat rodeos before and it ain't pretty.

"We'll have to tell our bureau chief what's going on. After all, she's the one you contacted. The three of us'll regroup tomorrow morning and start strategizing. We'll be in contact with you shortly."

"OK. I anticipated you'd want a list of everyone involved in the project, so here it is. I've included their positions and put a star next to those who you might want to investigate first – you know, the 'likely suspects'. Remember, this is very confidential just like anything else related to this lab," Treadwell said, handing a piece of paper to Michael.

Michael looked down the list. It was interesting that when it came to very important pieces of information, paper was still often used.

"You didn't put a star next to your name," Michael smiled.

"I assumed *you'd* put me at the top of the likely suspects." They both chuckled. Michael was glad she was loosening up.

"We'll have to be able to trust each other if we're going to solve this problem," Michael observed, smiling at her.

"I couldn't agree with you more, Detective Chan," Treadwell responded as she led them to the door.

Before she opened it, she added, "If we can't get to the bottom of the problem soon, we'll be forced to start using normal fetuses. After all, we've been using a population that isn't representative of recipients of the end product. This could be the root of the problem if it isn't sabotage."

Michael stopped and looked at her intently, "Understood."

On their ride to the dom district, Tony asked, "What do you think Michael?"

"No, what do *you two* think?" Michael countered.

"Well, obviously we don't have a crime, yet. As Treadwell described it, it's an incident, or better yet, a problem," Tony observed.

"Good," said Michael.

"I think she's in a 'cover-your-ass' mode right now," ventured Lenora. "She doesn't have a clue, her experiments aren't working and she's thrashing about for any explanation. Though sabotage is a possibility, and she probably does need our help at this point."

"I agree, Lenora. Did you notice the trump card left for the very end? By contacting us, she's exploring every avenue. So if all else fails, she tries normal fetuses. Use of termination-destined fetuses is legal from a Corporate stance – as long as it's furthering the bottom line. But she'll have to justify moving to normal fetuses. She knows full *well* she'll be *treading* on thin ice. Pardon the pun." They all had a weak smile at this one. "The Corporation won't like it, but they'll like lack of progress even less. So they'll go along with her if she's been diligent in trying to solve the mystery."

After a period of silence, Lenora spoke in a trembling voice, "It broke my heart to see those little live bodies. I kept thinking they should be home with their mothers, safely tucked into their beds, dreaming about the day's activities. Could you imagine the public walking through that place?"

"That's why that place is so well guarded and top secret," Michael responded, adding, "It speaks volumes of Connie's trust in us to handle the situation well. It's highly sensitive – and it's the stuff internal politics is made of."

Michael looked over at Lenora and then in the rear-view mirror at Tony. They were both very quiet. He pulled over and began, "Back in the day, in my first training session as a policeman, one of our instructors was a really old guy, or so it seemed to me then. He'd been a cop forever. And he told us something that I have never forgotten. He said police work is blood, sweat and tears. That to keep your sanity, you have to keep in mind that you're always dealing with the seamier side of life. You do your work each day then reenter real life, and put aside that dark world. You go home to your spouse and kid and get in touch with reality again. He said that the ones who couldn't do that were the ones who became alcoholics, spouse-beaters and suicides. I know you've already seen this in your former police work.

"But the advantage of regular police work is that even though you're dealing with the seamy side of life, you tend to be dealing in blacks and whites. There's an accident, you write it up. A man beats his wife, you take him to jail. There's a break-in, you race to the scene to catch the perp." Here Michael paused and looked out into the dark of the night and at the outlines of the abandoned buildings where only ghosts continued to shop.

"The Bureau's more like dealing with that out there," he said waving his hand at the scene before them. "It's a world where there are no blacks and whites – only grays – dark grays. It's a world of ghosts, or soon-to-be ghosts, and you're rooting around in that gloom trying to figure things out – to make sense of things – to solve problems that rarely have real solutions. You just move along in the gloom and do your best."

Here he turned back to his colleagues. "And the reason you do your best is because at some point you'll look back and those ghosts will be staring at you in the gloom. And you'd better be able to tell them you did your best or they'll tear you apart."

Michael realized he had gone too far. They were still just "kids" – maybe a little older than his daughter. They were visibly shaken as they stared out into the darkness.

"Hey, come on. Important lesson: listen to everyone, believe no one, and then make up your own mind. And last lesson of the night: get a sense of humor – it helps."

Michael dropped them off at Market and Montgomery and said, "See you bright'n'early."

As they waved and walked off into the night Michael felt incredibly tired and sad. They both still had feelings – they still had souls. He wondered how long that would last. As he watched them disappear, Michael wondered if he still had a soul.

Michael drove home and had a stiff snort'n'a'sniff before he went to bed. He knew he'd be waking up in the dead of night – escaping from a dream of his newest ghosts – those little, live bodies.

Chapter 11
MONDAY, JULY 6

Today was Founder's Day, honoring Kenneth Rechner, the first Chief Executive Officer of the Incorporated States of America. By celebrating Founder's Day close to Independence Day, it emphasized the importance of the founding of the Incorporated States of America, next to the independence of Americans from Great Britain. Independence Day was increasingly taking on the idea of independence from the tyranny of the dysfunctional government of the United States of America. By adding Founder's Day, President's Day was no longer necessary, so it was eliminated as a holiday.

There were no holidays for CBI detectives when there was important work to be done. Michael had hoped that he could have taken it off to enjoy the day with Julianna, and maybe his daughter and her boyfriend, but this case was high priority. When he walked into the bureau suite of offices in the restored Lucky-Platt building on Main Street, things were pretty quiet. Most agents were managing to take the day off. But Lenora and Tony were already at their stations, apparently 'sponding some training programs. Good for them. He walked over to them.

"Get a good night's sleep?"

They looked bleary-eyed. He felt for the rookies.

"Yeah, me too. You're going to see things all your career that are disturbing. It's part of the job. Leave the question of the ethics of LEPGen's research techniques to others. We have one job to do: determine if a crime has been committed. And if so, who did it. Any time someone intentionally adversely impacts the success, and therefore profit, of a corporation, and in turn The Corporation, a crime has been committed.

"Always think motive. Why would someone do something to cause their experiments to fail? Look for the disgruntled employee, the corporate spy. Look for possible links to terrorist organizations.

"Start by checking for criminal records of the people on the list. Slim chance, but you never know. Then try 'sponding their LEPGen records to see if Treadwell has gotten us clearance yet. If so, start poking around. I see Chavez is in so I'm going to go talk to her about the case.

"By the way, we're going to be working hot'n'heavy on this for the foreseeable future, so make appropriate adjustments. Tell your significants you'll be largely unavailable for a while.

Lenora and Tony nodded. Michael walked through the stations to Consuela Chavez's office. As the Poughkeepsie bureau chief she had a large, corner office. Michael thought it funny how the CBI still copied the old corporate practice of having corner offices for the big shots. The stations most agents worked at were in an open area but could be visibly and audibly tuned out for privacy. Solid walls, doors, sound proof glass and closeable shades were all totally unnecessary with today's technology, and therefore an unnecessary expense. Something the efficient Corporation should be doing away with. *But the director and executive levels still had to show that their dicks were bigger than yours,* Michael chuckled. *Hmmm. What appendage would that be in Connie's case?*

Connie saw him through the glass and waved him in. "Michael, that's what I like about you. You're always smiling! Come on in and close the door."

"Morning Connie. Yeah, I was just pondering some old customs."

"Sit down. Give me the scoop on LEPGen."

Michael briefed her and concluded with, "So agents Davis, Ragusini and I'll strategize and start checking the records of likelies."

"OK, keep me posted. Remember, you're a chief inspector now. Solving this case can give those agents their detective stripes – and you, more people. So keep them actively involved. Oh, and keep Davis pushed forward on this one."

"Gotcha." Well, it was clear who Davis's mentor was. Asking if he should keep Ragusini pushed forward too would be blatant insubordination – not that that had ever stopped him before. He just wasn't in the mood to get the ole raised eyebrow this early in the morning.

He walked back to Lenora and Tony and asked them whether they had had any luck.

"No criminal records. We have access to the LEPGen records now," Tony told him.

"Good. Let's start getting familiar with the likelies first. I'll take Treadwell and a few others. I'll also contact the location manager at CaringMother to get access to their LEPGen contact's records."

Michael sat down at his station and tuned in. He 'sponded into the LEPGen records and quickly got to Treadwell. He willed the mid-level detail with oral rather than written report, then selected the universal symbol for background information and settled back to listen.

Nowadays it was much more common to select the oral rather than written form in receiving information. Keeping eyes free to observe one's environment was safer, and people just preferred oral communication. They had been moving away from the written word for a long time. "Oral" was more like listening to an internal voice, like talking to oneself, rather than actually hearing it externally. Just as "written" was also totally internal, more like imagining seeing something written.

Yep, I was right. Divorced, one dog, no kids, but "nieces and nephews" (children of friends) she's fond of. Outdoor activities, Michael observed. *Only child of Chinese immigrants. Well, it looks like The Corporation will have to replace her with more Chinese immigrants, because she won't be helping out on the kid front. Hmmm, was married to a guy named Treadwell. Interesting that she took his name, and kept it when they got divorced. Doctorate from Harvard Corporate University. Smart cookie. And a Buddhist.*

At this Michael willed a pause and walked over to the window and looked down Main Street at the late 1800's and early 1900's restored buildings without really seeing them. He was never interested in religions, but he had received a certain amount of force feeding and osmosis on Buddhism from his wife and daughter. He knew that the original Buddha, Siddhartha Gautama, taught that all life is suffering and that we continue to experience this suffering through a cycle of rebirth and death. He said suffering is caused by human desires so the ultimate goal of humans should be to reach a state of nirvana, which means the "blowing out of desires", a state of wisdom and peace. Having reached a state of nirvana in life, one finally attains perfect nirvana in death, finally passing beyond the cycle of death and rebirth.

He knew that Buddhism was a very peace-loving religion and was big on doing no harm. One should eliminate suffering wherever possible. The image Michael had of the typical Buddhist was the Tibetan monk walking down the street, picking up insects and delivering them to safety at the side of the street before continuing along.

So how did this gel with Treadwell? He just couldn't see a Buddhist experimenting on those little bodies. Was she secretly sabotaging her own experiments? Consciously or unconsciously? She was undoubtedly the person with the most unquestioned access to the lab. Or was she a Buddhist in name only; maybe Buddhist because her parents were? Michael shrugged. He was a Corporate Christian because of where it could get him, not because of deep beliefs. He'd have to quiz Julianna about how a Buddhist would handle certain hypothetical situations. He knew his wife could never be a Treadwell.

Michael walked back to his station. He wanted to be sitting when he reentered the LEPGen records and began concentrating again. At this point he went into Treadwell's employment records. She had begun working at LEPGen Technologies in 2067 as a first-line, limited-production manager in Poughkeepsie. Limited production was typical for first-run quality control, before full production was farmed out. She then did a stint at headquarters in Westchester County. Someone there obviously liked her because she came back to Poughkeepsie as a director of development.

Then after only seven years at LEPGen she became director of transponder research. This was the company's jewel, so she was obviously held in high regard and must be considered beyond suspicion. She had consistently received "1", or highest, ratings with extremely complimentary comments, along with a number of impressive awards. They obviously loved her there.

Michael then moved into her prior employment record. Post-doc work at a university in China. Returning to the US began working for Xenton

Corporation in R&D. Unfortunately, he couldn't access her records at Xenton without their permission. She then moved on to NuTense Corporation, again in R&D, but again, no performance records. And from there on to LEPGen Technologies, where she had been the longest and obviously done very well.

But hadn't she said that NuTense was LEPGen's main competitor in transponders? Funny she didn't mention that she had worked for NuTense in her last position before coming to work for LEPGen. Could she be a NuTense mole, working her way into a position where she could cause real problems for LEPGen, and then pulling the lever? Na, Michael couldn't buy that. But yet?

He again paused her records and went to the NuTense Corporation main site and watched the spiel about the nature of their business. NuTense was a newer technology company that specialized in weapon guidance technology (read: they had a lock in this area with The Corporation and the army). Michael willed a demo, which showed a soldier thought-guiding a rocket into the middle of a bull's eye, then boom! Going back to their main spiel, they said they were an aggressive, up-and-coming corporation, looking to compete with, and unseat, the old guard.

Obviously they were after the lucrative transponder business with The Corporation. Given LEPGen's history with the transponder and The Corporation, they wouldn't stand a chance – unless, of course, LEPGen showed incompetence in development. He'd have to get access to Treadwell's NuTense employment records without tipping his hat.

After going through the rest of Treadwell's record, he decided to keep his findings and thoughts to himself for the time being – not telling Lenora, Tony, or Connie. He didn't want them to unconsciously treat her with suspicion when they were around her. At this, he decided to take a break and see how "the kids" were doing before tackling CaringMother.

"How's it going?"

"Nothing concrete yet, everyone seems to be performing well in their positions. No laggards, but no stellar performers either. No outside activities that seemed suspicious. So far, all have passed periodic security checks," said Tony.

"Any memberships in quirky organizations?"

"Just the usual, some sororities and fraternities, volunteer work, sports clubs," Lenora responded.

"What kind of volunteer work?"

"You know, the regular stuff – helping out the lower bands."

"Careful with those do-gooders; they can get carried away. Do some cross referencing on their volunteer work, see if there's any commonality. Also, do a cross check on their prior employment, see if there's any commonality there. Actually, give me a list next to the names of where they had previously worked and when."

"Will do."

"Religions?"

"Mostly Corporate Church. Then a smattering of all the others. Nothing stands out. No quirky ones."

Michael, would you come here for a minute? Connie 'sponded while he was winding down with Lenora and Tony.

"I've got to see Connie. Keep digging."

Michael walked into Connie's office and closed the door.

"We're going for a ride. Dr. Treadwell recounted your meeting with her to her site general manager, including that you wanted to check on the CaringMother contact. Well, the general manager called her good buddy, Rebecca Colson, CEO of CaringMother, and she wants to meet with you, me and Treadwell."

"Fuckin' Hell! Why did Treadwell alert her?!"

"Why did you brief me? She had to."

"Yeah, I know," Michael responded reasonably, but fuming. "So now the cat starts leaking out of the bag!" In spite of his anger, Michael couldn't help but grin at his mixed metaphor.

"Michael, come on, you knew it was just a matter of time."

"You know damn well that Colson's going to throw up major road blocks to the investigation to keep any sniff of wrong doing away from CaringMother. What should have been a simple side investigation on my part is going to turn into a pissing contest. Goddamnit! The good ole girls' club at work! You know they say it's twice as bad as the good ole boys in the olden days."

"Now Michael, don't start going sexist on me!"

"Just remember how many men were involved in this case when things start getting all fucked up!" Michael fumed as he opened the door and stormed out.

"Colson has a limo picking us up in ten minutes. Cool down and ready up!" Michael was pissing Connie off. But he was right. This was where things would start getting all fucked up.

Chapter 12

Michael realized that his temper worked against him and flying off the handle just wasn't Chinese. He chuckled. Had an Irishman or Italian slipped into his ancestry?

The good ole girls weren't any worse than the good ole boys had been, though they sure weren't any better. But damnit, once executives started getting involved, they'd start directing the investigation so in the end the results would come out in their favor. And bucking for an executive-level position, Connie would be only too happy to oblige. If justice was done in the end, it would only be by luck.

Connie leaned over his chair. "The limo's here, Michael. Let's go. Lenora and Tony, sorry you can't go along, but CEOs like Colson always want limited audiences. Keep plugging away and we'll see you when we get back."

As they were dashing from the cool of the building to the limo, Michael sized it up in a flash. A Duesenberg! Top of the line! While builders of cars had gone out of business or consolidated, many of the luxury brands were still in business and doing well catering to executives. Owning a top-of-the-line BMW or a Bentley wasn't good enough for many execs, so the Duesenberg brand, one of the ultimate signs of luxury and excellence from the early 1900's, was resurrected. As Michael stepped into the salon seating, he positioned himself toward the front. The failsafe organic intelligence driving the limo made a chauffeur totally superfluous.

"Dr. Treadwell. We meet again so soon!"

"Good morning, Detective Chan," Treadwell responded, as she drew back further into her corner. "I'm sorry if my GM's calling Colson is complicating the investigation, but I have no control over her."

"Don't worry about it," said Connie. "Let me do the talking when we meet with Colson."

Michael knew Connie was relishing the executive exposure she was about to have.

"We're heading out to Colson's home in Millbrook. I think she'll want to know what the situation is, how it relates to CaringMother, and to tell us how she wants interactions with CaringMother to proceed."

As the limo moved them beyond the dom district, they were immediately in the older, often dilapidated sections of Poughkeepsie. This was where the exurban refugees were living till they could get into an apartment in the dom district. And, of course, where the lower bands had permanent residence.

Beyond the Poughkeepsie Corporate city limits they traveled past derelict buildings that were not within the restructuring definition and were slowly disappearing due to the ravages of weather and nature. About 10 kilometers out they passed the attractive, wooded enclave where Connie lived. The large, director-level family homes were built to withstand the ravages of modern-day weather extremes. Most directors were in jobs that supplied cars and toll fees as a perk, enabling their commute.

They soon crossed under the old stone structure of a Taconic Parkway bridge and pulled up at a Millbrook Executive Patent checkpoint. Since two of the three passengers were with the CBI and they were traveling in an executive's limo, there were few questions and after a quick scan they were on their way again. They immediately found themselves riding through the scenic rolling hills of what had been the northeastern part of Dutchess County. This was an area of large, prosperous farms and wooded hills till the second half of the 1900's when well-to-do New Yorkers began buying up the farms and turning them into weekend-getaway horse farms. The large old estate manors were expanded to suit the tastes of the new owners, including modern conveniences, while keeping to the same style of the originals.

This area continued to be the weekend destination of the rich and famous from New York City, so when The Corporation took over they defined its boundaries and renamed it the Millbrook Executive Patent. Anyone who could afford it could buy an estate here and live here. Most owners were executives, usually CEOs, of corporations or executives in The Corporation. There was the occasional small Corporate village, like Millbrook, with old stores turned into boutiques and fine restaurants to cater to the executives.

After a drive of 20 more kilometers, they pulled up to a large, old, but sturdily-built arched stone gate and gate house combination. It reminded Michael of the fortified gates of old European cities. As they drove through the gate, Michael looked up and saw a coat of arms with a stylized mother holding a baby. They went over an old stone-arch bridge, built where the large lake on the left narrowed down into a stream running under the bridge. *Cool! Just like the moats of old! Good way to keep the riff-raff out!* Michael smiled.

As the Duesenberg took them up a tree-lined, cobblestone drive, they looked out at the lake where swans and ducks were dipping for fish or seeking shade among the ancient trees along the bank. Ahead they saw a huge, castle-like mansion, built of the same stones as the gate house and bridge. *This could have been the country estate of royals in England!* Michael thought as they pulled in under the *porte cochere* and up to the massive, granite front steps.

Two man servants in tails (*How quaint!*) came out to greet them and help the women out of the limousine (*Chivalry isn't dead!*) and held their arms as they walked up those massive front steps. Michael trailed along behind them, alone (*Sexism isn't either,* he smiled). They were led into the great entrance hall and escorted into a parlor with fourteen foot ceilings (*One would never be so crass as to refer to their height in modern metric terms!*) which was furnished with federal-style furniture. All except one item.

Michael walked over to the grandfather clock against one of the walls. *Oh my God, a Thomas Tompion tall case clock!* Michael thought as he studied the dial, admired the fine workmanship of the cabinet and listened to the solid, even "tick-tock" of the passage of time this grand time piece pronounced.

"I see you appreciate my Tompion, Detective Chan," said a strong, feminine voice behind him. Michael turned around to see a matronly woman smiling at him. Though she looked like the quintessential grandmother, Michael noticed her piercing eyes studying him for any telltale nuances.

As Michael bowed and she introduced herself as Rebecca Colson, Michael responded, "Antique clocks are a hobby of mine. I've only seen one Tompion before this. It was in the clock collection at the Metropolitan Art Museum. Tompion made the greatest clocks ever! I am in awe. May I stand here in its radiant grandeur for a while?"

Colson had a hearty laugh. "You certainly may! I often feel exactly the same way. I originally bought it for its beauty, even though it is English and doesn't technically fit in this room of American federal furniture. But I soon came to appreciate its magnificent mechanical works and the heavenly sound of its chime and strike as well."

Chavez and Treadwell were standing on the opposite side of the large room looking out the floor-to-ceiling windows at the lake. They walked over and introduced themselves, expressing their love of Colson's home.

"I'm glad you like it. It's home to me. I came from humble beginnings. My father was a university professor and my mother an elementary school teacher. When I eventually ascended to become CEO of CaringMother I felt I had reached a point where I should treat myself to the house I wanted. And this was it. This was the old Montbatten estate. It was run down when I bought it seven years ago. But I loved the spooky old place and have spent the time restoring it and furnishing it to my liking."

"You've done an exquisite job. It's just unbelievably beautiful!" gushed Connie.

"Well thank you. Although the manor and grounds look very staid and properly English, it's had quite a past of eccentric inhabitants. Timothy Leary, the 1960's LSD profit lived here, as did Bob Dylan, the famous song writer, as well as Uma Thurman, the actress from later in the 1900's. The great Sufi poet, Rumi al-Ghazzali lived here back in the 2040's. In fact, he wrote his *Reflections* while he lived here."

Ms. Colson asked them to take a seat and take refreshment. Maybe it was the surroundings, but they all requested tea, English Breakfast.

Connie proceeded to give Colson the overview of the situation at the LEPGen labs while Treadwell filled in some of the more technical details. Finally Connie said, "You know, Ms. Colson, we can't do a proper investigation unless we at least check out the CaringMother contact, and, if necessary, interview him."

"I understand, and I wouldn't dream of interfering with your investigation. However, remember that CaringMother is *the* wombcare and postnatal care choice of many young women, and even a hint of scandal could destroy their confidence in CaringMother. That would destroy us.

"We appreciate our business dealings with LEPGen Technologies. Our supply contract with LEPGen is important to us and we do not want to jeopardize that. I'll speak directly to the location manager in Poughkeepsie and tell her to cooperate. But at this point I'll only give you access to the contact's records and permission to interview him if necessary."

"Understood," Connie jumped in before Michael could voice any objections.

"If you need further access, I must insist that you get my permission directly."

"Certainly," Connie responded again.

"Oh, and be sure to keep me posted on the progress of the case."

"We will."

"One last thing. If this does turn out to be a crime and the criminal or criminals are caught, I don't want it to go to trial. Solve the problem and make it disappear."

Connie studied her face and carefully responded, "Ms. Colson, I understand your desires. That's the direction all of us are inclined toward. But it'll be resolved in a manner that's most advantageous to The Corporation. If a terrorist plot, The Corporation may choose to make it an example by holding a public trial. That all remains to be seen."

Colson's scowl indicated she didn't like Connie's cautious response. She was obviously used to people taking her direction without questioning. But she also had to understand Chavez's constraints in the matter.

Finally she smiled and said, "Well, thank you so much for coming out on a holiday. I know it was inconvenient. But it was important to me to make my wishes very clear and in person. Like you, I'm very concerned about the ramifications this case could have, not just for CaringMother, but for the whole wombcare and postnatal care industry as a whole."

Michael had uncharacteristically kept his mouth shut during the meeting, knowing how important the lime-light was to Chavez. He was using the proceedings to better size up Colson. On the surface, she seemed very pleasant. She expressed her directions clearly and distinctly. But there was something lurking under her surface that made him uneasy.

What was a CEO doing getting involved in a possible crime committed at the R&D facility of another corporation – even if it could be related to one of her facilities? He didn't like it. She'd be staying involved and on top of this case, bending and twisting it so that she and CaringMother would come out unscathed in the end.

Colson watched the Duesenberg glide down the drive. Turning to her assistant, she said, "Start selling CaringMother's LEPGen Technologies stocks and start buying NuTense stocks with the proceeds. Do the same with my LEPGen stocks. Yours too if you wish. But keep it at a pace that'll keep what's happening under The Corporation's radar. Also, start slowly selling my CaringMother shares and warrants and put the proceeds into bonds and floating credits. Then arrange a holoplay call with Thomas Watson-Finlay, the CEO of NuTense. Not a 'spond. I want it eyeball-to-eyeball."

As her assistant turned to walk out of the room, Colson glanced at his cute little butt and said, "You know, Hud, it *is* a holiday. Before you start doing all that, let's take some time to relax. Why don't you go upstairs, turn down my bed, and get yourself ready."

Hudson attempted a smile and said, "Sure thing, Bec." He had jumped at taking this rotating assignment as Colson's assistant. He knew that if he performed his duties well, she'd reward him with a generous leap in level in his next position. But at what cost? He had already lost his fiancée, not to mention much of his self esteem. Well, his assignment would end soon, another young stud would take his place, and he'd be off and scrambling further up the corporate ladder.

Chapter 13

At the tip of the island the Native Americans called Manna Hatta, lay the bustling Dutch new-world city of Nieuw Amsterdam. It was perfectly located in a great natural harbor, was protected on three sides by water, and on the north side by a defensive wall. Breede Weg, the widest street in the city, ran from the fortress at the southern tip of the island, up through the city. This broad way passed through the gate in the wall and followed the Native American and deer paths up to the northern end of the island, where one had to cross over by boat to Spijt den Duyvil, or "spite the devil", a place descriptive of the attitude one needed for the treacherous currents.

After passing by Bronck's farm, the way meandered through gentle hills and by lazy kills, past the Jonkheer's settlement, up through the craggy wilds of the Hudson Highlands and into the fertile lands of the Mid-Hudson Valley. When the English took control of Nieuw Amsterdam and Nieuw Nederlandt and renamed them New York, this connection of paths was broadened further and extended to the settlement of Albany. It was named the King's Highway. After independence, it was renamed Albany Post Road, and in the age of automobiles it was renamed New York Route 9. Now, on Founder's Day in the Tricentennial year, it was officially renamed the Founder's Way, in honor of Kenneth Rechner.

Siobhan stared out the windows of the tram that ran north up Founder's Way. She and Ian had just passed the Roosevelt and Vanderbilt mansions. She could catch glimpses of the stately Staatsburgh mansion perched on its hill overlooking the Hudson. Ian enjoyed the scenery too, but he couldn't help glancing at her occasionally, wondering about this woman who seemed so friendly on the surface, but maintained a distance that he so wanted to overcome.

Before leaving Doodletown on Saturday, he understood the mission he had committed to and its importance, so technically he could function on his own. He had no need to know more about Siobhan's other activities nor the names of any of her contacts. In fact, the less contact they had with one another, the safer each of them would be.

Their boat trip back up the Hudson had been a quiet one, both deep in thought as they gazed at the sights going through the Highlands. Ian had looked for a clue from Siobhan as they left the boat, ready to head their separate ways. But she had merely bowed and thanked him for the wonderful day. She again told him how thankful she was to him for agreeing to help with Spencer.

Yesterday Ian had waited till afternoon, hoping Siobhan would 'spond him. When she didn't, he took the initiative and 'sponded her, saying he had something important he wanted to discuss with her. She suggested they get together on Monday and agreed when Ian suggested they take a tram ride up the Hudson. They had met at the tram stop at the Poughkeepsie levtrain station late this morning and were just now pulling into their destination: Rhinebeck.

Rhinebeck was a Corporate village. It had long been a popular tourist destination. So PleaseCo Corporation had eagerly bought up most of the old, quaint shops. There were numerous excellent restaurants and activities such as watching "movies" in the cozy, 1930's-era Upstate Films theater that still showed independent, non-Corporate "films" (usually in 3D wallplay format now). One could also easily walk around the village and enjoy seeing the old Victorian and early twentieth century houses that were so lovingly maintained.

Since it had cooled down a bit today and the terrain was relatively flat in the surrounding country side, Ian and Siobhan rented bicycles to take a circular ride down by the Hudson before returning to the village to shop. They headed south on Founder's Way. Past Landsman Kill they turned southwest onto Mill Road. The warm, gentle breeze felt good through their UV-protectant clothing, as they used natural sweat to cool themselves.

As soon as they turned west on to Morton Road they saw the towering, gothic Wilderstein Mansion. Like many estates along the Hudson, Wilderstein had fallen on hard times in the late 1900's, and it had been taken over by a private foundation with the objective of restoring it and opening it up to public use. During the Great Restructuring, The Corporation took ownership of these estates and thanked the foundations for their many years of stewardship. It then evaluated all Corporate-owned estates, including prior federal- and state-owned ones. Estates that were less likely to turn a profit (income from visitation fees and souvenir sales vs. upkeep costs) were sold off to corporate executives. For estates like Wilderstein that could turn a profit, The Corporation put their concessions out to bid. PleaseCo was the only serious bidder, so they won the concession rights for a very low bid price for most of the estates.

Ian's great grandmother had been one of the original members of the Wilderstein foundation. The tradition of membership and volunteer work had continued on in his family. Ian had enjoyed coming up to visit and doing volunteer work. But after The Corporation took over he seemed to visit less and less. He was disappointed to see that the grounds were looking unkempt and overgrown. The mansion looked shabby.

Fees were automatically 'sponded from Ian's and Siobhan's accounts as soon as they entered the grounds, the mansion and as they entered each room. Each amount was small in itself, but they all added up to a sizeable amount by the end of the self-'sponded tour. But Ian wanted to show Siobhan through this place that had meant so much to his family. In each room he pointed out work a member of his family had done or contributed to.

"Those beautiful stained-glass windows were what got my great grandmother interested in becoming a member in the first place. She loved their beauty and craftsmanship, but they were buckling and would soon fall apart. They needed immediate attention," Ian commented.

"They are beautiful," Siobhan agreed. "And I love that this mansion has a true 'family' room that was used for family gatherings every day. So cozy and different from the formal parlor! I can see the family gathering around the piano to sing songs in the evening. The warm quirkiness of this house, I hate to say mansion, reminds me of Roosevelt's Springwood, or van Buren's Lindenwald in Kinderhook. They're so different from the sterile grandeur of estates like Vanderbilt."

Walking up the steps to the third floor, Ian observed Siobhan's eyes brighten as she saw that the entire floor was a large nursery/playroom for the children. As they walked around, she studied the many toys and cribs. Siobhan instinctively picked up one of the teddy bears and fondled it thoughtfully. She carefully replaced it when an automatic 'spond told her touching artifacts was not allowed. Ian saw a quiet longing in her eyes that lingered when she looked up at him and smiled.

When they went into the tower and looked out the windows toward the surrounding countryside and down the Hudson, Siobhan mused, "How idyllic! And how those children must have been loved!"

After touring the house and then the gardens, they walked down one of the paths to a quiet cove on the Hudson. They could have been a nineteenth century suitor and the woman of his desires enjoying a quiet, romantic spot on the Hudson – a scene that was so popular in many of the Hudson River School paintings.

But Siobhan's dreamy look hardened. "Well, this should be remote enough down here," she said. "What did you want to discuss?"

Ian instinctively drew back and stared at Siobhan as he mentally shifted gears. "After I got home Saturday, I reread Spencer's composition on independence several times. It's quite critical of The Corporation. If it fell into the wrong hands, like some corpo wanting to score some points, he could be in real trouble. I want to encourage him to explore all his thoughts unencumbered. But I don't want him to get into trouble. I'd like you to read it and tell me what you think." Ian took the folded paper out of an inner pocket and handed it to Siobhan.

She read through the composition and then stared across the Hudson toward an old monastery. "This should be read by the other students and used in class discussion. But you have to be sure it doesn't get outside your class. Ian, you just can't stifle Spencer. You'd be preempting the corpos if you did – doing their job for them." She was quiet for a moment. Her voice tightened. "But this could be construed as inflammatory and insurrectionist. Maybe discuss with Spencer how to tone it down for his own safety. And for his mothers' too."

Siobhan frowned. "You're an outstanding, experienced teacher, Ian. You already know what to do. Why did you want my help in the matter?"

"I guess to confirm the direction I'd take in handling Spencer." Ian could feel himself reddening. "But I have to admit that it was a good reason to see you again."

Siobhan smiled. "Ian, you're sweet. But we're colleagues only – working on our shared mission – Spencer. Anything beyond that would be a mistake. That's the way things are handled in our organization – unwritten rule number one. If we got emotionally involved and something went wrong, I'm afraid we'd end up dragging each other down. And maybe Spencer as well."

Ian felt her eyes were telling him something different.

"I understand." Then he laughed, "Ah, my vanity after being picked up by a beautiful woman!"

Siobhan laughed too but then said more seriously, "Ian, we just can't jeopardize Spencer's future. We have to concentrate on him, not ourselves."

But then her eyes softened again. "After Saturday I convinced myself that I wasn't going to contact you again, other than to get periodic updates from you. But then you 'sponded me about getting together, and my convictions flew out the window," Now reddening herself, Siobhan continued. "Of course, I immediately agreed not only to meet but to make an outing of it! That's how focused I am!

"Well, we're here – so why don't we just have a fun, unencumbered time together!" she added.

Chapter 14

After Wilderstein, they rode north up Morton Road to Rhinecliff, a quaint river hamlet that time had forgotten, though not The Corporation. With advanced information, PleaseCo bought up most of the small shops in the town before it was incorporated into the village of Rhinebeck. Ian and Siobhan ate a late lunch on the deck of the Victorian PleaseCo Rhinecliff Hotel, enjoying the views up and down the Hudson, before riding back to Rhinebeck. There they rode through the streets and admired the old houses. After returning their bicycles, they visited many of the old shops on Market and Montgomery Streets.

While they were in a dark, cluttered antique shop looking over its many treasures, a large, dirty, old shelf clock caught Ian's eye. As he was looking it over, the owner came up to Ian and said, "Chauncey Jerome."

"Pardon?" Ian said turning to the grizzled, old man who looked like he could have been one of the antiques.

"Chauncey Jerome. 8-day, weight-driven, OG shelf clock. Circa 1860. Here, let me show you." The man opened the front door of the clock. Inside was a nicely preserved paper label. "They never put manufacturing dates on these clocks, but if you're lucky enough to still have a label in it you can usually date it by where it was manufactured and by the label printer's name. Here, you can see Jerome had already moved production from Bristol to New Haven, Connecticut. Yep. Just about 1860. Jerome was a pioneer in manufacturing good-quality, affordable clocks. This one was probably sold to some farmer here in the Mid-Hudson Valley. The poor bastard might have had a year or two enjoying his new possession before going off to get his ass killed on some god-forsaken battlefield in the Civil War," the old man mused.

"Does it work?"

"Sure. Here, let me show you," the owner said as he cranked the weights up a bit and started the pendulum going. "See? Works fine. Just needs a good cleaning and oiling and I'm sure it'd appreciate a little restoration of the case. Yeah, these things were built to last forever as long as they're maintained. This old workhorse was around long before we came on the scene and will be ticking away long after we're gone. It's been waiting dormant on that shelf for years, waiting for someone with a heart like you to come along and start its ticker going again."

"But how do you clean and oil it?" Ian asked.

"You're from the valley? There's an active antique clock collectors association in Poughkeepsie. They'd gladly take you under their wings and help you out."

As he stared at the clock, Ian thought about how the Mid-Hudson Valley had looked back in 1860. He thought about that farmer going off to war and his widow passing the clock on to their children. *What's that clock been through over the past two centuries? How did it end up on this shelf? And it still works!*

Ian had to have it.

Siobhan had been looking at some antique post cards, but when she saw that Ian was still talking with the old man, she walked over.

"Look what I just bought!" Ian said, beaming.

"What is it?"

"Civil-War-era clock. It's beautiful!"

"Yes, it is," Siobhan said, admiring the hand-painted floral design on the dial and the soft patina of the finish evident under the layer of grunge on the curved, mahogany veneer. Then she added, "Large, robust and shamelessly dirty. Yet somehow amazingly feminine."

Ian removed the two 8-pound weights and put them into his day pack, hoisted the clock under his arm and they walked out the door and down the street to a bistro.

As they sat eating a light meal, Ian kept glancing down at his new treasure.

"Well, at least I now know where I stand," Siobhan teased him. "How soon we poor women are cast aside and forgotten when new toys come along!"

Ian looked up, embarrassed. "Sorry, I'm just so happy."

"What's the fascination?"

"My grandfather took me to the American Clock Museum in Bristol, Connecticut once. Connecticut was the epicenter of American clock making in the old days. I can still see this old Dutch *stoelklok* from the 1600's, sitting on a shelf, ticking away. I was fascinated with its age. I could imagine it coming over from Holland in the 1600s like my family. It was a working piece of history – each "tick-tock" somehow tying us to our past and taking us into the future. And I've been fascinated with antique clocks ever since, always telling myself I'd get into clock restoration some day. I guess today's the day!" Ian said smiling, sneaking another admiring peek at his clock.

When they got off the tram in Poughkeepsie, Siobhan, lost in thought, instinctively started heading toward home. But then she turned back and looked at Ian, standing with his clock under his arm. He had a hurt look. From the distance he looked like a little lost boy holding his teddy bear. Siobhan wanted to run back and throw her arms around him. But she didn't. Instead she walked back to him. "Ian, I'm sorry. I have a lot on my mind. I'm glad we got together today. It was the most fun I've had in a long time. Thanks so much."

After an awkward pause, Ian asked, "When will I see you again?"

"Ian, this is all I can handle right now." But after seeing the disappointment on his face, and against her better judgment, she added, "From a 'working-learning' standpoint, there's a place I'd like to show you that's quite the opposite of the life those children had had in Wilderstein, and of your school. Will you be free about 3 o'clock Thursday afternoon?" When Ian said he would be, they agreed to meet at the Shakespeare Garden at his school.

As Ian reached for Siobhan, she stepped back and bowed. "Enjoy your beautiful new clock and see you Thursday afternoon."

Siobhan turned and walked rapidly away from Ian. But she felt that with each step she was moving away from a world of warmth and light toward her one-dimensional grayness. She willed herself not to look back, but just as she was disappearing into the twilight's gloom, she glanced back. Ian was still standing with his clock in hand and his lost-boy look.

He waved. She smiled. And she was gone.

Siobhan sat in her easy chair drinking East Friesian tea. She was happy she didn't feel the need to drink Lapsang Souchong tonight – maybe that was an indication that she was beginning to move on. She looked up at the works of her famous resident ghost. She knew he was telling her to celebrate life, to open up to love in whatever form it takes and to be strong enough to accept the consequences of this greatest emotion. Without it, she wasn't really living. And she knew she hadn't been for years. Yes, she was working in her small ways to try to better the world she lived in. But she needed someone for herself – to love again, to fill that void – to relieve that sadness that had filled her being for so long.

She thought back to Saturday and how she had felt so incredibly sad at the creek in Doodletown. But then came the first inklings of release. She hadn't understood it at first, but when they headed back down the path toward the river, walking along in silence, enjoying the peace of the valley, she knew she was beginning to leave the dark valley she'd been in for so long. She was beginning to wonder if she really was deserving of happiness – if she could find it. And would she with Ian?

She felt a lightness, a hope. It was the magic of *Dodendal* that had caused her to impulsively take Ian's hand. To walk hand-in-hand toward a future beyond her dark valley. A risky, unknown future. But a future.

Yet once they were back on the boat and pulling away from that enchanted valley, she began to have doubts again.

And then came the dream.

After an emotion-filled day, she had come home Saturday evening and went through the motions of reading poetry. But eventually she decided to go to bed. She was emotionally exhausted. After trying to tune down her racing mind, she finally fell into a restless sleep.

She dreamed that she was walking though a dark valley. There were steep, rocky mountains on either side, so only one way forward. The gnarled, ghostly trees on either side reached down, trying to grab her. It was getting darker. She had to keep moving; she couldn't stop. But she was afraid of the unknown that lay ahead.

After some time she thought she saw a clearing though the trees. Yes, there was a clearing and she caught a glimpse of water in the distance. Siobhan soon came upon a decrepit wrought iron fence. Finding the gate, she walked through and realized that she was in a small, very old cemetery. Some of the tombstones had the ornate tops that were common among the early Dutch settlers. But Siobhan didn't stop to read any. She was drawn toward the body of water she had spied before.

She walked out the far gate and came to the edge of a pond. At first she didn't know where she was. Then she realized she was in the Valley of the Dead, but on the opposite side of the pond she had been on with Ian. The feeling of hope she had felt with Ian was now replaced by doubt and dread. As if to confirm her fears, the sky grew still darker.

Suddenly she saw Ian come crashing through the underbrush on the other side of the pond. Was he being chased? By whom? He at first halted and gazed around, as if to orient himself. But then he entered the pond, trying to get away from his adversary. Siobhan wanted to call out but she felt frozen, unable to move.

Then Ian saw her. She saw the longing in his eyes. He moved toward her, ever deeper into the pond. When he was up to his chest, he reached his hand up, silently asking for help. But she was still unable to move.

Instinctively, she looked behind herself toward the graveyard. She knew whom she expected to see, but he wasn't there. She would no longer see him, but she would feel him in her heart. Always.

When she turned back toward Ian, he was thrashing and struggling. She desperately wanted to run into the pond to help him. But an evil force locked her into place. She could only scream in her mind and watch as Ian was slowly dragged under the water. The water filled over where Ian had been. She *watched as the smoothing water gave witness that Ian was not there. As if he never had been.*

Siobhan had woken up crying. She had already had her heart ripped from her. Could she survive if she surrendered her heart to Ian and lost him too?

Now, as Siobhan finished her tea, she still felt terribly conflicted. She knew she needed to sort out her feelings by Thursday when she'd see Ian again.

Siobhan stood up and went to the stairs. As she walked up the steps, each creak spoke of the many lives who had climbed these treads – who had gone before her in this house. Sensing comforting presences around her, she wondered what they would have done.

As she walked toward her bedroom, she paused and looked into his room. She saw herself sitting in the rocking chair as she had so many times before. And in the shadows she could almost see him. But then she reached for the knob and slowly closed the door. *I'm sorry. I'm sorry. I don't love you any less. But I have to live again.*

Chapter 15
TUESDAY, JULY 7

" ... All of you have done great work on your compositions – writing and rewriting them. This session lasts the whole morning, so you'll have time to work your way through the first two compositions I'm handing out: Linda's composition on the rise of The Corporation and Spencer's on independence. I thought both of these were outstanding and will be an excellent starting point for reading and discussing the papers.

"Intense reading like this is not easy now-a-days, so if you have a problem with any passages or words, come and discuss them with me. I'm also handing out what were called 'number 2 pencils' that students used in the old days. Use them to write comments on the paper in any blank space. They'll help you when we discuss these papers tomorrow.

"To get the full experience, I want you to tune out while reading." This elicited groans from the students. "Hey, guys, you need to concentrate on this stuff. Students had external devices in the old days that they could tune in to, but they were not allowed to use them while working in class. Teachers would even confiscate them! If you need a break, put the compositions down and take a short tune-in break. Just raise your hand so I know you're tuning in.

"In about an hour, Jane Addams-Alvarez will be visiting us. She's a retired professor who was born on May 3, 1976, shortly before the Bicentennial celebrations. " This reminder perked his students up. "We have a lot to learn from her about the old days. Ask her questions, but listen and learn."

Ian watched them get down to work. A typical mix: 10 females and 6 males. 4 whites, 4 Hispanics, 4 Orientals (3 of whom were Chinese), 3 blacks and 1 "other". Racial designations were an anachronism since so many people had more than one race in their background and the ISA was supposedly "post-racial". But when whites became a racial minority, they, more than any other racial group, had insisted on keeping racial designations.

Though he had no children of his own, these young people always awakened fatherly feelings in Ian. He wanted to protect them but also wanted to see them grow, to learn to make their own way. They were mostly 15 or 16 years old – still kids, but approaching adulthood.

Being in the upper form school, most of them came from well-off families. Their parents were typically executives, or at least directors. As a result they came with a lot of "executive-class baggage", as Ian called it. They parroted their parents' unquestioning support of The Corporation (more so than the typical person on the street). They felt they deserved their life of privilege and disdained those who were less fortunate. But they were also under intense pressure to succeed and had incredible difficulty accepting any kind of failure on their own part.

Up till now, their exposure to history had focused on the terrible times before The Corporation took over the government and all the good it had done since. They would be the leaders of tomorrow, and Ian was a good teacher. So he always felt an urgent need not only to make them more aware of history – the good *and* the bad – but more importantly to encourage them to become aware, thinking human beings, able to feel some compassion. He never drove them, but he did push.

At her invited time, a very old woman assisted by a younger woman walked into the classroom and greeted Ian. Although she was petite and frail, she presented herself with an aura of authority. Her engaging smile and bright eyes belied her frailness.

Ian had met Jane Addams-Alvarez on an architectural tour at the school. After a short time it became obvious that she was very familiar with the campus. At one point she corrected the middle-aged docent's comments on a particular building. When he became huffy, she said, "Young man, I was teaching at this school and knew every building well before you knew what architecture was. Check your records. You'll see I'm right." Ian admired her assertiveness when she knew she was right – not letting the docent's incorrect information slide. After the tour, Ian talked with her, learned about her interesting past and asked her to attend one of his class sessions.

"Hello Ms. Addams-Alvarez. We're so pleased to have you attend our session today," Ian said, making a quick bow and leading her directly to a seat in the circle of the class.

"This is a pleasant change from my drab routine," she responded as she looked around the room, smiling at the young people. "And just call me Mrs. Alvarez, or even Jane."

"OK, Mrs. Alvarez it is," Ian said, looking at his students so they got the message – no first names with this lady!

"And this is my granddaughter, Sabina Havard. She helps me out a lot."

"We're so glad you could attend as well, Ms. Havard," Ian said.

Ian could tell his students were awed by meeting such an old person who wasn't from the executive level. With the downward health trend of the population and the financial limitations to health care under privatized health insurance for the elderly, it was rare to see a person this old.

After the students each introduced themselves, Ian said, "Well, Mrs. Alvarez, as we discussed, this is the upper-form, first-year historical awareness class. In this class, the students explore many areas of history. They have just completed a written composition on an historical topic of their choosing and its relationship to our current day. So we all thought it would be great to have a centenarian come in and give us direct insight into the past century."

Mrs. Alvarez smiled. "I don't know how much insight I can give you, but let me start by telling you a bit about my background. As Mr. Vanderkill indicated, I'm a bit over 100 years old. I was the second of four children, and named after the great humanist, Jane Addams, who did so much for poor immigrant families in Chicago 200 years ago. My parents told me we were related to her.

"I went to college, got my Bachelor of Arts degree in modern languages, and went on to get my doctorate in Spanish language and literature. While teaching Spanish at New York University in Manhattan, I met my future husband, Hector Alvarez, who was originally from Chile, and was a professor of international business at the university. We got married, had two wonderful children, and moved up to the Mid-Hudson Valley for its beauty and quality of life. Hector continued to teach in the city, while I took a position as a professor of Spanish here, at what used to be Vassar College. In fact I taught many classes in this building. It brings back fond memories," Mrs. Alvarez said as she wistfully looked around the room.

"I retired from teaching in 2046. My husband died two years later. But fortunately, I have my other family members and friends (much younger friends!) who bring me such happiness," she said as she patted her granddaughter's hand.

"Now, why don't you tell me what you'd like to talk about, and let's see if I have something to say on the subject?"

After a pause, Alicia Nguyen raised her hand and asked, "What were the boys like when you were our age?"

Mrs. Alvarez laughed. "Oh pretty much like today, I would say. But they were certainly more forward. About getting to know girls and expressing their desires. But boys and men have to be much more careful today because of laws and social pressures. We had a saying back then, that boys always just wanted 'to get into your pants'."

At this the girls giggled and the boys reddened and took an interest in their shoes.

"Why do you go by 'Mrs. Alvarez' and not 'Ms. Addams?" Alma Gonzales wanted to know. "Isn't that a double sign of subservience to your husband?"

"Well, that was a tradition, although it was changing. I took his last name because I loved him and wanted to be with him the rest of my life, and 'Mrs.' because I wanted people to know I was married and proud of it."

"How did you deal with being oppressed as a female? How did you manage to get a doctorate back then?" asked Linda Xiaobo, adding sympathetically, "It must have been very difficult."

Mrs. Alvarez turned to Ian. "Mr. Vanderkill, what *have* you been teaching these young people?" At which Ian held up his hands helplessly.

Mrs. Alvarez continued, "Women in America were never oppressed. Certainly blacks and Native Americans had been. But women? No. For centuries, maybe forever, women and men had a convenient working relationship.

Women had babies and raised them, and men protected them and provided food and shelter. This became especially true in the industrial age. But that's when that convenient social structure started breaking down. When divorce started to become more than just a blip on the radar in the 1950's, women needed a different arrangement, more independence, more outside work opportunities. Society resisted as it does to any change. So women fought for change, and got it, conveniently using the myth of oppression to spur change along."

The students looked shocked by Mrs. Alvarez's unorthodox views and bluntness. Linda turned red and said, "Mrs. Alvarez, I think history would say otherwise. It's well-known that men were brutal oppressors of women."

"Linda, right? Look Linda, relationships between the sexes, including marriage, have never been easy. For various reasons on both sides of the equation. Reducing the past to oppression is too simple." Mrs. Alvarez could see that Linda and the others were still skeptical.

"How many of you have read *1984* by George Orwell?"

Many of the students raised their hands.

"Well, many of Orwell's works emphasize his idea of 'groupthink', the idea that humans in groups and societies tend to think alike, and if influenced or engineered to an extreme they become almost a single organism with one pattern of thought.

"Within a short period of time it became 'politically correct' to assume women were oppressed. Men by their evil, domineering nature were always trying to oppress them – or 're-oppress' them. Unfortunately, this 'groupthink' about men and women became increasingly ingrained and is still firmly entrenched today."

"With all due respect, Mrs. Alvarez, I think you're belittling the progress the women's movement has made," Linda said sharply.

Mrs. Alvarez smiled at this young version of herself. "I'm thankful to the original feminists who really did create change and made things easier for women like me. But many young women my age balked at the extremes of the 1960's and 1970's feminists. Some chose to be stay-at-home mothers, for example, even though they were looked down upon by their working peers.

"I think my generation started getting the right balance with men. More women than men were going to college and were gaining in financial equity, though they still tended to pursue lower-paying fields of work. Just as many women were getting doctorates as men, including becoming medical doctors. We weren't oppressed. But then the neo-feminists of the teens and 20's made a powerful comeback, creating new myths of oppression."

The students were still skeptical and a short stretch of silence ensued.

Finally, Ester Quon ventured, "Please let me know if I'm getting too personal, but you had your children before artificial wombs were developed. What was it like having to carry your children for nine months inside you and then give birth to them? Didn't that make you more dependent on your husband and make you feel terribly op... uh, vulnerable?"

Mrs. Alvarez's expression softened. "Carrying and giving birth to a child was no easy task. But I don't think I was ever happier. Sure, it made me more dependent on my husband and sometimes I felt vulnerable. But my husband loved me and would have done anything for me. I knew it so I felt safe and protected. That's the point of love; you help each other along, especially in time of need – as I helped him in his final days." At this Mrs. Alvarez paused and looked out the window.

Then she continued, "After the artificial womb came along, women lost that close intimacy of carrying and giving birth to their children. And in needing their husbands less, they also lost that vulnerability and need for protection which, when given, created such a strong bond.

"Now-a-days, young women and their husbands just go into some place like CaringMother, drop off their eggs and sperm, come back in nine months to peak at the new arrival, then leave the little one there for another three years while they both go off and pursue their careers. We've lost control over our children and our ability to protect and nurture them.

"But don't you think the artificial womb was critical in freeing women from their biological prison so they could develop their true potential?" Ester countered.

"As you know, Margaret Dwyer became President in the late '20's just when artificial wombs were becoming a viable option. Like many well-intentioned Americans, she saw this as an opportunity to free women from the biological burden of pregnancy and the vulnerability and dependence that went along with it. With every good intention, and with the urging of the neo-feminists, she and congress passed laws requiring access to artificial wombcare for all women and three years of post-natal care for their children.

"The problem is artificial wombcare stopped being one option. 'Groupthink' soon made it the only option. What woman would want to go through the inconvenience and health risk of pregnancy and make herself vulnerable and dependent by becoming pregnant? And when The Corporation took over, all conditions surrounding artificial wombcare became codified, including mandating terminations for defects."

Then after a pause and gazing out the window again, she continued, "Our children are no longer ours; they're The Corporation's. We've become the perfectly-engineered society, a single organism of thought and actions; like an ant's nest – serving the queen ant who hatches her babies – and the worker ants at wombcare and post-natal-care facilities care for the nest's offspring."

Rochelle Redfern's raised her hand next. "Mrs. Alvarez, you have a low opinion of the neo-feminists of the late teens and 20's. But weren't they the ones who did battle to retain women's reproductive rights, when men were trying to take it away?"

"Rochelle, women had gained the right to birth control, including abortion, in the late 1900's. But in the early part of this century political forces – made up of as many women as men – did try to take that away. This gave rise to the neo-feminists. They fought to retain those rights for women. In the end they were successful in getting the Women's Choice Amendment added to the constitution. I was a great supporter of the neo-feminists in this effort. Unfortunately, after that victory, they continued with an extremist agenda."

Mrs. Alvarez looked at the puzzled faces. *Damnit, these aren't kids anymore; they're young adults and future leaders. They should be thinking!*

She concluded, "Anyway, those are some of my thoughts on the subject. It doesn't mean I'm right or wrong. And you shouldn't take my words as gospel, and I'm glad you obviously don't! You should all question what I've said just as you should question whatever anyone else says, including Mr. Vanderkill and your other teachers. Think for yourselves. Discussions like this should make you want to explore history further."

Changing direction, she asked, "Hey, how about you young men, what are your questions?"

This seemed to jolt the boys. After a short pause, Jonathan Stuart asked, "What were those gasoline-powered cars like? And what was it like to be able to just hop in a car and take off down the road and not have to pay tolls?"

Mrs. Alvarez laughed again. "It was great! Young men like you dreamed about what 'muscle machine' they would buy to go ripping down the street, impressing the girls. Of course, we were incredibly wasteful with resources back then. But, oh the freedom of being able to get up and go with no toll or geographical restrictions!"

Then after a thoughtful pause, she continued, "Back in the old European days, they built walls around their cities to keep their enemies out. Now we draw boundaries around cities to keep people in and around executive patents to keep people out. And to assure control, we have toll roads that are unaffordable for most, even if they could afford a 'lectroscooter."

"But don't you think it's much healthier to walk, as The Corporation encourages us to do?" Jonathan countered.

"Oh yes! Humans were becoming too weak and lazy. But now we walk everywhere and never drive. Just think of how convenient that lack of wider mobility is for the government – it knows everyone is in her place."

After another pause Spencer asked, "What would you say was our biggest mistake in the past 100 years?"

Mrs. Alvarez stared at him. "What's your name?"

"Spencer Galloway."

"Well, Spencer, that's an excellent question and one I've thought about a lot. The biggest mistake the USA made was to squander our wealth on wars rather than on education and related development of our youth; especially 'wars of choice', like Vietnam and the Middle East Oil Wars. We couldn't afford to do both. As we were policing the world, countries like China and India were investing their wealth in developing their youth and infrastructure.

"After the turn of the century, these and most other developed countries were pulling ahead of the USA in education. That soon became manifest in technological development. By 2020, the USA had fallen far behind in research and development and production as well as services. It was rapidly moving toward becoming a third world country.

"Fortunately, we had been China's main customer so we had developed an inextricable, symbiotic relationship with them. They were sitting on piles of American money from their one-sided trading relationship with us. They couldn't let their biggest customer slip into oblivion, so they invested in the US – their money and their people. Of course, this investment came with dramatically lower wages for Americans.

"As you know, most American corporations are Chinese-owned, are Chinese subsidiaries or have large Chinese investments in them. Many grumble that we've become a colony of China. But I shudder to think of where we'd be today without the Chinese. We owe them a lot."

She looked around the room. "How many of you have a Chinese background?"

Three hands went up.

"And how many of your ancestors came to America after the year 2000?"

The same three hands went up.

"Well, you are all part of China's investment in America. I thank you." She smiled and gave a slight Chinese-bow from her seat.

The three looked embarrassed, but the others laughed and applauded.

Then Mrs. Alvarez said, "It's a huge irony that American capitalism funded Chinese communism in the 1980's through the first part of this century, only to have Chinese communism end up saving American capitalism later in this century."

Allison Schiller raised her hand and asked, "How have you managed to survive to be 100? You know, I don't mean just health-wise, but economically as well?"

Mrs. Alvarez nodded. "Health-wise, I guess mostly the luck of having good genes. I've lead a healthy life style. Fortunately, I've weathered the ups and downs of my investments. And being fairly healthy I felt I could buy affordable, high-deductible health insurance policies over the years.

"Of course, if I had gotten very sick or contracted a disease not covered by my insurance I would have run out of money long ago and would have made the choice to visit a "sleep palace", as they're so euphemistically called."

Turning to her granddaughter, she said, "I would never allow myself to be a burden on my family."

Randal Buckley raised his hand and asked, "What's the best thing The Corporation has done since gaining power?"

"Getting us out of our cycle of wars that was bleeding us dry of our youth and wealth. Wars make no economic sense, and The Corporation, operating on the principal of economic sense, realized this. By the time The Corporation took over, the large majority of corporations were international, and so they understood the importance of international cooperation. The world had become intertwined economically, and a war any place could have negative economic consequences across the whole planet.

"The Middle East Oil Wars and the Second Mexican War almost took us under. So it had become obvious that we had to get out of the war business. That wasn't too difficult to do, given the economical interrelatedness across the world and the mood in America."

Ian looked around the room and could tell the students were totally absorbed, though he could see skepticism in many facial expressions. He was glad that they were listening, but voicing their differences where they had them. She was indeed an historical figure presenting a different perspective. He let the questioning and answering go on for another 15 minutes, making sure that everyone got to ask at least one question. Then he could tell Mrs. Alvarez was tiring, so he finally said, "OK, time for one more question."

Spencer raised his hand and asked, "From your point of view, how could things change to make life better – you know, society, The Corporation?"

Mrs. Alvarez again studied Spencer intently, "All of you have asked such great questions and listened so intently and respectfully. With leaders like you, tomorrow will be in good hands. Spencer, the way we can improve things is to do exactly what you just did – question.

"I've seen a lifetime of changes – some good – some bad. But there's always change. There was much bad about the USA, especially in its declining years, but much good as well. The same goes for the ISA. Don't ever think the ISA is perfect. You are future leaders, the agents of change. Always be asking yourselves and others exactly what Spencer has just asked.

"One thing I think we've lost since the days of the USA, certainly since my parents' and grandparents' time, is a belief that all people should have certain rights – like the Bill of Rights in the old constitution. Certain rights were guaranteed to everyone, but those rights are now subservient to The Corporation making a credit. That should change back to the way it was in the USA.

"Also, there should be a minimum financial safety net to catch people when they lose their job, and to support them in their old age, like we had with the old unemployment benefits and social security.

"With birth control rights and the wombcare option, women gained control of their bodies. Now they should gain control of their destinies. They should truly be made to feel they can carry and bear their own children and spend more time with them after they're born.

"Men should be released from their legal and social straightjackets – this doesn't mean to run amuck, but enough to feel comfortable around women again – and to be equals with women again."

And then after a pause, she said, "Oh, and finally, I'd get rid of the corpos."

At this last statement, every one gasped, including Ian. *Oh, shit, I'm going to hear it on this one from the parents and the director!* He thought.

Mrs. Alvarez laughed and said, "Hey, look, you don't make it to a hundred without being feisty! Seriously, though, each of you should be looking at the world you live in and deciding what changes are needed for the better, and then work to make them happen. You aren't just future executives; you're human beings shaping the future. Don't turn around and see my ghost chasing you with a switch in the years ahead. I want you to see me smiling at you."

With this, the young people went up and surrounded her, thanking her for coming in. Ian stood back and smiled, thinking, *Well, I may catch hell on this one, but I'm glad I did it. It sure gave the kids a lot to think about.*

He saw Mrs. Alvarez and her granddaughter out to the waiting cab. When he returned to the classroom, some of the students were busy reading the compositions. But some were staring out the window deep in thought. This pleased him. And he was pleased to see that Spencer was one of them.

"Thoughts, comments?" Ian asked.

"Well, she needs a good lesson in women's history! We *were* oppressed!" Linda said immediately.

"But she *is* women's history!" Randal countered. "Sure she's speaking from her own experiences and observations. But it sure didn't sound like oppression to me."

"She said not to believe her without questioning," Allison added. "But that goes for other sources as well. Meaning don't just take what you're fed as the truth. Investigate the past on your own and come to your own conclusions."

"She's blatantly anti-feminist," Rochelle added. "She'd have us chained to our biology again, barefoot and pregnant in the kitchen, begging our husbands for credits for food! God, that boils my blood! She's a nice old lady. But how could she be so backward?"

"No, she just thinks women should have a choice on how they'll have their children. Natural child birth should be a real option. It shouldn't be looked down upon and automatically discounted as it is now-a-days," Ester countered.

"Man, I almost fell out of my chair when she said to get rid of the corpos!" Jonathan said laughing. "That's gutsy! As the saying goes, the only sure thing in life is death, taxes and the corpos. Nah, they aren't going away,"

"Why not?" Spencer asked. "She said the only sure thing is change. Why couldn't the corpos be gotten rid of? Or at least changed for the better? Yeah, I thought she made a lot of sense in everything she said. Though I tend to agree with Rochelle on her point. I wouldn't want to be pregnant. "

Ian continued to refrain from joining the discussion. The students were doing a splendid job on their own. Finally, noticing the time, he reminded them that they needed to complete their reading before the end of the session.

When the morning session ended, he collected the papers as the students filed out. Ian asked Spencer to stop by his office before he went home for the day.

Chapter 16

"OK, let's see what we have," Michael said to Tony and Lenora. Since today was a regular work day, there were more agents in, so they were in the small conference area with raised electronic walls for privacy.

"Any criminal records?"

"None," said Tony.

"Did you check with Interpol, including any records from normally non-participating countries?"

"Yep," said Lenora.

"Good. So what'cha got?"

Lenora brought up a wallplay 3D matrix chart she and Tony had prepared, summarizing the important elements of the likelies list, with pictures and summary symbols but also written comments. Michael glanced through it for several minutes.

"Nothing that really jumps out at you," Lenora said. "All good-to-exceptional performers. All Corporation-approved outside organizations and religions. Most typically married with Corporation-approved one child. Good, Corporate citizens."

"Yes, but if you have a kid, and love it, wouldn't it bother you to see those little bodies? That might be a motive for sabotage," Michael observed as he continued to study the chart.

"But if you have a kid to support and want it to do well in life, you're not about to bite the hand that feeds you," countered Tony. "If it really bothered you, you could request a transfer to another area."

"Good points. Keep that protection, or repulsion, motive in mind as we move along. You'll understand it better when you have kids of your own.

"Look at the number of people that had worked for NuTense before coming to LEPGen. Does that fall outside of statistical norms?" asked Michael.

"No, we checked that. It's within norms." Lenora responded. "Of course, we're working with a small population."

"How about if you add in Treadwell?" Michael asked. "She worked for NuTense too."

Lenora and Tony looked surprised. Lenora observed, "Hmmmmm. That certainly would bring it to the edge, if not outside, given she's the director and had recruited her team."

"Keep that in mind as we move along. I'm going to discuss it with Connie, though I'm sure she'll nix requesting NuTense for access to records unless we have a really good reason. Plus, I don't want to tip off Treadwell and the others who had worked for NuTense, not yet anyway."

"Anything else we should know about Treadwell?" asked Tony with a new interest.

"She was married, that's where she got her name, but divorced with no kids." Michael answered. "Buddhist, which is a 'do-no-harm' religion. Conflict with her work? Potential motive, but no 'bingo'. We have a number of other divorced people among the singles. Statistically normal?"

"Yes," responded Lenora.

They continued for some time looking at the chart, discussing their observations, and drilling down in the third dimension. In the end they found themselves tired and frustrated.

Finally, Michael concluded, "OK. Look, ya done good. I like the chart. Keep it updated and 'spond-ready, and start another with our observations, especially with tie-ins to possible motives. Like Treadwell's 'do-no-harm' Buddhism. I'll ask Connie if she's received permission for us to access the CaringMother contact's file."

After a thoughtful pause Michael added, "If we had any solid indication that an actual crime had been committed at this point, I'd say we were missing something. With no indication of a crime, all we can do is keep fishing and prodding. If we don't come up with something soon, we're going to have to prioritize likelies and start interviewing. As soon as we do that, the cat'll be out of the bag and the perp (if there is one) is going to clam up and stop what he's doing. Then it could get even more difficult to catch him. Last resort is the interview center. You know what that means."

Lenora and Tony nodded their heads.

Michael studied the chart one more time then said, "OK, when all the high-tech security measures and analysis, and bureaucratic bullshit record keeping of the corporations and The Corporation fail to produce what you need, you go to the mountain. Take a few hours off. Tonight we're going to go see the Oracle."

Tony and Lenora looked perplexed at each other then at Michael.

"The Oracle?" Lenora asked.

"Yeah," Michael grinned. "When you've turned over every stone and found nothing, it's time to start crawling under them."

Like many older, restored buildings, Ian's office had solid walls and a door. Given his historical specialty, he liked that – along with the tall ceilings and the musty, old-wood smell from the oak trim and original oak flooring in his office. He was gazing out the window at the statue of Matthew Vassar when Spencer came in through the open door.

"Hi Ian. You wanted to see me?"

Ian turned around. "Hi Spencer. Yes, come on in and close the door."

Ian studied Spencer as he walked over and took a seat. Tall, lanky kid. He'd probably had a growth spurt in the past year, along with other changes, and communicated it in the way he walked. Kind of smooth and gliding – as if hoping no one would take notice. His strawberry blond hair, blue eyes and smooth, oval face gave him an almost angelic look, which certainly endeared him to his mothers and other older women. Not the fan base a young man would aspire to. Spencer probably stood in front of a holomirror every day looking for some sign of masculinity – facial hair, jutting jaw, developing muscles.

"Spencer, you're an exceptional student. And I don't mean just in intelligence and ability. You question the way things are. You look beyond. Mrs.

Alvarez picked up on that too. Don't ever lose that quality." After a reflective pause, Ian continued, "But now, the 'however'."

Spencer pursed his lips.

"You're fortunate that you're attending an upper form school and I'm fortunate that I'm teaching at one. This gives us latitude to explore and discuss topics and ideas that would not be tolerated in a middle- or lower-form school. The Corporation wants future leaders to be able to think, to be able to envision. Like Mrs. Alvarez said today, life is change, and The Corporation knows that leaders need to be able to navigate and shape that change.

"But that's at a high, almost theoretical, level. When you deal with The Corporation at a lower, local level, their representatives don't always believe that. They often think of The Corporation as a static, non-changing monolith that will always be as it is now. They're threatened by anything that challenges that perception."

"You're talking about my paper. That I went too far," Spencer said looking at Ian intently.

"Spencer, I don't want to discourage or stifle you. But you need to keep in mind what I just told you when you're exploring ideas, especially in the more permanent, accessible form, whether transspond, wallplay or written. I'll always defend your expression of your ideas. But my defense, or others', might not always be enough. So glance back over your shoulder when you're expressing your thoughts. You have to protect yourself and those associated with you, like your mothers."

Spencer let out an exasperated breath and his one leg started nervously moving up and down.

"Your paper on independence is very well thought out and thought provoking. I'm sure it's challenging the other students to think independently. But some people would see it as a challenge to The Corporation. As you move toward adulthood they'd increasingly see you as a threat. So do continue to think and speak your mind. Just keep your audience in mind."

"But how do you change things if you can't express your ideas?!"

"You can! But understand who your audience is and craft the expression of your ideas appropriately. As you move forward in your schooling and in your career, you'll want to be viewed as a strong leader with good progressive ideas, not as an outlying rebel. Sometimes you'll have to soften or even hide your ideas, till you move into positions where you can affect changes. It's ... 'adult finesse'," Ian said, hating his final, but accurate, choice of words.

"OK, but how do I do this without becoming a hypocrite?"

"Well, for example, in your paper, you said, 'The current government ... must be amended to address the following shortcomings.' This has a confrontational tone. Some might say rebellious and threatening. Try something like, 'The following are suggestions for improvement." This invites people to have a non-emotional discussion.

"Look, I'm not telling you to change your paper. But in future compositions, try using more ... finesse," Ian continued, feeling hypocritical in choosing that same word again. "I think you'll see that it gets you further than confrontation. And guard your back."

Spencer settled back in his chair, looking resigned. "The corpos. I understand. It's just that I see things that aren't right, get mad and express my feelings." He looked down in thought and then looked up with a wan smile. "I guess I can't do much good if they come and drag me off in the middle of the night. And I sure don't want to do anything that could endanger my mothers. OK. I get your point."

"Speaking of expressing yourself, what got into you the other night at the Walkway? You had me and the others scared for you."

Spencer dropped his head and said sheepishly, "I guess it was one of those times when I had to spout off about the way things are. People just don't get it!"

"But alcohol? Spencer, you were blitzed! Luckily, people and that cop just took you for what you were – some drunk kid. Put on a few years and they won't think it's so harmless and funny. And it didn't impress anybody. It scared your classmates – but they stuck with you – they cared."

Spencer looked up and said, "Do you think they do? Care?"

"Sure. I know they do. Allison 'sponded me later on asking if you were OK. She was worried."

"She did?" Spencer said beaming.

Ian studied his face and continued, "Spencer, being drunk or high may give you false confidence, but it doesn't impress anyone. If you're interested in someone, you have to let them know. You have to make more than a superficial contact. And then take an interest in them as a person.

Spencer reddened and said, "Well, I've learned my lesson with alcohol. I woke up the next day with a splitting head ache. I won't do that again."

Spencer stood up and walked to the door. He turned around and said, "Ian, I really do appreciate your thoughts. I'll try to do you proud." He smiled and walked out the door.

Ian nodded and watched him leave. He hoped he had handled things right.

"Saint Ian of Edinburgh!"

Ian looked up, stood up and saluted. "General Sherman!"

The two men laughed and hugged.

"What brings you over to the land of the arts?" Ian asked.

"I was wondering what had happened to you. Ruth and I had been hoping to see you over the fourth. But you disappeared," Walter Sherman said as the two of them settled comfortably into chairs. Walter was a tall, thin black man pushing the later stages of middle age. His father had been a Presbyterian, but his mother a member of the local Reformed Jewish congregation. They had raised Walter in both religions. Not easy, Walter claimed. But he joked it was the best way to learn tolerance.

Although he taught math and physics and as a result rarely ran into Ian, the two men had hit it off the first time they had met at a faculty social gathering. Ruth had said it was their easy-going but thoughtful temperaments that had brought them together. But Ian felt it was also their shared values and true affection for their students.

"I know. Sorry. But the good news is I've met someone, so I've been spending my free time with her."

Walter's eyebrows arched. "Tell me more."

"Well, it was a chance meeting last Friday. And we ended up spending a lot of the weekend together, having a good time, getting to know each other.

"So what's her name; what does she do?"

"Siobhan Carlson. She works for EvalProm developing student assessment programs. She lives in a nice old house south of Hooker Avenue that she's convinced is going to fall on her head one of these days."

"Well don't tell Ruth about her till you're sure you really like her, because she'll be pushing the two of you down the aisle before you know what's going on," Walter said, laughing.

"I know," Ian said laughing as well. "I like her a lot. I hope it works out."

"Hope to meet her soon."

After a pause, Walter continued, "Are you waiting for someone? Some students stopping by?"

"Actually, Spencer Galloway just left. You have him too, don't you?"

"Spencer? Yeah, for physics. My best student. That kid's a natural in the sciences. Have you ever been in a position where a student was teaching you? That's Spencer. I can't imagine he's having trouble in your class."

"No. We just discussed a composition he's written. Sometimes he just stops by to talk."

"He's done that with me too," Walter nodded reflectively. "He'll ask me about a few points related to physics, but I'm sure he knows the answers. Then he'll segue into more personal areas. It's hard making your way in a woman's world."

Then continuing, "You know he has two mothers, no father. I think he craves adult male companionship, or at least a man he can go to with questions."

"I'm glad your office is open to him too," Ian said. "He just needs a little advice and guidance. He's a very gifted and outstanding student, and he has a good heart. I think he has huge potential. I'll want to stay in contact with him as he moves on."

"I agree. He really is exceptional."

Ian gazed out the window then back at Walter. "I hope you'll stay close to him as well. You're a good, solid influence. Especially if I weren't around, I'd want to feel he wasn't left hanging."

Walter looked surprised and said, "You goin' some place, bud? I hope you aren't thinking about taking that position in Manhattan."

"No. But you never know. I could drop dead tomorrow."

"Well, if you do, I'll take enough interest in him for the both of us," Walter said chuckling.

"I mean it."

Walter's smile left his face. "Ian is everything OK?"

"Sure."

Ian reddened, and thinking about Siobhan again, he asked, "Tell me something, Walter. How did you know Ruth was the right one for you?"

"She told me she was!" They both laughed. "I dated a lot of women, but always hesitated to move on to a more serious level. Invariably, they were always very intent on their careers, which always came first, as they let me know. I didn't fault them for that. But I always had the feeling there wouldn't be much 'second place' left over, so I guess I figured getting more serious wasn't that attractive. And they sensed it and moved on. That was OK too.

"But with Ruth I could tell she was different from the beginning. She was always interested in me – as I was in her. Though she told me on our first date that she worked for InterSpan, she didn't talk about her work. I didn't find out till our third date that she was already a director!

"We talked about life and what was important to each of us. I guess our personalities, values, interests hit it off. So when she popped the question I didn't hesitate."

"Walter, I've never pried into why you never had a child, but can I ask you now?"

Walter looked down at the floor for several moments. "Ruth didn't trust the wombcare corporations. She wanted to have a child naturally. Her friends told her she was nuts. And her colleagues told her it would do irreparable damage to her career. But she was adamant. When we got permission to have a child, we tried for several years, and then tried invitro, with no luck. With The Corporation's iron-clad control of births and one-child law, there were literally no kids to adopt. So the only possibility was wombcare.

"But she just wouldn't have it. I wanted a child as much as she did, but I understood her feelings and agreed with her in the end. It's been especially hard on Ruth. Even though we both decided against wombcare, she was the adamant one, so she blames herself. Plus, I have 'my kids' here at school."

"I'm sorry Walter. And I'm sorry for prying."

"Hey, don't be. It's good to talk to someone else about it. We've both accepted the way things have turned out. What's important is we have each other – and good friends like you."

The conversation turned to politics at school and upcoming social events. Finally Walter said, "Hey, I'd better be heading back. Take care. And keep me posted on how things develop with Ms. Carlson. I'll only be able to hide things from Ruth just so long!"

"Thanks Walter," the two men stood up and hugged each other.

When Walter reached the corner down the hall, he stopped, turned and looked back intently at Ian, as if something about their conversation was nagging him. Finally, they both silently raised their hands and waved as Walter disappeared around the corner, heading to the exit.

Chapter 17

Michael relaxed with Julianna over a dinner of chicken fricassee, forbidden rice and bok choi. Julianna was surprised by his 'spond saying he'd be coming home early. She quickly 'sponded up the special dinner. As a special touch she lit candles and opened a bottle of Hudson Valley chardonnay. She put on a pastoral wallplay set to the dreamy music of Erik Satie. They mostly talked about their daughter's wish to have a traditional Buddhist wedding in addition to The Corporate wedding.

Michael began quizzing Julianna on Buddhism. As he kept digging, Julianna interrupted him and asked, "Is this related to the case you're working on at LEPGen?"

"Yes."

Julianna stared at Michael for several moments before she continued. "Michael, you're a good father. And I know you love our daughter. But I wish your questions about Buddhism had been prompted by your desire to know her better and not by your work. She'll soon be married and starting her own family, so we'll see her less and less. It's time to think of her happiness. Don't lose this opportunity."

Michael reached across the table, took her hand and said he was sorry. They let the chardonnay and Satie take them to a place of relaxation.

After supper and quiet moments spent with Julianna, Michael went into his clock room and started cleaning the works in his newest acquisition, a very high-quality black forest mantel clock made by Winterhalder and Hofmeier in the early 1900's. He already had a W&H mantel clock which he dearly loved. The cabinet was solid mahogany, in a rounded gothic form with a hand-engraved, silvered-brass dial. The massive brass works showed such high-quality, loving workmanship, that it was obvious that this clock would be still running hundreds of years from now. The cathedral gongs rang out their reechoing Westminster chimes on the quarter hour, and the hour gong strike told you in no uncertain terms what hour it was.

His new W&H was also made of solid mahogany, but was squarish and had thick, beveled glass panes on the front, top and sides for viewing the exquisite brass works. Rather than using a pendulum to meet out time, it had a balance platform mechanism, jeweled with rubies to ensure virtually no wear. And instead of Westminster, it chimed out the quarter hours on two cathedral gongs.

Michael loved collecting and restoring antique clocks. Each clock was a work of art from when hand craftsmanship had been a way of life. Each marched along through time with its constant "tick-tock", ignoring the petty scurrying about of its current caretaker. Each was a reminder that its heart had been beating long before Michael's and would be beating long after his had stopped. Michael's clocks were a world of certainty he could escape into from his daily world of nebulous gray zones. He sometimes disappeared into this room for hours at a time to work on a new restoration project. Julianna didn't begrudge the clocks, because he always came out refreshed and more sure of himself.

Michael enjoyed listening to music while he worked. Baroque music complemented clockwork so perfectly with its clear, majestic certainty, announcing the greatness the human mind was capable of reaching.

As he worked on his new clock he paused to listen to Bach's "Prelude and Fugue in G Major", to Michael, the greatest work of music ever written – from the first flourish of the organ announcing the theme, through the ever-mounting chords of light, surging with absolute certainty toward its inevitable coda, and trumpeting out its final, brilliant, massively-powerful chord. Michael felt that this work was the perfect combination of power, beauty and grandeur – perfection that had always existed and always would on a plane beyond the impermanence of man. Bach had brought it down from that plane and given it mortal life for humans to hear so they would know that perfection did exist.

As Michael admired the works of his new clock, listening to Bach, he pondered the ancient Greeks' belief that there was a harmonious relationship among the planets, indeed among all heavenly bodies throughout the universe. This *musica universalis*, or "Music of the Spheres" was the glue that held the universe together, that gave it order, that kept it from flying apart. Mere mortals couldn't hear or see this harmony. It existed on a plane that was beyond human comprehension. But they sensed it, and the great mortals attempted to give it human form through mathematics, geometrics – and most magnificently through music.

Michael's clocks began to strike eight, and he knew he had to return to the imperfect world of man, and deal with that paragon of imperfection, the Oracle. He chuckled. After his Bach purification, he could again deal with the crazy comings and goings called reality. Michael was thankful his parents had brought with them from China a love for western, classical music. He was proud that it was the Chinese immigrants in this century who were largely responsible for the revival of classical music in America. With a satisfied sigh he 'sponded Lenora and Tony to meet him in his lobby.

While he finished cleaning the pivot holes, he thought about Colson's Tompion tall case clock. Man, that had cost her more credits than Michael could earn in ten years. Thomas Tompion's clocks, built in London in the late 1600's, were near-perfection in the antique clock world. And they always had at least one additional feature that one would rarely, if ever, find in another maker's clocks. He noticed that Colson's had two minute hands, one to show the standard, mechanical minute, but the second one to show "true noon".

Due to the earth's variations in relation to the sun, "true noon in relation to the sun" varied by up to seven minutes either side of mechanical noon, depending on the time of year. So Tompion had built this "true noon" mechanical feature into some of his clocks when requested by customers. This was, of course, a vanity feature showing that a person had a more perfect clock than others. But what thought and skill had gone into creating this feature!

Michael didn't trust Colson. Her brilliance was surely self-serving. Her hard work for CaringMother had one end – to earn her more credits so she could buy more Tompions, or their equivalents. He had 'sponded Corporate information on Colson and found out that she had built CaringMother up from a regional corporation to a national, and then to an international one with operations in 23 countries.

Even though she looked like a typical grandmother, she had never had a child. She had been married several times, each time to a much younger man, and each time divorced with millions of credits in "amicable" divorce settlements – a pittance for her, but enough for each ex-husband to leave without ruffling the feathers of the executive world.

As with the other wombcare corporations, there had often been accusations made by 'oggers of improper care of fetuses in unsanitary conditions at CaringMother facilities. And there was the occasional disclosure on Corporate communications of fines being paid by CaringMother for minor infractions found by Corporate health inspectors.

But Colson had had a number of awards, including "Executive of the Year" in *ExecWorld* the prior year. Michael had 'sponded the issue she was featured in and saw her soft, matronly face smiling out at him. He would never trust her with a child.

Michael stepped off the elevator to find both Lenora and Tony waiting for him in the lobby. "Whoa, you were both quick. Hope you weren't waiting long."

"Nah, we both got here about the same time, only a few minutes ago," responded Tony.

As they exited from the lobby into the hot blast of the outside air, Tony continued, "So where are we going and who is this Oracle?"

Michael smiled and said, "We're going to Mario's Restaurant at the corner of Market and Main. Have you eaten there before?"

When the other two shook their heads, Michael wasn't surprised. He continued as they walked in a northwest direction along the walkways, "It's a retro diner. They serve 1950's American food with an Italian bent, the way they always have. You know, burgers and fries, but also steak sandwiches on

Italian bread with tomato sauce. Pretty good food, nice "unhealthy" change from your regular fare. It's been owned and run by the same family since it opened in the mid 1900's. Somehow the corporations didn't get their hands on it – yet. And even though it's at the epicenter of Poughkeepsie, not many people know about it. Anyway, that's where we'll find the Oracle."

"OK, and who the hell is this Oracle?" asked Lenora, having waited long enough to find out.

"The Oracle, born Dan Schmitt, is a go-to source of street knowledge in Poughkeepsie. When you want to know the mood of the street he's the one to go to. He's not an informant or a snitch, but as his adopted name indicates, he's a 'seer of truth, and giver of knowledge', as he likes to say of himself.

"Sometimes listening to him is like 'sponding your horoscope – kinda vague. But he usually does give you direction. Even though you can't give him the specifics of the case you're working on, he'll take your vague words and run with them. And a day or week later he'll come back with more information that'll point you in the right direction.

"A lot of cops and agents dismiss him as a 'bag o' beatnik bullshit', but he's helped me out on some important cases; I think because I show him some respect. Did you have any sources like him in your prior police work?"

"Just snitches," said Tony.

"Well he's different. Not a snitch. But I believe in working with any source that'll help me get to where I need to go."

"Where does the beatnik come in?" asked Lenora.

"The Oracle prides himself in 'living-off-the-grid'," Michael said. "His transponder's been inoperable for years now. Technically, he could be fined, but he's considered a potentially useful source by the police so they just let it go. An inoperable 'sponder here and there is no big deal. Since it's virtually impossible to function in today's world without an operable transponder, people always get them fixed immediately. In essence, they police themselves.

"So unfortunately you can't 'spond him to get ahold of him. You have to know where he'll probably be when you want to meet with him. He usually 'holds court' about this time of night at Mario's. I think he likes Mario's because it's so 1950's which is when the beatniks lived."

"And who were the beatnik's?" asked Tony. "I've heard the name, but beyond that ... "

"They were whites who 'dropped out' of the 'rat race', loved jazz and lived life as 'cool cats', the way they believed black jazz musicians would. You'll see that the Oracle is a 'cool cat', very low key, and speaks a beatnik jargon."

"How does he survive? Does he have a job?" asked Lenora.

"Not that I know of. A real beatnik would disdain regular work. He has space at his mother's in the old section of houses south of Hooker. I'm sure she helps him out, you know, breakfast, a few credits now and then. But mostly I think he survives by his wits, helping out the cops and others with useful bits of knowledge from time to time for a few credits here and there.

"Here's what I'm bringing him as an offering." At this Michael pulled out a small, white package with a large, red bull's eye.

"What is it?" asked Tony with the curiosity of a little boy.

"Lucky Strike cigarettes, unfiltered," said Michael proudly.

"Cigarettes? Those have been outlawed since before my time. Where did you get them?" asked Tony, reaching like a little kid for forbidden fruit.

"Black market. Real tobacco, no filters. And Lucky Strikes. You can't get any more 50's than that," Michael said proudly, pulling the package away from Tony's reach, while smiling at his little treasure before he put it back into his pocket.

They rounded a corner on to Market Street and headed north toward Main. Mario's Restaurant was in the darkening shadows cast by larger buildings. Michael thought back to last fall when he and Julianna had walked by on a cold, dark evening. He had looked into the brightly-lit interior at the several customers sitting around the counter, with the current "Mario" waiting on them.

He had been struck by how much it reminded him of that iconic painting, "Boulevard of Broken Dreams" by Gottfried Helnwein. In it James Dean, Humphrey Bogart and Marilyn Monroe were sitting at a counter while Elvis Presley waited on them. They were in a light-flooded, diner-style restaurant on a dark, deserted street corner. It was as if they had been suspended in an eternal 1950's world. That's the way Mario's customers had looked – suspended in the 1950's.

Michael shook off the image as they walked through the door at the corner of Market and Main. He said to the others, "Let me do the talking. The Oracle might be leery of two new faces."

"Hey, Mr. Chan, haven't seen you in a while," said Mario.

"I've been away on assignment. I'm here to see the Oracle tonight, but I'll be back for one of those great steak sandwiches, Mario."

"OK, I'll hold you to that!" Mario said smiling.

Michael did a thumbs-up as they headed to the back corner booth, tucked behind a corner of the kitchen.

"Hey, man, it's Charlie Chan, the corpo man!" said the Oracle with a big grin on his face.

Michael flinched when Lenora and Tony chuckled. *Damn! Well someone had to call me Charlie Chan in front of these two. Might as well be the Oracle,* he thought. He also didn't like being called a corpo.

"Oh great Oracle!" Michael joked. "I bring you an offering to be burned!"

The Oracle nodded to the couple sitting in his booth, maybe his current girl friend and one of his followers, "You cats split, so I can jam with my man." The two reluctantly got up and walked off, eyeing Michael and the others suspiciously.

As Michael, Lenora and Tony settled into the booth, the Oracle said, "So, I hear you been doin' a gig with the propaganda types and just made this scene again."

"Yeah, I've made chief inspector and these are my people, Lenora and Tony. We wanted to stop by to say hi."

"Boss, man! Gimme some skin!" the Oracle said as he swiped his palm across Michael's, beatnik style, as he eyed Lenora.

"So, whacha got?" the Oracle asked, looking Michael over like a kid anticipating a present.

"I brought you a little souvenir I got while on assignment." At this Michael pulled out the pack of Lucky Strikes.

"Oh daddy, far out, fags!" The Oracle took the pack, fondled it, smelled it, and said, "Can I open 'em?"

"Sure, they're yours."

The Oracle opened the pack and peered down at the tobacco at the end of the cigarettes. When he inhaled the aroma, his eyeballs rolled up.

"Wow, man, like this is hep! Can't wait to have a drag where there ain't no flat foots around to pinch me!"

Michael smiled.

"Still hopped up on classical?" The Oracle asked.

"Yeah."

"Pops, ya gotta start groovin' to jazz: Davis, Mulligan, Coltrane. I got a new vinyl with Mingus playin' a gig in Harlem in the late 50's. Man, that cat could slap his axe!"

Lenora and Tony looked mystified, while Michael wondered if "groovin'" wasn't hippy talk from a generation later.

"Hey, I dig you daddy," Michael said. "I was just 'sponding Davis' *Birth of the Cool* the other day. I dig it, man! And Brubeck, he da mammy jammy!"

The Oracle laughed and slapped Michael on the back. "Charlie, you're a gas! Brubeck, huh? He's pretty good – for a white cat."

Then looking at Michael intently, he said, "Yeah, Brubeck's definitely the place for you to start."

As the Oracle took another long smell of his offering, he looked up at Michael. His eyes narrowed and he said in a more serious tone, "So Michael, what brings you to my digs?"

"To get the lay of the land from you."

"Hey, things are cool, man, cool," the Oracle said, but after eyeing Michael a little longer, he added, "A more specific lay of the land."

"What's the word on the street?"

The Oracle glanced around the room and proceeded in a confidential tone, "The word is there's a shortage of quality drift-off drugs at Euthanesta, so they're pumping in the heart arresters before the clients are in the zone. Causing some nasty scenes. Rumor is DomFab's going to bring in illegals to work on the next phase of doms. Nothing new there. They're running fewer transmobiles out to the Executive Patent, so longer waits for servants both ways. A lot of grumbling about that. Supposedly LEPGen will be off-shoring more jobs – you know, BAU."

The Oracle continued along these lines for some minutes, studying Michael's reactions. Then, as if by instinct, he hunched over and looked into Michael's eyes. "I also hear there's dissatisfaction at the CaringMother facility. It seems the CEO, that Colson chick, sticks her fingers in where she shouldn't, treating the facility as her own exploratory lab on how to increase profits. You know, the standard, trimming pay and other benefits, working fewer people longer hours. But also takin' a walk on the dark side to make more bread."

"Like doing what?"

"No specifics." He sat back and studied Michael's face. "If you're interested, I could do some sniffin' around. But I'll need some resources."

Michael nodded. "We'll transfer 25,000 credits into your account tomorrow. Keep your ear to the ground on LEPGen too."

"You snap da whip, I make da trip!" the Oracle said, shifting back into beatnik slang. "But the credits gotta be free-floaters. I'll drop you a dime when I hear somethin' fine. Thanks again for the fags, man. Gimme some skin." They did their beatnik palm swipe again.

"And Ms. Lenora, it was so nice to meet you! I hope I'll be seeing you again soon!" the Oracle said with a wide grin on his face. "You too, man," he said glancing at Tony.

As they got up to leave, Michael paused. "Hey Dan, do what you can. But be careful."

The Oracle smiled. "I'm cool, man, I'm cool."

As they stepped out into the heat of the night, Michael glanced back at the restaurant – at the several customers sitting at the counter in the flooded light, all contrasted by the now dark and largely deserted streets. Michael wondered. Did Dan have dreams, or was he already fading into that painting?

Chapter 18
WEDNESDAY, JULY 8

"Most of you wrote comments on your copies of Linda's and Spencer's compositions. Well done! Take out your copies." Ian watched the students search through the stack one at a time, obviously unaccustomed to this activity.

When they each had their copies and were going through them, refreshing themselves on the content and their comments, Ian said, "Why did I choose these two compositions to read first? Because their subjects are so different, yet inextricably related. Linda's is a portrayal of the rise of The Corporation and its extensive involvement in our lives. Spencer's discusses the essence of humans and their 'unalienable' rights.

"They both should have raised the question in your minds: what *is* the right balance between the government and individual rights, including the pursuit of happiness, or 'flourishing' as Spencer put it? They both agree on the good The Corporation has done: saving the country from economic collapse, reducing extreme civil strife, and steering us away from wars.

"But Spencer's raises the question of where do we go from here? As Mrs. Alvarez pointed out yesterday, the only constant is change, nothing remains static. The question is how will things change and how will you influence that change? Have we formed a 'perfect union', or are there changes that should be made as Spencer mentions?"

After a short pause, Luisa ventured, "Well, we have to have effective government, otherwise we drop back into the chaos the United States was experiencing before The Corporation took over."

"But what *is* 'effective', Luisa?" Spencer asked. "Although The Corporation has done a good job over all, there are areas where it could improve. Like in creating more competition. Too many corporations have virtual monopolies. That isn't effective. People like to pretend that we have a capitalist system. But real capitalism demands competition. Where's the competition? Corporations are more like monopolistic divisions of The Corporation.

"At best you'll find a small number of corporations controlling a market. But because of their small number and broad reach, they naturally stifle competition. They're like the oil corporations back at the turn of the century. That wasn't capitalism, or at least not a good, effective form of it.

"And I think we've sacrificed our individual rights at the expense of The Corporation making a credit. This should be changed."

"But money makes the world go 'round, as the saying goes," countered Viswatham. "If The Corporation doesn't make a credit, then we, as a country, go bankrupt as the United States almost did."

"I agree," said Spencer. "But it can still be profitable if our rights are guaranteed, and not subordinate to profitability."

"Like what rights?" asked Viz.

"Like freedom of speech."

"But we have freedom of speech. What are we doing right now?"

"In this room," countered Spencer. "We're granted this latitude here because we need to learn how to think and reason so we can better run the corporations tomorrow. But do people have this freedom in general? Try having this discussion out on the streets and see how long before the corpos, or their cadet wannabes, come along."

"Spencer's right," said Alma. "You don't have a right if it's not guaranteed."

"But look at what Hobbes said. If humans don't have a common power to keep them in awe, then they descend into war, every person against every person. You submit to the power of a sovereign to guarantee your survival," countered Linda.

"But he also said that people's submission to the sovereign lasted only as long as he was able to protect them," Spencer said. "Jefferson went further in the Declaration of Independence and said that governments derive their powers from the consent of the governed. And that whenever a government 'becomes destructive to these ends', in other words doesn't derive its powers from the consent of the governed, they have the right to alter or abolish it. He envisioned a world where the people were the sovereigns, not the government.

"The question is, should The Corporation exist to serve the people, or should we exist to serve The Corporation? I believe the former. And to attain this we need to alter it, not abolish it."

"Along these lines, I like Spencer's ideas on the pursuit of happiness, or "flourishing". Allison said. "I agree with him that all people should have the opportunity to reach their potential. We shouldn't be banding young children based on their parents' bands."

"But how'd we ensure that we had the needed labor force at each level of work?" Patricia countered.

"Well, maybe we start with the needs of people, rather than the needs of The Corporation and corporations," Allison responded.

"That would never work," Patricia said in a huff.

"What did we do before The Corporation came along with banding?" Allison asked rhetorically.

"There was no predetermination before," said Spencer. "But it wasn't a perfect world. At one point the United States had a system of strong, public-funded schools. But as schools started running into problems, instead of working on fixing them, the better off started pushing for vouchers to support private schools that they set up and could afford to send their children to. In the end, the children of those with money got good educations and, in turn, the good jobs. Those whose parents had less money were left to wallow in the failing public systems, predestined to get lower paying jobs, perpetuating their situation.

"Each person should have an equal chance in life. You don't get that when you are your band, you are your work, you are what you bring to the betterment of The Corporation and corporations. Humans need to develop and exercise their minds; that is their essence. If that's stifled, they are not fully living. Why, I bet that most corpos are closet 'eudaimonians'! After keeping the likes of us in place, they have that place they go to let their minds flourish, whatever that place might be."

Allison laughed. "So Spencer, what's the place you go to to let your mind flourish?"

Spencer looked at Allison and blushed, but he quickly and confidently responded, "Music. Mostly classical music, especially Bach."

And then for the first time that Ian could remember, Spencer addressed Allison on a personal level, "And where do you go to, Allison?"

It was her turn to turn red, but she recovered quickly as well. "I often sit back and think about what direction I'll go in my career. But mostly I dream about what type of man I'd want to marry. And of having a child, a family."

Allison looked around the room at the reaction of the others to her last words. Reddening again, she continued, "I guess I'm kind of old fashioned."

"I like that – you being your own person." Spencer said supportively, still looking at her intently.

You go boy! Ian thought.

Ian let the discussion carry on for another half hour. These "kids" knowledge and intellectual maturity was well beyond their years, and it reflected in their discussions. Most had begun some sort of instruction within their first year of life. Their exposure in home and school to all subjects was astounding. Even more impressive was that Spencer usually appeared to be ahead of the others in spite of his non-executive background. But, Ian pondered, emotionally they were still kids, no further advanced than any other youths their age. Maybe less so, given the protection and pampering they received.

He had purposely stepped back and stayed out of the discussion, thinking about Siobhan's advice. He wasn't surprised that Spencer had given the discussion direction, at first defending the ideas he had expressed in his composition, then leading the other students in a constructive, thought-provoking exploration of the nature of human existence.

At one point Ian almost stepped in when the students were pointing out that special interests had done so much harm to the USA. But then Randal Buckley, one of his black students, objected saying that if it hadn't been for the NAACP, blacks would never have gained any rights. Then Spencer pointed out that *the* most influential special interests had been the corporations. So hadn't they done the most harm to the USA in having their interests met?

Finally, at a convenient juncture, Ian said, "I hate to say it, but I think it's time to bring this discussion to a conclusion. Not much consensus on where we should go from here as a country and government, but there were plenty of ideas expressed – a lot of 'eudaimonia' going on! Best of all, you were all able to present your views, often opposing views, to others, and yet keep a civil atmosphere. Something the congress of the United States was unable, or unwilling, to do in their final days. Congratulations, you are true adults!

"For the rest of this morning's session, I'd like you to start reading the next two compositions. The first is Juan's, 'The Second Mexican War'. Pay close attention to Juan's main contentions – I want to discuss them tomorrow. First, that Mexico did have a right to take New Mexico, Arizona, Southern California and most of Texas in that war, since most of that land, and more, had been taken from Mexico in the first Mexican War of 1846-1848. This 'succession from the union' was supported by the plebiscite of 2032 in which a majority of people in those areas voted for independence from the United States so they could realize their destiny as an Hispanic culture.

"Interestingly, those pushing for succession quoted Jefferson Davis's thoughts on states' rights leading up to the South's succession and the resultant Civil War. Davis, of course, was the President of the Confederate States of America, and ironically, he had fought as an officer in the First Mexican War. As Juan points out, Davis had said that the federal government was a 'creature of the States; as such it could have no inherent power, all it preserves was delegated by the States, and it is therefore that our Constitution is not an instrument of limitations, but of grants.' In other words, the states were supreme and could rescind those grants whenever they determined that the federal government no longer met their needs.

"Second, that Mexico won that war handily because the United States was totally consumed by the Mideastern Oil Wars, and was dependent on Mexico for production of key defense components. Juan contends that those facts, in addition to the historical fact of ownership and the plebiscite, gave Mexico all the important advantages – they just walked in and reclaimed some of their land. There wasn't much the US could do about it.

"And third, that it was the trauma of losing a part of the United States in a war on top of the devastation of the oil wars, that lead to people readily accepting the takeover of the government by The Corporation and the total incorporation of states into one, truly-indivisible entity – the Incorporated States of America. Focus on and think about these points and we'll discuss them tomorrow.

"When you're finished with Juan's composition, start reading Allison's, 'The Biarchal Ideal'. Similar to Mrs. Alvarez's thoughts, Allison contends that we have gone from being a patriarchal society a hundred years ago to, in essence, a matriarchal society today. She says that women had not been content with the social structure in the US and had organized to change it in a way that was more congenial to their needs, basically giving them more power and status. By organizing, they were able to influence politicians to pass laws supporting them, and influence the media and society to support their cause.

"But instead of meeting at a place of equals with men, 'the biarchal ideal', women continued to surge ahead while men became increasingly marginalized to the point where things are at today – women hold the vast majority of mid- and top-level, influential jobs in corporations and government. And society views men as the 'y-chromosome anomaly', a problem to be dealt with severely, but whose solution has yet to be found.

"She further contends that men's subservient position in society today is their own fault. That other than in isolated instances, they allowed themselves to be pushed aside, being either too stupid or too 'macho' to organize to improve their status; to help other men and in turn themselves. And now, given The Corporation's disdain for special interests' complaints, it may be too late to move back to a balanced, 'biarchal' society.

"At the end of her composition, playing the devil's advocate, Allison raises the provocative question whether there's a defect in men's genes, maybe their 'competitiveness gene', that has rendered them simply incapable of organizing to improve the status of all men, indeed to compete in the world as it exists today. Have men simply gravitated to their inevitable level of subservience?

"After your reading, please organize and hold a debate, with the young women in the class supporting the proposition that 'Men are second-class citizens in today's society' and the young men arguing against the proposition." A number of groans echoed around the room. "Stick to the proposition at hand, collecting data and other 'proof' to support your position. We're debating whether men are second-class citizens based on empirical evidence, not whether their status is right or wrong. We'll discuss the more philosophical questions raised by Allison's composition separately."

Ian concluded, "As future executives you'll increasingly find yourselves having to argue one side of an issue or another, often a side you don't agree with. Debates are great preparation for that. I'm going to grade your team on how well you argue your side, so don't do it half-heartedly if you don't agree with it. So get reading!"

Ian smiled at the additional groans but saw how quickly they all began working on the assignment.

Chapter 19

"Let him sweat a little before we go in," Michael said to Tony and Lenora.

They had Jonathan Raston in a solid, soundproof, interview room at the CBI offices in the Luckey Platt building. It was very much like the old-fashioned interrogation rooms with the one-way mirror and one-way intercom. This was still the best setup for interrogations, though they were now euphemistically called interviews. This was the only such room in the downtown offices. The main interview center was located ten kilometers northeast of Poughkeepsie in a more remote location and was a state-of-the-art facility. But that was used for serious interrogations, which usually lead to disappearances.

"Let me do most of the talking. But I want you two to get some experience too, so go ahead and join in when you think appropriate. If I keep looking at him while you talk, I'm OK. If I look at you while you talk and don't say anything, it means to shut up. Tony, you're good at the tough, Italian New Yorker routine, so you play the bad cop. You know, 'Yo, ya wanna sleep widda fishes?'" They all laughed. "This'll keep him on his toes and dependent on me. Lenora, you can play both, good and/or bad, whatever seems good. Go back and forth to keep him off guard. I may get tough with him, but I'm always the good cop in the end."

Since Raston was the only CaringMother person of interest at this point, and the only one Colson had given Michael permission to interview, Michael had decided to bring him here instead of interviewing him at the CaringMother facility. This way no other CaringMother employees would see them and get suspicious; and bringing persons of interest "downtown" made them sweat without scaring the hell out of them. They knew that if they didn't cooperate, the next step was the Poughkeepsie Roach Hotel, as the main interview center was called on the streets. "The roaches check in, but they don't check out."

Raston's manager had accompanied him and had wanted to be present for the interview. Michael sized her up: she was young and new to her management position, so he decided on intimidation – he'd kept them both in the interview room, occasionally popping his head in and giving them angry looks. When she had cooked long enough, he called her out of the room and suggested that it would be much more productive if she weren't present. And after all, it was just routine questioning. When he said that he would be glad to have a driver take her back to CaringMother, she nervously agreed.

"Take a good look at him. He looks like the classic case of a good Corporate citizen innocently caught up in a situation, but he doesn't know what it is. He's sweating, fidgeting, eyes darting nervously around, especially at the mirror. He knows there's trouble in River City and is trying to figure out what it could be. You can tell he's never had a run in with any levels of the law. OK, let's go in and get to know Mr. Raston."

The three of them walked into the interview room and sat down at the solid metal rectangular table on the solid metal chairs. They had just enough cushion to keep pain away, but ensured discomfort. Michael sat directly across from Raston, Lenora on Michael's left and Tony on the right. The walls were bare and painted what Michael called "sweat-swamp green". The finishing touch was the old-fashioned incandescent light hanging down on a wire from the ceiling with a metal lampshade that dispersed the light onto these sitting at the table. About as hokey as you could get, Michael figured, but it seemed to have the desired effect on those being interviewed – it made them sweat.

Michael gave his best Jackie Chan smile and said, "Hello Mr. Raston. Thank you so much for coming in. I'm Chief Inspector Chan and this is Agent Lenora Davis and Agent Tony Regusini," Michael said nodding at the others individually. "Before we get started, would you care for something to drink? Coffee, tea, soft drink, water?"

Raston said in a raspy voice, "Coffee?"

"That sounds good to me, too." Michael turned to Lenora and said, "Agent Davis, do you think you could get us some coffee and something for you and Agent Regusini as well?"

Lenora looked surprised, but recovered quickly and said, "Sure."

As she walked out the door, Michael couldn't help the additional comment, again with his cutest Jackie Chan smile, "Be sure to get a fresh pot, and maybe some of those tasty little glazed donut holes as well." He noticed her back stiffen as she closed the door. He looked over at the mirror and wondered if Connie was on the other side fuming at him right now. Tony put his hand over his mouth. Michael mentally lashed himself with a neo-feminist whip. But everything so far had the effect of disarming Raston. Being more relaxed now he'd cooperate fully.

"Mr. Raston, I want to be totally frank with you. The reason we asked you to come in is related to your work as the CaringMother-LEPGen liaison for the LEPGen transponder research project. There's been a statistically significant lack of progress in that research. LEPGen has not been able to pinpoint the problem yet, so they're concerned. I know that you've checked and rechecked with your quality control people, and everyone appreciates your diligence. But the problems persist. LEPGen has asked the CBI to get involved, fearing sabotage."

Raston kept glancing over at Tony's glaring face. He turned visibly pale when Michael said "sabotage". "How can I help?"

"First, would you please describe the operation you are involved in at CaringMother?"

"Sure. We have a quality control team that culls out defectives. They look for evidence of debilitating defects like Down syndrome as well as severe retardation which often is a result of technical problems. And, of course, predictors of anti-social behavior, especially indicators of male-pattern aggressiveness. Anything that could prevent the fetus from being a productive member of society if they were born. I don't do actual quality control work, but I know that we only hire top notch people in that area and they adhere strictly to quality control protocols."

"How do *you* know they're top notch and strictly follow protocols?" Tony asked in a belligerent voice.

Raston looked nervously from Tony to Michael, and back to Tony again. "Well, that's my understanding and I've never seen anything to indicate otherwise."

"Hmmpf!" Tony countered.

"Severe retardation due to technical problems?" Michael asked. "That's the first time I've actually heard it acknowledged."

Raston again glanced nervously back and forth, obviously wondering if he had said too much. "It happens, though not that often. It's ... not common knowledge." After a pause, "Fetus conception and development has always been perilous. Especially before artificial wombs. We have much better success rates now. And, of course, zero women die from carrying and delivering children." Raston added proudly.

"Hmmm," Michael said just as Lenora came back in and plunked down the coffee, other drinks and donut holes. He noticed she had brought in some kongo lango for herself. Good. He could never get used to that popular drink from Africa, but the mild alcohol in it would probably mellow her out. "Oh, thanks sweetie," he said as he glanced up at the mirror with a smile.

"So they cull the defectives out. Then what?"

"Well, in general they're then disposed of and the expectant parents are notified. But a statistically representative sample is set aside for use at LEPGen in their research. When there are enough for a delivery, or when LEPGen contacts us for more fetuses, I step in and make the arrangements. Usually it's LEPGen contacting us for a limited number of fetuses with specific defects."

"How do you know that they aren't normal, healthy fetuses?" asked Lenora.

"Good question, Agent Davis," Michael commented.

Raston wore a shocked look on his face, "Well, I'm not the expert here, but I believe that would be illegal. The label on each of the womb containers lists their defects in code, as well as the control lists I receive in hard copy. Nothing has ever been out of order. I keep one copy and the other goes with the shipment. I accompany the shipments to LEPGen to ensure there are no problems along the way, like temperature fluctuations, or leakage. But it's only a distance of about five kilometers."

"How long have you been doing this job?" Tony asked.

"A little less than two years. Almost since the program's initiation. I've been with CaringMother for fourteen years. There had been other programs similar to this in the past, but they were just pilots and were disbanded." Raston said nervously, looking at Tony who was now contemptuously ignoring him, counting holes in the acoustic ceiling tiles.

"And do you have a delivery protocol that you follow?" Tony again asked, glaring at him again.

"Oh yes, in fact I developed the protocol and procedure check list. It's now recognized as the CaringMother standard," Raston said proudly.

The others looked at each other somewhat puzzled.

"What do you mean as the CaringMother standard?" Michael asked.

Raston glanced around at all three of them and said, "Well, my procedures are what are used at all CaringMother facilities worldwide when they have to make similar deliveries."

Michael gasped and looked at Lenora and Tony. He thought Lenora was going to lose it, so he jumped right in.

"Worldwide! Wow, that's impressive. Did you receive some kind of recognition? Like an award or something?"

"Well, not specifically for that. But I did get a high performance rating last year when I developed it, as well as a corporate Inner Circle Award with credits last year. It was obvious what they were for," Raston beamed.

"So CaringMother uses this worldwide. At all facilities?" Michael asked.

"Oh, I don't know if it's actually used anywhere else. That's very confidential." Raston must have realized he might have gone too far again.

"Well then how do you know it's the standard worldwide?"

"My prior manager told me when she gave me my appraisal. And she said I might get some 'sponds about it for clarifications."

"And did you get some 'sponds?"

"Several. From Europe, Middle East: Israel, Egypt. China, Japan. Most were translation questions - like what this or that meant."

Michael could tell that Raston was getting more nervous with this line of questioning, so he decided to shift gears, "What function are you a part of? Quality Control?"

"Yes."

"Who's head of QC at your facility?"

"Kaneesha Johnston."

"How long has she been in that position?"

"A couple years."

"Has she always worked for CaringMother?"

"No. She was hired in from the outside when she took over Quality Control."

"Where did she come from?"

"Hmmm. I believe from NuTense Corporation," Raston said. Then after a pause, "Yes, NuTense."

Michael and the others looked at each other; then Michael continued, "NuTense? Are there any other people working in your area who also came from NuTense?"

"Oh, I don't know. I only knew about her because you always get that kind of scuttle-butt about the new big boss. You know."

"Oh sure."

Finally, Michael said, "Do you have any ideas of possible problems going on at CaringMother that could be causing or contributing to LEPGen's lack of success?"

"No. My delivery operations have always gone smoothly. But I'm just the 'doorman'. I can't answer for the other areas. You'd have to interview people from the QC work area to get a better idea."

"Understood. Well, Mr. Ralston, thank you for coming in. You've been most helpful. Do not discuss any of this with anyone other than your manager. Do not tell anyone else, including your wife and child, that you have been here today. We may call you back if we need further information."

"I'm always ready to do my duty to The Corporation," Raston said enthusiastically. As he went out, he kept his distance from Tony, who continued to scowl at him.

The three of them stared out of the window, looking down on to Main Street, and watched Raston scurry toward the tram stop.

"He's clean," Michael finally said. He frowned at Lenora. "I thought you were going to lose it when he said his procedures are used worldwide," Michael said looking at Lenora.

"I just about did. God, Michael. Take the nightmare we saw from the other night and multiply it how many times? And what are they using these fetuses for? I wanted to cry."

"I'm glad you didn't. He would have clammed up if you had. To him, it's probably BAU at this point.

"Tony, thanks for being my right-hand tough guy while Lenora was out. Ya done good!"

"Yezzah, while ah wuz jis out tha getting' da massah's coffee! Yezzah!" Lenora said sarcastically.

"Oh, get over it, Miss Pretty Two Shoes! Look, before we went in there I figured this guy for a typical, straight-up Corporate citizen. Meaning he'd feel intimidated by a woman, and a black woman at that. Who do you think Kaneesha Johnston is? So I had to put him at ease. Let him know you were my lowly wonk and then remove you from the scene for a while. He lightened up when you went out. And Tony did his tough Italian routine. He didn't go having a hissy fit over me stereotyping him. I wanted to keep Raston on his toes, not overwhelm him."

"OK, point taken. Oh, Connie was in the observation room while I was out there."

"Thanks for the heads up. She'll be after my balls on this one," Michael said resignedly. "Look, this was a good start to the interviewing. I just wonder how widespread this fetus business is. And how much CaringMother is making from it. I'd like to dig deeper into CaringMother now, but Colson'd fight us every inch of the way.

"I've 'sponded Treadwell that we'd start interviewing the LEPGen people tomorrow at their facility. Too many to parade in and out of here. She said she has a secure, discrete conference room for that. But she wants to know who we'll be interviewing. So draw up a prioritized list of the most likelies. Include all the ones who came from NuTense. I don't like the pattern I'm seeing."

As they walked back to their stations, Connie popped her head out of her office and said, "Michael Chan, get in here!"

Michael rolled his eyes, turned and said, "Coming dear!"

Chapter 20

The Oracle walked along listening to one of his favorites, Jerry Mulligan, playing his baritone saxophone. *Man, he can he can really blow a lot'a deep soul out'a that bari sax – for a white cat!* he thought. He was listening to an old fashioned device inserted into his ears. Great sound from a tiny chip containing his favorites. It was the best alternative to 'sponding the music, which he would not do, even if his transponder were operable. Dan Schmitt had always been a rebel against the system. From early on he had gotten into trouble with his teachers, questioning things too much for his own good.

There had always been tension in his home life. His parents were always fighting – usually about finances. One day when he was ten years old his father suddenly disappeared. No explanations. His mother was obviously distraught but would never talk about his disappearance. But Dan knew that fathers didn't just suddenly disappear.

As each day, week, month, and year passed with no word, Dan became increasingly convinced that The Corporation had disappeared him. The few times he brought up his suspicions with his mother, she'd change the subject. He soon learned not to bring it up. But it was always that nagging thought, ever-present in the back of his mind.

In his mid teens he was swept away by jazz. He couldn't remember an exact moment when it happened or which piece of music had caused it. He had always liked all kinds of music, except the crap The Corporation pumped out. But suddenly, there it was, jazz! And with each passing day he had to hear more.

In the end, it was the greats of the classical period of the 1930's to 1960's that captured his heart – Davis, Mingus, Peterson. And around this love he built his personality of a devoted beatnik. He wasn't idealizing the past – he certainly wouldn't want to be a black back in those days. Rather, he was building his ideal world, dropping out of The Corporate world, and into a perfect world of jazz.

To further model himself on the beatniks of the 1950's, Dan started hanging out in the clubs of the hard-scrabble north side of Poughkeepsie, and as a result developed his street smarts. In spite of his escapism, he had a natural, easy way with people and soon gained a reputation as a go-to man. The police soon found it useful to "consult" with Dan and were willing to pay him in free-floating credits.

When agents from the Poughkeepsie office of the Corporate Bureau of Investigation approached him, Dan was very reluctant to work as a consultant for them. As the enforcement arm of The Corporation, he had always blamed them for his father's disappearance. But by chance, the first corpo who approached him was Michael Chan. Their personalities clicked and they became "arms-length working associates", if not friends. Dan told Michael he wouldn't snitch. Michael respected that.

Like with the police, the work Dan did for Michael steered him in the direction of solving his cases and away from unnecessary damage. At least, that was how he rationalized working for Michael. Dan disliked and refused to work for most corpos. He soon got a reputation as being a burned-out beatnik. Few consulted him, which was fine with Dan.

As Dan walked up Clinton Way among the doms, he passed an old square, and studied the statue of the Civil War soldier that stood gazing into the setting sun. He always wondered why The Corporation had left that old square and statue when they built the doms. They didn't fit. He paused and read the battles that the Poughkeepsie Union soldiers had fought in. He was vaguely aware of the circumstances of that war and that hundreds of thousands of men on both sides had died.

He looked up at the determined look on the statue and wondered just how determined those men had been. *I bet they weren't that sure and were scarred shitless,* he thought as he shook his head. Yet they had found courage and done what they had to. He wondered if there were any people like that today. He shrugged, and walked off to the sounds of Mulligan. Cool.

As he exited the dom district, Clinton Way became the old Clinton Street. Dan studied the dilapidated buildings in front of him. Though it wasn't common knowledge yet, Dan knew that this would be the next area where The Corporation would be building doms. Soon this whole neighborhood would disappear and in its place would stand the sterile, efficient cubes that were the symbols of The Corporation.

After several minutes he saw the old, three-story apartment building. It was probably built in the early 1900's to house the poor working in nearby factories. It was obviously beyond fixing up, and a new dom in its place would be a functional improvement. Unfortunately, the inhabitants of the current building would not be able to afford living in the new dom and would have to scramble to find other shelter, hopefully in no worse condition.

Walking up the front steps onto the porch that stretched to either end of the building, Dan studied numerous items. The easy chair and rocking chair were typical of the old north side. People still sat out on the porches as the evening cooled and watched life go by, calling out to acquaintances. Once the baking sun was down, these chairs would be occupied. Like the numerous toys on the porch, the chairs were so run down that the owners never had to worry about them disappearing.

Dan pushed the buzzer to apartment 3C and waited, watching a squirrel peek out of a hole in the porch roof. Soon a tinny female voice rasped out over the speaker, "Who is it?"

"It's Dan Schmitt, Ms. Maltos, you know, Jimmy's friend."

"Come on up, Dan," Alvira Maltos said as the front door buzzed open.

Climbing the stairs, Dan was surprised that there wasn't much clutter. The walls in the halls were dingy, but the windows had obviously been cleaned in the not-too-distant past.

Ms. Maltos was waiting at her door for Dan, greeted him as he walked in, and then closed and locked the door after him. She was probably in her sixties and had that tired, resigned look of someone who had toiled all her life, with the knowledge that she would have to work till the day she dropped dead.

Dan looked around at the small but tidy apartment. Family pictures on the walls. Obviously no wallplays or holoplays here. There was the obligatory Jesus on the cross and picture of the pope, as found in many Hispanic homes.

And the outdated picture of the long-deceased husband with black cloth draped around it. There were toys neatly arranged in a corner, probably for visiting grandchildren.

"Jimmy said you'd be expecting me." Dan figured it best to soften his beatnik talk and mannerisms if he wanted to gain her trust.

"Yes, but I thought you'd 'spond before you came over."

"Ms. Maltos, my 'sponder hasn't worked in years."

Ms. Maltos seemed relieved but said suspiciously, "How do you get away with that."

"You'd be surprised about what you can get away with, if you try."

Ms. Maltos looked intensely into Dan's eyes. Finally, she said in a tentative voice, "Jimmy said you might be interested in information related to CaringMother. He told you that I've been a servant in Ms. Colson's household for years?"

"Including in her newest one in Millbrook?"

"Yes." Then after a pause, "Dan, you have a good reputation. And Jimmy's recommendation means a lot to me. Before we get into what I have, I'm going to tell you some things, give you some background. I'm a good person, not a rat. I want you to understand why I'm doing what I'm doing."

And then after another pause, "You know, Dan, over all these years I've never existed in Ms. Colson's houses. When I was hired by her assistant many years ago, Ms. Colson would look at me with suspicion. But once figuring I was harmless, I faded into the background. I became a useful tool attending to her comforts. That was fine with me, I didn't expect more from her.

"But being invisible has its advantages. Over the years I've been the fly on the wall during many of Ms. Colson's meetings; the in-person ones, and the wallplay and holoplay ones as well which have been the main ones since she started living in her Millbrook estate most of the time. Much of what I've seen and heard in recent years has chilled to me to the bone. But being a good servant I've been discrete and have dutifully 'forgotten' those meetings.

Ms. Maltos stood and walked over to the picture of her husband, as if to gain strength from his memory. "About four years ago my daughter told me she and her husband had gotten permission to have a baby. She was so excited. They had wanted this for years but had never been able to build a business case and gain enough credits to convince their managers to sign off.

I contributed some of the credits I'd been investing for retirement to them – you know, to get them over the hump. They refused at first, but I insisted. I'd never retire so those credits would just be wasted anyway – they'd just revert to The Corporation.

"My daughter and son-in-law made arrangements at the local CaringMother facility. Soon after her egg was fertilized they informed her that the egg had split into identical twin girls. With current technology, this is quite rare. And it's one of the rare 'abnormal fetus' conditions where parents are given the choice to terminate or not. My daughter and her husband chose not to terminate. They wanted those little girls so much."

After some reflection, Ms. Maltos continued, "Well, the girls were born. We were overjoyed. They were so precious. But early on it became obvious that they had developmental problems. My daughter was beside herself. She felt trapped. Both my daughter and her husband are lower bands like me. She knew they needed to keep working overtime to pay for two children. So she put the girls in lower-band post-natal care, when what they needed was her. They needed my credits now more than ever, so I started working longer hours to help them out. I couldn't quit or retire and take care of the girls. We felt trapped."

Dan heard the grief in her voice as she continued, "Given the path they were on, I knew those little girls wouldn't make it." She gasped and wiped her eyes with her hands. Dan resisted his urge to go over and put his arm on her shoulder.

Regaining her composure she continued, "I thought of trying to get help from some of the staff in Millbrook, or even from Ms. Colson. But what a foolish mistake that'd be! I'd be viewed as a problem and dismissed immediately."

Ms. Maltos hesitated as if unsure about proceeding.

Dan said, "Ms. Maltos, what you're telling is safe with me. I'm no rat. If I was, Jimmy'd make a quick end to me."

Seeming to be convinced, Ms. Maltos continued, "One day, Ms. Colson was having a holoplay meeting with the quality control director at one of the CaringMother locations. The director briefed her on some of the quality problems they were experiencing and the developmental problems they were causing the fetuses. She flew into a rage. She told him to find a fix to the damn problem and get on with things. But he'd better be damn sure word didn't get out, or he'd be out on the street and unemployable. Even on the holoplay I could see he was sweating.

"I quietly put her tea tray down as she fumed about that meeting wasting her time. She flung the tray onto the very-valuable, restored antique Persian rug before she stormed off. I ran quickly to get water, cleaner, brushes and rags and frantically worked on the tea stain. I knew that if the stain set in, she'd eventually notice it and tell her assistant to discipline whoever was responsible. That would mean me.

"I went home that night, thinking about that holoplay, thinking that my granddaughters' problems could have been caused by CaringMother. Colson couldn't have cared less if she had known. It was then that I knew what I had to do. Jimmy got me a black market techie who set me up with a recording device so I could record all of Colson's holoplay meetings at her Millbrook estate. And I've done that over the past two years."

With those words Ms. Maltos sat back and let her words sink in with Dan.

"You've recorded all of them?"

"Yes. If they were to pass into the wrong hands – or right hands – they would be very damaging to her, to CaringMother and to many corporations she's been cutting deals with. And to The Corporation."

Dan was silent for several moments. Finally he said, "Whew! What do you want for them?"

"I've been storing them up, knowing my trove was becoming more valuable each day. I know they'd be priceless to certain individuals and corporations. But I also know I can't advertise and put them up for auction. Obviously, I can't black mail Colson or the others. I'd be dead in no time and the recordings would disappear. I don't want that. But my primary concern is to get help for my granddaughters – but I'm running out of time. So I'm willing to let them go for 100,000 credits – free floating."

"That's a lot in free floaters."

"No it's not. But like I said, my granddaughters are running out of time with each passing day."

"I'm not disputing their value. It's just that coming up with that much in free floaters isn't easy. I'll have to consult with my client and see what he's willing to do. Is LEPGen Corporation one of the parties?"

"Yes."

"You're putting yourself in a very dangerous position. I wouldn't rat on you. But it's not me you have to worry about. If this ends up in the right hands and is discretely used, you could be safe. But if it made it into the public realm, it wouldn't take Colson and others long to put two and two together, and you'd be dead."

"I've thought all of this through a thousand times. Dan, have you ever found yourself floundering and then one day realize what you had to do? Well, that's how it was with me.

"I have two choices. Let my granddaughters fall further behind and watch my daughter and her husband sink into despair; or I can sell my recordings and get them the help they need. My days may be numbered. I'm realistic. That doesn't matter. I've lived a long life and have always had the love of my family. I'm ready for whatever happens to me. The free floating credits will prevent a trail leading to my daughter."

"Does your daughter know?"

"No. She wouldn't want me to do it if she did. I don't want the free floaters to touch me in any way. I already have a hermetic account set up for them that only my daughter and her husband will be able to access, when I tell them about it."

Dan reflected for some time, and finally said, "OK, you know I need to sample the wares. Show me something significant – something related to LEPGen."

In a minute Dan was watching Colson in a holoplay meeting with the head of LEPGen Technologies research and development. He watched in disbelief as the meeting proceeded. Toward the end he looked over at Ms. Maltos in horror.

When they were done she could see Dan was visibly shaken. Maybe for the first time in his life he was speechless.

"Dan, I'm only a band 2. But I am religious and do understand certain things about life, and I believe there is evil in this world. I can't judge whether Colson is evil; that's for God to decide. But she is doing evil things.

"Many would say she's just been a successful business woman. I don't know if it comes with the territory of driving a large, international corporation – you know, driving more business and profits – or moving out to that old estate in Millbrook and living cut off from humanity. But over the past several years her actions have become evil.

"And what you've seen tonight is just a small sample."

Michael moved quickly along Market Street in the cooling influence of the night. There wasn't anything playing at the Bardavon. Most of the shops had closed, so the street was becoming increasingly dark. Just the street lights and the lights from the few open late-night clubs along the way parted the darkness.

As he approached Mario's he looked up and gasped. There was the Oracle sitting at the front counter gazing blankly out into the darkness. There were a few other customers at the counter and Mario waiting on them. That image! He couldn't get it out of his mind. It spooked him. It was as if Dan were already finding his place in the painting. Just then Dan saw him and smiled. Michael shook off his dread and walked in.

"Hey Charlie, how they hangin'?" Dan asked.

Mario greeted Michael too as the other customers looked up from their dishes.

"Let's like split this scene," Dan said as he handed Mario a free floater and told him to keep the change.

As they walked out into the night, Michael said, "I got word that you wanted to see me. Damn, I wish you'd get your 'sponder repaired! I could've been here an hour earlier."

"Cool it daddy. Come on, let's keep walkin'. You didn't have a tail did you?" the Oracle asked as they headed down Main Street toward the river.

"What's this about? I've got a long day tomorrow and I'd hoped I was going to have a quiet evening."

"I dig ya man, I dig ya," the Oracle said as he looked back anyway. "Look, I've come up with a source that's got the goods on Colson and CaringMother."

"What do you mean by 'the goods'?"

"Big time goods. Like that Colson chick has been arranging some dirt with a lot of other corporate big cats. Including LEPGen. I saw Colson cuttin' a deal with an exec from LEPGen in a holoplay. It'd make your balls shrivel up. And there's a lot more."

Michael thought about what he had seen the other night at LEPGen.

"How do you know it's real and that there's more?"

"It's real, man."

"OK, and how much?"

"A hundred K in free floaters."

Michael stopped. "Are you nuts? Look Dan, let me clarify the scope of this investigation. We believe there was a crime of sabotage committed at the LEPGen R&D facilities on South Road – on a project that CaringMother is tied into. I'm not out to hang Colson or any other execs. Have you come up with anything specific that could be related to sabotage at the LEPGen R&D facilities?"

"Simmer down, man. Look, I've found something big connecting CaringMother and LEPGen R&D, and a lot more. Don't rag on me!"

Michael realized he wasn't handling things well. "Hey, Oracle, I'm sorry," Michael smiled. "I know you're trying to help me ferret things out. And I do feel I'm in the dark on the CaringMother side of the equation – but Colson's gonna block me every step of the way.

After scratching his head in thought, Michael continued, "My boss'll have a fit, but I'll transfer you another 25K first thing in the morning. But that's all I can do at this point. And you'll have to make do with that for now. Get a better idea of exactly what your source has. And if it's good, work on bringing down the price."

"Yeah, yeah. But that 25K along with the original 25K ain't gonna cut it."

"Dan, you've always come through for me. Keep pluggin' away – CaringMother and LEPGen."

Dan shrugged with half a smile and said, "Hey, you know me, Michael me laddy. I'll keep on it and drop you a dime when I've got somethin'."

Michael watched the Oracle walk off and disappear into the fog coming up from the river. He couldn't get the image of that painting out of his mind.

Chapter 21
THURSDAY, JULY 9

Michael was still groggy from his restless night. He had to get his wits about him so he, Lenora and Tony could strategize on how they'd handle the interviews with the LEPGen employees. He looked around the windowless conference room in the LEPGen R&D labs.

"Tony, are you sure the room's secure?"

"Yeah, Michael, I checked it out the first thing when we came in"

"Oh, yeah. Where's the list of the people we see today?"

"Right in front of you, Michael. I gave it to you five minutes ago," Lenora said as she glanced over at Tony, giving him a "what-the-hell" look.

"OK. Look, I didn't sleep well." Michael walked over to the coffee dispenser and picked up a cup. He flashed back to his dream. Mario's restaurant. The Oracle sitting at the counter. James Dean, Marilynn Monroe, Humphrey Bogart, and Elvis Presley waiting on them. None of them saw Michael standing outside. He had to warn Dan. He banged on the window, shouting to Dan to be careful, but Dan didn't see him.

He finally woke up, shaking. It was early morning. He saw Julianna's shadow next to him, breathing deeply. He didn't want to disturb her, and he knew he'd drop back into that dream if he went to sleep again, so he got up and went into his work room and polished the mahogany on his newest Winterhalder and Hofmeier to a soft glow.

"Michael, are you OK?" Lenora asked.

"Yes," Michael finally said, snapping out of his funk, taking a drink of his coffee, and walking over to the conference table. "Let's try the approach we did with Raston yesterday. We're here interviewing these people. We appreciate their help in figuring out what's going on. If we run into a tough guy, Tony, you're the bad cop again. I'm the good cop. Lenora, you're the floater between the two, do what seems to be best with each person. But remember, like with Raston, your being a black female can be intimidating. In general, we want them to be comfortable and open." Then he smiled and added, "By the way, you don't have to go out and fetch the coffee today."

"Oh thanks. And why not?"

"Because it's already in the room," Michael said laughing, as Lenora reached over and swatted him.

Just then Emma Treadwell walked into the room. "I hope I'm not interrupting something."

"Just a little department joke." Michael said, smiling at Lenora and Tony. He really liked these two rookies.

Michael continued, "Can you give us a status?"

"No real changes," Treadwell said. "We did have two more fetuses expire since I last spoke with you. But that's part of the pattern we've been seeing. A statistically abnormally high number of fetuses have been expiring under these experiments – there's no apparent cause. They just drift off. It's hard to explain. It's like an older person finding peace letting go.

"The organic injections put a certain amount of stress on the fetuses. We keep a close eye on the progression, which often involves stress tests along the way. We also do a large number of different types of transmissions to them along the way and test their level of reception. You'd expect a certain amount of expiration as a result."

"When you said you were running a low rate of success, I didn't realize that that included an abnormally high rate of 'expiration'," Michael said.

"Well, yes. That goes with the territory. Just varying the makeup, quantity, and placement of the injections causes a certain amount of predictable expiration. And all of the experimenting along the way causes a certain amount as well. But the level of expiration is high, especially on the more developed fetuses," Treadwell observed.

"How do you know the expiration rate is abnormally high?" Michael asked.

"That's part of the problem. Fetus experimentation is relatively new. It's been done on and off over the past number of years, but on a very limited, highly-confidential basis, so there are very few statistics to go on."

"So you really don't know whether your failure rates, as well as high expiration rates, are abnormal, and therefore have no real grounds to believe that a crime of sabotage has been committed?"

"Well, no solid proof. But based on the limited history we have, we believe sabotage has been going on. And based on gut feel as an experienced scientist as well. Like the way many of the fetuses drift off and expire with no apparent cause. It doesn't make sense."

"Does it happen while certain experiments are being done? Or while certain people are doing those experiments?"

"Again, it seems to be more prevalent in the more developed fetus. And this is at a stage where we do more transmission testing."

"What kind of transmissions?"

"Speaking, especially with educational content; alerts, like weather and fire; all kinds of music. Anything you might receive in a regular 'spond."

"But no discernible patterns?"

"No, we're monitoring things more closely now. But nothing yet."

"Are only certain people working on the advanced fetuses?" Tony asked.

"No. Everyone's trained in most areas and performs many duties at most stages of development. It's much more economical to have things structured that way."

After some reflection Michael said, "It's good that you haven't seen any changes. We can assume that if sabotage has been going on, it still is. After our interviews, if you see an improvement in your success rates, then you probably do have a saboteur. Or, if we're lucky, the saboteur may tip his hand in another way. Like overreacting during a "friendly" interview; changing his work patterns; or even confessing or bolting. You never know."

After a brief pause, Michael handed her a copy of the list and continued, "Here's the list of people we'd like to interview. We've gone through their LEPGen records as well as external records and have selected and ordered them according to points of interest. Take a look and let us know if there's anything you'd change, like who we should interview or in what order."

After looking down the list, Treadwell said, "Looks good."

Smart woman, Michael thought. She knew she's under scrutiny as well, and any change could be construed as an attempt on her part to mislead them.

"OK, we'd like you to get each person on the list in the order we have them. We have them ordered by shift as well and we'll be here for each shift, though we'll have to knock off around midnight, and pick up tomorrow. To start, give us about fifteen minutes while we prep for the first interviewee, Isabella Hernandez."

"Why Isabella first?" Treadwell asked, but then immediately added, "I mean, there's no problem with that. I was curious."

"She's the first shift lead so carries more responsibility to have an overview of what everyone's doing. She may be able to give us more insight into the others," Lenora said.

"Oh sure, alright. By the way, I understand you interviewed the CaringMother contact yesterday. What did you learn from him?"

Hmmm, who told her? Michael thought. "That's right. According to him he's been following proper protocol. We have his receiving contact here on our list to interview."

"OK. I'll send in Isabella in fifteen minutes."

As she rose, Michael added, "Dr. Treadwell, LEPGen has transponder R&D in the Euro Swiss division, right?"

"Swiss, yes."

"Are they doing similar experiments on fetuses?"

No. That would be redundant, which would be uneconomical. Though if we don't start having more success here, they might have to ramp up over there."

"How about other locations; Middle East, China, Japan? Are they doing similar experiments?"

"No, why?"

"Just curious. Trying to fill in your situation in my mind. Thanks."

As she walked out, Michael couldn't help but notice how nicely the shape of her backside came through on her expensive, well-designed slacks. As she closed the door, he caught himself and looked over at Lenora who was giving him a knowing, arched-eyebrow glance.

"What? I was just admiring her taste in clothing!" Michael said defensively.

"Yeah, that and much, much more!" Lenora exclaimed.

"OK, let's look at what we have on Hernandez," Michael said looking toward the wall as a 3D wallplay popped up. On the left was a rotating 3D view of her head as well as a rotating full view, with a brief summary of her dimensions: age, height, weight and true hair, skin and eye colors. On the right at the top was a summary of symbols relating to her: female (unchanged), Hispanic (unchanged), married (hetero) with one daughter (also unchanged), Poughkeepsie resident, member of the Corporate Church, etc.

Underneath that were bulletized rectangles with comments about her, each with drill-down detail behind it: valedictorian of middle-form high school, graduated from Corporate Institute of Technology with honors, worked for NuTense before coming to work for LEPGen about half a year after Treadwell started at LEPGen. Worked briefly in weapons R&D before moving over to transponder R&D. Worked as technician before taking over as shift lead, first night shift then day shift.

Michael took it all in within a minute, and then drilled down to the employment interview, which included interviewing with Treadwell who had glowing comments about Hernandez in the conclusion. Consistently top ratings since being hired. Hmmm ... that seemed odd. Normally initial ratings were lower. "Look at those ratings. Either she's been a consistent superstar, or someone has been padding her performance," Michael commented as he looked at the others.

"Yeah, and look who signed off on most of them – Treadwell," commented Tony.

"Methinks there be a cozy connection here!" Michael observed.

After doing a few more drill downs, someone knocked at the door. Michael glanced at the elapsed time as he killed the wallplay. "Five minutes early," he commented.

Tony went to the door and let Isabella Hernandez into the room. As she walked to the table, Michael saw that she was an attractive, youngish-looking, middle-aged Hispanic woman. Hmmm, they all seemed to be attractive. He glanced over at Lenora, who had seen the writing on his face and just rolled her eyeballs. But in his defense, Michael did notice that she had long, flowing dark hair, with large, dark-brown eyes – the kind you could get lost in. Oops.

Introductions made, Hernandez bowed to each of them and took a seat.

"Would you care for a drink Ms. Hernandez?" Michael asked.

"Water?"

Michael got a sealed glass of water and brought it over.

"Did Dr. Treadwell mention why we're here?"

"She said she had asked your help in trying to get to the bottom of our lack of progress on the transponder experiments," Hernandez said quietly.

"Exactly. She thought our investigative techniques might be able to help."

"But you're with the CBI. Doesn't that imply that a crime has been committed?"

"Not necessarily. We sometimes get called into situations as, well, consultants. We're all one big Corporate family. We're just here to help if we can." Michael looked at Tony who gave him a "you bullshitter" look. "Do you think a crime has been committed?" Michael added, a bit too sweetly. Lenora gave him the eye.

"I don't know. But it's hard to explain our lack of progress."

"As shift lead, can you give us some insight based on your overseeing responsibilities? Have you noticed suspicious or out-of-the-ordinary actions or activities in any of the technicians on your shift?"

"No."

Michael noticed she was stiffening up. Shit. She probably thought he was trying to get her to rat out colleagues on flimsy grounds. He'd better change directions.

"What seems to be going on in the experiments that seems out of the ordinary, other than just having a high failure rate?"

She hesitated, so Michael encouraged her, "Whatever comes to your mind, no matter how unscientific, or whacky it may sound. Believe me, we've seen it all."

Hernandez finally volunteered, "We started this line of experimentation a few years ago. We had had a lot of success with animals, so it was time to move on to the next stage. At first, we seemed to be having some success, you know, with the more elementary work. But it was as we moved forward to the more advanced work; that's where we started running into problems. You know, 'sponder nets failing, high expiration rates, that kind of thing."

"So you've been on the project since it started?" Tony asked.

"Yes, I started as the third shift lead, pretty much a skeleton crew. I took over as first shift lead about half a year ago. It was more responsibility, more people, so I got a promotion," Hernandez beamed.

"Who did you take over from?" Lenora asked.

"Indira Japore."

"What were the circumstances? She's still on first shift as a regular technician now, right?" Lenora pursued.

Hernandez caught her drift and continued, "She's just had her new baby delivered from CaringMother – she wanted to have more time to be with her. Indira's a top notch technician and is always very diligent in her work."

"Were there any other significant changes in personnel in the past two years?" Tony asked.

"No. Emma, Dr. Treadwell, had assembled the entire team before we kicked off this phase of the experimentation. It's quite an honor to work under her and does pay extra due to the high confidentiality of our work. It's been a consistent team, some changing of shifts, but coherent. Of course, everyone's background was checked out and they were all briefed on how important and confidential the work is. It's a privilege to work in this area so not much turn over."

"Not much? So there has been some change?" Michael asked.

"Well, about the time I took over as first shift lead, a woman named Christina Sessions left."

"Left?"

"Yes. She'd been having trouble. You know, this isn't easy work. It's not for everyone. You have to be able to focus on the objective and remember the importance of what we're trying to accomplish. Well, she couldn't do that. After a number of meetings with Dr. Treadwell, it was decided that it would be best if she left."

"Did she go to work in another area of LEPGen?" Michael continued.

"No, she left the corporation."

"So what's she doing now?"

"I don't know. None of us ever heard from her again. She just kind of disappeared." Hernandez immediately put her hand over her mouth. "Not *that* kind of disappeared. I mean, she just left the corporation and I believe Poughkeepsie. I've heard that she's working for another corporation down in Manhattan."

"But you don't know for sure?" Lenora asked.

"No, just word of mouth."

"Has anyone else left this project that you know of?"

"No."

"Is there anyone else that has developed a problem dealing with their work?" Lenora pursued.

"Not on my shift. We have periodic discussions with each person and evaluations to be sure there are no problems developing."

"How often does that take place?"

"At least every half a year – during their performance evaluations."

"How many of the technicians on the project have children of their own?"

"Most do."

"Do you think that could be a source of conflict?"

"Well, it could be."

"Do you have a child?"

"Yes. She just finished her first year at Corporate Tech, my alma mater," Hernandez said.

"That's great," Michael said. "I have a daughter too. She's doing very well in her career and has applied for permission to get married *and* have a child."

"You must be very proud of her. And before you know it you'll be a grandfather!" Hernandez said. Then she added wistfully, "They grow up so fast! It just seems like yesterday when CaringMother delivered my daughter to me."

Michael moved closer, stared intensely into her eyes and said, "Ms. Hernandez, does having a child cause a conflict for you in your work?"

Ms. Hernandez sat back and blinked twice. "These fetuses all had problems that would have otherwise lead to a termination of their gestation. They're at least making a contribution to the betterment of humankind." But after a moment she continued, "But I'd be less than human if I didn't add that sometimes when I gaze down at the little faces of the post-natal fetuses I do step back and pause. They tug at my heart. But then I remind myself and I move on."

Michael said, "Ms. Hernandez, I appreciate your openness." Then after another short pause. "Going back to your observations on the failures – sorry, lack of success. You said that the problem was greater in the more advanced work. Can you elaborate?"

"Sure. The problems are more pronounced in the fetuses in which the 'sponder nets are fully developed. Once the net is developed you'd expect the failure rate to drop. But it increases rather than decreases. The fetuses receive 'sponds, but then their openness to reception starts to drop off, and then closes up."

"Is that when they expire?" Tony asked.

"Often, but not always."

"What happens when they expire? Do you think it's caused by the stress of the experiments?" Tony continued.

"In some cases it's stress. But in most, it isn't stress related. At least it isn't obvious when we do the autopsies. If anything, it's seems to be the opposite. They seem relaxed and at peace when they expire." After a pause she continued, "I think what's causing the failures is external to the fetuses. Some external agent being introduced, probably purposely. I've voiced my thoughts to Emma."

"I've noticed you've referred to Dr. Treadwell by her first name. Is that typical here at LEPGen? Is she a personal friend of yours?" Lenora asked.

"Oh yes. We're all on a first name basis on the team. That's common in LEPGen. I've known Dr. Treadwell for a long time, going back to when we both worked for NuTense. In fact, she recruited me into LEPGen from NuTense and has been very supportive in my advancement here."

"Did she recruit others to the team that had also worked for NuTense?" Lenora pressed.

"Yes, in many cases. But she's also recruited others from the outside. Mostly people she knew from school or from other places she'd worked at. She also recruited internally, of course. People she knew well." At this she looked at the others and then added, "But external recruitment is typical, especially in R&D."

"What was her criteria for recruiting?"

"You'd have to ask her that. But I would say, highly capable, diligent people. Sorry if it sounds like I'm bragging. And loyal. People like me who admire her and believe in her visions for the future."

They concluded the interview, thanked and excused Isabella Hernandez. Michael went up to the dispenser, poured more coffee and took a long, reflective drink. He finally turned to the others and asked, "What can you conclude from our discussion with Ms. Hernandez?"

"Well, first, you have a thing for Hispanic women," Lenora said. They all laughed.

"Agent Davis, your powers of observation are definitely improving toward detective grade! And here I thought I was hiding it so well," Michael exclaimed.

"She thinks there's sabotage going on," Tony observed. "But beyond that, nothing definite."

"Like Treadwell, she did observe that the fetuses seemed to just give up; 'expire in peace'," Michael added. "Two things I want to push hard on in these interviews. First, the NuTense connection. A lot of them came over from NuTense, usually recruited by Treadwell. Find out those circumstances. Second, dig down into the feelings of the people who have children."

"One thing's clear. Treadwell assembled a loyal team. That certainly fits into her mission. In fact, it's probably critical to the project's confidentiality and success," Lenora added. "It's amazing that the whole team is still intact, except for that one defection. The roaches check in, but they don't check out."

"Good points, both of you. Let's be sure to 'spond up Christina Sessions when we get out of here and see what she's up to. I'm becoming more convinced that something beyond the ordinary is happening, but I'm just not convinced that it's sabotage. It's frustrating that we don't have anything solid yet. But beyond Treadwell, we've only interviewed Raston and Hernandez. So let's keep plugging away.

Chapter 22

"Hi Ian, can I come in?"

Ian snapped out of his thoughts and looked up at Spencer in the doorway. "Sure. I was thinking about some upcoming class activities. Take a seat.

"So how are things progressing on debate preparations?"

"Pretty good. We've listed the points we want to cover, and discussed how to argue each point. Which brought up questions about conducting debates. Can we borrow your book on the rules of debate?"

"Sure," Ian said, taking down an old volume down from a shelf. "But be careful with that. It's one of the last copies ever printed of that book back in the 30's. Why don't you just 'spond the rules?"

"Things were pretty fuzzy when we 'sponded. You know, debating's a lost art, so it's actually difficult to 'spond a consistent set of rules. The girls are cherry picking the rules they want from the different sources they're 'sponding. We figured if we had a solid copy to refer to during the debate, we could insist it be used as the sole source. Making us use hard copy sources in writing our compositions kind of rubbed off on us," Spencer said smiling.

"Good idea. So what are some of your points? Technically I shouldn't be asking since I'll be the judge of the debate and need to stay neutral. But I'm also here to help, and I'll do the same for the girls if they want help."

"Well, the first one is this: The Corporation has banned all favoritism, whether race, ethnic background, or sex. But that's part of the problem we're running into. The Corporation *says* that all people are equal, so shut up, go away and be equal. But if you look at all statistics, you can only conclude that men *are* second-class citizens, whether you're looking at positions of power and influence in government or the private sector, or at wealth accumulation.

"Or if you look at the way laws are written and adjudicated, it's very clear that they're very biased against men. And look at society's jaundiced view of men in general. The girls are going to have a slam-dunk in this debate. We were wondering why you didn't let the guys support the obvious, that men are second-class citizens, and let the girls defend the world that their foremothers created for them."

"Spencer, anyone can debate a side that they believe is right. That's easy and you don't learn anything from it. It's when you're supporting a position that you don't believe, or that's hard to support, or better yet both, that you learn to debate. To argue a point of view in a civil, structured manner.

"Tell the guys they need to step up to the girls' challenge. Remember, the girls have to argue that men are second-class citizens. They'll have a lot of those statistics so they'll have to use them, even though it may cause them discomfort. Maybe they'll gain some empathy.

"Look, if statistics on power, influence and wealth support the position that men are second-class citizens, then avoid them. Same with laws and societal views. Build your argument that men are not second-class citizens based on other statistics and observations. Like, even though women may hold most executive positions, which can be boring and are certainly stressful, men often excel in many of the fun or interesting jobs, especially jobs that require physical strength or danger, like construction or police work. Poke around on those statistics and see what you can build around that."

"Shift the paradigm?"

"Right. And how about looking at non-power, non-financial aspects of living, like quality of life. You could argue that since men often have less demanding jobs, they have more time to pursue other interest. That they have a more balanced life."

"OK, I see what you're getting at. Thanks, we'll work on that."

"You don't need the best statistics and points to be made. You just need to do the best job of presenting those you have."

Spencer looked down at his hands for a few moments, and then said, "Our discussions in getting ready for the debate have been taking some digressions into more basic questions. Like what it means to be a man today, or a woman for that matter. That was much more easily answered in the old days, when women had babies, cared for them, and men supported them by earning a living and protected them.

"As Mrs. Alvarez said, now you deliver your eggs and sperm to a wombcare center, see the baby when it's born, and then occasionally at the post-natal care center. If anything, men care for the children more than women, since they typically have the less demanding, less time-consuming jobs. But other than obvious physical differences, there isn't much difference between men and women. Except when it comes to society predetermining what'll happen to you and how far you'll go in your life based on your gender."

Ian studied Spencer and let out a puff of pent-up breath. "Spencer, I'm probably not a good one to pontificate on what it means to be a man, but I'll give you my view. But don't take what I say as right. You have to find your own way and figure things out for yourself. And that's one of your greatest strengths – always asking questions but then deciding for yourself. Ask others who you admire. Ask Walter Sherman – being a happily-married man, he can probably give you a better answer than me.

"Now, given those caveats, I believe you shouldn't view yourself as a man or as a woman, but as a human being first. The question is what does it mean to be a human being? What it means to be a man, or a woman, should be a minor question. Should, if we were to reach the "biarchal" ideal as Allison put it. Neither patriarchal nor matriarchal.

"Society has always put artificial expectations and demands on each sex, what men and women are, what's expected of them. And, of course, that's changed dramatically over the past hundred years, swinging from one extreme to the other. Like Ms. Alvarez said, we had seemed to reach a good balance in the early part of the century, but the pendulum kept swinging and here we are."

Ian hesitated a moment, and then continued, "You know, in your paper on independence you emphasized 'eudaemonea', the idea that the essence of being human is to allow your intellect to flourish – that every person should have that freedom – it's the pursuit, the intellectual activity, that is happiness. You were so right.

"But there's another side of being human that you didn't address in your paper or in the class discussion. I think there's a part of each of us that I'd call the yearning of the heart – or of the soul. The need to love and be loved. This is our other half. We have an emotional need for others, and in particular for a special other.

"This is where gender comes into play. If you're a straight male, that special other will be a woman. If you're gay, it'll be a man. Poems, songs, religions – so many times you'll see the idea that humans as individuals are not complete beings – that they aren't complete till they meet a special other who will become their mate and make them complete."

"Like John Donne's 'No man is an island, entire on itself'?" Spencer interjected.

"Yes, exactly. I don't know if I go along with the idea that someone else can make you complete. Only you can do that. Or maybe human beings by their nature are never complete – they're always yearning. I don't know. But I feel that that special person serves to enhance your life, to broaden it. You break each other out of the boxes that are your lives and you take each other somewhere else that's more meaningful, that makes you happier. You need each other to help find that place, and once there you never want to go back. And that means that you can't live happily without each other. That you always want to be with her, and she with you. You commit to each other.

"I know you like music. Did you ever hear of Bruce Springsteen? He wrote and performed music around the turn of the century."

"I've heard of him but haven't listened to his music."

"Well, 'spond up the recording of his 2007 Dublin concert, and let's listen to "If I Should Fall Behind". Especially the first and last verses. Those words express what this special relationship means to me." Ian and Spencer synced up and listened.

> We said we'd walk together, come what may,
> And then come the twilight, should we lose our way,
> If as we're a'walkin', our hands should slip free,
> I'll wait for you, and should I fall behind, will you wait for me?

There's a beautiful river in the valley ahead,
There 'neath the oak's bough, soon we'll be wed.
Should we lose each other in the evening's trees,
I'll wait for you, and should I fall behind, will you wait for me?

"That's beautiful, Ian."

"But that's me. Most people would call me an incurable romantic."

"Ian, why aren't you married? I think you'd like to be."

Ian laughed. "That's why I gave you those caveats earlier. I'm definitely not the best role model!"

"When I was in high school – we still called it that in the old days – and a little older than you, there was a girl who was special. But I lacked confidence – I figured I never had a chance with her. So I just admired her from afar. But now, many years later, I wish I would have at least tried to get to know her better.

"Maybe that's the best advice I can give you. If you find someone special, let her know how you feel. Pursue her. It takes guts, but if you're shot down, at least you tried."

Spencer nodded his head.

"Say, I have to meet someone in the Shakespeare Garden. Why don't you walk that way with me and we can continue our discussion."

"Sure, who are you meeting?"

"A woman I met last week. You might know her. Siobhan Carlson."

"Oh sure, she ran a fall camp I attended. We all liked her a lot."

As the two of them walked out into the brilliant sunlight and toward the Shakespeare Garden, Ian thought back to last Saturday in the Valley of the Dead. He pictured himself and Siobhan walking down that overgrown dusty road toward the river, into the purple hues of twilight, and toward a future they couldn't yet see. Taking each others' hands and committing themselves to this young man walking beside him. Would they make that same commitment to each other?

We said we'd walk together, come what may,
And then come the twilight, should we lose our way,

If as we're a'walkin', our hands should slip free,
I'll wait for you, and should I fall behind, will you wait for me?

There's a beautiful river in the valley ahead,
There 'neath the oak's bough, soon we'll be wed.
Should we lose each other in the evening's trees,
I'll wait for you, and should I fall behind, will you wait for me?

It was a perfect day. The sky was a cloudless, Bavarian blue. The temperature and humidity were comfortable. Just when Ian felt himself getting too warm, a gentle, cooling breeze would come along, or they would walk through the cooling shade of a tree. Ian looked at the granite gothic structures of the library and Skinner Hall of Music, and at the Romanesque chapel. He was struck by their perfection. Watching the young people playing boomerfriz on the lawn, or reclining under a tree 'sponding a lesson against the background of the buildings, transported Ian back to a gentler, though he knew idealized, time. Some of the students noticed him with a wave and a "Hi Ian".

This was a small, perfect world in which Ian found profound happiness – a world which he would never leave for the likes of Manhattan or any other place. Ian found himself slowing down so as not to miss anything. What a wonderful day! He wanted to enjoy it so he could remember it in future not-so-perfect days. As a nagging reminder that this perfection would end, he caught glimpses of the dom district in the distance in between the buildings and trees.

Ian and Spencer were walking in increasing silence. It seemed so appropriate.

At the Shakespeare Garden, Siobhan came into view. She was admiring a patch of English bluebells. She looked up and waved. Ian felt a strong desire to rush to her and hug her – she was such a completion to the perfection of the day.

Did he see the same desire in Siobhan's expression? He awkwardly took her hand, squeezed it gently and let it go.

"Hi Ian." And turning to Spencer, "And Spencer. What a surprise!"

"Hi Siobhan. I was meeting with Ian when he told me he was coming here. So I was happy to tag along so I could see you again."

"I'm glad you did. Ian told me he had you in class. How've you been? And your mothers?"

"Great. I had applied to get Ian for Historical Awareness. I've learned a lot in his class. You can learn a lot from history that's applicable to better understanding and improving the present for a better future."

"Hey, you quoted that from the class syllabus!" Ian joked.

"Well, maybe I did. But it's true. There's nothing boring about history," Spencer said.

"Well, I just wanted to come along to say hi. I have to get back to my team and work on our debate preparations. Ian drives us pretty hard!"

"Oh come on! I'm a push-over!" Ian objected.

Ian and Siobhan watched Spencer as he walked toward the garden exit. Just before he disappeared around the hedge, he turned and waved. Ian and Siobhan waved in unison. Ian had a strange feeling, as though he and Siobhan were Spencer's parents, watching the gulf grow between them as he went out into the world to find his way. He looked at Siobhan and thought he detected the same feeling in her expression.

"I was surprised to see Spencer with you. My first reaction was that something had gone wrong and you had to bring him along to meet with me."

"No, he dropped in just before I was ready to call it a day. I thought he should come along and say hi to his benefactor." They both smiled at his last word.

"How's he doing in class?"

"Outstanding. Others notice his exceptional abilities too; the students, class visitors. My friend Walter Sherman has him in his physics class and realizes how exceptional he is. He's taken a real interest in Spencer as well. I asked him to keep it up, especially if anything were to happen to me." Ian looked into Siobhan's eyes, wondering what the future held in store for them.

"I'm glad I had you read Spencer's paper. It created a lot of good discussion in class. But I did have that talk with him and will make all traces of it disappear after we've finished discussing all the compositions."

Siobhan nodded thoughtfully.

Looking down she said, "Look at these English bluebells! I can't get them to grow this nicely at my house. I wonder how they do it here?"

"No idea. But I do know the head grounds keeper. I'll ask him."

"Would you? Thanks."

As they continued, Ian saw her admiration for the plant life. She named and described each plant as they passed. He had always been consumed by history and here, at the school, by the historical architecture of the buildings. But now, through her, he was beginning to see the beauty that was so lush in this garden – a place he hardly visited. It was as if she were a sprite lifting a veil before his eyes, giving life and meaning to each plant as they progressed.

"And here's my favorite. Sweet William. So exquisitely beautiful! They fill me with joy for life every time I see them. But they're so small, so fragile." Siobhan reached down and gently held one of the small blossoms. "This little guy reminds me to slow down and grasp life's beauty."

Soon the clock tower struck four and Siobhan said, "We'd better get going, the little ones know it's time and will be waiting for us."

Chapter 23

The gothic armory was a massive, foreboding, sandstone structure which had been built in the late 1800's to house and train the Mid-Hudson Valley militia. It continued to accommodate the local National Guard through the early part of this century, but then the Guard decided that the building was too large and inefficient, so they found smaller, more modern accommodations elsewhere. After that the armory remained an empty, brooding hulk for many years till it was used again, for storage. When CaringMother was looking for a building in Old Town in which to set up a post-natal care facility, they bought the armory from the city for the price of one credit.

As with most people who lived in Poughkeepsie, Ian was aware of the armory; its huge hulk was impossible to ignore at its well-traveled location at the corner of Market and Church Streets, just where Church tapered off into the pedestrian walkways of the dom district. But also like most, he wasn't sure what it was used for. He knew it was still called the armory, and there were no signs outside to the contrary, so he had assumed that it had military uses. But this conflicted with the large number of shabby adults with raggedy children that he always saw going in and out of the place.

Ian taught young people in an idyllic setting, youth who had pampered upbringings and were lavished with many resources by The Corporation because they were the preordained leaders of the future. Now he was to see how the first stages of life were for the lower bands, those who would be the servants, day laborers and menial factory workers of the future.

After Ian was cleared as a non-pedophile, he and Siobhan entered the great hall. Ian instinctively stepped back from a sense of confusion and disgust. There before him was a crowded sea of little bodies, which appeared at first to be moving about in chaos, though he soon realized that there was a sense of order. But the heat, humidity and stench left him reeling. Coming in from the outside on a beautiful day, he had thought the hall would be cooler.

Ian looked around and noticed there were no ceiling fans and he didn't notice any flow of air to indicate air conditioning. He wondered if the bathroom facilities had been updated since CaringMother took the armory over. And there obviously weren't enough teachers to change the younger children when needed.

Siobhan saw Ian's expression. "Welcome to the world of the lower bands. No pleasantries of life here. Most of the volunteers are upper bands like me. Not too many director/executive bands show up, though. We try to give the children some individual attention in the 4-to-6 time slot. I volunteer on Tuesdays and Thursdays."

Siobhan was immediately mobbed by little children like planets swirling around a warmth/life-giving sun. As Ian found himself ever further toward the edge of this "solar system" looking in, he felt the children's attraction to Siobhan. She indeed glowed as she gazed down on the little ones with her warm smile. The late afternoon sun streaming in through the high windows added to the effect. She caressed each one just as she had done to the Sweet William.

"Let's all play Ring-Around-The-Rosie! Now we all join hands! No pushing or shoving. That's right." She was soon in a large circle of laughing, singing, fast-moving children.

While she was organizing the children to play London Bridge, Ian noticed two of the CaringMother teachers glaring at Siobhan. They also kept a close eye on him. Even though he had been cleared as a non-pedophile, did they think him to be one in waiting? Ian was careful not to come into contact with any of the children.

As more of the children were picked up to go home, the "planets" circling around Siobhan diminished to a more manageable level. Soon a sweating, exhausted Siobhan said to the children. "I think it's time for stories! Each of you get your rug and your favorite book and we'll take turns."

While the children scrambled, Siobhan said to Ian, "They love Mother Goose and Grimm's' fairy tales the most. I think it's the rhyming in the Mother Goose – such fun, silly rhymes. And even the sanitized Grimm's tales seem to activate their imaginations and give them courage. Especially the ones who sleep upstairs love 'The Three Billy Goats Gruff'. They identify with the smaller goats being challenged by the troll under the bridge and squeal with delight when the big goat gently pushes the troll into the stream, in which he floats to a land where he can no longer threaten little goats."

"Read us Cinderella! Read us Cinderella!" Some of the little girls were crying.

There was no objection and a lot of enthusiasm, so Siobhan said, "OK, sit down on your rugs and we'll start as soon as everyone's quiet." She seated herself on a small chair and said to Ian, "I read this even though it's politically incorrect."

Ian watched as Siobhan, with exaggerated expression that the kids loved, sounded out the voices of sweet, hardworking Cinderella, the greedy step sisters and step mother, and of course the prince, when he swept Cinderella off her feet and saved her from poverty. At the end of each page Siobhan showed the book's pictures. He watched the children listening, totally transfixed.

After "Cinderella", and some nursery rhymes, there was only a handful of children left. Two little girls, identical twins, went to Siobhan with their tattered book and mutely showed it to her. "'Hansel and Gretel'," Siobhan said. "I don't think we'll have time to read it today. It's pretty long." When she saw the disappointment on their faces, she said, "But you know what? I know that story, so I'll tell it to you."

The little girls' faces brightened as Siobhan sat down on one of the children's rugs. The twins each nestled up against Siobhan as she put her arms around them. The other children pushed their way in close too. Siobhan told of Hansel and Gretel being separated from their poor, hardworking peasant parents, getting lost in the forest, encountering the witch whom they reformed in the end and brought her, and her wealth of food and goodies, into their family. Ian chuckled at the sanitized ending.

Ian found himself shifting into a different dimension – one removed from the hopeless stench of lower-band life in a humid, gothic fortress – a dimension of imagination. As he watched, Siobhan and the children moved beyond the mad, hectic world of those around them, and into a secure realm.

As Siobhan smiled radiantly at the small, adoring faces, with her arms still around those two little girls, Ian knew where he was. It was like paintings he'd seen in art museums and 'spondings. Paintings of Madonna and Child, of children playing in fields while their mothers watched over them. Artists had captured the spirit of what he was seeing now in real life.

Ian recalled a little boy lying in the darkness feeling a dull sadness he didn't understand. As if by magic, the door opened and the soft hallway light shone in. Haloed by the light was the figure of his mother. When she sat down and held him in her arms, he knew she had come in because she had sensed that longing in his heart. She sang him a lull-a-bye and assured him that she loved him and always would.

When she stood again in the light of the hall and paused one last time before closing the door, he knew she had also felt that same longing in her heart. This was what had brought her to him. He went to sleep, knowing he would always be loved.

Ian was now in a world beyond the daily, crushing grind of The Corporation. It was a world that existed because of Siobhan; because of her love for these little children. And Ian was the Joseph giving witness to what was before him. He knew it would always be there, haunting him, reminding him that he had glimpsed a perfect world that existed beyond the confines of time.

As the story ended, the twins' waiting mother stepped forward and thanked Siobhan for her kindness. Ian noticed Siobhan's longing gaze and ever-so-slight hesitation in letting go of the girls. This perfect world was slipping beyond her grasp.

Siobhan continued to watch the girls leave as Ian helped her off the floor. "I always wondered why they loved 'Hansel and Gretel' until one day they asked me if I could change it to 'Marina and Bella', their names."

As the twins disappeared out the front door, Siobhan shook her head. "They aren't developing like normal children, as much as that's possible in this place. They hardly interact with the other children, and they barely speak.

Life's pretty harsh for the lower bands. I'm afraid of what it has waiting for them."

Ian was surprised at how few people were on the Walkway, considering it was such a beautiful day. Of course, it was only early evening so most people would have stuck to their regular schedules, avoiding the normally hot late afternoon temperatures. He was glad they had the Walkway largely to themselves as they walked out over the river. There was a constant wind coming up out of the highlands. It was refreshing. Siobhan gazed down river toward the highlands as they strolled. Ian caught her smiling.

"Something amusing?"

"I was thinking about last Friday when we first met out here. You were pretty cagy about being picked up. Obviously you were wondering what my motives were. But you did handle things well, retiring little thing that you are." They both laughed before she continued, "I appreciate your not running out on me when you found out my motives."

They proceeded to the middle of the Walkway and then stood at the rail, gazing toward the south. The highlands were already turning deep purple in the shadows cast by the sun. They too would soon be in the shadows of the cliffs on the western side of the river. Far below, the paddlewheel was docked at Wayrus Park, taking on a group of laughing, already intoxicated people for an evening cruise. Under the dominant smells of the river, they could occasionally catch a sweet fragrance of honeysuckle.

"How did you get involved in volunteering at the armory?" Ian asked.

"A few of my friends talked me into trying it. The armory was a good location between work and home, so I volunteered there. I've been doing it for a couple years now. I feel like I'm helping out the parents and I hope I'm doing some good for the children. Being around children does me good as well."

"You're a natural with them. They adore you."

Siobhan stared at the distant highlands. Ian sensed that sadness in her that he had caught glimpses of when they first met.

Ian cleared his throat. "Why don't you have a child of your own? Why aren't you married?" As the silence grew and she continued to look off into the distance, Ian began to fear he had gone too far and that she'd walk off without saying anything.

But then she turned to him. "When I got out of school and started my first job, I was very career oriented. Like most girls I wanted to make my way up the ladder of success. I told myself that love, marriage and having a child could wait. Oh I dated and had fun. But I was always guarded. You know the old neo-feminist saying: *Love Dependence equals Subservience.*

"About six years ago I met Guy. He was exciting and very good looking. He started hanging with a group I was in – you know, twenty/thirty-somethings having a good time with no commitments. All the girls were attracted to Guy and started pursuing him. But he played one off against the other. Maybe because I was the only one that didn't chase him, he took an interest in me.

"Soon we were seeing each other away from the group. We had a fun time together and were very compatible. I was doing quite well in my career. I had recently turned thirty and started thinking about love, marriage and children. I loved Guy. I felt he was the right one so I asked him to marry me and he accepted.

"When we got permission, we didn't waste any time. We had a civil ceremony at the Bureau of Life Changes and invited our friends to attend. At first, the other girls were jealous, but then they became excited since we were the first ones in our group to get married. I already had my house in South Poughkeepsie, so Guy moved in with me.

"The first year was great. We still hung with our group. Each day we kissed goodbye and went our separate ways to our work. It was ideal.

"But after a year, I started dropping hints about having a baby. I had thought it through – the responsibility, the expense, possible impacts to my carrier and Guy's as well. But I felt a growing emptiness inside me, and felt that it was my yearning to have a baby. Guy thought we should put it off for a while. But he eventually gave in. He was sweet; he wanted to make me happy.

"So after applying and getting permission, we went down to CaringMother and started the process of having a baby. After several days, they 'sponded us to let us know that we had a successful fertilization. I was overjoyed. At that point all my motherly instincts kicked into high gear. Even though my baby was growing in an artificial womb at CaringMother, I felt as if he were growing inside me, in *my* womb – or maybe my heart. I even wanted to buy some maternity clothes!

"Guy was less thrilled. He also thought I was nuts for wanting maternity clothes. First of all, they are virtually impossible to find. And secondly, I wasn't pregnant! People would think I was either nuts or just showing off.

"Of course, I agreed with him that maternity clothes were ridiculous. But that was the way I was feeling. I knew my baby wasn't physically inside me. But somehow he was inside me; spiritually. I felt a definite connection to him. Many days at work were a complete waste, because I'd just sit there thinking about him. Reaching into myself and out to him. Luckily I had an understanding boss – she'd turn a blind eye, though eventually she'd remind me that I was behind in my work.

"I'd go down to the CaringMother facility and sit in the customer waiting room just to be close to him. I 'sponded my mother upstate every day. She was the one person who seemed to understand."

At this point Siobhan's wistful smile visibly melted into an expression of remorse. "In the eighth month, when I was finishing up the room we were making into a nursery, I received a recorded 'spond from CaringMother that the gestation had been terminated because they had detected a tendency toward male-pattern aggressiveness in our baby. Of course, Guy had received the same 'spond. He came into the nursery.

"At first, we stared at each other in shock. This couldn't be true! Then I started crying and couldn't stop. Guy held me, but I was inconsolable. I laid down on the love seat next to the crib, turned my face to the wall, curled up and cried. Guy sat next to me, rubbing my back, trying to comfort.

"So many confusing thoughts were going through my mind. My baby was still inside me; he wasn't gone! I blamed myself. If I had carried my child naturally, I could have protected him. And how could CaringMother terminate the gestation? They had no right! Guy and I should have been the only ones deciding whether to terminate or not. And I never would have terminated for male-pattern aggressiveness.

"When I had recovered enough to go into the CaringMother facility, they were cold and bureaucratic and explained that they had followed prescribed procedures. And furthermore, we had understood that gestations were terminated when abnormalities were detected. Unfortunately, male-pattern aggressiveness tendencies were typically not detected till late in the gestation, so a late termination was necessary. I was furious. Guy had to take me out before I totally lost it.

"All of my friends and colleagues were very sympathetic. But in the end, they very tenderly told me to get over it, move on, and try for another baby. Guy held off for a while, but then he started with the same message. But I couldn't. How could he just dismiss what CaringMother had done without our knowledge and consent?

"He wanted to try for another baby; he thought it would help me get over my loss. But I told him I couldn't while my baby was still in me. And if I were ready for another baby, I'd never trust a wombcare facility again. Guy argued that natural birth would devastate my career and our finances, so it wasn't acceptable. I was overreacting.

"Our differences eventually drove us apart. We tried to find common ground through counseling, but couldn't. Our divorce was finalized two years ago."

Ian had been listening, not daring to interrupt. Very cautiously he put his arms around her. He thought he would feel her shaking with emotion, but instead he could only feel her tension. He continued to hold her as she stared into the distance.

"It was about that time I became involved in the association, with our mission to improve life through individual initiatives. That's what prodded me to help out at the armory when my friends mentioned volunteering. And, of course, why I took a great interest in Spencer, not just letting him continue down his life's path unguarded. I threw myself into my work, volunteering and association work. But I never let my child go. Until last Saturday."

At this point Ian could feel her begin to tremble and see tears welling up in her eyes. Siobhan took a deep breath and continued, "It was when we were at Doodletown and you took me up to the brook. I sat there in total bliss. Watching the water move along and listening to the music, I could feel peace and acceptance creeping into my being. I hadn't felt that way in a very long time.

"I was scared at first. I wondered if the spirits in the Valley of the Dead were taking control of me. But then I slowly gave in. At the point that I was totally at peace, I felt myself opening up – letting my fears, frustrations and regrets go."

Siobhan turned and looked up into Ian's eyes. "And, finally, I let my son go. He had grown in my mind to be about three years old. I felt him leaving me. I could almost see him as he went up the path and into the shadows. And in a flash of sunshine, he was gone. I felt a terrible, almost unbearable wrenching of my heart as he left."

Breathing deeply, Siobhan continued, "Since then I've felt my heart healing more every day. But I know a sadness will always be with me."

Ian continued to hold Siobhan as she cried. He hoped her healing process would lead to her opening her heart to him.

Chapter 24
FRIDAY, JULY 10

Michael had had a more restful night. But he still couldn't shake the image of the Oracle in the restaurant and his strong emotions. He'd have to get a status from him tonight.

He walked over to the drink dispenser, but before he got his typical cup of coffee, he turned to Lenora. "Is that kongo lango I smell?"

"Yeah."

"Hmmm. Let me give it a shot," Michael said turning back and dispensing a cup of the warm, muddy-looking liquid. He took a swig and frowned. "I just can't get used to the taste. Do you really like that stuff or is it just because it comes from Africa, and you're an African Queen?" Michael quizzed her with a sly expression.

"Hey," she protested. "It's the drink of the future – millet-based, so it's good for you. And just slightly alcoholic, so it settles your nerves but doesn't impair your senses. I guess it's like developing a taste for coffee. Plus coffee is so twentieth century. Do you drink it because it's retro, or do you really like it?"

"Good point. But us old folks need a kick in the butt in the morning, not a 'settler-downer' like you whipper-snappers do."

"Whipper-snappers?!" Lenora exclaimed, looking over at Tony. They both laughed. "Michael, where *do* you come up with these terms from? You're so twentieth century – or earlier!"

"OK, OK, you got me!" Michael surrendered before he turned more serious. "What did Natalie come up with in her observations of our interviews yesterday?"

"Not much more than we did," Tony said. "She's warning us not to get too focused on the NuTense connection, but she does like the parent connection – given human emotion. You know, throw in a little human emotion and Organic Intelligence thinks it has things figured out. But no suspects."

"How about her observations on body language, glistening sweat, that kind of thing? That's what she excels at."

"Nothing out of the ordinary. You know, all within statistical bounds of nervousness."

"Big help she is! When are we going to get a decent OI model?! We really are like the shoemaker's children. If the general population knew how chintzy The Corporation is in giving us the tools we need to do our job, they'd walk all over us."

"Well, she *did* notice your interest in the attractive females and is considering reporting you to internal affairs on charges of sexual harassment," Tony said looking over at Lenora, who was glancing down at her cup of kongo lango, trying to hide her smile.

"What?" Michael exploded. "That sanctimonious bitch! You tell her to do her fuckin' job of observing the interviewees and that's it!" After a few moments, he said in a quieter voice, still laced with tension, "Did you ever watch that old classic film *2001, A Space Odyssey*?"

"No," They both looked at each other wondering what Michael was talking about.

"It's a 1960's version of the future. The computer on board a space ship starts stepping beyond its bounds and eventually kills people. In the end, the lone survivor shuts it down, one module at a time, in essence 'killing' the computer. Humanity prevails. Well, if Natalie doesn't produce and oversteps her bounds again, I swear I'll track her down and pull her apart, one noodle at a time!"

"My, but we're touchy! Tony, cut off his coffee rations!" Lenora said.

"Just once I'd like to get some useful help from OI!"

After a deep breath, Michael continued, "So what did you find out about Sessions?"

"Nothing. No indication that she ever existed," Lenora said. "I 'sponded the interview center to see if someone there at least remembered her.

Nothing. If her disappearance is tied to this job, then someone here with pull at the CBI was displeased with her. Or afraid of what she might do on the outside. The roaches check in ..."

Michael looked at the wall, staring beyond it. Finally he said, "You know, I wish you wouldn't use that roach hotel saying. It gives the CBI a bad name, though maybe deserved." After a brief pause, he continued, "But I think you nailed an important element of this whole situation here under Treadwell. LEPGen's scared to death of unfiltered word getting out about what they're doing. If someone like Sessions went to an 'ogger and spilled the naked beans, it could severely hurt LEPGen's reputation. After all, they're a well-respected corporation.

"We may never get a truly honest response from any of Treadwell's people, either from loyalty to her or from fear. I'm going to ask Treadwell about Sessions, just to see what her reaction is. Let me do the talking on this." Then after a brief reflection, Michael said, "OK, play the first on the docket."

The wallplay on the next interviewee appeared. While they observed the contents, Tony made the following comments, "Hiro Yamaguchi. Born Harold Gucci, Caucasian, Italian decent, but always felt he was a Japanese trapped in a Caucasian body, so he had a transethnic operation performed 5 years ago.

"I 'sponded the unofficial scuttle-butt site. Word is that he really wanted to work on this project, but didn't make the final cut. So in the end he implied that he'd accuse Treadwell of being an anti-transethnicist if she didn't include him. If you look at his background, he's certainly well qualified. She probably felt cornered into letting him join the team. Nothing can kill your career quicker than being accused of being anti-something. So I'm betting there's no great love between the two."

"Good idea on hitting the scuttle-butt site," Michael said grinning. "You see a lot of whites transenthnicing to Chinese hoping for advancement. But this is the first time I've seen one transing to Japanese. I wonder what's behind it." But then he turned to Tony and Lenora and giving them his cutest Jackie Chan grin he continued, "Only thing I've always wondered about transethnics to Chinese – how could the operation ever turn them into sexual tigers?"

"Boy, are you full of it!" Lenora said laughing.

"Wait till I tell Natalie!" Tony said a mock-indignant voice.

"You know it's true!" Michael joined in, feigning hurt feelings.

Upon concluding their wallplay review of Yamaguchi, Michael said, "This one's mine with Treadwell, too."

Tony went to get Treadwell, and the two of them returned in a few minutes.

"Have you uncovered anything from your work yesterday?" Treadwell asked.

"Well, the interviews were very helpful in getting the lay of the land. But we've gotten the distinct impression of reluctance to open up to us. Through loyalty to you. Or fear," Michael said.

"I don't understand that. I told all of them to cooperate fully."

"Hmmm, yes," Michael said. "Tell us about Christina Sessions."

Michael could see a nervous jolt in Treadwell's expression.

"Ms. Sessions left our employment over a year ago. She couldn't possibly be responsible for what's going on."

"But she was part of your core team. And if she wasn't happy here, she could have planted the seed of discontent in others. Or she could still be in contact with someone on your team. We tried to 'spond her records here at LEPGen, but didn't have any luck."

"Those records are highly confidential. When employees leave in unpleasant circumstances, we have to guard ourselves against uncomfortable eventualities."

"So please tell us about the 'unpleasant circumstances'."

"I didn't recruit her. She applied to work on the project, had an excellent work record, and came highly recommended. So I brought her on to the team, though reluctantly."

"Why reluctantly?"

"It was a gut feeling. She appeared enthusiastic about joining the team. But I sensed an element of aversion on her part when I described the circumstances of our work. When we started the project I kept a close eye on her. I didn't notice anything out of the ordinary and was beginning to think maybe my concerns were unfounded.

"Then one day she came into my office at the end of her shift and asked me if what we were doing was legal. I told her yes, it was, otherwise we wouldn't be doing it. Then she hit me with: was it morally right? I reminded her that these fetuses would have been otherwise terminated due to their defects; that this way they were serving humanity. And furthermore, she had known the circumstances when she joined the team. If she had had any reservations, she shouldn't have come to work for me. But she did and was now an integral part of our 'family'. I knew then that I had made a big mistake letting her join the team.

"After that I had periodic informal 'sit downs' with her. She voiced the right words in our discussions. But I could still tell she was wrestling with her feelings."

At this point, Treadwell darted her eyes from Michael, to Lenora and Tony. "All of us have feelings and struggle with them. Sessions just seemed super sensitive. I've seen it in younger women especially. They work on building up their careers and start having fantasies about having a child. But they realize they don't have a husband yet, let alone a boyfriend. On their technician's salary they know they wouldn't get permission to have a child on their own. Understandably, they feel trapped, which might put their natural feelings into overdrive."

Michael nodded.

"Finally, a little over a year ago, she came into my office, closed the door, broke down and said she couldn't do this work anymore. After a long discussion I determined that this was not a passing phase. I wished that I could have sent her to the site psychologist, but couldn't because of the sensitivity of our work. I talked to her about taking another position in LEPGen, and she indicated that she was amenable to doing this. But in the end, we decided the best solution was to terminate her employment with the LEPGen Corporation."

"Who's 'we'?" Michael asked.

"Why, our site general manager and me. Given the sensitivity of my project's work, I report directly into her.

"Why was termination the best solution?" asked Tony.

"We felt as long as she worked for LEPGen she'd probably continue to be reminded of her difficulties. So we decided it was best for her to start over afresh somewhere else."

"Did you help her find a job with another corporation?" asked Lenora.

"We don't usually do that with terminations."

"So where did she end up working?" Lenora asked.

"I don't know."

"Did she have any friends here who might know?" Tony asked.

"We're all friends on the team. But she didn't have any close friends that I know of."

"Well, could you check with the members of your team to see who might know where she ended up? We'd like to interview her too," said Michael.

"I'll ask around."

"Oh, and please get us access to her LEPGen records as well."

"I'll try," Treadwell said. "Why don't you just 'spond her up after you leave here to find out where she is?"

Michael studied her for several seconds, and then leaned in close to her face. "Because, Dr. Treadwell, we did try and she didn't come up. It seems she's *disappeared*."

Treadwell instinctively moved back. "Oh. OK. I'll see what I can come up with."

"Thank you. And please remind your people to cooperate with us fully. They have nothing to fear." He couldn't resist this last jab, but he was sure that Treadwell knew that Sessions had been disappeared, had probably been involved in the decision to make it happen, and was obviously not cooperating with him. He had taken Treadwell down a notch. Now for the next notch.

"Today we're starting off with Hiro Yamaguchi. We've played his stats and record. What can you tell us about him as his director?"

"He's competent and does his job well."

"Only competent? I thought you only had the very best joining your team," Michael said.

"He does his job, but he also has somewhat of an attitude problem."

"How so?"

"He thinks he's entitled to more than the others without excelling. He's wanted to be shift lead. He felt passed over when I gave the latest open lead position to Hernandez. Somehow he thinks he's special."

"Because he has an oriental background like his director?"

Treadwell frowned. "Oh, he's not oriental. He's transethnic."

Michael feigned surprise and turned to Lenora and Tony and said, "How did we miss that?"

They shrugged.

"Is his transethnicism a problem for you?" Michael asked.

"No, of course not, I treat him the same as everyone else."

"Nor that he's a male? All your leads are female."

"What are you implying, Detective Chan?"

"I'm trying to determine if this guy has a grudge against you before I interview him."

"I'm sure he has a grudge against me! Oh, he's never displayed it openly. But I've caught the occasional hostile glance. I didn't select him in the first draft for the team. I'm sure he holds that against me." Treadwell took a breath and smiled. "I've heard that he wants a sex change now. I say go for it! I'll be happy for him."

"Oriental female. It sounds like he's trying to emulate you. You're not flattered?"

"I hardly admire people who bend and twist themselves into something they're not."

"Thank you Dr. Treadwell. We're ready for Mr. Yamaguchi. Would you please send him in in about fifteen minutes?"

"Yes," she said as she stood.

As she was about to open the door, Michael said, "Oh, by the way, Dr. Treadwell, I didn't see mention of any other surnames in your records. Was Treadwell the name you were born with?"

"I was born Emma Choi. Treadwell was my ex-husband's name."

"All the holes we're finding in the records! You should really get that one corrected. Just out of curiosity, why did you take your husband's last name when you got married and keep it when you divorced?"

"Took – tradition. Kept – convenience." And she walked out and slammed the door after her.

"Touché, Michael," Lenora said.

Chapter 25

"You were mean to her," Tony said.

"All for good reasons. If she comes up with Sessions' records, good. If she says she can't locate them, then we know she's being straight forward. But if she doesn't get back to us, we know we can't trust her. She's not on our team.

"If in a day or two I'm told to back off Treadwell, then we've made the influence connection between her and the Poughkeepsie bureau and her willingness to use it. We'll know her intention's to keep us from delving too far into what's going on here. Find the bad guy – nothing else.

"As for Yamaguchi, we got a handle on her feelings toward him. Maybe we can use that to pry more out of him. But be careful. Don't give him the impression that you're in anyway prejudiced against him. He'd clam up."

After finishing their preview of Yamaguchi and the day's line up, there was a knock at the door. Tony opened the door to an average-sized, oriental-looking man.

"Welcome Mr. Yamaguchi," Michael said as he stood and gave a deeper-than-normal bow. Lenora did likewise. Michael saw on Yamaguchi's face that he appreciated this sign of respect. If he had passed Yamaguchi on the street he would have thought he was Japanese.

"Please make yourself comfortable," Michael said indicating a chair. "Something to drink?

"Green tea, please," Yamaguchi said in an agreeable voice.

Michael looked to Tony to get some. "This is an informal discussion to help us determine what might be preventing progress on your team's project. Please be forthcoming with whatever comes to mind, even if it seems insignificant. Also, our discussion is confidential. Specifics do not go back to the shift leads, or to Dr. Treadwell."

"I want to help if I can."

"Great. We appreciate that. Do you have any theories as to what's causing the team's problems? Or who might be causing them?"

"Are you recording this discussion?"

"Yes, but only for use with our OI analysis. Beyond that, no one sees it."

"Can you stop the recording? I'd feel more comfortable if you did. So I can be more open."

"Absolutely," Michael said as he 'sponded a halt to the recording. "Done."

"And none of what I say will go back to Dr. Treadwell directly identified with me?"

"You have my word on it."

Yamaguchi studied Michael's and the others' faces for several moments, then he began, "I'm not convinced there is a problem, other than trying to meet committed timelines and budgets."

"Others have voiced those reservations as well," Michael said supportively, though not accurately. "Can you expand on your thoughts?"

"Sure. This level of fetus experimentation is pretty new. So there's no extensive history to use in setting up solid statistical parameters on what to expect. If you add in the complexity of our experiments, there's no solid predictability. With no overt, identifiable sabotage going on, we only have gut feel to go on. But gut feel isn't solid or scientific. There's no reason to believe that any sabotage has been committed." Yamaguchi said, pausing to study Michael's take on what he had said.

"Mr. Yamaguchi, thank you for your clear, succinct assessment," Michael said nodding while turning to the others. They did the same. *Yes, Yamaguchi's the type who wants to be the go-to-guy, the one who really understands the situation,* Michael thought.

"So tell me about timelines and budgets."

"This is a large, very costly, project. So LEPGen wants to see progress. Two years and we don't have anything solid to show for it. Our failure rate's so high that there's no hope that we can use this approach with the general population. If you look at our project's tactical timelines, you'll see where we've continued to miss milestones; they've been continually pushed out to the right. And that's not good."

"What impact has this had on Dr. Treadwell and the rest of the team?" asked Lenora.

"It's really stressing everyone out, especially Dr. Treadwell. At first, she was very 'executive-like' in running the project. You know, delegating, keeping the high-level overview. But over the past several months, she's been more involved with the daily work. Way too many hours, micromanaging everyone. That adds to everyone's stress. It's not good. You can tell that she's in panic mode now, and that's rubbing off on the entire team. Things are falling apart.

"There are rumors that she's in talks with NuTense about going back to work for them, implying that she'd take her best people with her, and let the rest of us 'go down with the sinking ship'. Of course, that's just a rumor. I'm only telling you so you can get a feel for the atmosphere here."

"Why would NuTense take her back if her project's a failure?" asked Tony.

"Dr. Treadwell's a very capable and well-respected scientist. I'm sure NuTense hated to lose her and would love to get her back. But first she'll have to convince them that she's been successful here. To do that, one of two things needs to take place. Either she shows progress here very soon. Or she demonstrates that her project has been sabotaged, the guilty identified and removed, and after a short 'recovery period', during which time she 'cooks the books' to demonstrate that progress is beginning, she bows out and goes to NuTense. Of course, for the second option she needs a scapegoat."

"Scapegoat? Not saboteur?" Tony asked.

"My gut tells me it's not sabotage. Believe me; she and the supervisors have been looking hard, along with the rest of us. Nothing even remotely solid has turned up."

Everyone sat back and digested what Yamaguchi had said.

Then Lenora asked him, "Mr. Yamaguchi, does it bother you that you're doing experiments on human fetuses?"

"Yes. But I view it as in the old war movies, where the commander's willing to sacrifice some of his men to storm and take the pill box, so the army can move forward. It's a necessary evil."

"Do you have any children of your own?" Tony asked, knowing the answer.

"No. Never been married. I guess I'm too independent."

"So you buy the 'party line' that these are fetuses that would have been terminated anyway due to their defects?" Michael asked.

Yamaguchi's mouth formed a faint smile. He remained silent.

"What?" Michel asked wondering what his expression meant.

Yamaguchi leaned in toward his three questioners. "All the defects are coded by letters. Male-pattern aggressiveness, the most common, is coded an A. Down's syndrome a B, and so on. These codes are in their records and are also identified by labels on the artificial wombs. Sometimes fetuses have more than one."

"We noticed the labels," responded Tony.

"Those defects aren't relevant to us technicians in performing our duties. We do our injections and perform our tests, and the results are recorded against each fetus. Specific defects mean more to Dr. Treadwell and her 'inner circle' in doing their analyses. They keep a close eye on how the different defect categories perform. We technicians are aware of how different categories perform, especially when we're briefed each week by Dr. Treadwell.

"Several months ago, after it was obvious that we had entered panic mode, we started getting a new category: 'O'. There was no notification or explanation. Just 'O'; there it was. We technicians don't have a 'need to know'. So no one asked directly, though we've asked each other informally, 'Hey, what's this new category?' 'No idea'.

"Well, at a weekly briefing, I asked Dr. Treadwell what the 'O' category was. She looked annoyed – she doesn't particularly care for me – and said, 'Other', and proceeded with her briefing. We all looked at each other – not much of an explanation. So I asked her what 'Other' meant. She said it was a category reserved for all other maladies a fetus could have. Then she stamped her foot, which is her way of signaling 'end of discussion'. So I shut up and she moved on, quickly ending the briefing. Normally she'd stay to answer questions or even mingle. But that day she left for her office.

"Of course, there are other defects that can lead to terminations. But it makes no sense to toss in a bunch and label them as "other". By not identifying each defect individually, you're making the experiment on those 'other' fetuses meaningless. We were all confused."

Yamaguchi leaned in even closer and said in a very quiet voice, "After a while, the rumor started that the 'other' category was being used for normal fetuses. That in her desperation, Treadwell had CaringMother send over perfectly normal fetuses."

Lenora gasped. Yamaguchi sat in silence. Michael's mind raced ahead, thinking of an appropriate response considering the legality of using normal fetuses.

If her experiments included normal fetuses but succeeded and lead to the implementation of organic transponder implants, she'd be considered a hero by LEPGen and The Corporation. LEPGen would have extended its lock on the industry, and the program would save The Corporation billions over the years.

If they failed and her methods were discovered, and she didn't have the parents' permissions for using the normal fetuses, it's possible she could be tried for murder – at least for the 'post-birth' fetuses. More likely, she could be disappeared.

Michael sat back in his chair. "Mr. Yamaguchi, that's a serious accusation."

"I'm not accusing. I'm just relating a rumor – one that's impacting morale and potentially performance. If it isn't true, Dr. Treadwell could have avoided a lot of consternation if she had chosen to be open with her team. As I am trying to be with you."

"Point taken. And we do greatly appreciate your openness. No matter where it leads." Michael studied Yamaguchi's face for any sign of gloating. He saw none. "Have there been any better success rates in the 'other' category?"

"Not that I know of, though it may still be too early to tell."

After further questioning, Michael concluded with, "One last thing. Did you know Christina Sessions?"

"Sure. She was a member of the team from the beginning."

"Your thoughts of her?"

"She was a very good technician. Did her job well. Everyone seemed to like her."

"Did you? I understand she was quite attractive," Michael said.

"Yes I liked her. But she wasn't my type."

"Hmmm," Michael said. "What did you think of her dismissal?"

"We weren't told it was a dismissal. We were told she had chosen to leave the corporation in order to pursue other interests. But it was obvious to us that she had been fired."

"Why fired?"

"She had increasing moral problems. She'd ask us others if we did too. Obviously it got her into trouble, and poof, she was gone."

"Did you or any others keep in contact with her after she left?"

"I didn't. No one really mentioned her after she left. You know, *persona non grata*. But she did seem to have something going with a guy working the graveyard shift; midnight to 8."

"Who was that?"

"Guy Crawford."

Michael turned to Tony and said, "We interviewed him just before we wrapped up last night. Our stats didn't connect him to her and he didn't mention her, did he?"

"No," Tony answered.

"Let's circle back to Mr. Crawford tonight."

"Can I ask why you're more interested now?" asked Yamaguchi.

Michael was going give him a flippant "it's confidential" answer, but then he reconsidered. "We'd just like to discuss her concerns with her. But we've had difficulty locating her."

"Well, you won't get hold of Crawford here tonight. He works the regular graveyard shift; meaning today was his last day for the week, so he won't be in till Sunday at midnight. If you want to see him soon, you'll have to track him down outside of work."

"OK, thanks. We'll probably just wait till early Monday morning," Michael said.

With this, they all stood, bowed, and Hiro Yamaguchi left the room.

Michael continued standing, looking reflectively at the door, and then he said to the others, "Well, to quote Alice, this case is getting curiouser and curiouser. Let's chase the rabbit further down the hole."

Chapter 26

From where Ian and Siobhan stood on Mount Beacon, the Hudson was only partially visible as it ate its way through the Highlands. Just beyond Mount Taurus they could see the massive stillness of West Point and pick up the river again at World's End not far from Bear Mountain and Doodletown. In the far distance was Manhattan's faint skyline, looking insignificant and ephemeral in the haze. Below, the ruins of Bannerman's Castle peeked out of the Hudson where it stood partially submerged on Pollepel Island. It still appeared to be a haunted, foreboding sentinel, guarding the entrance to the Hudson Highlands between majestic Mount Beacon and the ever-brooding Storm King Mountain. To the west the granite ridge of the Shawangunk Mountains ran northward like a knife, ever closer to the Hudson, till it appeared to slice into the towering Catskill Mountains in the north. In the northeast, the Taconic mountain range ran down the eastern edge of the Mid-Hudson Valley to join up with the Highlands and complete the enclosure of the valley.

Ian's eyes followed the line from the Stormville Escarpment, along Breakneck Ridge toward where they stood and finally rested on Siobhan, who was no longer looking at the vistas, but at him. "What do you see?"

"A kind, supportive man. Ian, thanks for bringing me up here after yesterday. It's beautiful." She gave him a hug and a peck on his cheek.

"You are an enigma, lady. I'm glad you told me what you did, yesterday."

"I'd let life harden me. Now I'm trying to break out of the shell I've created. Thanks to you, I think I'm making progress. But enough analysis. Let's have fun!" Siobhan laughed as she closed her eyes and twirled around enjoying the warm, dry breeze and the alternating brightness of the sun on her face.

Two days in a row with a break in the typical heat and humidity allowed them to stand unprotected on the top of Mount Beacon, enjoying the full-circle views of the Hudson Valley as the golden sun sank deeper. They had taken the levtrain from Poughkeepsie twenty miles south to Beacon, the only other Corporate city on the eastern side of the river in the Mid-Hudson Valley. From the train station they had taken a tram to the foot of Mount Beacon, and ascended to the top on the inclined railway.

This railway had originally been built in the late 1800's but had fallen into disrepair and was finally abandoned around the time of the bicentennial. In the early part of this century a group of industrious Beaconites started a foundation to rebuild the Mount Beacon Inclined Railway. When it was completed, Mount Beacon became a favorite destination, along with the Walkway over the Hudson.

"If we're going to hike the long path down, we're going to have to start now," Ian said.

"But we just got here!"

"Next time we'll have to come on a day when we're not working. Or leave even earlier from work. But I had to get you out tonight after yesterday." With this Ian grabbed Siobhan's hand and led her toward the long path. Observing the long line waiting for the railway, they were glad they were walking.

As they descended into the shadows of gullies and woods, Ian talked about how important Mount Beacon had been during the Revolutionary War. Since it was the highest mountain in the Hudson Valley south of the Catskills, fires, or "beacons", were lit to warn the people of the valley when the British were coming. That was their only warning. After his brief history lesson, they walked along in silence, enjoying the views and cool of the shadows.

They soon reached a secluded overlook that was a short distance off the trail. Ian enjoyed the immediate fragrances of the mountain laurel and pine needles, as he listened to the less immediate din of life proceeding without them in the streets of Beacon down below.

The views were so distant that nothing seemed to move; not the several boats on the Hudson, nor the white, puffy clouds over the Catskills so far away. In this stillness Ian imagined being in a Frederic Church painting of the Hudson. So still, so perfect, so idyllic. He and Siobhan locked in suspended happiness, still holding hands, observing the valley as Henry Hudson might have almost 500 years before.

Suddenly a red-tailed hawk swooped by, reminding him that they weren't in a painting, and that this moment was fleeting, being poked apart by the hawk and the sounds and smells of reality.

Ian sighed.

His sigh broke Siobhan's own reverie. "What was the sigh for?"

"I was transfixed in a still-life dream, like a Frederic Church painting. But then reality struck."

Siobhan looked intently at his face and asked, "Was I in your dream?"

"Yes, you were beside me. Like now. But we were in an ideal world."

After a few minutes, Siobhan asked, "What else do you dream about, Ian?"

"Consciously, mostly about my students. I guess that's the teacher in me. I dream about what they'll do, what they'll become, what life'll be like for them and whether they'll leave a better world."

"Do you have dreams for yourself?"

Ian gazed off into the distance. "When I was younger I'd dream about being a great teacher. I think I've managed to become a good one. I could also imagine getting married – and having a child. But the years went by and I never found anyone. As those dreams faded, I became content with devoting myself to 'my children' in my classes.

"I sometimes wake up in the early hours of the morning and a quiet voice says, 'perchance to dream'. I ask myself where my dreams have gone. But then my thoughts scatter into the reality of the day. Soon I'm walking out the door, heading to school for another day with my students. But there remains that nagging, subconscious voice saying 'perchance to dream'."

Turning to Siobhan again, he asked, "Siobhan, do I dare dream about you?"

Siobhan studied his face and began, "As I looked out across the valley, like you, I saw us standing together, looking out on this scene as it might have been hundreds of years ago, having found happiness together. I can still see it in my mind.

"But we don't live in that idealized past. We're alive now, dealing with today's reality," Siobhan said looking back out over the valley.

After a short, thoughtful silence, she continued, "After my son's termination, I committed myself to improving this world in any small way I could. No matter what the consequences to me. But I have a terrible feeling that someday the path I've chosen will catch up with me." And turning back to Ian, she added, "And I don't want you to be hurt."

Ian began slowly, "When I committed to helping Spencer, I was also committing to your effort – to you. I understand that I could end up being hurt – or worse. I can accept that. But since I've met you, I've felt that I dare to dream again. And I don't want to lose you, to let you go." And after a reflective pause, "I've chosen a path too – to stay at your side whatever happens. As long as you want me there. Do you want me there?"

"Oh yes!" Siobhan said as she flung her arms around Ian. "But I don't know if I can take another loved one being hurt."

"All that's important to me is that 'Oh yes!'" Ian said, as he dared to kiss her for the first time.

They each knew that despite their fears, they had found someone to love, someone who would love them back. With a burst of youthful joy, they ran down the long path, holding hands, laughing, much to the astonishment of the sedate, orderly hikers they quickly overtook. Once they reached the bottom of Mount Beacon, they quickly made their way through the winding streets of the sloping, old section of the City of Beacon, and out on to Main Street.

As with Poughkeepsie, The Corporation had drawn Corporate limits around Beacon. Anything outside that line would lose support by utilities' maintenance. So when electric lines failed, they would not be restored to use; when gas lines broke, gas feed would be shut down; when water lines broke, they would not be repaired.

Beacon's dom district had been started to the north of Main Street and was then expanded to the south side. As in Poughkeepsie, the revitalization of Main Street had begun in the early part of the century, so that when The Corporation took over, the street was already a thriving shopping and entertainment district. The Corporation only had to tweak it to meet its objectives.

Even though Ian and Siobhan got to the restaurant about fifteen minutes before their reservation time, their table was ready. Ian was pleased it was tucked away in an alcove in the back as he had requested. The building had originally been a late 1800's bank, but long ago had been converted into a restaurant, with the massive, now open-door vault serving as a wine cellar

"Well, I guess they don't have to worry about any one stealing their wine!" Siobhan joked as she took her seat.

"Yeah, that thing is massive! I'd like to bring my students in here so they could see where hard currency was kept safe. They have a hard time conceiving of credit value being tangible. I've shown them old dollar bills and coins, but they can't figure out how paper could have any value. They understand gold and silver better."

After the waiter lit the candle on their table, giving their little world a romantic glow, Ian reached across the table, taking Siobhan's hands. For several moments they just stared into each other eyes. "You know, this is an anniversary," Ian said.

Siobhan said, "Our 'weekiversary'? Of course, in a way, I've known you a little longer," Siobhan said, looking down in embarrassment.

"When you had learned about me through Spencer's mothers' comments and checked me out, why didn't you approach me at the school, colleague to colleague?"

"I couldn't have just walked into a Corporate school and blurted everything out! I needed to get to know you better first. Get your confidence. And then decide. Plus, after hearing such glowing accounts of you from Spencer's mothers, 'sponding more on your background, and sizing you up through your holoplay, I admit I wanted to get to know you on a social basis."

"Oh, for my body and good looks!"

"Vanity, thy name is man!" Siobhan said, and they both laughed. "Yes, I did some scheming and stalking before we met on the Walkway."

"And now a stalker! Who is this woman I love? OK, 'fess it all up!"

"I frequented some places you might go, per Manhunt's list of your haunts. You know, the Bardavon, the Adriance Library, the museum. But that didn't work. Then I thought of following you home from school to learn your route and then, well, drop a hanky or something."

Ian burst out laughing. "I believe you dropped this, me lady!"

"Hey, you guys have had eons figuring out how to pick up women. We've only had a hundred years!" Siobhan said.

"Finally, I figured it out. Because of my work I still had access to Spencer's assignment lists from his teachers. I saw that you were giving extra credit for students to physically go out and view the fireworks, and extra-extra credit for doing it from the Walkway. I hoped you'd practice what you preached, because if you did, I knew I had a lock on you. There was only one way on to the Poughkeepsie side. So I waited patiently around the entrance to the Walkway and voila!"

"So refined, patient and determined!"

"So I 'fessed up. Now it's your turn. When did you first feel attracted to me?"

"Immediately, on the bridge. I admit it, I'm a cave man! Really, it was your smile; it has such an air of confidence and grace. What a combination! And those qualities came out even more as we carried on our conversation. But I was really hooked when we went into the light of Anna's. I have a genetic weakness for women with dark flowing hair, light blue eyes and fair skin. You know, that classical Irish look. Did you notice that I stammered a bit?"

"Yes. I was afraid you were disappointed when you saw me in the light – and that I wasn't taller and more 'svelte'. That's a trait that's prevalent on my Swedish/German side. Just my luck I didn't inherit those genes, which disappointed me enormously when I was a short teenager."

"Men are always physical in first assessments," Ian admitted. "I like petit and shapely. I also like tall and svelte. Either isn't high priority with me. But like I said, I can't resist raven hair against fair skin and light blue eyes. I'm your man slave! Your boy toy!

"It was really your strength of character that hooked me in the end. Your determination to help and protect Spencer. Your love for the children at the armory," Ian said more quietly as he took hold of her hands again.

As they were finishing their desert, Siobhan said, "Now, tell me why we're going to go to a production of *Frankenstein, the Musical*? 'Frankenstein' and 'musical' just don't seem to fit together."

"Well, it's not light and airy, but a faithful rendering of the Frankenstein story, set to music. You know, man creating a monster then chasing it down to destroy it. And in between learning the lessons of his actions – the cost to love. I hope it's not too heavy, but the ratings were good.

"Also, it's being put on to honor those who rescued the theater. It had originally opened in the 1930's but almost became derelict in the late 1900's. In 2010 an entrepreneurial acting group embarked on renovating it. To kick off the renovation effort they presented this same musical. So this year they're remembering those creative people whose efforts did so much to help in revitalizing Beacon."

"You always impress me with your knowledge of history. That background information will help me enjoy the play even more," Siobhan said as she looked across the street to the old theater. They each 'sponded a generous tip for the waiter on their way out.

As they walked though the dimly-lit streets of Siobhan's neighborhood of solid, old houses in the southern part of Poughkeepsie, more stars became visible in the clear, warm night. Star gazing had always been one of Siobhan's hobbies, so she was happy to display her expertise by pointing out key stars and constellations. As she was explaining the importance of star identification to humans in earlier times, she wondered what she would do when they reached her front porch. She had a deep desire to invite Ian in for some romantic music and wine, and then perhaps let herself go and make passionate love to him.

She almost laughed as she continued to explain the importance stars had had in navigation, while she was imagining luring Ian into her bedroom and throwing him on her bed and ripping his clothes off. Well, maybe removing them quickly and lustily. *It's good 'sponders still don't enable mind reading,* she thought. *Hmmm, or maybe I wish they did at times like this.*

But Siobhan felt conflicted. She'd had such a wonderful day. It had been so enjoyable and uncomplicated. And she wanted to keep it that way. At least for the moment. She knew that making love would deepen, and therefore complicate, their relationship. She knew Ian was ready to make love. Men always were, or were at least ready to have sex. But did she really want to move from the pleasurable, 'innocent' level to a more serious one right now? In the end, she decided to let herself go and see what would materialize when they reached her porch. Maybe Ian wasn't ready to do more than kiss her goodnight and leave.

When they turned on to her street and the light on her porch became visible in the distance, they both fell into an awkward silence. They held hands as they walked, eventually looking at each other and laughing shyly.

In a dark stretch of the street, before reaching the light of her porch, Ian stopped, pulled Siobhan back and kissed her passionately. After a long embrace, they turned and walked toward her house, still holding each other tightly. Even more than before, Siobhan was willing to let circumstances and passions take their course.

As they approached her house, Siobhan noticed that her old-fashioned swing was slowly swaying back and forth; maybe just the cooling breeze of the night. But then she saw a figure was sitting on the swing. She looked up at Ian as he down at her. Finally, they reached the front porch, and Siobhan froze on the first step.

Part 3
MUSIC OF THE SPHERES

I could compare my music to white light which contains all colors. Only a prism can divide the colors and make them appear; this prism could be the spirit of the listener.

Arvo Paert, *Alina*

Chapter 27

"Guy, what are you doing here?!"

Siobhan's ex-husband stood up. "Siobhan, I have to talk to you."

"After all this time? On my porch?" Siobhan fumed. "This is really awkward, Guy!"

"I have to. Now, tonight. Please." Guy had a nervous, hunted expression on his face. Siobhan had never seen him like this.

"Can't it wait till tomorrow?"

"Tomorrow may be too late. There's no one else I can trust," Guy said.

"What about your girl friend? Christina?"

"She's disappeared." He darted his frantic look from Siobhan to Ian.

"Oh, I'm sorry. Ian, this is my ex-husband, Guy Crawford. Guy, this is my very good friend, Ian Vanderkill."

The two men bowed.

Ian finally said, "Look, Guy, it was good meeting you. You want to talk with Siobhan alone, so I think I'll make my way home. Siobhan, will you be OK?"

"Yes, but let's go down the street a little. I want to say good night."

As they walked, they spoke quietly.

"Siobhan, what's going on?"

"I have no idea. But I know him pretty well, and I'm convinced he's in some kind of trouble."

"Do you still love him?"

Siobhan looked nervously at Ian and said, "I still have feelings for him. He was going to be the father of my child. But you're the one I love. Look Ian,

I'm so sorry that this happened tonight of all nights. But I have to help him if I can."

"I understand. Are you sure you'll be OK?"

"Yes. Guy's always been a gentleman. Like you in that sense. And he knows that we'll never start a relationship up again. Don't worry about me."

Ian wasn't sure how to say goodbye in this situation, so he hugged Siobhan and said, "Good night. I'll 'spond you in the morning." And then with a tighter squeeze he said, "I love you."

"I love you," said Siobhan as she stretched up and gave him a passionate kiss.

Ian smiled, turned around and walked down the street. Siobhan watched him go. Their growing separation hurt. At the end of the block, Ian turned around and waved. She waved back.

As they entered her house, Guy looked around at the still-familiar surroundings.

"I was so sure you'd have sold this place after our divorce. You really shouldn't have stayed here."

"I couldn't leave. There were too many memories."

"Did you remodel his room?"

"No."

"Oh Siobhan. I'm so sorry for the way things worked out."

"I am too. I've been sorry every day. But I've met Ian and I'm beginning to think I can get my life together again."

"I'm happy for you. And I am sorry that I never felt things as deeply as you did. I've always admired you for that, and always will. It's as if you existed on a different plane. I think that's what really drove us apart. I've always regretted it, but learned to accept it." Guy instinctively started to reach for Siobhan – to put his arms around her.

But she drew away and said, "Do you still like to drink Lapsang Souchong?"

"Sure, do you have some?"

"Yes, not dispenser-ready, so it'll take me a few minutes to brew some."

"You never liked it. Im surprised you have some."

"I bought some a while ago. It's funny, but it brings back good memories. So I drink some once in a while."

Guy followed her into the kitchen and sat down at the table.

While she got the strong, smoked, black tea ready to brew, she said over her shoulder, "What's going on?"

"You knew that I had continued to work for LEPGen, down on South Road. Well, a couple years ago, I got accepted to work on a highly confidential program. It's very prestigious and pays well, so I was happy to do the work. Several months after I joined the project I started seeing Christina Sessions, who was also on the team. We were 'friends with benefits'. We never got serious – you know, we just had a good time. After you, no other woman measured up."

Siobhan didn't turn around as she finished brewing the tea.

Guy continued, "As soon as I started seeing her, Christina told me she had qualms about the work we were doing. Wondering whether it was legal, or morally right. I think that's what attracted me to her. She had a heart," and after a pause, "a soul. Like you."

"I repeated the words that had been drilled into our heads; that what we were doing would be a great help to society and to The Corporation. I also told her that it was alright to talk to me about her concerns, but not to others, and certainly not to management. Well, she was soon talking to our coworkers and eventually went in and discussed her concerns with our director. Of course, our director was upset and soon Christina 'had decided to pursue career opportunities elsewhere'; in other words, she was fired."

"Well, what kind of work have you been doing that upset her so much?"

"I can't tell you. It's confidential."

Siobhan nodded.

Guy proceeded, "She visited me at my apartment a few times after she was fired. She was relieved and said she was going to look for work in Manhattan. Now that she was gone from her old position, she was even more convinced that our work was wrong. She thought of contacting an 'ogger about it. I told her she could get into real trouble if she did that, and anyway, who would believe her without some kind of proof?

"She tried to convince me to leave LEPGen and go with her. When I told her no, that I was going to stay where I was at, she just looked at me sadly, gathered up her things, and in a matter of minutes was gone." And with regret, "I almost went after her.

"I tried 'sponding her a number of times after she left, but she had me blocked. In the end I gave up. Several months later I hoped she had cooled down and tried 'sponding her, but the message came back that I was trying to connect with a non-entity. I tried 'sponding several sources, but the 'non-entity' message always came back. She had disappeared."

Siobhan poured the brewed tea into two mugs. She set the mugs on the table and sat down. They both knew what "disappeared" meant.

"I was upset, but I knew not to ask questions. I would have if we had been more than friends, but we weren't. I told myself she had brought things on herself. But what she had said started sinking in. About the work we were doing. So to ease my conscience I guess, I started altering my procedures in an insignificant and, I believe, non-detectable, way.

"Our project was in a very new area of research. We weren't making good progress before I altered my procedures, so I don't really know if what I did had any impact. But we certainly haven't made good progress since I made my changes.

"Several months ago a sense of panic set in at work. It started with our director and made its way down. She and the supervisors were checking and rechecking everything. Everyone kept looking for a cause for the lack of progress. But there wasn't any explanation. And that led to talk of sabotage and an intense level of suspicion on everyone's part. So finally the corpos came in this week to help in 'solving the problem'."

"Oh God, Guy! You know the corpos won't stop till they find someone to pin guilt on. Why didn't you switch back to your standard procedure? You have to do it now!"

Guy smiled sadly. "Switching back now could make matters worse, or could tip them off. And anyway, I couldn't. I'm stuck."

Siobhan studied his face, "You couldn't? Why? Guy, you're going to have to tell me what's going on if you want me to help you."

Looking down at the table, Guy said, "Our project has to do with developing an organic transponder with the objective of being able to inject it into fetuses; possibly even as early as the point of conception. If this works out, it could save thousands of lives of children who currently die from complications from implanting electro/organic transponders as we currently do. The organic transponder had been developed and successfully tested on animal fetuses, so now we had to test it on human fetuses. We only use fetuses that have been identified as having defects that would have lead to their terminations. You know, things like Down syndrome."

Siobhan felt the muscles in her face hardening. "Do these defects include male-pattern aggressiveness?"

"Yes."

Siobhan slumped back in her chair. "That could have been our son!"

"No. These experiments didn't start till later."

"That's not my point! Those are someone's children, someone's dreams. Just as we had dreams!"

Guy slowly moved back in his chair, dropped his head, and quietly said, "I know. I felt conflicted from the beginning. Our testing was causing stress and pain, especially to the post-natal level fetuses."

"Post-natal? You're experimenting on live babies?!"

"Please hear me out," Guy interjected. "I thought of our son. I saw their torment. And I thought of a way that might alleviate their suffering, but didn't implement it out of fear. Finally, after Christina left and disappeared, I decided to try it."

After a short, reflective pause, he continued, "Do you remember how I used to come home tense from work? I'd 'spond up Indian karnatic music to relax. The continuous, soothing sound of the drone mellowed me out. So I tried it on several of the fetuses. I interjected a harmonious, karnatic drone to the classical music that was fed into their 'sponders. Only a trained musician would have been aware of the drone. It was there, but barely.

"At first I didn't notice any difference. But soon, usually after moving on to other tests, I began to notice a greater peacefulness in their expressions and reactions. I thought it was helping. So I started using the drone in all the music on all of the fetuses. It seemed to have a positive, soothing effect. As I said, without coming out in the open and testing it, I don't know if it's had an effect on our work, or if it has, whether it was a negative *or* positive effect.

"But I couldn't let them revert back to the suffering I saw on their faces. And that's why I can't stop. I couldn't carry on if I did."

Guy tilted his head and rubbed his neck. "Several months ago, after the panic mode had set in, we started getting a new category of fetuses in from CaringMother. Supposedly fetuses with "other" defects. A rumor started spreading that they were normal. That in their panic to find out why we weren't making progress, management decided to start testing totally healthy subjects, hoping that using fetuses with defects had been the problem. We technicians don't have the means to test them for defects, but on the surface they do seem to be healthy."

Siobhan stared at Guy, feeling only incredible sad. She again went through the realization of why she and Guy could never have stayed together after their son was terminated. Guy's actions in his lab had been to put a bandage on Dr. Frankenstein's creation. Did he understand that?

"Siobhan, I'm sorry."

Siobhan reached across the table and took his hands. "So am I." She recalled the man she thought she had married in another life.

Siobhan quietly said, "Guy, what are you going to do?"

Looking very tired he said, "That's why I came to you. I needed your strength to overcome indecision – my fear.

"They disconnected the recording memory in our 'sponders when we started the project. And they have a scanner at the entrance to check them, both when we enter and leave. But with some help I learned how to reconnect and disconnect on my own. One day I reconnected the memory in the lab and recorded a snack as I ate it. You know, something totally innocuous so if discovered I could protest innocence, that it must have been a glitch. Then I disconnected it before I left. Nothing happened. I tested it several more times. It worked.

"I'm ready to record what's going on in our lab. But that's as far as I've taken it. I don't have any 'ogger contacts. Can you help me?"

Siobhan knew that in the next breath she would be locked into a conspiracy with her ex-husband. There would be no turning back. Could she even trust him? He could be a corpo informant.

"When can you do it?"

"Tonight. I'd normally be off, but I'm covering for someone. It's the graveyard shift and a weekend – the best time."

"Do it. Who knows if you'll have an opportunity later on? Then come by after your shift tomorrow morning. Be careful not to record anything that could identify you, though we can edit that tomorrow. We'll make a copy of your recording, delete your 'spond memory, and then add your voice-altered commentary. I have contacts that can get the final work to a phantom 'ogger. I'll figure out the details tonight so we can complete it and get it out of our hands quickly. That's the safest way.

"Guy, Christina was right. What you're doing is wrong. We have to let people know what CaringMother and LEPGen are doing with their children."

"I know." Guy finished his tea, stood and headed toward the door. Before he opened it, he turned. "Do we have a chance of pulling this off? Unscathed?"

"I don't know. But Guy, that doesn't matter. We have to do what's right."

Guy nodded, hugged Siobhan, and walked out the door.

As Siobhan watched him disappear into the night, she wondered if he would carry through. She hoped she had given him the support he needed.

But in a corner of her mind she hoped he wouldn't. She imagined him not showing up tomorrow, or any day after that. She imagined Ian coming over tomorrow and the two of them spending another perfect day together. Maybe going down to Doodletown to where they had first held hands. And then tomorrow night, picking up where they had left off when they discovered Guy on her porch.

But she knew that was a dream to push away. Guy would return. They would do what they had to do.

Chapter 28

"Wasn't that that Crawford guy who knew Christina? I thought he wouldn't be back in till Sunday night," Tony said as he, Michael and Lenora rushed out the front entrance of the LEPGen labs.

Michael glanced back and said, "Looks like him. 'Spond the work schedule to be sure he's supposed to be here tonight. But right now you two secure the Oracle's house while I head to the hospital."

The three of them jumped into their cars, and sped off into the darkness. Michael was thankful he had requested loaner cars for Lenora and Tony to use. Goddamnit, why hadn't he hunted down the Oracle last night to get an update? He'd been too damn tired and it was late.

They were reviewing today's interviews when Treadwell's assistant said that Vassar Hospital was urgently trying to get ahold of Michael. When he went out of the secure area to 'spond the emergency doctor, he was told that a Daniel Schmitt had been found severely beaten in the north side of Poughkeepsie. He'd asked the doctor to get ahold of Michael.

Michael pulled up to the emergency entrance and ran in. At the admissions desk, he flashed his CBI holobadge and said, "Detective Chan, I need to see Dr. Lopez right now!"

"She's expecting you in ER2, that's the second room down that hall."

Michael ran down the hall and burst into the room. He saw a youngish woman manipulating medical records on a wallplay. Near her was an emergency room bed with a sheet pulled over a body. The woman looked over at him.

"Dr. Lopez? I'm Detective Chan from the CBI."

"I'm sorry Detective Chan, but Mr. Schmitt didn't make it." Studying Michael's face, she continued, "Was he a friend of yours?"

Michael lifted the sheet. He immediately recoiled from the display of extreme brutality he saw. He finally exhaled a long breath, carefully replaced the sheet, and said, "Yes. He was helping me on a case. What happened?"

"A couple discovered him in an empty lot off Parker Avenue. I did what I could for him. But he was pretty busted up. I tried to get some information out of him, but he was delirious when he came in."

"How long do you figure he had been in the lot before he was found?"

"Maybe half an hour. If his 'sponder had been working ..." Dr. Lopez trailed off as Michael nodded. "I did get his name out of him and that's when he mentioned you. So I 'sponded you immediately, but couldn't get ahold of you."

"I was in a secure facility."

"Luckily, one of the policemen who brought him in was able to track down where you were, so we 'sponded LEPGen."

"Exactly what did he say about me?"

"'Detective Chan, CBI. Please,' was all he said. He did a lot of rambling. I can holoplay from when he was admitted to the time he expired."

"Please do."

Michael watched the holoplay as the Oracle was rolled in and Dr. Lopez tried to help him. Some bastards had really done a job on him. It was hard for Michael to watch. He kept flashing back to his dream in which he tried to warn Dan. He felt guilty.

Suddenly he said to Dr. Lopez, "Please play the last half minute back."

He watched as the Oracle said, "Tell Michael, take the A train."

"Again, please."

After he watched it, he said to Dr. Lopez, "Did I hear it right? He said 'Tell Michael, take the A train'?"

"Yes, does it mean anything to you?"

"I'll have to think about it."

Michael watched the rest. Most of it was Dan mumbling as he became increasingly exhausted. And he watched as Dan died.

"Could I be alone with him for a few minutes?"

"Sure. I'm sorry about your friend. He was terribly disfigured. Are you sure it was him?

"Yes, it was Dan Schmitt."

"Any relatives or friends that should be notified? I couldn't tell without a 'sponder."

Looking back down at the bed, he sighed and said, "I'll let his mother know."

Dr. Lopez walked out and closed the door. Michael couldn't lift the sheet again. *My friend?* he thought. *Yes, you were my friend. You made the job interesting. Man, what a character! Oh, I dig you daddy! Underneath that beatnik façade you were a good person. I'm sorry I didn't listen to you more closely when you told me about those Colson recordings. I'm sure she's tied up in this somehow. Dan, I'm sorry I got you involved in this.* Reaching down, Michael put his hand on Dan's shoulder. He exhaled deeply and said goodbye.

Dr. Lopez was in the hallway.

"Thank you for doing your best. Did the policemen who brought him in indicate that there was any evidence, witnesses?"

"No. They're back out checking the scene and talking to people in the area."

"Any other emergencies tonight?"

"No. But a woman was killed in her apartment not far from where Mr. Schmitt was found. She was taken immediately to the morgue.'

"What was her name?"

"Just a minute," and she 'sponded some records. "Alvira Maltos."

On the way over to the Oracle's house, Michael 'sponded Lenora and Tony to be sure they were alright and had secured the house. He found the two of them sitting with the Oracle's mother in the old fashioned living room.

Ms. Schmitt's eyes looked pleadingly into Michael's. "Is Dan – ?"

"Ms. Schmitt. I'm so sorry. Dan didn't make it."

She broke into mournful sobs. Lenora put her arms around her.

"People made fun of his love for jazz. They said he was just a put-on beatnik. But he had a good heart. He always looked out for me," Ms. Schmitt sobbed out in between gasps.

"I know he was a good person, Ms. Schmitt. And I know he loved you. The doctor told me his last words were, 'Tell my mother I love her'." Lenora looked up and nodded approvingly, as Ms. Schmitt renewed her heart-rending sobs.

Michael signaled to Tony to go with him into the other room, and when there, asked him to recount what had happened since they got there.

"When we rolled up we could see some figures moving around in the house, but they scampered out the back immediately. We pursued them for a few hundred paces. We'd seen Ms. Schmitt tied up in the corner as we ran through, so we 'sponded the Poughkeepsie police for a manhunt and went back. We untied her and got the story.

"She'd been at home when the front door burst open and three people wearing Kenneth Rechner masks rushed in. All were dressed in black and were large. She was pretty sure two were men and one was a woman. They immediately whacked her on the head and bound, gagged, and blindfolded her. She was conscious shortly before we got here, but too afraid to move. She could hear them yelling out to each other. They were obviously searching and scanning the different rooms. You can see the results. Dan's room upstairs is a real mess."

"What time did it start?"

"About 11:30. We got here at 12:25. I'm figuring they scanned each room, and when nothing came up they defaulted to the old fashioned search. She couldn't give us any more on what they were looking for. But they kept each other appraised of their progress as they moved room to room, apparently separately. They sounded like pros to her. We advised her to go to the hospital but she said she wouldn't leave till she heard if Dan was OK. So what's the story on Dan?"

"They may have been professionals, but they were unrefined brutes. Obviously, when Dan didn't give them what they wanted they resorted to old fashioned physical pain. They did what they could at the hospital."

Tony nodded as he looked into the other room at Lenora and the grieving mother.

"Hey Tony, ya done good."

"Thanks, Michael."

The two of them walked back into the living room. Michael began, "Ms. Schmitt, I'm so sorry about Dan. He was my friend. He was helping us on a case. I have some important questions to ask you that might help us zero in on his killers. But we also have to take you to the hospital to have you checked out."

"I'll go to the hospital later. Ask me your questions. I want to help however I can. And my name's Elizabeth. Please call me Beth. "

Michael smiled warmly and said, "Michael. You know Lenora and Tony." The other two nodded.

"Beth, did you know that Dan had been doing some work for me?"

"I figured that much, though he didn't tell me directly. Yesterday morning, Thursday, hit me up for some free floaters. He said he'd pay me back. And he always did pay me back when he said he would."

"How much did you give him?"

"Ten thousand. I knew he had about fifteen or twenty thousand of his own, but not a lot more."

"Did he say what it was for?"

"No. But he took off early in the afternoon and didn't come back till late Thursday night. He seemed pleased. I told him I'd make him some supper, but he said no thanks and went straight downstairs."

"Downstairs?" Lenora asked.

"Oh yes. To his man-cave, as I call it. That's where he spent most of his time." After a pause, she said with a wan smile, "Those bastards were looking in the wrong place when they tore his room apart. He didn't keep anything up there."

"Are you up to taking us downstairs?"

"Sure."

They went through the kitchen into a hall leading toward a rear pantry. Beth opened a door on the right, turned on a light and took them down wooden stairs and into the basement. It was an old fashioned basement with stone walls. Very well built as was typical back then. Michael could see that there had been shallow, narrow trenches dug and cemented in along the walls which lead to a sump pump well near the bottom of the stairs. And there were two dehumidifiers. It was a very comfortable temperature with just the right humidity.

Along the one wall on the right, but not against it, were shelves of old fashioned vinyl record albums. Michael guessed maybe two to three thousand. There were also a number of old fashioned '45's' and even '78's'. Along the left wall was a long workbench with some books and papers piled up. Covering most of the wall was a long, smooth board that had hundreds of old fashioned notes stuck to it.

On the far wall were shelves filled with books, and in front of that was an old fashioned easy chair, with reading lamp and side table. A bit off from the chair, toward the record shelves, was an antiquated stereo set, with large speakers. A pair of headphones hung over the easy chair, with a wire connecting them to the stereo equipment.

"Cool," Tony said, obviously impressed.

Beth smiled. "Dan was very proud of his record collection. Many of these are over 100 years old, and the rest are immaculate reproductions. He spent most of his time down here. He only slept in his bedroom. Sometimes he'd fall asleep in his easy chair and sleep here all night. His books are mostly about jazz and its golden age in Harlem."

Michael walked over to the wall with post-its. "What are all these?"

"Dan used this wall to post little reminders or important points to remember when he was working on a project. Old fashioned, but very practical, to him anyway."

"Had he posted any of these in the past week?"

"Oh, I don't know. This was his domain. He wouldn't even let me clean up down here. He did all the cleaning himself. Spotless, isn't it?"

Turning back to Beth, Michael continued, "Beth, Dan told the emergency doctor, 'Tell Michael, take the A train'. Does that mean anything to you?

"'Take the A Train' was a piece written by Duke Ellington. But the A train's a subway that takes you from lower- and mid-Manhattan up to Harlem. The message in Ellington's song is that if you want to have a good time, hear some great jazz, just hop on the A train and come up to Harlem."

"Did Dan have a connection to Harlem – the A train?

"Harlem was Dan's Mecca. When he was old enough (or he thought he was, because he didn't tell me) he took the Hudson Line down to Grand Central. He could have gotten off at 125th Street, the main street in Harlem, on the way down, but no, he had to take the A train up to Harlem. His journey had to be authentic, pure.

"Well, he was very disappointed. Harlem was full of white and oriental people. The buildings had all been restored to their original late 1800's condition. The few jazz clubs he found were just cheap tourist traps out to make a credit.

"The only saving grace of that trip was he found a small, basement book and record shop that specialized in jazz and Harlem in an old brown stone across the street from the Morris-Jumel mansion in North Harlem. The owner was a transplanted Minnesotan, an older white man, who had also made a pilgrimage to Harlem as a young man. He had also been disappointed in what he had found, so he had opened his shop to keep history alive. Dan bought some books and records from him and he's been a source for Dan over the years. I think kind of a mentor too."

"What was the name of the shop and the owner?"

"It was called The Word or The World, I'm sure you'll find mention of it if you go through some of these things. He told me the man's name a couple times, but it wasn't a common one, and I'm starting to get a little forgetful. I do remember thinking his last name was German."

Looking at the others' puzzled looks, Beth continued, "Jazz, Harlem was Dan's world and he didn't let me into it much. When Dan's father left us, it was very difficult on Dan. He blamed me. I did fight a lot with my husband. We were like fire and ice. Later, Dan started believing that the corpos, I'm sorry, the CBI, had disappeared him. He couldn't accept that his father had just walked away one day. After that he had his Harlem historian, and you, Michael. You're a bit younger than his father would be but 'old enough'. And he respected you a lot.

"There wasn't a lot of help for a boy like Dan. So when he'd get into trouble or try to reach out to a father figure and it wouldn't work out, he'd come home frustrated and blame me. He'd storm in the door and go up to his room. I was so happy when he started fixing up his own domain down here. He'd still storm home, but he'd come down here for hours, and come up relaxed, and even happy. Somehow he'd work things out in his world.

"He let me know that was his world and I wasn't a part of it. I accepted that. But he occasionally shared it, especially if he had bought a new album."

After a reflective pause, she continued, "He came to accept that *his* Harlem, his perfect Harlem, only existed in his mind – a Mecca of the mind, he put it. That it was an ideal place that gave him inspiration, peace."

Michael slowly put his arms around Beth's shoulders and held her as she cried again.

After several minutes she stopped, wiped her eyes and looked at the others and said, "I'm sorry, I went way off on a tangent. But I think that A train comment was about music – not the physical subway and Harlem. If you're looking for something related to that comment about the A train, it's probably down here."

After getting a visual hint from Lenora, Michael said, "Beth, this has been very helpful – it'll put us on the right track. Lenora, would you please take Beth to the hospital and have her checked over? Tony, 'spond the Poughkeepsie police and see if they have any developments yet. Tell them I want this house secured and put under twenty-four hour protection as a site important in a CBI investigation. But I don't want them entering yet. Not till we're done. While you're doing those things, I'll stay down here.

"Once the police have the house secured, let's knock off, get some shut eye, then meet back here late morning. Lenora, when you're done at the hospital, please take Beth to the Grand Hotel downtown."

"Can't I come back home?" Beth asked. "I'd sleep much better in my own bed."

"Michael, I can camp out here after we get Beth checked out," Lenora offered. "I don't think those guys will be stupid enough to come back with the police and myself here."

Michael looked at Beth then at Lenora and finally gave the OK.

After the others went upstairs, Michael stood in the silence and looked around the room. He smiled. "Man cave!" A term you didn't hear much anymore, but the expression sure nailed this place. It was so easy to imagine the

Oracle sitting on his raggedy old throne with his headphones on listening to some great jazz recording.

He walked over to the record shelves and was surprised at the amount of classical, country, rock'n'roll, Celtic and other types of music that was interspersed. Not surprisingly, no Corporate music. He realized that the albums were arranged alphabetically by performer or composer. He saw the Duke Ellington section but left it untouched. He'd wait till later after they had done a thorough multi-scan of the room.

Michael went to the workbench and looked at the books and papers stacked on it. Again, he was reluctant to touch anything till after the multi-scan, but he peered at the titles on the book bindings. Mostly on jazz and Harlem. One on the Mid-Hudson Valley during the revolution. He finally looked up at the hundreds of post-its on the wall, but he was too tired to concentrate. It would have to wait till later.

In a few minutes, Tony came down and told him that the police had shown up to guard the house and that they didn't have any new developments. Michael took one last look around the room before they went up the stairs.

Chapter 29
SATURDAY, JULY 11

"What do the multi-scans tell us?" Michael asked looking around the basement, still groggy from his restless sleep. He was surprised he hadn't dreamt about the Oracle. Instead, it had been his wife and daughter who were in danger and he was trying to protect them from a nondescript adversary. He had finally woken up flailing and gasping for breath, realizing it was late morning and Julianna was out with friends.

"Well, nothing on the scans upstairs," Tony began. "No suspicious OI devices. And of course, the guys who broke in made such a muck of the place that we couldn't get a reading on chronological disturbances. But we did come up with DNA that wasn't Dan's or his mother's. Pros would've wiped themselves down with a DNA disturber. But we're sending the DNA samples in for analysis.

"As for down here, also no OI's. Though all the electronics and recordings did confuse the hell out of the scanner. It wasn't made to deal with stuff this old. Only Dan's and his mother's DNA. And a few of our flakes, of course. There was nothing on the chronological disturbance scan."

Michael looked at Tony and said, "What?"

"Yeah. It's kind of weird. Did you notice how spic'n'span everything was down here? It wouldn't have looked like this if it had been my man-cave. I mean, it would have had chronological piles of plates and half-eaten food lying around," Tony observed.

"So I figure Dan might have cleaned the whole place and wiped it all down to prevent any bad guys figuring things out with a scan. The only problem is now it makes things difficult for us."

"So that leaves us with good old-fashioned detective work," Michael said. "OK, let's take a look at Ellington's recordings, first with the ones that include 'Take the A Train'. Tony, put your gloves on and help me. Lenora, 'spond up a list of other artists who did recordings of 'Take the A Train' and compare it to recordings down here. Those'll be next."

Michael and Tony carefully removed the Duke Ellington albums from the shelf and put them gently on a desk. Three of the seven albums had a recording of 'Take the A Train'. They inspected the first three albums very carefully, first with the disturbance scanner, then visually on the outside. Then they removed the records and carefully inspected the insides of the jackets and sleeves. Nothing. They then played each recording of the 'A Train". All three were different. Two included vocals, which didn't tell them anything useful.

"I like the music, but I think things are going to get boring fast," Tony said.

"Hold on to your butts, boys. There are nine more albums by other artists down here that include recordings of 'Take the A Train'," Lenora said.

While Michael and Tony methodically checked out the remaining Ellington recordings, Lenora put on gloves, pulled out the other albums that had 'A Train' recordings, and carefully put them on the desk. For a few minutes after that she watched the two men who were engrossed in their work. Finally she said, "I'm going to go upstairs and check on Beth."

"Hmmmm," Michael said as he carefully looked inside an album sleeve.

"Good idea," Tony said, as he sorted through the pile of nine, never looking up.

"Men!" Lenora said as she went upstairs to talk to a human being.

"We had a good talk. She felt better after that," Lenora said when she returned after half an hour.

"Good," Tony said, listening to the lyrics in another vocal recording of "Take the A Train."

"Hmmmm," Michael said, carefully inspecting the outside of the next album jacket.

Lenora shook her head. She walked over to the workbench and, putting her gloves back on, began to inspect the books that were lying there. Nothing. She then started carefully going through the papers that were on the desk. They were amazing – actually hand written. Cursive. Since handwriting, especially cursive, was so rare, she struggled with reading it.

She turned to ask Michael for help, since he was older and probably had had more exposure to hand writing, but he was engrossed with the albums. So she struggled through alone. She determined that they were biographical write ups of jazz greats. It looked like Dan had been putting together a collection of their lives. But for what? Surely not a book!

Lenora put the papers down and began perusing the hundreds of sticky notes stuck to the walls. At first, it just looked like an indecipherable jumble. But having learned something about Dan's scrawl from his papers, she slowly was able to make out more and more words. The notes seemed to be important reminders to himself. He must have had some method.

There were all kinds of topics covered; some appeared to be related to the jazz-greats writing he was doing. Others were on other subjects, such as the Declaration of Independence. Then she started noticing notes interspersed throughout the wall with C/M or L or both on them. CaringMother? LEPGen? Maybe his order was no order. Maybe this was the way he thought. Or maybe this was his way of covering up his work, at least superficially, to confuse others looking at it. There were notes like, "L – comp: NuTense, QuantroPhan" and "C/M ←→ L, NuTense, FlenRite, Probelon, Phalanx". She figured comp was competition, and the two-way arrows probably indicated a working relationship of some kind. Lenora continued, getting used to deciphering Dan's hand writing. "

Suddenly she paused and studied a note that read "C/M →L, unhappy customer". This one had her puzzled and therefore intrigued. Was LEPGen an unhappy customer with the "products" they've been receiving from CaringMother? Likely. Was there another unhappy corporate customer involved? Was an unhappy customer of CaringMother somehow gaining access to LEPGen? And doing what?

"Hey, guys, come here."

They ignored her as they continued to inspect the albums.

Finally, "Would you *please* come over here!"

Michael and Tony both looked up. "God. Don't get so testy!" Tony said. He and Michael put their albums down and went over to the wall.

"Take a look at that note and tell me if it means something to you."

Both men leaned forward, squinted, and finally Michael said, "What does it say?"

"'C/M arrow L, unhappy customer'. I figure C/M is CaringMother and L is LEPGen. Does that say anything to you?" Lenora asked.

"Not yet."

As they all continued to stare at the note, Lenora continued, "Well, I was thinking. What if we, and Natalie, got it wrong. What if we shouldn't be concerned about parents. They're the happy CaringMother customers. What if we should be looking for an unhappy CaringMother customer employed at LEPGen? Maybe we should be looking for an employee whose child's gestation at CaringMother *didn't* work out. Either it failed or was terminated for one reason or another. Like the fetuses at LEPGen."

A light seemed to go on in both of her colleague's faces. "Good point, Lenora," Michael said as he nodded. "'Spond Kaneesha Johnston at CaringMother. Remember, she's head of quality control. I know she's aware of what's going on. 'Spond her a list of everyone working in Treadwell's organization and ask her which ones, if any, had had an unsuccessful gestation at CaringMother, either here or at any of their facilities. And tell her we need it now."

"I'm on it," Lenora said as she slowly walked away from the wall to avoid distraction during her 'spond. Michael and Tony continued to pour over the wall.

"Man, I don't know how she could read this stuff. I can't make it out," said Tony.

"It is hard. I remember reading cursive handwriting when I was younger. But look, a number of them do have C/M's and L's," Michael observed as they continued looking over the notes. After a while, the two of them got used to the handwriting, helping each other out as they went along. Michael turned around and saw that Lenora seemed frustrated. He didn't want to interrupt her 'sponding so he just gave her a "whazzup" look.

Lenora finally said, "I could only get ahold of Johnston's assistant. She wanted to know what our need to know was. I explained and said that Johnston was aware of the importance of our case. She in turn checked with Johnston and came back with: we didn't have a need to know."

Michael was furious. "I'm gonna haul her ass into the interview center and she'll damn well find out what our need to know is!" After calming down he 'sponded Chavez and enlisted her help to get what they needed. "This job! All the bullshit! Look, Lenora, ya done good. Real good. Keep pouring over these notes for any others that might be of interest. Tony and I'll finish up on the albums. Grab us if anything else catches your eye.

"We've all had a long, hard week, so we'll finish up here and call it a day. I have a hard stop at five. My daughter and her boy friend have invited us over to his apartment for a special dinner. My wife thinks they have a big announcement so I can't be late."

Michael watched both of them as they turned back to their work. He knew they were as exhausted as he was; not just the hours but the emotional ups and downs they had been going through in the past week.

When he had first started with the CBI he was as fresh and innocent as they. Another time, another world. Before he had gained his following – of ghosts. Old Marley in "A Christmas Carol" had forged a chain in life. Michael had forged a "chain" of ghosts, except he knew he had the chain while he was still alive. And now he had one more link. He turned to the threadbare easy chair and could almost see Dan sitting in it, happily listening to his jazz. Michael turned around, looked at the stairs, glanced at the ceiling, and finally walked up the stairs to talk with Beth.

Forty-five minutes later Lenora came rushing up the stairs with Tony trailing behind. They stopped at the entrance to the living room. Michael was talking softly to Beth, holding her hands. She was laughing with tears streaming down her face. Michael looked up. "Beth and I were just sharing some good times with Dan. I told her about our paying homage to the Oracle the other night and that he took a real shining to you, Lenora."

Beth said to Lenora, "I hope he wasn't too forward with you. His unconventional ways seemed to attract some girls. I told him to be careful, that he could get himself into trouble if he was too forward with more 'conventional' girls. He just said, 'Screw convention.' That was his attitude."

"Beth, I found Dan very charming. I'm sorry I never had the opportunity to get to know him better."

"I think I've found where he may have helped us on a case we're working on. If I can borrow Michael for a few minutes."

Michael excused himself, and he, Lenora and Tony returned to the basement.

"Johnston's assistant got back to me. Only one person on the list had had an unsuccessful gestation. Guy Crawford. That was three years ago. A divorce a year later – which would indicate that the termination probably caused problems for him and his ex-wife, a Siobhan Carlson. Couple that with his relationship to Christina Sessions and I think we've got a likely."

"What were the circumstances of the termination?" Michael asked.

"That's another aspect that supports him being a likely. It was a late-term termination. Male-pattern aggressiveness. You know, there are certain circles that believe MPA is a bullshit defect, that it's never been proven that you can accurately detect the tendency, nor that it necessarily leads to violence against women. Some say it's just a Corporate conspiracy to selectively breed a more docile male population."

Michael stared coldly at Lenora, "I'm one of them."

Lenora looked surprised, but then continued, "Late term is always hard. It can't be easy experimenting on those fetuses, knowing they'll be terminated in the end, and having your son's termination in the back of your mind …"

"Did you check out the work schedule to see if Crawford was supposed to be there last night?"

"Yes, he was covering for someone who wanted last night off. You know, working the graveyard shift is the perfect time to sabotage an experiment and not get caught."

Michael nodded.

"What do you want to do?" Lenora asked.

Michael looked at Lenora and then at Tony and said, "You're supposed to be getting experience that'll lead to your making detective rank. So tell me what you two think we should do."

Lenora began, "I think we have good reason to have him picked up and taken to the interview center for questioning."

Tony nodded in agreement.

"You're right. And we all know that. But that's not what I asked you. I asked you what you think we *should* do, weighing what we have vs. what'll happen to him at the center."

"I don't think we have a choice," Tony finally chipped in. "Indications are that a crime of sabotage has been committed and we have a likely suspect with a motive. I think we have the duty to bring him in."

"Indications, but no solid proof," Michael said. Staring intently back and forth at each of them, he continued, "And, by the way – you always have a choice."

Michael could tell "the kids" were taken aback at his reluctance. Up till now he had probably seemed decisive to them. But they were about to lose their innocence, to begin their chain of ghosts, if they had any humanity, which he knew they did. No one had asked him to think before he had first sent a suspect to the interview center. He wanted them to at least think about what they were doing.

"I think we should have him picked up and taken to the interview center," Lenora finally said, with Tony nodding in agreement again.

Michael looked at them and said, "You're right – and you're wrong." And after he got the desired puzzled look from both of them, he added, "You'll understand better every time you have someone picked up. OK, arrange it. As usual, have it done when as few people as possible are around. Let's get it done tonight. And tell them at the center to just loosen him up at this point. I don't want them to put the worm on him till I give the go ahead. Understood?"

"Gotcha," Lenora said.

Michael added, "And guys, ya done good." But the lack of conviction in his voice and the sadness in his eyes said otherwise.

Chapter 30

The elevator door opened to the lobby. "Hey, Ian. Off and running?" Bill asked as he stepped back to let Ian out.

"Yes. Out for the evening," Ian responded, though his thoughts seemed to be elsewhere.

"Have fun. By the way, I'd like you to meet Caitlin's parents, Michael and Julianna Chan."

Ian broke out of his distraction and smiled. "Pleased to meet you," Ian said as everyone bowed and the Chans countered with pleasantries. "Bill's one of my favorite people and I'm very impressed with Caitlin. She's a real go-getter. Knows what she wants."

"Yes, she's always been very determined," Julianna said. "Made for heartburn when she was a teenager, but I think it's helped her as an adult. We love her."

"She's a good person. And so's this guy," Ian said indicating Bill.

"Thank you," Julianna said.

Michael was quiet. Preoccupied.

"Well, it was very nice meeting you and I hope to see you again," Ian said as they all bowed again and said their goodbyes.

"What's his story?" Michael asked as the elevator door closed.

"He lives on the eighth floor. Nice guy. Teaches at the Corporate upper-form school. History. He knows a lot about Poughkeepsie and the Mid-Hudson Valley. We've had some good talks."

"Hmmmm," Michael said absentmindedly as the elevator door opened and they walked down the hall to Bill's apartment.

Recognizing Bill, the door opened and all three went in. Caitlin was standing, facing the door. "I'm so glad you could come tonight! And Dad, I especially appreciate you making it. I know you've been tied up with a case."

"The older I get, the more I realize there's a time for everything. I wouldn't miss an invitation from my daughter and her boyfriend," Michael said as he hugged is daughter.

"Well, the reason we asked you over was to let you know that Bill won't be my boyfriend much longer. He'll soon be my husband! We both received permission this week to marry."

"Congratulations!" Michael and Julianna both said almost simultaneously and there were hugs all around. "But I bet your mother already knew," Michael said ribbing his daughter, knowing the two of them confided in each other on everything.

"No, not yet. We wanted both of you to find out at the same time," Caitlin countered.

"Then I *am* glad I came today; otherwise I'd never have heard the end of it!" Michael said.

"You'd better believe it!" Caitlin said.

"So what are the plans now?" Michael asked.

"Mom's been helping me put together preliminary plans. Now we can lock in a date at the temple. As soon as possible. The Buddhist ceremony's what's important to us, so we'll just lock in the Corporate ceremony at the Bureau of Life Changes around that.

"But right now we've got a bottle of Champaign to celebrate!"

They walked into the kitchen alcove where the bottle was on ice. Bill cautiously opened it and poured the Champaign into the glasses.

As they clinked, Michael said, "Here's to your happiness together. We love you both. And as the saying goes, 'May the sun always be on your face, and the wind at your back.'"

"Wow Dad, did Buddha say that?" Caitlin kidded.

"No, me sainted Irish muther did!"

They all laughed and drank the first toast.

"Now, Bill, man-to-man, do you understand what you have to do for the wedding?" Michael asked.

Bill looked confused. "I think so."

"You have to do two things. One, show up. Two, say 'I do'. Oh, and I forgot, you have to say "yes dear" to all the plans and to everything else for the rest of your life."

Julianna looked exasperated. "I knew you'd say that!"

"If there's one thing that's a God-given women's territory it's weddings," Michael countered. "It's OK for women to ask men's opinions and even have them help work out any special words to be spoken. But then they go and do whatever they want anyway. And it's a wise man who understands that. I'm just trying to get Bill off on the right foot." Michael smiled his mischievous, Jackie-Chan grin that he knew his wife couldn't resist. But she rolled her eyes.

"Points well taken, Michael," Bill laughed, "Though I think I've already learned that lesson.

"But before we drink the rest of our Champaign, I'd like to let the other shoe drop. When we received permission to get married, we were also granted permission to have a baby."

"I'm so excited!" Julianna said and hugged both of them. "I can't wait to have a grandchild!" Tears of happiness were welling in her eyes.

"But we want to wait till after the wedding before having the baby." Caitlin interjected. "You know, it's more traditional. I've been having my eggs harvested, so I'll be ready to go. Dad, what do you think?" Caitlin noticed that Michael hadn't said anything and seemed to be holding back on displaying any emotion.

"Honey, I think it's great. But don't you want to hold off a little longer? You know, till you've had some time getting used to being together?"

"We know each other well enough. Come on, Dad. Be happy!"

"I am, Honey," Michael said, though the scowl on his face belied his words. "Where are you going to have the insemination and gestation done?"

"Here in Poughkeepsie. At CaringMother. You know there aren't any other options. It's the only wombcare in town," Caitlin responded. "You don't think I should go to Manhattan, do you? You can't beat the options and service down there, but that would be a real time commitment, not to mention expense."

"No, no," Michael said. But he didn't add that Poughkeepsie CaringMother would be fine.

"Dad, what's the matter? I thought you'd be pleased too."

"I am. Very pleased. I'm like your mother. I can't wait to have a grandchild. But I want it to be right."

"What do you mean right?"

"Well, have you ever thought about having a baby the natural way?"

Caitlin and Julianna stared at each other and then back at Michael. "Dad, are you serious? No one does that anymore. It's just not done! I can't take the time off – delivery, post delivery – and what if there were complications during pregnancy and I had to take time off? What would happen to my career?"

Michael didn't want to spoil the evening, so he said, "I'm sorry Honey. I guess I was just thinking some old-fashioned ideas out loud. Yes, I'm happy, very happy." And then, lifting his glass and doing a 'Godfather', Luca Brazza voice, he said, "And may your first child be a masculine one!"

With this, they all laughed, clinked their glasses and downed the rest of their Champaign.

Caitlin and Julianna started getting the dinner ready while talking about the wedding plans and babies. Michael and Bill sat down in the living area and talked about sports. They were both die-hard Mets fans now that the Yankees had moved to Atlanta. Bill asked the obligatory question, "How can you have a team called the Yankees in the heart of the Deep South!" before they moved on to the Mets' line up for the next game.

But though Michael was talking Mets light-heartedly on the surface, he felt a growing dread in his heart.

Siobhan had felt dread in her heart for a long time. It came and went depending on what she was currently involved in. Sometimes it almost evaporated, like when she was with Ian in Beacon yesterday. But even then, it lurked, ready to rise again. It was like having a kink in her neck – nagging at her, till she'd reach up and massage her neck, acknowledging its existence.

Her dread had now returned in full force. She took a sip of her Lapsang Souchong, trying to recapture happy feelings. She looked out the window at the brooding sky, wondering how long it'd be before it rained torrents. Wondering how much longer her old house could tolerate the abuse of weather it hadn't been built to withstand.

The house had been on the registry of historical homes because Walt Whitman had lived here for a month with a Vassar College music professor while they collaborated in putting Whitman's poems to music. But the registry had largely been abandoned. The Corporation found history to be, well, inconvenient.

Siobhan looked around at the kitchen and out into the hallway toward the parlor and dining room. She loved this old house. How many lives had passed through it since it was built? Each life had left its breath. She felt them.

Siobhan sometimes went into her son's room, imagining her son playing with toys modeled after antique muscle machines. Maybe playing with heavy-equipment toys. Maybe playing with dolls. But he had always looked up at her and smiled. For this, too, she had loved the house. This was why she hadn't been able to leave it.

But now, she knew he was no longer here. He had left her in the Valley of the Dead, not as a punishment, but as a release. Now he was a sweet memory. Now she had Ian – and a wish, though maybe not yet a hope, for a future.

If only the dread weren't there. Like the old house and the pounding weather, she wondered how much more dread she could withstand.

She was jolted out of her thoughts by the ringing of the antique door bell. It couldn't be the corpos; they weren't that fast. And the Phantom'ogger hadn't even gone online yet. Probably not for another hour. So she walked down the hallway, and seeing Ian through the translucent curtain, she opened the door.

Ian's perturbed look immediately turned to concern when he looked her over. Siobhan looked down at her light skin. It was beyond pale now, almost translucent in the light of the gathering storm. She managed a distant smile as she reached up and hugged him for a long time.

"I'm so glad you're here," Siobhan said.

"Are you OK? Why did you block my 'sponds?"

Siobhan released him, looked up and down the street, and then said, "Come in."

They went inside. Siobhan turned to him and said, "It's done. Now all I do is wait."

"Wait for what?"

"The knock at the door. Or not. Every minute the knock doesn't come, is better. Till finally I can almost hope it won't come. But then I do something else, and wait again."

"Siobhan, what are you talking about? What happened with Guy?"

"Guy needed my help. We did what was right."

She touched his open lips.

"I can't tell you what, Ian. Your only hope if that knock comes is not to know what happened. I can't live with the thought of the corpos coming for you too."

Ian took her in his arms and hugged her for a long time, kissing her cheeks and forehead. He could feel her trembling at first but that subsided.

"Why do people always think I'm so strong? You, Guy. I'm not. I'm weak and I'm scared. I do these things and then live in dread," Siobhan said still holding Ian.

"Siobhan, most people are too scared to act in the first place. Strength is doing what's right in spite of your fears. That's what I admire about you. And I'm sure that goes for Guy and many others as well. You are the essence of strength to me."

Siobhan rested her head against his chest. "When I was a little girl, we used to go to church. I loved the sunny days when the light would stream through the stained glass windows. One was a beautiful Tiffany window called 'The River Jordan'. It must have been five meters tall, but narrow, only about a meter wide. At the top was a blue sky with puffy, white clouds. The sky merged with the yellow, gold and orange of a setting sun. There were mountains of purple in the background with a deep blue river streaming toward the foreground and tall trees in green fields on either side. I loved that window and would stare at it during the service. I'd imagine myself being with Jesus at the River Jordan. I felt so safe and loved sitting there between my parents. They'd look down at me and smile. I could see their love.

"But one Sunday the minister read the Psalm about walking through The Valley of the Shadow of Death. Somehow that stayed with me. I think that was when I began to realize that the world wasn't all sunshine and being with Jesus at the River Jordan. I began imagining walking through the Valley of the Shadow of Death. It was all dark brown and black rocks and mountains on either side, totally devoid of life. There was only one path through and I had to walk down it. I was a little girl walking alone, trying to be brave one step at a time.

"There were no lurking monsters; I think I could have handled that. What tore at my soul was being alone. My parents weren't there and never would be. I kept saying, 'I will fear no evil, for thou art with me. I will fear no evil, for thou art with me', but I couldn't imagine God or Jesus being in a place like that. I was alone as I walked through the valley.

"Don't get me wrong. I had a wonderful childhood with loving parents. I wasn't morbid. But I did walk through the Valley of the Shadow of Death in my mind; alone. I came out stronger, more self-sufficient, wanting to avoid caring about being alone.

"When I met Guy I began to open up again. And then we were going to have a baby! Oh God, I was so happy. My life was perfect. I was drenched in sunlight.

"But then my world crashed and I was alone again; empty." Looking up at Ian, she whispered, "Till I met you."

Ian looked deeply into her eyes. "I promise, you'll never be alone again." And he kissed her passionately.

After the kiss, Siobhan began moving her face against his and whispered, "Ian, I want you to make love to me."

The storm began tearing at her house as they walked up the dark stairway.

Undressing in the growing darkness of her bedroom, Siobhan recalled lines from Whitman's poems:

Behold me where I pass, hear my voice, approach,
Touch me, touch the palm of your hand to my body as I pass,
Be not afraid of my body.

Stop this day and night with me
And you shall possess the origin of all poems.

That night Siobhan was not afraid of the storm engulfing her – she embraced its passion and fury. As she straddled Ian and felt the warmth that was in her, she relived the now-delicious splendor of sunlight streaming through the skies over the River Jordan. And she was no longer afraid of the Valley of the Shadow of Death because Ian was with her.

Chapter 31
SUNDAY, JULY 12

Siobhan was jolted from a deep sleep by an almost imperceptible, yet well-defined short series of 'sponded pings. She sat up. "They've picked up Guy." Ian moved in his sleep. Siobhan gently massaged his face. "Ian, wake up, they've picked up Guy."

Ian propped himself on his elbow. "How do you know?"

"I gave him a 'spond alert to set off if the corpos came – a one-shot unit that gives off a short series of non-traceable pings before degrading into dust."

Ian looked at her intently. "Where did you get something like that?"

"How in God's name did they zero in on him so quickly? They must have been on to him already – ready to pick him up." Siobhan 'sponded the time and said, "It's 2:30am. If he's not back by about noon, it means it's more than just a 'downtown questioning', it means they've taken him to the interview center."

Ian sat up. "How'll you know if he's back and OK?"

"He has a similar 'all clear' unit that's well hidden.

"It's time to prepare for the worst while hoping for the best."

"Siobhan, I understand you thinking ignorance is the best protection. But I need some understanding. I won't let you face this alone."

Tears welled in Siobhan's eyes as she kissed Ian and then held him tightly. After several moments she said, "General knowledge can't hurt at this point. Set your 'sponder to search mode for the Phantom'ogger and let me know when you've found it and locked in so we can sync up."

Ian looked at her, mystified, but did as she said. After a few moments he said, "OK, I've got it." They began receiving the 'spond in sync mode. The 'spond started with an outside view of the LEPGen Technologies Research and Development facility on South Road just south of the Corporate limits of the City of Poughkeepsie. An obviously-disguised voice announced the location to the viewer, and went on briefly to describe some of its R&D programs.

But, the voice continued, there is a highly secret and highly restricted area within the facility that is doing experimental research involving living human fetuses, some of which were at the post-natal stage of development. As this description proceeded, the view shifted to an internal lab setting and closed in on rows of transparent artificial wombs, and finally to the individual fetuses at various stages of development within the containers.

The voice commented that the fetuses were obtained from the Poughkeepsie CaringMother facility, without the knowledge of the parents. The parents had only been told that the gestations had been terminated due to detected defects in the fetuses. These defects may or may not have been real.

At this point the view shifted to the rows of 'post-natal fetuses' lying naked in individual coffin-like beds, and zeroed in on their sleep-like angelic, sometimes tormented, faces. Siobhan looked over at Ian. He was continuing to concentrate on the 'spond, visibly trying to stifle his urge to cry.

The commentary continued, describing the types of experiments that were being performed on the fetuses, many of which caused pain and suffering. Toward the end of the 'spond, still images of Treadwell and the general managers of the LEPGen and CaringMother facilities came up, telling the viewer who the individuals were, and that the research was going on with their full knowledge. The voice also said that the knowledge did not stop there but went to the tops of those corporations and to the top of The Corporation.

The 'spond lasted about half an hour, and repeated automatically. It was obviously unmanned to prevent connection to the initiators. It would continue indefinitely till the corpos tracked it down and destroyed it. In the meantime, the corpos would try to jam the 'spond, but it would shift to a different frequency.

Shaking with tears on his face, Ian looked at Siobhan. "Now I understand. When I first came over yesterday I wanted to convince you to stop your activities – to let others carry the burden. But now I understand. I'm sorry I doubted you." And he took her in his arms.

After some minutes he said, "What do we do now?"

"We have to leave. If they're taking Guy to the interview center, he'll only be able to hold out so long. The trail will eventually lead to me."

"So let's go to my place. You haven't been there before, and our relationship isn't general knowledge. We should be safe there at least for a while."

"Yes, good idea. I'm going to pull together some things." She got up and noticed Ian studying her body. He got up and went to her, pressed his body up against hers and started running his hands over her.

Should she try to talk some sense into him? No! She had lived on the edge before and knew that she had to take advantage of precious moments. Siobhan welcomed his desires, his advances. When her breathing became heavy and raspy, Ian led her back to bed.

Siobhan leaned on her elbow and looked down at Ian's face and studied it. "No matter what happens, I know that I've been fulfilled, made whole. I can face whatever comes, because I've met you." Ian was about to speak, but she put her finger on his mouth. More words at this point could only diminish her message. She kissed him again and then rose, took a quick shower and got dressed.

While Ian showered, she began packing some essentials in an overnight bag, not wanting to attract attention when they walked out. When Ian came out of the shower, Siobhan was just putting a small package into her bag. Its tell-tale shade of purple caught Ian's attention.

"What's that?"

"Just some feminine supplies."

Ian pulled the package out of her bag and studied it. "I thought I recognized the Euthanesta purple. 'Premium Home Solution Kit'. What are you doing with this?"

Siobhan looked down at the package. "Ian, I know too much and have too many contacts. And now I've got to protect Spencer. I could never let the corpos find out about him. I have to keep them on hand."

"Them, you have more?"

"A few backups."

Ian walked over to the closet, found another of the purple packages, and put it in her bag. "If this becomes necessary, you won't be leaving this world alone," Ian said firmly.

Siobhan looked dejectedly at the package and sobbed, "This is why I didn't want to get romantically involved. The only thing keeping me going now is thinking of you still being alive if I do end things. I can't lose you."

"You won't. I'll be with you."

Ian held her as she cried softly.

Then Ian added, "And remember, I know about Spencer too. I wouldn't let those ghouls take him. I swore this to myself in Doodletown."

Siobhan finished packing, zipped the bag closed and Ian picked it up. As they walked down the hall, Siobhan looked into each room. Downstairs she also looked into each room, saying goodbye to all who had lived there, saying goodbye to her home. They both turned their transponders completely off, which made them untraceable but would also be considered an admission of guilt by the corpos if they were looking for them. As they walked out and closed the door, she thought of Whitman's words.

> Full of life now, compact, visible,
> I, forty year old the eighty-third year of the States,
> To one a century hence or any number of centuries hence,
> To you yet unborn these, seeking you.

Michael parked his car and rushed into the CBI building. The holoplay time indicated 4:52am. Connie would be pissed, but it couldn't be helped. Tony was already in the conference area, and judging from his concentration was replaying the 'spond. He saw Michael. "Looks pretty bad. I was trying to see when and who recorded it. Nothing yet. Did you get ahold of Lenora and Connie?"

"Yeah, Connie'll be in by 5:30. I always pegged you for the wilder one, but Lenora was still out partying. She should be in in a few minutes. Sorry I had to call you back in now."

Just then Lenora came in looking disheveled.

Michael smiled. "Ah, sweet Lenora – as pure as the driven snow – across a pile of coal!"

"... across a pile of coal? Has anyone living ever seen a pile of coal? God, Michael, where *do* you get these sayings?" Lenora said, holding her head.

Oh man, Michael thought, *now I'm going to have two bitchy females on my hands. Three counting Julianna when we were woken up at 3 o'clock.* He decided to back off. "Well, you do look like you had a good time. But like I told Tony, I really am sorry I had to drag you two back in this morning. Who knew a shit storm was going to start?

"The CBI 'spond monitors contacted me at 3. They had picked up this Phantom'ogger 'spond soon after midnight. They're working on tracking and shutting it down. They checked the roster and saw that I was working a case at the LEPGen facility on South Road, so they contacted me. I viewed it once and contacted Connie. She wanted to meet with the three of us here ASAP.

"By the way, I checked and Crawford had been picked up about 2:30," Michael continued. "They're softening him up as we speak."

While they were discussing the 'spond for any clues, Connie Chavez walked in looking cranky. She headed directly to the beverage dispenser to get a cup of coffee. Michael noticed Lenora didn't get down on Connie for being old fashioned in her drinks.

"OK, what's the status?"

"It's still cycling. No report on when they think they can shut it down. Even though the labs are indoors with no windows, the monitors could still analyze the ambient light and believed the recording was done at night. Given there didn't appear to be any other people around, it was probably done on the graveyard shift. But no idea how long ago – yesterday morning or when."

"What about that likely, what's his name?"

"Guy Crawford? They picked him up at about 2:30 this morning, but they haven't gotten anything out of him yet."

"How about the worm?"

"We'll be heading to the center as soon as we're done here. We'll see what they have and determine if the worm is necessary." When Connie gave him her questioning 'What?' look, he continued, "Look Connie, I want to be comfortable that softening didn't work. If he's done something there's still a chance he'll 'fess up with just the softening. Once the worm's turned on, there's no turning back. He'll just be an empty shell by the end. So if the worm doesn't work, as sometimes happens, we'll be screwed. Also, if you use the worm, taking him to trial is no longer an option."

"It's your call. But as soon as we're done, I'll have to 'spond Treadwell and Colson. If they haven't heard yet, the shit'll hit the fan then. So that's when the stopwatch starts for you. Colson will demand a meeting today and expect this to come to closure then. We can't control the tracking down and elimination of the Phantom'ogger 'spond. But she'll want some heads on a platter by then. So you'd better have something good. I'll 'spond them when you leave here, and I'll try to give you twelve hours, which means a 6pm meeting. We'll probably have to head to her place in Millbrook, so plan on at least 45 minutes travel time."

Michael knew that both his job and career were on the line. And he also understood that Connie was not the one who controlled his professional fate. Colson did. Whenever an executive was involved in a case that closed well, she would either move on, leaving those in charge with a job and future potential. Or she'd give the nod and they'd be considered for a raise and possibly a promotion. But if things didn't go well, the exec would certainly give a thumbs down. He knew Colson wouldn't want to hear that he'd been working with fluff so far. Until the 'ogger 'spond, which was a crime, they had no solid proof that any crime had been committed.

Well, at least he had twelve hours to lock up this case. This was an infinity when dealing with an executive and things weren't going well. He appreciated Connie watching is back, though her skin was in the game too. She wanted to give him as much time as possible to lock things down; it would make her look good too. If Colson wanted something unreasonable, like to have a meeting by noon, they'd be doomed.

Just as Michael, Lenora and Tony were ready to head out the door, Connie came out of her office. "I 'sponded Colson's assistant. He said she has a dinner party tonight at 6 at her Millbrook estate, so he said we'd have to meet with her at 5 at the latest in Millbrook. Keep me posted during the day, but be here at the latest at 3:30 for a briefing and strategy session. I don't want to do it in the limo she'll send us. She'll have it bugged."

Chapter 32

The Mid-Hudson Valley Interview Center was located about ten kilometers northeast of Poughkeepsie. Since Poughkeepsie had the largest population concentration in the valley and was in the middle of the valley, it had been the logical place to locate the center. At ten kilometers, it was close enough to be convenient and far enough out to be rarely seen by anyone.

It was a state-of-the-art facility, built from the ground up in an abandoned subdivision. Its windowless cube-design spoke of order and efficiency for the diversity of activities that took place inside. This was where people were brought for anything beyond routine questioning. There was the reception area where interviewees were processed, administrative offices, interview rooms, advanced interview rooms, holding rooms, cells, overnight accommodations for interviewers working on important cases.

The "great hall" extended out the back from the main building. It contained evidence for the short period required, as well as the remains of the individuals who had been disappeared. Beyond, and detached from the main building, was the site crematorium. A tall electrified fence ran around the perimeter. Beyond that, surrounding woods had been encouraged to grow to keep curious eyes away from the site.

As Michael, Tony and Lenora pulled up to the guard at the gate, Michael shuddered involuntarily, recalling the first time he had visited. The center was a necessary evil, most of his colleagues would say. He glanced at Lenora and Tony. They seemed to be in awe, like Hansel and Gretel coming upon the witch's house in the forest. He wondered how they'd feel when they left.

"Director Fitzgerald will meet you in the lobby," the guard said after all three in the car had displayed their holobadges.

As they approached the front entrance, Michael remembered how the drab, dirty, pale gray exterior pronounced "All hope abandon, ye who enter here".

The surrounding woods looked deceptively beautiful. Green, brown, lush with birds calling out. But that was another world, beyond the surrounding fence. For most, those woods would be the last thing of beauty, of nature, they would see.

The large, dark, recessed entrance way opened up to swallow them.

The lobby was small by contrast to the exterior doors. There were several easy chairs and couches placed around. Sean Fitzgerald was waiting for them at a counter, across from a stern-looking guard in uniform.

"Michael, good to see you again – and after only a week! All these years, and now we're bumping into each other all the time!" He and Michael bowed but then Sean put his arm over Michael's shoulder.

"Sean, it's my pleasure," Michael said as he turned and introduced Lenora and Tony.

"Michael's *the* master detective. Pay close attention and you'll learn everything you need to know. Michael and I were colleagues, but I always viewed him as my role model. He's a natural.

"They call me director, but as the new kid I'm just an assistant director, one of three. That's why I'm here on the weekend. We AD's take turns doing weekends and nights. There's always a director on duty here since there's always activity, day and night. Director-level decisions have to be made," Sean said. "Well, let's get you processed and we'll go in."

In contrast to Sean's cheery disposition, the guard wore a permanent scowl as he processed each of them.

After processing, the large internal door made a swooshing noise, sounding like an old-fashioned vault opening up. Michael looked back through the front glass doors to catch a glimpse of the last natural light he'd see while at the center. The door swooshed and clicked shut, locking them in to the massive vault that was the interview center.

They walked down a narrow, dirty-yellow corridor. On either side were cell-like processing rooms. Judging from faint voices, most appeared to be occupied. A busy night. One door opened and they caught a glimpse of utter terror on the face of the woman being processed. Michael saw concern registering on Lenora's and Tony's faces. Michael thought sadly, *You ain't seen nothin' yet, kids.*

At the end of that corridor, they paused before another large door. Once they were scanned, the door clicked and swooshed open. Now they heard faint crying and screaming that even extensive insulation couldn't block. *Was that the desired effect?* Michael wondered. *Don't let the place sound like Bedlam, but let enough sounds through to send a message.*

After zigzagging down several corridors, Sean paused in front of a door. It clicked open for him, and they walked in. It was a long, narrow, dimly-lit room, with only a table and several chairs placed around it. Three of the walls were bare, but the fourth wall was a built-in mirror.

Sean invited them to sit. "This is nothing new to Michael, and I'm sure you two heard a version of it at the academy, but since this is your first time here, let's make sure you understand some of the basics. As a general rule, 'street agents' do not come here. You do your work. Then we pick up the suspects, interview them, and handle them from there.

"This solid wall between us? It's there for a good reason. The Corporation wants you out there using your well-developed detective skills, ferreting out those who are, or may be, committing crimes against The Corporation. Once you've done your job, you can move on to your next case. That's the way it should be.

"The Corporation doesn't want you wringing your hands about what's going to happen to the perps after we pick them up. Agonizing over whether someone's guilty isn't your worry; we'll take care of determining that. No distractions. No losing your edge. Can't let the criminals get away, can we?

"You're here because this is an important, high-profile case that needs to be resolved quickly. In fact, as I understand from Connie Chavez, by 3:30 this afternoon. That doesn't give us a lot of time, so we're expediting the case, and have your suspect in an advanced interview room next door," Sean continued as he glanced over at the mirror. "Now, we're going to change the mirror to see-through for us.

"You might ask why we don't just use virtual walls in a state-of-the-art facility like this, instead of old-fashioned one-way viewing mirrors. Well, the design of everything here has been thought through in great detail to achieve greatest effect. If we used a virtual wall, a perp would not necessarily know he's being observed. Plus virtual walls give a sense of openness, of freedom, of the possibility of escape.

"Psychologists have found that people have watched so many old crime movies with one-way mirrors, that using them makes the perps feel vulnerable and at a disadvantage. You know, 'they can see me, but I can't see them'." Sean paused and asked if there were any questions.

When there weren't, Sean stood up and went over to the mirror. Once he pushed a button, they were able to see into the advanced interview room. It was a bare, cinderblock room with a rough tile floor and a drain in the middle. There was a hose and bucket in one corner and a long narrow table along the wall.

A naked, drenched man sat on a stool at one end of the room. His feet were perched up on the rungs. His face was bruised, as if repeatedly slapped. No other bruises were apparent on the rest of his body. Michael looked at Tony and Lenora. He could imagine what they were thinking.

"Normally we take suspects to interview rooms first. They're often so scared that they confess everything right away. But if after a day or two, we don't make any progress, we move them to an advanced interview room like this for more aggressive interview techniques.

"Typically we strip them first and make them sit on those uncomfortable stools. Humiliation works very well for many. So for men, we use women interviewers and for women, men. After quizzing them for some time, the interviewer leaves the room. Alone for the first time, the suspects will often relieve themselves in the drain. The interviewer comes back in and berates them for what they've done and hoses them down, tells them to get back on their stool, and leaves the room again. The rooms are kept cool, so the perps will typically start shivering at this point. You'd be surprised at how many holdouts confess at this point.

"But if they don't, we move on to enhanced interview techniques like waterboarding and mild physical inducement – mostly slapping. We also use threats, like rape or castration, though we don't carry through on them, of course. I hate to see things move to this level.

"It is all perfectly acceptable and legal. The Supreme Court ruled long ago that none of this so far is torture, but necessary interview techniques. Fortunately, a large majority of the remaining perps confess at this point.

"As you can see, we've accelerated your suspect's interview to a level in a matter of hours that would normally have taken a day or two. By the way, your preliminary report was very helpful in guiding us."

"Looking at his profile and initial interview, I'd have expected him to confess by now. But he's toughing it out. 93% of perps would have snapped by now, and 98% of the 'soft types' like him. We'll get through to him."

Michael 'sponded the time. It was almost 8:30. He cleared his throat. "So what do you suggest next?" Michael's voice seemed to break Lenora and Tony out of a trance.

"Normally, some form of torture, which I really hate. It'd be hard to bring him to trial then, if that's what you decided you wanted to do. And I just don't think he's going to crack quickly, so it'd probably just be a waste of precious time."

"So what you're saying is you need to move on to the worm," Michael said looking intently at Sean.

"Yes. Unfortunately. It's so much better to get conscious, free-will confessions and disclosures of colleagues. We only use the worm as a last resort. It's only about 75% effective and it's irreversible. If it doesn't work, at the end his mind will be so far gone that you'll have lost any chance of retrieving what was in there through other means."

"How about truth serum?"

"Less effective. People can just game it. Plus it takes time."

"Damn!" Then after a few seconds, Michael asked, "Do you have an OI analyzer trained on him?"

"Sure, we always do."

"A good one? Not that worthless Natalie model?"

"Natalie!" Sean said laughing. "God no, we got rid of her years ago!" When he looked at their pained expressions, he continued, "You're not still using her are you? She's just an incompetent, self-righteous bitch!"

"Tell me!" Michael said.

"We have the newest model, Sofia, an S model."

"OK, make sure she's zoomed in on him. We've got one shot at his flank before he can adjust his guard. Put me on the intercom and disguise my voice."

"OK, push that red button and hold it while talking,"

Michael looked at the others, and then down at the button he pushed. "Hello Guy, this is a friend speaking."

Guy Crawford looked up, startled. "Who are you?"

"A friend who doesn't want to see you hurt. Guy, you know that they'll keep advancing their techniques on you till they get what they want. But each level does more permanent damage. Won't you tell them what they want?"

"Fuck you! I didn't do anything!"

"Guy, I fully understand why you did what you did. Having lost your son in a termination, I fully understand why you sabotaged the research at LEPGen."

Guy said nothing, but a slight flinch was visible to Michael and the others.

Michael took a wild stab in the dark. "It was even more difficult for your wife, so I understand why she helped you."

Guy's brow dropped slightly, and it appeared that tears were welling in his eyes.

"Look, Guy. Confess. We already know everything and understand. There were enough clues in the Phantom'ogger 'spond to prove that you did that recording on your graveyard shift. So please confess and save yourself suffering."

Guy just continued looking down at the floor.

Michael released the button and said, "OK, have Sofia do a total analysis of his reactions and have her 'spond me her results. I hit a soft spot. In fact two. His son and his ex-wife. Then start on a mild truth serum. Not that super stratum crap. That'll scramble his brain as much as the worm. It remains to be seen whether we'll take him to trial. I want to be convinced before you use the worm that he's the saboteur, or we'll just be facing the same problems down the road with the real perp. Get what you can out of him on the serum, zeroing in on his child and his ex-wife. And get back to me by 2 on what that produces. We're going to pay his ex-wife a visit."

Just as Michael, Lenora and Tony walked out the door, Michael turned back to Sean. "Why don't you dry that poor son-of-a bitch off and put some clothes on him. At this point a little humanity might be in order."

Chapter 33

"I can't get a lock on her location," Tony said looking at the holoscreen in Michael's car as they were driving back into Poughkeepsie. "Her 'sponder's either inoperable or she's turned it off. God, I wish they didn't have that 'off' option!"

"Yeah, but remember when they tried that model with no 'off'? And those hackers started frying people's brains? Ya gotta have an out." Michael countered.

"Well, if she's turned it off, she's got something to hide."

"You can assume that," Michael said. "Any 'spond tracing available?"

"No. Apparently she was never a person of interest, nor any one 'sponding her. So we'll have to work with the Corporate Security Agency. You know how bureaucratic they are. It'll take days."

"OK," Michael said as he looked over at Tony. These were the first complete sentences any of them had spoken since they left the center. Michael could only guess what was going through the minds of these first-time visitors to the center. On the surface they both looked despondent. He'd have to lighten up the mood if he were to keep them charging ahead.

"Let's go directly to her house and see what we can find there. Is Sophia done with her analysis yet?"

After a pause, Tony said, "In a minute."

"Have her tri-spond it to us in audio format as soon as she's done. I'll control the pause mode; I don't want it to interfere with my driving," Michael said as he studied the road ahead.

"Why don't you just put the car in auto-drive?" Lenora said in an irritated voice from the back seat.

"Call me old fashioned but I've never really trusted auto-drive. It's supposedly fail-safe in the higher-end models, but these lower-end crates have always had glitches."

"Oh, you're way beyond old fashioned, Michael. You're a Neanderthal! You're just too macho not to have personal control of your car – as well as other moving objects!"

Michael studied her face in the mirror and thought he detected a slight smile at the end. Maybe he could wedge in some levity at this point. "Hey, don't insult the Neanderthals! They were very easy-going, loving, family men, even though they were a bit on the husky, hairy side – like their women. If it hadn't been for the leavening influence of their interbreeding with Tony's European ancestors, Tony here would be a friggin' serial killer!"

"Sheee-it! Says Genghis Khan over here," Tony said laughing. "I'll have you know, the Neanderthals never made it down to Sicily, where most of my ancestors came from!"

"There ya go! If they *had* made it down there, maybe we wouldn't have had to deal with the Mafia!" Michael said grinning at Tony.

"Yo, Guido! Dis bum's gonna be sleepin' wid da fishes tonight," Tony proclaimed.

"Boys, boys, Sophia's trying to 'spond us!" Lenora interrupted.

Still chuckling, Michael accepted the 'spond and they all listened to Sophia's report. Sophia's fine-tuned analytical abilities were far beyond the N models like Natalie. But she also had a slightly deep, breathy voice with a hint of an Italian accent. Michael and Tony listened with both concentration and dreamy smiles on their faces. The OI modelers had found that an exotic name and exactly Sophia's voice was the best way to get male agents' attention. She got their attention. The problem was keeping them on message. That would be improved in the new Teresa model.

Lenora listened intently.

Sophia apologized for taking so long, but she had wanted to be thorough and explore every angle and nuance. She reported that when Michael had mentioned Guy Crawford's son, 23% of his reaction was due to remorse and sadness combined, but fully 47% was his concern about being discovered hiding something. The rest was various categories, each of which registered as non-significant. Moreover, when Michael mentioned his ex-wife, 21% of his reaction was due to remorse and sadness, but a full 41% was registered as concern about being discovered hiding something, *and* 17% was a wish to protect her from looming harm.

Sophia concluded that Crawford had been involved in a crime and that it was a statistical certainty that his ex-wife had helped him in some way. She further let them know that this was just a high-level summary – that she was 'sponding them a complete, detailed report in trial-evidence formant.

Michael 'sponded back to Sophia, thanking her for her help, that it had been a pleasure working with her and that he looked forward to working with her when she became available out on the street.

"Why thank you, Michael. I've certainly heard a great deal about you. That was a very astute way of ferreting vital responses out of your suspect. I admired your subtle touch in calling his ex-wife his 'wife'. That enabled his true feelings to surface, where saying 'ex-wife' could have connoted negative feelings, enabling him to continue to hide his emotions. Michael, I hope you don't mind me saying that you are a real master at what you do. I admire your skills and abilities a great deal."

"It's very nice to be appreciated, Sophia," Michael 'sponded back, beaming as he looked at Tony and Lenora. "You're a true model of a perfect lady. If I weren't married and you had human form, I know how and where I'd be concentrating my attention!"

"Michael, you *are* a naughty boy! Goodbye till we meet again."

"Goodbye, sweet Sophia."

"Oh my God, Michael! 'Perfect lady'? 'Sweet Sophia'?" Lenora said shaking her hear. "You do know that she's just a bunch of noodles, don't you!"

"Yes, but she's also an ideal of perfection. That's the way the modelers designed her," Michael shot back.

"Think about those modelers' objectives," Tony said, looking out the window at the passing scenery. "She's perfect alright – a perfect inquisitor. She was probably trying to get a better read on you in case she has to work on you some day."

"Hmmpf!" Michael puffed out as he whipped around a curve faster than was safe.

They pulled up on a side street about a block from where Siobhan lived. From there they could observe her house without being too obvious. They tried 'sponding her, tried to get a fix on her whereabouts, all to no avail. While observing the house, they 'sponded more information on her.

Carlson had not remarried, did not have a steady boyfriend, or other known close friends, for that matter. She had kept the house in the divorce settlement. She worked for EvalProm in their student assessment division. Excellent work record. She had never had a run in with the law and seemed to be a model citizen. "I hope we're not chasing up the wrong tree here. We don't have time," Michael said exasperated.

Finally he said, "OK, Lenora, get your rain gear on and walk at a normal pace over to her house and knock on the door. If she's there, identify who you are and that we would like to ask her a few questions. If she's not there, back off a few steps till we have a chance to scan the outside immediately around the door.

Lenora hopped out of the car and quickly put her rain gear on. Although last night's storm had moved out, there continued to be periods of stinging, driving showers that required effective rain gear for exposure to weather for more than a brief moment. Michael and Tony watched Lenora intently as she walked down the street toward Siobhan's house, also watching the other houses for signs of nosey neighbors. Everything looked normal as Lenora walked up the steps and rang the bell first. She then tried knocking. When no one answered, she backed off a few paces and 'sponded them.

Michael and Tony walked up to the house at a normal pace and went up the steps. "Did you notice anything of interest on your way over or while you were knocking?" Michael asked.

"Her neighbor to the left seems interested. The curtain in the side first-floor window moved a bit."

"OK. Tony, scan the area around the front door. Try to be discrete."

Tony did a quick scan and said, "Nothing. Not surprising with this weather."

Michael looked briefly up and down the street. "Vibe the door."

Tony put the scanner back in his raincoat pocket and pulled out a lock vibrator that would simultaneously vibrate open the old fashioned lock and disable the security alarm the scan had detected. After Tony popped open the door, the three of them went in. Tony proceeded to scan the front hall, dining room and parlor.

"A lot of recent activity in the hallway but not in the front rooms," Tony reported. So they moved toward the back and into the kitchen. "Recent activity in here. And I'm picking up three recent, separate DNA's. No known perps. I'll get an analysis going as soon as we get back to the office."

Even after all these years, Michael still felt creepy searching through someone's house without their permission or knowledge. This house was quiet for such an old one; very quiet. He was surprised that he didn't even notice any rattling windows from the whipping wind outside. It was almost as if some presence that didn't like them being there were sucking the air out of their surroundings. As they walked back into the hallway, Michael went to the front door and opened it.

"Michael, what're you doing? An open door could make people curious. Plus you're disturbing the scan," Tony said in an irritated voice.

"Just wanted some fresh air. It's stuffy in here," Michael said as he reluctantly closed the door. He felt confined again. He was probably just spooked from being at the interview center this morning. That place always gave him claustrophobia for a day or two.

As they walked up the shadowy stairs, he would have liked to hear them creak. But there was no sound. He was having a hard time breathing. He felt he was being watched; stalked while he was stalking.

"It's stuffy in here," Lenora remarked as they walked toward the front bedroom. "These old houses always give me the creeps; all those past lives."

As they approached the open bedroom door, Tony said, "Only two recent DNA's up here."

Scanning the made bed, Tony reported that there was still ambient warmth in the bed; somebody or bodies had slept here last night. They looked around the room – decorated with a feminine touch – soft yellow, lace, many pillows. Looking in the closet, all the clothing was women's, apparently of the same petite size. Poking further back in the closet, Tony produced a single, purple package.

"Hmmm. Euthanesta Premium Home Solution," Tony read.

"Any more back there?" Michael asked.

"Nope."

Michael studied the package and said, "With her excellent work record, I'm sure she's designated a high-priority asset by The Corporation. So she can't have that legally. Only low priorities can get those if they prefer to terminate at home. She must have gotten that on the black market. So it's contraband in her possession. Put it in my trunk when we leave. We may need it as evidence."

"Probably prefers that to being dragged into the interview center," Tony guessed as he continued to read the label, adding, "I know I would."

"Don't jump to conclusions on why she has that kit," Lenora said from the doorway. "Come and take a look at the next bedroom."

The three of them went into the next bedroom. The light blue room had one wall decorated with a rainbow and puffy clouds painted above a green field. Friendly animals romped around in it. Spaced around the room were shelves, a chest of drawers, a dressing table, a rocking chair with reading lamp, and a baby bed with a mobile of birds suspended above it. Tony scanned the room and found no recent activity in it, though there was no evidence of dust.

"A well-maintained shrine," Tony observed. "How long ago was their son terminated? Over two years, wasn't it?"

"Or a dream deferred – or terminated," Lenora said in a soft, sad voice. "Maybe the Euthanesta was there in case she couldn't live with this anymore. I could understand that. But I can't understand how she could have stayed here after what happened – the termination and divorce. I would have been long gone. She's either a very strong individual – or devoid of feelings."

All three stood in the stillness, looking around the room, trying to figure out who this Siobhan Carlson was. Why had she stayed in this house and not remodeled this room? Did she come in here often, looking around the room, as they were, imagining a toddler playing with the toys now so neatly put away in the shelves? Did she sit down in the chair, rocking her child who no longer was?

They slowly backed out of the room, respectfully taking their leave. Quietly, they looked through the rest of the house. Finding nothing, they went to the front door.

"OK, we've got to get back to the office. Connie'll be waiting for us and we need to fill her in and strategize for our meeting with Colson. Tony, 'spond the Poughkeepsie police and tell them we want this place kept under discrete surveillance. Let's go out and make sure the door locks again. Under the slim chance she returns, I don't want her noticing someone had been here. But I think she's on to us and in hiding."

They went out, carefully checking the lock to be sure it was still holding. Then they hurriedly walked up the street toward Michael's parked car. Michael noticed a tall man wrapped up in his rain gear walking toward them but across the street. As he passed, Michael caught a glimpse of his partially-exposed face. Something about him rang a tiny bell in Michael's head, but he didn't have time to dwell on what it might be. He stored it for later.

Chapter 34

"So we've got one perp who's admitted to sabotaging the project and a suspect on the run?" Connie asked. She was well-rested and wide awake now.

"Crawford admitted to altering the music that was being used in testing the fetuses," Michael said slowly and deliberately, trying to be objective. "He said he had done this to alleviate their suffering, not to sabotage the project. He said he had done all this of his own volition with no help from anyone else. He further insisted that he hadn't done the recording for the Phantom'ogger.

"He said all this while under a truth serum. I didn't want to get more aggressive yet. Sophia, their new S-model OI analyst, believes he's telling the truth about altering the music, but not about the recording. She believes he's trying to protect someone – his ex-wife, if she was the one who helped him."

"Any luck on tracking down and stopping the 'ogger 'spond?"

"No, they're working on it. They hope to have it locked down by late day tomorrow."

"Colson's gonna be pissed. I wish we had better news on that front," Connie said looking thoughtfully at the table. "OK, Colson's limo is waiting for us outside. Again, let me do the talking. And let's keep things light in the limo. I have no doubt that Colson's assistant will be listening in to whatever we say. Treadwell's been out of town over the weekend and she'll meet us at Colson's. Oh, and guys, good work. I know it hasn't been easy."

The grandeur and opulence evident in the Millbrook Executive Patent never ceased to amaze Michael. It was hard to comprehend that each estate they saw tucked away in the scenic hills, with all its fields, woods, horses and other animals, stables, guest houses and stately manor contained only one executive and her family, if she had one. And her hired help. He couldn't help but admire the beauty streaming before his eyes.

He looked over at Lenora and Tony. Were they wondering what they'd have to do to end up out here? In their next thought they'd realize that their chances were zero, and then they'd think about rising to a director level like Connie so they could enjoy the amenities of a gated community. Michael had thought the same things when he first rode out to the Patent as a fresh CBI recruit. He smiled now at his naïveté; at theirs.

He pondered his contentment with what he had obtained. He wouldn't trade his life with Julianna for a life in any of these estates without her. Julianna. He wished he could be with her more right now; that he could tell her about his work, about the excitement of the detective chase, but also about his fears and nightmares. Julianna would be going with Caitlin and Bill to the Buddhist temple this evening. He wished he could be more spiritual, less cynical. Well, he guessed it went with the territory.

He was so proud of the direction Caitlin had found in her life. He was very fond of Bill and the support and love he showed for Caitlin. Now he'd be joining their family. And soon they'd have a little one running around! Michael envisioned himself sitting in a chair, reading to his grandson. Grandson? Why did he assume that? Didn't Caitlin say she was going to have a girl?

The chair was an old-fashioned rocking chair, like the one in Carlson's house. The reading lamp shed its light in their immediate area, while all around them was darkness. It was almost as though they were in the safety of a snow globe, protected from the world around them. Michael was happy and content with this image of his future.

But why was he sitting with his grandson in Carlson's rocking chair and not in his own easy chair at home? He had to get closer. As he did so in his day dream, the head of dark hair looked up. It wasn't him – it was Siobhan Carlson looking up at him, smiling radiantly. When the small head of dark hair looked up, he saw it wasn't his grandson. This little boy had light blue eyes like his mother.

"Michael, are you OK?" Connie asked.

Michael looked up and saw the concern on Connie's face. "Yeah. Just tired. Really tired. I'll be glad when this case is over." He had wanted to add he wasn't convinced justice would be done.

"Look, when this is over, I'm going to give all three of you some time off and a 'Night-Out-in-Manhattan' award, so you can go have a great dinner and see a Broadway show. Just hang in there a few more days and I'm sure we'll have it wrapped up."

Yeah, that's what I'm afraid of, Michael thought, though he smiled and thanked Connie. Michael liked her. She watched out for her people. But her career took precedence over everything else. And if that meant locking down a case with speed over justice, then so be it. He gave Lenora and Tony a reassuring smile and then looked back out the window of the cruising Duesenberg at the idyllic scenes that floated before his eyes.

As they drove through the massive gate at Colson's estate, Michael looked up at the hand-hewn granite relief of the CaringMother mother cradling her child and shuddered. He noticed that the swans were out of the water and huddling under the mature towering shade trees along the long, winding drive leading up to the manor house. They were probably frightened by the changing weather and especially the occasional bolts of lightning that could easily hit them if they were out on the lake.

As they pulled up under the *porte cochere*, he saw Colson herself out in front of the massive entrance way, directing the Hispanic-looking yard hands, who in turn were trying to chase the swans back into the lake. Off to the side was a gigantic, multiple-peaked, enclosed white tent with people scurrying in and out. Colson looked frustrated – not a good omen for their upcoming meeting.

"Hello Ms. Colson. As you requested, we're here to give you a briefing on the situation at LEPGen," Connie said as the four all bowed toward Colson, who did not bow in return.

"Do you have any idea how inconvenient this is?! Look at this mess! My guests will start arriving in half-an-hour and the weather is totally non-cooperative! I imported special oriental swans to decorate the lake for my guests to see when they come up the drive. But they're afraid of lightening and up under the trees! So *I* have to come out and get my lazy yard hands after them! And, of course, nothing's ready in the tent. It's a disaster! Now you! Well, come in. We may as well make things a complete disaster!"

She stormed in through the front door, her butler having opened it at the last second. The others followed, with Connie offering profuse apologies.

This time they went into a large library, with many old and expensive-looking volumes on the shelves. Emma Treadwell was already there, studying the titles. She turned and greeted them. On one wall hung a large, dark portrait of Dutch merchants. *Probably a Rembrandt,* Michael thought. *Original, of course.*

There was comfortable-looking antique furniture, but Colson turned around and said, "OK, let's have it," without offering them a seat. So they stood in a circle. Connie succinctly recounted the happenings of the past week, leading up to the arrest and interrogation of Guy Crawford and his admission.

"This Crawford guy works for you Dr. Treadwell?" Colson snapped.

"Yes, graveyard shift."

"This is a highly sensitive project. Don't you check out your people?" Colson asked, becoming even more agitated.

"Yes, thoroughly. You can't always predict the human factor in cases like these. Who knew he'd have been so upset about his son's termination?"

"It's your job to predict! How did you zero in on Crawford?"

Connie stepped in. "It was Lenora Davis here who finally cracked the code. She added up a number of vague clues and realized Crawford was their man. I'm going to see that she gets special recognition for her outstanding work and a promotion to detective as soon as the case is completed." Connie saw the surprised look on the others' faces and gave Michael a "Don't-say-a-word!" look.

Colson smiled. "It's good to see us girls getting ahead in a man's occupation. Men have dominated police work for too long! I'll be keeping an eye on your progress, young lady."

"Actually, Ms. Colson, we've worked as a team on this," Michael said much to the Connie's chagrin. "Lenora has done an excellent job and certainly is deserving of praise and promotion, but Tony Ragusini was also very instrumental."

Ignoring Michael's comment, Colson turned to him and said, "Detective Chan. You interviewed my employee, Jonathan Raston, without his manager being present. My understanding is you scared her off. That's totally unacceptable. I believe you got into restricted areas in that conversation. That presents a serious confidentiality problem."

"We needed him to be open and honest, not being restrained by his management. That's the way we've been interviewing Dr. Treadwell's employees," Michael said in his defense, ignoring Connie's barbed looks at him.

"And yesterday, you weren't able to handle a situation, so you ran to Connie and dragged her into your work."

"If you're referring to our requesting CaringMother information on Guy Crawford and your QC director blocking our efforts to get that information – then yes, unfortunately I had no choice but to get Connie involved. If we had been unimpeded, maybe we could have prevented the Phantom'ogger from getting ahold of the recording from LEPGen."

Glaring at Michael, Colson asked, "So what are you going to do now? We're in damage control, producing counter 'sponds to the Phantom. But immeasurable damage has already been done."

"The CBI 'spond monitoring division is working full speed at tracking the 'sponds down and stopping them," Michael answered. "They hope to have it done by this time tomorrow."

"Tomorrow?!" Colson fumed. "Do you have any idea how much damage can be done to CaringMother and LEPGen by then. Dr. Treadwell, is this acceptable to LEPGen?"

"Certainly not!" Treadwell said firmly, speaking her first two words of the evening.

"Ms. Colson, I'm putting every bit of pressure on the situation that I can," Connie interjected. "I'm in constant contact with the director of the monitoring division."

"Inspector Chan, what about Crawford and the fugitive?" Colson asked.

"Well, before we begin using more aggressive techniques to get the full truth out of him, we first have to determine if he'll be going to trial."

"Trial? Are you out of your mind? This problem must be concluded and disappear now!" Colson said loudly and firmly.

After a pause, Colson continued in a controlled, but seething, voice, looking from one to the next, "Here's what you're going to do. First, you will use any necessary means to pump the full story out of Crawford; then he will disappear. Then you will find his ex-wife and anyone else involved in this, pump them as well, and then they will disappear. Do you understand?"

Michael was about to remind her that it wasn't certain that Crawford's ex-wife was involved, but Connie headed him off and said, "Yes."

"And I want Raston to disappear as well," Colson said still fuming.

"Why, what's he done?" Michael demanded.

"It's not what he's done; it's what you've done. You pumped him for information he shouldn't have given out. Now he's tainted, unreliable."

"But you personally gave him an award last year. He has a wife and a child."

Colson turned to Connie and gave her a "get-control-of-your-employee!" look.

"We'll take that under advisement, Ms. Colson," Connie said.

"Good. Needless to say, I want you to keep me posted at each milestone; closing down the Phantom, breaking Crawford, disappearing all accomplices."

"We most certainly will, Ms. Colson!" Connie said as they opened the door and began filing out of the room.

"Just a minute, Inspector Chan." Michael stepped aside and let the others go out the door. He could hear their footsteps receding as they walked down the flagstone floor in the main hall.

When it was clear that they were out of earshot, Colson continued, "Chan, I had another unreliable employee who gave something of mine to one of your snitches. I'm holding you personally responsible for getting that back to me. Either you have it or you know where it is. I'm sure that weasel made you aware of it."

"If you're referring to Dan Schmitt, he wasn't a snitch or a weasel. He was my friend. And I don't know what you're talking about. But if something of yours turns up, I'll see that you get it back."

"See that you do," and just as Michael was ready to walk out she said, "You don't like me, do you?"

Michael stared at her for a few seconds. "You use up people and toss them carelessly into the trash heap, whether your employees, my friend, or those children, born and unborn, in the LEPGen lab and God knows where else. Tell me something. Where's your family, your husband, your children? Has all this grandeur bought you happiness?"

Colson studied Michael intently. "You admired my Tompion clock, didn't you? You said you collect clocks as well. Maybe we're not so different. We both appreciate and collect clocks, though in a different price range. But we both feed our collections on the lives of others. I, through my business transactions. And you, through the criminals you track down and make disappear. No. We're not so different."

Michael did not retort. She was right.

Chapter 35

Michael found the others waiting on the front steps under the *porte cochere*. "What did Ms. Colson want?" Connie asked.

"Oh, to extend her condolences on the Oracle's demise."

"Michael, don't get flippant with me! What's going on between you two?" Connie demanded.

"You'll be the first to know if I figure that one out," Michael said. "Where's the limo?"

"Apparently over at the neighbor's helipad picking up some of Ms. Colson's guests for tonight. We'll have to wait."

"Perfect," Michael huffed.

They watched the Bugatis, Pierce-Arrows, Duesenbergs and other resurrected super-luxury brands come drive up under the *porte cochere*, letting their passengers out. Two of the doormen ran down the steps to assist the passengers, while the one who remained pushed Michael and the others further away from the doorway till they were exposed to the drizzle.

Can't have the hired help crowding the doorway when the corporate gods are ascending, Michael thought. He finally walked off from the others in disgust. They were just the rent-a-cops to these immortals, just keeping the other riff-raff in line. *No,* Michael thought sadly. *Colson and I aren't that different. She just gets paid more for her inhumanity.*

As Michael strolled over to the protection of an overhang on one of the towers, he wondered what Julianna was doing at that moment. Probably getting ready to go to the Buddhist temple with Caitlin. They'd go without

Bill. Like Michael, Bill wasn't much into Buddhism; at least not yet. Knowing Caitlin's determination, that would change. He'd have to take Bill out for a few drinks and sniffs soon, and talk a little backbone into that boy! Michael chuckled to himself. Nah. He wasn't going to rock that boat.

He tried 'sponding Carlson again, just in case. Nope. She was definitely in hiding. But where? Michael thought back about their visit to her house. There wasn't anything incriminating in their quick peruse, nor any hints as to where she could have gone. They'd have to go back to the house tomorrow. He was too tired now.

He thought about when they had walked out the door and shut it. Somehow it had felt like closing the door to a tomb. Swoosh, click. Probably the willies from the interview center earlier. Or thinking about Carlson's survival prospects. He visualized his closing the door and the three of them turning around to leave.

Recalling that instant now, he saw that the man walking on the other side of the street had been looking at them but had immediately looked straight ahead when they turned toward him. *That's* what had caught Michael's subconscious attention. And in spite of the man being wrapped up in his rain gear, his face was partially visible. Now that Michael had a chance to drag that short glance out and look at it, there was something familiar with that small scrap of face he had seen. Something related to Bill.

He quickly 'sponded Bill and asked him the name of his friend Michael and Julianna and met yesterday.

Ian Vanderkill, was the response.

He said he was going out for the evening, do you know where?

No, but I would assume to his new girlfriend's.

And what's her name?

After a pause, the response came back: *Siobhan Carlson.*

Michael looked back at the others huddled together. He tried 'sponding Vanderkill, but like Carlson, his transponder was turned off or inoperable. They were at his place. He was sure. If he told Connie she'd have the interview center henchmen pick them up immediately. She'd then wait in the drizzle till she got the confirmation that they had been picked up, and rush breathlessly in to Colson's assistant and tell him to tell Colson that she had apprehended the fugitives and they were on their way to the interview center.

He'd risk not telling Connie right now. When they got back to the office and saw Connie off to her home, he'd tell Tony and Lenora. The three of them would go over and talk to Carlson. The end result would most likely be the same: a one-way trip to the center. But he just couldn't send Carlson without being somehow convinced that she had been involved. Maybe they could keep her "downtown" till they got some definitive answer from the center that the truth serums or the worm had worked on Crawford and she either was or was not involved.

He thought back to his vision of Siobhan sitting under her lamp, holding her son, looking up at him, so radiant, happy and fulfilled. She could have been his daughter.

Bill had automatically paused in giving the name of Ian's girlfriend to his future father-in-law. People were always cautious about giving information to corpos, even if they're related to them. But then he had. Now he was concerned.

Was Siobhan involved in Michael's case? And if she was, what were the implications for Ian? He really liked Ian and couldn't let this pass. Bill went out to the elevator and down to Ian's apartment. When he approached the door, a sensor recognized him and 'sponded Ian that Bill was there.

Ian slowly opened the door and looked both ways down the hallway. He smiled and said, "Hi Bill, good to see you." But he didn't invite him in.

"Ian, I don't know how to tell you this without sounding alarmist," Bill said gazing down the hall. "Listen, can I come in?"

"Sure," Ian said letting him inside the apartment just enough to close the door.

"You know my future father-in-law's a detective with the CBI. He's working day and night on a big case out at the LEPGen labs right now. Well, he 'sponded me out-of-the-blue a while ago and asked me where you were headed when we saw you yesterday. When I 'sponded that I assumed to your new girlfriend's place, he came back asking her name. I 'sponded Siobhan's name back to him. There was no explanation or response like 'OK, just curious.' Nothing.

"He's my future father-in-law, but you're my friend. I just wanted you to know." Bill saw the concerned look on Ian's face and added awkwardly, "Well, let me know if there's anything I can do."

Ian looked at Bill and said, "Thanks for letting me know. I appreciate it. You're a good friend." And to Bill's surprise, Ian reached over and hugged him. Bill then opened the door and stepped out into the hallway.

"Goodbye, Bill."

While he waited for the elevator door to open, Bill looked back at Ian's door. It was closing slowly. He didn't like the finality of that goodbye.

Siobhan came out of the bedroom and looked at Ian. They went to each other and held each other tight. "I'm sorry, it's my fault," Ian said slowly.

"It's no one's fault. It just is," Siobhan said.

Earlier in the day, Ian had gone to his school to destroy the students' printed compositions and delete them from the pads. So if anyone inquired about the compositions, they'd be "misplaced"; not just Spencer's. Siobhan hadn't wanted him to go out; she thought it'd be too dangerous. But Ian insisted that he had to get rid of Spencer's composition.

While at the school, he convinced himself that they couldn't just live in a vacuum, waiting. Their only defense was to know what was going on. So after finishing at the school, Ian decided to walk by Siobhan's house to see if everything looked normal. He saw three people came out of her house. One of them was Bill's future father-in-law, Michael Chan, a corpo. Chan glanced over at him but didn't appear to recognize him in his heavy rain gear.

When he got back he had told Siobhan what had happened. They both agreed that they now needed to prepare for the worst. Siobhan insisted that he had done the right thing. In fact, they should venture out later on and try to get more information. They couldn't possibly turn their 'sponders back on now; it'd be too risky. She had other ways of contacting help, but not from the vacuum of Ian's apartment.

After some moments, Siobhan continued, "Guy's way past the point of no return. Obviously they've already made the connection to me. And now me to you. I just can't figure out why they aren't here yet."

"Is there any place we can go? Any one we can contact?"

"They're most likely waiting for us outside to see where we'll lead them. I can't jeopardize others at this point." And then after a pause, she added, "I'm afraid we're trapped."

They continued to hold each other. Then Siobhan cleared her throat and said, "I feel so lucky that I met you, Ian. I'm so glad I took the chance and opened up to you, to life, again. This past week has meant so much to me. It just hurts so much to know I won't be leaving you safe and secure."

"I couldn't have stayed behind. I love you."

After kissing passionately, they held each other tightly again.

After a period of quiet, Siobhan said slowly and quietly, "Ever since my son was terminated, I've tried not to be afraid; to do what was right. I hope I have and that in some small way I've, we've, made a difference."

"You have. That's why I love you," Ian said looking into her eyes. "When I watched you telling stories to your children in the armory, I knew I was seeing something special – something magical. They *were* your children. Your love for them – nurturing, protecting them. Their adoration for you. You *are* their mother, Spencer's mother, the mother of those children in the LEPGen labs. Nothing will ever change that. Not the corpos. Not anything."

As they stood holding each other again, Ian's gaze moved from the floor and up to his front glass wall. He took in the nearby doms, the cliffs of Highland across the river, and the Shawangunks behind them. And finally, his eyes moved toward the north, to the distant Catskills, and to the notch in the mountains above the hamlet of Ashokan.

Chapter 36

"OK, vibrate the lock," Michael said. Tony had given the door a quick scan to be sure it wasn't booby-trapped. This was one of the most dangerous situations for agents – when suspects were in hiding and trying to protect themselves from being picked up.

The lock clicked open and Tony very cautiously pushed the door open with the remote on his vibrator. Then he carefully scanned the opening and continued to scan as he proceeded into the apartment with Michael and Lenora behind.

The apartment was quiet. Everything looked neat and orderly. They caught glimpses of the Hudson and the cliffs on the other side of the river. Michael was surprised to see a bust of Bach on a pedestal-like table and an antique clock on a shelf. He resisted his inclination to pause and study them. Tony walked up to the bedroom door and scanned it. It checked out and was not locked. Very carefully he opened the door.

In the dim, indirect light from the outside they saw the bed, and as their eyes grew accustomed to the dimness, two bodies began to take shape. Michael moved his hand upward and an indirect internal light began to glow. They looked down at the two forms lying before them. A man and a woman were laying face-to-face, holding hands, still staring into each other's eyes; even in death. Michael recognized Ian Vanderkill from their brief meeting yesterday and Siobhan Carlson from her 'sponded records. On the nightstands on either side were Euthanesta Home Solution kits, empty of their contents. The three of them instinctively stepped back.

Tony finally scanned them. "Time of death 7:42. Less than an hour ago."

"OK, scan the room well and then the rest of the apartment. Lenora, let's you and I do the visual."

Michael and Lenora started with the bedroom. They checked the bodies over briefly, then respectfully lay them back in their original positions. The kits had been set up to be activated by a holoplay. They would have to check that out. They then moved into the main room, first to the kitchen area, then dining and finally living area. They didn't find anything of interest. The apartment was a Spartan, typical single-male abode.

Michael studied the bust of Bach. One thing Vanderkill must have had in common with him, he figured. A person living in an imperfect world, searching for the perfect, the eternal, and maybe finding hints of it in the music of this great man. Now gone. What had he done? How was he tied up in this mess?

He walked over to the antique clock. *Beautiful but dirty. Pre-Civil-War. Running, but needs a good cleaning. I'm sure he wasn't a member of our clock society. I wonder if he would have joined. Another thing we had in common.* Michael shook his head and moved on.

While they were looking around, they received a 'spond from the interview center. They had wormed Crawford and could confirm that he had recorded the scene in the LEPGen lab early yesterday morning. His ex-wife had helped him in recording his voice-over and had gotten the recording to the Phantom'ogger. They tried to retrotrace her steps but found no indication that she had ever left her house. Like Crawford, she must have turned off her 'sponder.

Michael briefly 'sponded Connie with the center's report, about Carlson's connection to Vanderkill, what they had found at Vanderkill's apartment, and that they were still searching. He would send her a more detailed 'spond when they were done. Connie congratulated him on a job well done and said she would let Colson know what a terrific job he and his team had done.

After an additional half hour of searching the apartment, the three of them regrouped. The place was clean. Finally, Michael said in a somber voice, "A trail of ghosts. You can add these two to the Oracle, and by tomorrow you can add Crawford. And Raston, if Colson has her way. Think about whether you want to stick with it. You know you can bow out and go back to regular police work, where things are more black and white, or maybe into some other line of work."

"Michael, why did you stick with the CBI?" Lenora asked.

Michael paused thoughtfully before he responded, "Originally, the status, the pay. Protecting our way of life. The always-interesting cases. Thinking I could make a difference in a bloodless organization. But after a few years I stayed because I was there. You know, you get in a rut without really acknowledging it, and soon that rut becomes your life."

"Would you leave it now if you could?" Tony asked.

"I've always loved detective work. What would I do if I weren't here?"

Lenora and Tony nodded.

After a thoughtful pause, Michael said quietly, "Tony, 'spond the center goons to pick these two up later on when it'll attract the least attention. You know the routine. Lenora, 'spond the police to put the place under discrete surveillance till we can return. On your way out, both of you check out the lobby and around the building – just in case. But make it cursory; nothing to raise interest in others. Then get a good night's sleep, 'cause we'll be busy tomorrow.

"First thing in the morning, I'll pay a quick visit to Vanderkill's school; then I'll head over to Dan's place. Lenora, you're still with Beth and the police are still watching the place?" When she replied yes, Michael continued, "OK, sleep in a bit, and stay with her till I get there. Then go back to Carlson's and give it a good search. Tony, you give this place a good search in the morning. Then the two of you go over and check out Carlson's office and have a talk with her boss. I'll stay here for a while and replay the holoplay that triggered their Euthanesta kits. Might be some clues in it."

Alone in the apartment, Michael became aware of the silence surrounding him. These ultra-insulated, doms were cut off from all noises, all life, in the outside world. It was like being in a tomb. Apt description, Michael thought when he looked down at the two lifeless bodies before him. He tried not to look at them as he reset the holoplay to replay the scene that had activated their Euthanesta kits.

The holoplay began in darkness with the almost inaudible strains of a classical piece. Michael quickly realized it was Wagner – from one of his operas but in an orchestral arrangement. As the music started climbing out of its darkness, dawn came to a woodland scene with a brook running through it. Judging from the rocks and hints of mountains in the background, Michael thought it was somewhere in the Hudson Highlands.

As the music increased in intensity, the scene became more lush with life, with woodland ferns, grasses and mountain laurel shining with moisture. There was an explosion of flowers of all colors and shapes. Some wild and some domestic, planted long ago. Michael saw wildlife – grazing deer, chipmunks and squirrels in long-abandoned stone walls, rabbits assessing greens before eating.

The boughs of the towering ancient oak trees appeared to form a vaulted ceiling stretching out down an old dirt road, now merely a path. That, coupled with the shimmering, stained-glass-like surface of the river far down the valley, gave Michael the impression of being in a natural place of worship. Maybe the setting for an outdoors wedding.

As the music continued to mount, driving the intensity of the scene, Michael recognized the upward reaching strains of the "Liebestod" from Wagner's *Tristan und Isolde* where Isolde discovers the body of her love, Tristan. The music continued to build, expressing the passionate love Isolde felt for Tristan till it burst forth its climax of pure longing. Likewise, the woodland scene reached a peak of total idyllic beauty, with warm, almost-blinding sunlight reaching into every crevice to expose even the smallest insect in the stone walls. The stream gushed over the rocks, reaching the upper limits of its banks.

With these passions bursting forth from Isolde, she knows she cannot live without Tristan and kills herself. Michael noticed the trigger light in the holoplay that would have set off the Euthanesta kits at this point. As Isolde dies, the music begins its dénouement, moving from passion to an achingly-beautiful acceptance that this short life of turmoil and passion was ending and that Isolde would be with Tristan forever in a place beyond this world's reach.

The woodland scene slowly became less intense, but beautiful in a more subtle, enduring way. As the music moved ever more quietly toward its ending, the sun began to set, causing shadows which moved down the valley toward the river. Michael now recognized the Hudson at Iona Island, below Dunderberg.

The music built to one last question, which was answered with a rich harmonic chord that seemed to float on and on. Michael checked the holotime at which the music had originally ended: 7:42.

Knowing this was their time of death, Michael sighed and stood up. But the scene moved into darkness and a multitude of stars appeared. He sat back down, mystified. Music began again. But instead of the passionate, operatic grandeur of the "Liebestod", a simple, austere, yet beautiful duet played in time. Michael didn't recognize the piece so he 'sponded the title. It was "Spiegel im Spiegel", mirror in mirror, by Arvo Paert.

Where the "Liebestod" had expressed the height of passionate love, this piece was a slow minuet, an almost-halting waltz, between a piano and violin that seemed to express ongoing love. The piano and violin slowly waltzed forward, complementing and reflecting the beauty of the other. As the music moved on at its hypnotically-constant pace building patterns of prismatic triads, Michael could imagine Vanderkill and Carlson staring deeply into each other's eyes, waltzing into the distant stars till they were a unified point of light.

Slowly the stars came closer and parted on to other worlds, other galaxies, other universes. The music ended as it had begun, thus beginning a cycle that had no end.

Chapter 37
MONDAY, JULY 13

Michael rounded the corner of the armory and onto Market Street. It was dark, cold, windy and damp with drizzle. The sight of the foreboding gothic structure gave him a chill. So hard and unyielding. He shouldn't be here; he should be home in bed, warm and safe, sleeping next to Julianna. Why was he walking up Market Street at this time of night? What time was it, anyway? He tried to 'spond the time, but got nothing. If I were home, the striking of my clocks would tell me, he thought. But a harsh gust of wind reminded him he wasn't home.

He felt a growing dread in his heart. He knew why he was here and what was waiting for him. He tried to stop his forward movement, tried to turn toward home, but he couldn't. He looked for a way out, but there was none.

Ahead he saw the welcoming lights of the Bardavon's marquee, but he would soon pass them and move on to that one dull, lonely street light. Trudging past the opera house, his muscles aching from fighting his movement, he looked into the bright interior hallway. So warm and welcoming. But he couldn't stop. He couldn't slow down. As he walked out of the light of the Bardavon and back into the darkness, the opera house quickly seemed like a distant dream, a reminder of times of happiness that were now beyond him.

Just a short distance ahead was that cold, dull street light at Market and Main. As he approached it he could feel himself slowing down even more. Then he saw it; the glow of light coming out of Mario's window. At first it was faint, but it grew with each leaden step he took. And with each step, the terror grew in his heart. He knew what he would find there, but he didn't want to admit it.

The large, front window came into view. The first one he saw at the counter was the Oracle, drinking coffee out of an old-fashioned porcelain diner cup, looking knowingly out into the darkness. When Michael came closer Dan looked directly at him, smiling. The Oracle's eyes spoke, but Michael didn't want to hear, so he averted his eyes to what was coming next into view.

He saw Carlson and Vanderkill next, still holding hands and gazing into each other's eyes, happily oblivious to all that was around them. Michael wondered if they knew he was there. He hoped not.

As his feet took him inevitably forward, he could feel his heart pounding in mortal fear. He tried to turn his head away but couldn't.

Julianna and Caitlin were sitting at the counter. There was an empty seat between them. Like the Oracle, they were staring out into the darkness, but they looked terribly sad. And obviously they couldn't see him. Why aren't I in there with them? Why aren't I sitting in that empty seat between them? But he knew. That wasn't his seat. It wasn't Bill's, because he had left Caitlin. The empty seat was what was left of their dreams. Tears ran down Michael's face. He fought back sobs. He pounded on the window, but as he already knew, they couldn't hear him or see him.

He wasn't there.

Michael woke up trembling. He looked at Julianna sleeping peacefully in the faint, predawn light and yearned to touch her, to hold her. If only he could sleep like her.

Michael got up and walked out into the living room. He sat down in his recliner and pushed it back, not to go to sleep – he was too afraid of that – but to regain control of his emotions. He looked up at the stately old tall case clock next to him and let the slow beat of the "tick tock" bring his racing heart down to a comfortable rate.

A number of years ago their new puppy would curl up and sleep next to this clock. A veterinarian friend explained that the beat of the clock reminded puppies of the beat of their mothers' hearts, and gave them comfort. Michael soon after moved his easy chair next to the clock.

He called it his "love clock", which sounded silly to others till he explained its story to them. This was his oldest clock, and the only one he had acquired for free. He had "inherited" it from his old clock society friend, Henry Goss. It had been in Henry's family since it was made in about 1740 in Essex, England. It was a simple, yet stately and very well-made "provincial" clock. Though it had a beautifully hand-engraved brass dial and silvered chapter ring, it was not in the league of the great London clock makers of its time. But Michael wouldn't have traded it for the greatest Tompion ever made, because it had history. It had the story that followed a family down through over 300 years of its existence.

Henry's favorite story was that of his mid-1800's namesake ancestor who had been the poor relative of his uncle Edward Goss, a partner in a successful iron works. When Henry's parents died in his early teens, Edward took him in and raised him as the child he had never had. Henry eventually fell in love with the local pub owner's daughter, Hannah. Edward considered her family to be beneath their station and wouldn't allow Henry to marry her. Also, unspoken, was that Edward had wanted to buy some land from Hannah's father, who had refused. When Henry insisted on marrying her, Edward gave him an ultimatum: if he married Hannah, Edward would disinherit him.

Henry married Hannah and they moved into a modest, rented cottage in which they lived happily till the end of their days. When Edward died he left all of his wealth and possessions to his partner in the iron works except for one item. He left the family clock to Henry. Henry had always admired the clock, and apparently Uncle Edward had relented in one tiny corner of his heart. Or maybe he just couldn't let the family clock leave the family.

Henry's three sons eventually immigrated to America. His daughter remained behind to take care of him and Hannah in their old age. After the death of her parents and when she was aging herself, the daughter sent the clock to her brothers in America to be passed down through their families.

Henry often thought about that pivotal moment in his ancestor's life. If he had obeyed his uncle and not married Hannah, the current Henry wouldn't exist. Neither would the three brothers who had immigrated to America, nor their countless off spring. And the clock would have stayed in England continuing to reside with a well-off family who could have afforded to cast it aside when purchasing a newer, more advanced, more elaborately-worked time piece.

His ancestor had had the courage to follow the convictions of his heart. And look at what his convictions had produced. A line of thousands of lives in "the new world", each moving through their days, striving to find meaning, happiness and love. To Henry, the family clock was a reminder of that fateful act of love and the many lives that had followed as a result of it. It was his "love clock".

Finally, his health was failing and neither his daughter, nor any other close relative, was inclined, or in a position, to take the clock and care for it. Yes, his daughter had said she would take it, but he knew she would just stand it lifeless in a corner. The clock deserved a real caretaker who would appreciate it and keep it well-maintained and running. After more than three hundred years it had outlived his family. It was time for it to move on. And after getting to know Michael, Henry wanted to pass the clock on to him, knowing he would revere it, keep it running well, and eventually pass it on to the next right person.

Michael quickly said he would love to take on that responsibility. Henry hoped Michael would begin a tradition of passing it down through his family and also retain its history, which Michael assured him he would. And finally, Henry asked him to remember the love story of the clock. That life would go on long after he was gone. And that even though our lives were brief, we each had important decisions to make that would impact our families and others long after we were gone. So Michael should always listen to his heart in making those decisions.

Now, years later, his "love clock" had calmed his heart again, as it had so many times after difficult nights. He thought about Henry, and his words. And he thought about how much history had swirled around this stately old grandfather clock while its measured movements kept going on into the future, never pausing, always assuredly constant. It had existed before the United States of America, and after it as well. It was now moving just as constantly through the life of the Incorporated States of America, into a future that humans would also make; that Michael would.

Michael now felt he could get up and face the day. He went and dispensed some coffee and breakfast. After he ate, he showered, got ready, took one last look at Julianna as she slept, and quietly went out the door.

Michael walked into the school's main office, flashed his holobadge at the assistant behind the counter and asked to see the director. When Ms. Gunderson came out of her office, Michael said he'd like to talk with her about one of her teachers, Ian Vanderkill. Ms. Gunderson looked nervously at the students milling around and invited him into her office.

With the door closed, Michael explained that Mr. Vanderkill would not be returning to his duties at the school, that he would need access to his office, and when he left it would need to be locked and not opened again till he or another CBI agent returned. Ms. Gunderson said she understood and would follow his orders completely. Michael was glad she hadn't asked what was going on. The smart ones never did.

The office was what he had expected; the typical "professorial" teacher's office with shelves of books and clutter on the desk. He looked at the books on the shelf. Not surprisingly most dealt with history. He took down the classic *The Lives of the Great Composers* and leafed through it. He had a copy of it at home. Funny how only Bach and Dvorak seemed to have lead normal, happy lives. He chuckled at how prolific old Johann Sebastian had been with children as well as music. He had to crank out that music to feed all those mouths!

Michael moved on to the desk. Nothing of great interest – just a pile of papers which he leafed through quickly. Nor did Ian's wallplay directory come up with anything of interest. Well, he'd come back later and go through things in more detail. He wanted to get over to the Oracle's house. Ms. Gunderson had given him the old-fashioned key to the door. He liked it when these historic old buildings retained such quaint touches, though keys and locks weren't very secure.

As he walked out the door, he saw a student disappear around a corner. Just some curious kid, he thought. He locked the door and went back to the office. There were still a lot of students milling around, obviously curious who he was. He went directly into Ms. Gunderson's office and closed the door.

"Ms. Gunderson, this key is very out dated and not very secure, so I suggest that you personally keep an eye on it and the office until I tell you otherwise."

She nodded as she took the key and clutched it.

"The only thing you will tell the staff and students is that Mr. Vanderkill will no longer be teaching at this school. Nothing else, no speculating."

"I understand," Gunderson squeaked out in a raspy voice.

"I wish we had met in more pleasant circumstances. Goodbye, Ms. Gunderson," Michael said. He then turned and walked out. He smiled as he walked to his car. He admitted that he always got perverse enjoyment in reading the riot act to those on the periphery of a crime. They were invariably scared shitless, and would do what they were told.

It was for their own good. On the rare occasion that a tough guy didn't take him seriously, Michael would ask him if he would rather get his instructions at the interview center. That always straightened him out immediately.

Chapter 38

Michael gave Beth a hug.

"How are you doing?" Michael asked. He looked at Lenora who shook her head no.

"Oh, you know, Michael. One moment at a time. I know it'll become one day at a time someday – then maybe I'll be able to breathe without gasping. It's so hard. I'd like to go into his room and the basement."

"I know. We'll be done in a day or two. But it's important not to disturb those two rooms till then. That's why I've come over. To do some more looking."

"Beth and I've had some good talks," Lenora said putting a comforting arm around her shoulder. Finally she said, "Beth, I'll be back tonight. Michael will be here. And when he leaves the policeman will still be outside. You'll be safe."

"Oh, I'm not afraid," Beth said wistfully and then added, "Anyway, it's hard to care, with Dan gone."

Lenora gave Michael a knowing look, said goodbye and walked out the door.

"Would you like some coffee, Michael?"

"I'd love some," Michael said as they headed into the kitchen.

Beth dispensed a cup of coffee and handed it to him.

"Sugar, cream?"

"No thanks, I'm sweet enough without them."

Beth smiled slightly.

Turning serious again Michael said, "Beth, I'm convinced that Dan had some important information that ended up costing him his life. I need to find it but haven't been successful so far. I'm sure his words 'Tell Michael, take the A train' are an important clue."

Beth looked intently at Michael. "I've wracked my brain on that. I think back to when he walked in looking satisfied on Thursday. He went straight downstairs. I have a feeling whatever it is, it's down there somewhere."

"OK. We've obviously overlooked something, and it bugs me to no end," Michael said standing up. He took Beth's hand and squeezed it, then grabbed his cup and headed downstairs.

Michael looked again at the sticky notes they had studied. He was sure there were more clues in them, but they just weren't jumping out at him. He'd have to get Lenora back in here to look at them. She was sharp. Exasperated, he finally said, "Come on, Danny Boy, I need some help here!"

Michael turned to the shelves of countless LP albums and began perusing them again, starting with the A's. *Hmmm. Aderly. Cannonball Aderly. Interesting name, I'll have to 'spond him some time.* When he got to the B's, he was pleasantly surprised to see the number of Bach albums the Oracle had collected. Then he saw the words that made him gasp: *E. Power Biggs Plays Bach in the Thomaskirche.*

Very carefully he pulled the album out and looked at the picture of the Thomaskirche in Leipzig on the front. Then slowly turning the album over, and looking below the picture of the statue of Bach in front of the church, he saw what he knew he would see in the list of works: "Prelude and Fugue in G Major ('The Great'), BWV 541". *The greatest recording of the greatest work of music.* Michael very carefully removed the record from its jacket and gently placed it on the stereo system's turntable. When he had turned the system on, he carefully placed the turntable arm on the record. This was the first time Michael had heard the piece externally on vinyl. They really never had improved over vinyl.

Michael listened to the piece a few times; enjoying each time as if it were the first. Finally, he carefully replaced the record in its jacket and continued on. Count Basie – Dave Brubeck. *Oh yeah, there's the* Time Out *album. Probably the best introduction to jazz that ever was – something anyone could "dig".* Of course, when he had told the Oracle the other night that he was listening to Brubeck, Dan had dismissively said, what was it? Oh, yeah, "He's pretty good for a white cat." Michael chuckled.

He again couldn't help taking the album out and listening to it. He knew he couldn't continue his investigation in this manner. But what a treat. Listening externally and on vinyl. "Blue Rondo a la Turk" in its unique 9/8 time. And "Take Five"! Michael's head kept bobbing up and down as he listened to that cool music. What else had he said? Michael paused and saw the Oracle's eyes looking at him intently as he had said, "Brubeck's definitely the place for you to start".

Michael continued looking carefully at the Brubeck albums. After several, he came upon one that he hadn't heard of. The title was simply *Dave Brubeck, Berlin, 1966.* Michael carefully removed the album from the shelf and studied the grainy black and white photo of the Dave Brubeck Quartet on the front. It appeared to be a bootleg production of that performance. When he turned the jacket over, Michael's heart skipped a beat.

At the top of the list of pieces was a ten minute version of "Take the A Train". They hadn't studied this album in their investigation on Saturday. He quickly went over to the work bench and found the list of "A Train" albums Lenora had put together. This album wasn't on it. Not surprisingly, if it was a bootleg.

He again took up the album and intently studied the outside of the jacket. It looked very old – it was probably an original. Nothing caught his eye. He then very carefully removed the record still in its sleeve and studied the sleeve; nothing. Then he removed the record and, sweating with nervousness, he gingerly put the record on the turntable and ever-so lightly placed the arm on the record. At once he heard those now-familiar strains of "Take the A Train", but in a definite "Brubecker" rendition.

God, Brubeck's light touch on the piano, improvising off into the stratosphere, Michael thought. *Paul Desmond playing that sax so cool and fluid, Eugene Wright's soft thumping and riffs on the string bass, and the head-nodding beat of Joe Morello on the drums. How could anyone not love jazz after* listening to these guys – these cool cats? On the surface, their easy-going music couldn't have been more different than Bach's "Great". But underneath there was that building inevitability driving toward the end, with one final flourish of the theme. Bach would have "dug" Brubeck, Michael was sure.

Michael imagined himself in a 1960's smoke-filled jazz club in a shady part of town. Hey, maybe in 1960's Harlem. Everyone was sitting around wearing "shades" even in the interior gloom, with cigarettes hanging out of their mouths, heads moving up and down to the music.

But the "A Train" ended too quickly, making Michael realize he hadn't listened to it analytically at all, so he replayed it listening for any clues. There were no words in this instrumental version, so no verbal clues.

As "Take the A Train" ended the second time, Michael took the jacket over to the reading lamp next to the Oracle's easy chair. He held the jacket under the intense light and looked inside. The cardboard structure on the inside was rough and course, indicating the low quality construction of a bootleg jacket. The paper fibers were coming loose; disintegrating.

Then Michael noticed a fiber that appeared to be slightly larger than the others. He opened his self-assembled detective kit and got a magnifying glass and tweezers out. He sat in the easy chair and again pried open the jacket, peering into it. With the magnifying glass, he saw that that fiber was indeed slightly larger than the others. It seemed loosely woven into the cardboard, not pressed.

A freeze-dried Organic Intelligence "noodle"!

Michael sat back and stared at the jacket. Standard procedure would be to take it to the CBI lab for analysis. But he wouldn't trust them to come clean with what they had found. If this was what Dan had died for, Michael was going to figure it out first hand.

He went out to his car and got his portable holoplayer. Back inside the house he noticed that Beth was dozing on her couch. She lifted her head. "Oh hi, Michael. I guess I'm a little tired. I think I'll go up to my bedroom for a nap."

"I hope the music downstairs didn't bother you," Michael said.

"Oh no. It was almost as if Dan were home again," Beth said sadly.

"Can I use one of your bowls?"

"Sure. Help yourself to more coffee and food while you're at it."

"Thanks."

Beth climbed the stairs.

"Have a good rest."

Michael watched her disappear upstairs and then grabbed a bowl, put some warm water in it, and returned downstairs. He sat back down in Dan's easy chair and proceeded to carefully free the OI strand from the surrounding cardboard fiber. OI strands were pretty tough, so he wasn't afraid of breaking it, but he didn't want to nick it, because that could cause some data loss.

Once he had freed it, he carefully lifted it out with the tweezers and placed it into the bowl of warm water. It immediately expanded, which was a sure indication that it was an OI noodle. After about five minutes Michael lifted it out of the bowl with the tweezers, and placed it on a hard, clean surface to let the excess water dry off. When that was done he placed the strand into his holoplayer and turned it on.

Michael sat down in the Oracle's easy chair and observed the holoplay. It was a series of meetings between Rebecca Colson and high-level executives and CEO's of other corporations. In each case, Colson was discussing the terms for delivery of fetuses: where the supply would come from and to which facility, warranty and quality assurances, and, of course, price. Pricing was two-tiered: one price for fetuses with defects and a higher price for fetuses without defects. Most agreements were being made for deliveries within the ISA, but a large number were with foreign corporations for delivery to their facilities from one of CaringMother's foreign locations.

Of course, what the fetuses would be used for would be an important determiner in setting the parameters of the warranties, so their uses were discussed at length. LEPGen Corporation would use the fetuses for developing and testing organic transponders.

NuTense Corporation needed fetuses for testing advanced weapons; for example, the impact of sterilization rays on fetuses at different stages of development. Colson was firm in setting the warranty expiration on these fetuses to the time they were delivered and quality tested at NuTense's receiving dock.

Probelon Corporation was developing intelligence suppressors for lower bands and intelligence enhancers for the children of executives. They were also developing genetic "drop dead" DNA switches, so lower bands would drop dead at about their typical retirement age of 70, since they usually had few credits invested for retirement. Upper bands would have a few more years to look forward to before their "drop deads" kicked in. Of course, any unused credits would revert to The Corporation. They were also testing life expectancy enhancers for executives since they had abundant resources to use in retirement, and by law, their unused resources would be passed on to their children, tax free.

The executives reminded Colson that they were subcontracting to The Corporation, obviously in hopes that they could secure better terms and prices from her. They tried to portray themselves as victims of Corporate directives, willing to do what was necessary as good Corporate citizens, though they were certain to lose money in this current endeavor.

Colson typically laughed at this point and reminded them that they would cook their books and overcharge The Corporation for their work. Then, when their products were developed, they would charge The Corporation and/or other customers exorbitant monopolistic prices/fees for their products and services of questionable quality. They would do this by keeping their details proprietary and fighting competitors, and even The Corporation, with their armies of lawyers, knowing that corporate law was the one area of the law that actually worked in the ISA and other Corporate countries. Colson said she was merely trying to get a piece of the pie, doing her job to maximize profits for that corporation which had been entrusted to her: CaringMother.

Of course, she continued, if the other corporations weren't happy with her terms and prices they were free to go to a competitor, knowing full well that CaringMother was the only wombcare corporation with the reach and quality capable of meeting all their fetus needs.

Once she had delivered her "gotcha", the other executives sheepishly smiled and acceded to her demands.

And The Corporation would in turn smile upon all of them.

Seeing that the recording would go on for over fifteen hours, Michael shut the holoplay off. He had seen enough. This had been his dread ever since he had gotten involved with the LEPGen investigation a week ago. Just as in his dreams of Mario's, he had sensed that his waking nightmare would lead to this. He was beyond horror now.

He slowly looked around the basement, at the records, at the wall of sticky notes, at the stereo equipment, and finally at the Oracle's easy chair that he was sitting in. To what extraordinary lengths had Dan gone to get this recording? And he had paid for it with his life. Dan Schmitt, confused as a child and frustrated growing up with so little help, had somehow managed to make a life for himself in the streets. And in the end, had found the courage to care and the determination to do what was right. Michael now understood Dan's gaze at him from the restaurant.

Michael began to notice things. He could hear the slight whisper of his breath as he looked down and watched his belly calmly rise and fall. He felt the smooth fabric of his pants. Gabardine, wasn't it? He smelled the musty dryness of the warm air, and in licking his dry lips he was surprised at the saltiness of the taste.

He noticed that the basement was growing lighter. He looked up and saw sunlight streaming through the small windows and was amazed at how bright the sunbeams were. He slowly stood up and walked over to one of the windows and put his hands in the beams. Such brilliance!

Michael had been in a dark place for a long time. Had he entered this Dantesque world when those Muslim men were falsely executed for acts of terrorism? Was that the first level? Had he been traveling downward ever since, with the LEPGen/CaringMother case being the latest, deepest and darkest level in his netherworld?

With a flood of calmness that he hadn't felt in a long time, Michael let out a sigh, knowing that his struggle was over. He was almost buoyant. He watched his hands calmly pick up his portable holoplayer and its contents and felt his legs move him forward and up the stairs. He was no longer fighting them as he had in his dream.

When Michael emerged from the house, he was amazed at how stunningly blue the sky was, how bright the sun, and how varied the greens among the trees, shrubs and ground cover. He reveled in the heat of the sun on his face and heard the songs of birds as if for the first time. And he smelled sweet scents as he looked at the multi-colored blossoms at his feet. Why hadn't he noticed them before? He felt a sense of sadness when he realized how long he had not experienced any of this, and how fleeting it now would be.

Michael walked over to the policeman to tell him that he was leaving, but more importantly that Ms. Schmitt had been sleeping all of the time he had been there, hoping this would help protect her later on. He then walked to his car, got in, and willed his 'sponder into the off position as he drove away.

Chapter 39

Michael gazed out the window from his seat at his work bench. The other buildings were washed in a golden glow from the setting sun. Michael was already in a twilight – that last grasp at the day before he would enter the night – that time of dreams. But he was no longer afraid of what dreams would come.

Julianna had gone out with the girls after work and wouldn't be back till close to midnight or even the wee hours. He had never understood why they would go out after work regularly on the first night of the work week. Julianna said it was so they had a reason to look forward to Mondays on Sundays. It had become a ritual with them.

They were a wild bunch. Except for Julianna. She was much more solid than the rest of her friends. She had always been such an anchor, a stable force, for him, for Caitlin. Maybe she needed an occasional relief from her responsibilities. He smiled as he imagined Julianna laughing with the rest of them, making comments about their husbands and boyfriends. He now wished he had woken her up this morning to say goodbye.

Michael continued working on his newest Winterhalder and Hofmeier. He was determined to complete his work on it and was almost done – just final adjustments to the cathedral gongs.

At about 6pm he had turned his 'sponder back on. There was a message from Tony, but he didn't answer it. The CorpiLeaks transmission had started. He watched the now familiar figure of Rebecca Colson pacing about as she negotiated terms and prices with her corporate counterparts. This one would be harder to chase down and stop than the Phantom'ogger, since CorpiLeaks was international and had had many years of experience in transponding and disappearing. And this one would have much more impact.

Jimmy had been very nervous when Michael first showed up. But Michael told him that this was what Dan had died for – that they owed it to him. And when Michael assured Jimmy that there would be no tracing of the recordings from him to Jimmy, Jimmy looked deeply into Michael's eyes and understood.

Michael smiled as he tuned the transmission out. He knew what each next step would be and he was no longer fighting it.

Finishing the W&H, he tested the strike on the gongs for perfection of sound and set the clock running on the work bench in front of him. He sat admiring the beauty of the solid mahogany and the job he had done restoring it. Then he observed the movement of the shining brass works through the beveled glass on the top and sides of the case. How many proud owners had observed these exquisite works ticking in measured beats, often not realizing that they were only caretakers – keeping the heart of this work of art beating till it was time to pass on its care?

Michael wondered who would accept the care of his clocks after he was gone. His gaze turned to the "love clock" out in the front room. He hoped it would be someone in his family. Maybe his grandchild?

His clocks started striking nine. As he listened to the slow, definitive strike on the iron bell in the love clock, he reflected, *It tolls for thee*. Each strike was a step into the future, a future he had set in motion and now could not stop. A future he now welcomed.

While he was walking around admiring all his clocks one last time, a 'spond came in from Connie.

Michael, where are you?
Michael knew she knew. *At home. Where are you?*
At the office. Michael, where have you been?
Michael didn't respond.
Look Michael, stay right there. We're heading over.
We? Are Lenora and Tony with you?
Pause. *Yes.*
OK. I'll be here.

He 'sponded Lenora's and Tony's locations. They were both at Carlson's house. They must have gone back there after checking out her office. Well, it obviously hadn't taken Colson long to be alerted to the CorpiLeaks transpondance and figure things out. She was smart, quick and decisive. *Guess that's part of the territory in being an executive.*

Michael walked over to his three calendar clocks, stopped their pendulums and then set their dates. He wished he could 'spond Julianna now or even leave her some kind of note. At least the calendar clocks would tell her he had been there. Her only protection would be to be totally ignorant of what had happened.

She'd come home, find him gone and wonder where he was. Later she'd 'spond him to find out what was going on, and her heart would freeze when the response would come back, "unknown entity". She'd then 'spond Lenora and Tony, who wouldn't answer, and finally Connie.

That's when Connie would start the cat-and-mouse game with her. Connie would have forbidden Lenora and Tony from communicating with Julianna. And Julianna's 'sponds to Connie would be met with silence. In frustration, Julianna would go to the office in the morning and demand to see Connie. Connie would be unavailable. But Julianna would be observed and recorded and then analyzed by Connie and Natalie. They'd observe her true agitation, frustration and fear in not knowing what was happening.

They'd conclude that Julianna really had no knowledge of what Michael had been up to and decide to leave her alone. Julianna would now know for sure that Michael had disappeared, and that she'd never be given the truth, no matter what she did. And she could be endangering Caitlin and Bill in addition to herself if she continued pushing the issue, so she would finally give up and learn to live with her pain.

Watching the entrance down below, Michael saw Connie get out of her car and walk toward the building with a couple interview center goons he recognized. *Like clockwork,* he thought. He turned, sat down at his bench and began the flow of the contents of the Euthanesta Premium Home Solution Kit into his arm as he 'sponded Bach's "Prelude and Fugue in G Major".

He felt the initial rush of the kit building into his body as the four notes of the prelude theme sounded. The rising four notes that lifted one's eyes to the heavens. The theme that carried on ever surging, ever building, ever lifting.

Michael found himself sitting in a cavernous cathedral with bright sunshine streaming infinite hues of changing colors through the stained glass. The structure's massiveness convinced him that he had to be in the Cathedral of Saint John the Devine in Manhattan. But when he looked to the sides, there were no confining windows of glass; there was only blinding light and ever-changing colors. Then the music pulled his gaze upward and he saw a serene, deep-blue sky with occasional billowy clouds gently drifting by.

Noticing movement in front of him, Michael's gaze moved downward, and peering forward through the seemingly unending nave, Michael saw Bach playing the prelude on a massive organ console with pipes lined up infinitely behind; his fingers popping and legs flying. Michael burst out with a hearty laugh. Johann Sebastian threw his head back and laughed along with Michael, sharing in his utter joy, but still never missing a beat.

He couldn't miss a beat, because Michael knew he was no longer listening to the earthly prelude played by a human performer with his slips of imperfection. Michael had moved to the plane where this music existed beyond the mortal confines of brief human existence and imperfection. It had always existed here and always would, beyond the birth and collapse of physical universes.

Michael slowly turned around, fearing he would see his chain of ghosts, but they were no longer there. Only the love clock was there as the prelude ended and the fugue began. Its stately beat sounded out in time with the music; each beat reminding Michael of the story of a simple human listening to what the beat of his heart told him. He couldn't see Julianna, but he felt her presence. By the old clock. *I'm sorry Julianna.* He hoped she would come to understand.

The fugue was more complicated than the positive joy of the prelude. Its stated theme didn't begin with the uplifting four notes of the prelude, but with a pestering, questioning repetition of the same notes. It was asking him something human, yet somehow immortal and eternal. It drew his gaze forward again, and this time his focus settled on a figure of Mary holding her child. Her gaze down at her son was that of pure love and protection, a love that had always been and always would be. With the fugue coursing through its labyrinth of questions and emotions that were all too human, Michael became uneasy. He realized that Mary wasn't a cold, stone statue, but mortal; fragile. Would her mortality crush her and conquer her love? How could this frail, temporal being protect her child?

The music began to even out and build and drive toward its perfect, unquestioning ending. As he stared at Mary and her child, Michael saw that she was Siobhan Carlson looking lovingly down at her son. With the fugue building toward its last powerful question, Michael found himself overcome with emotion. His heart asked Siobhan for forgiveness for what he, The Corporation, and life had done. Siobhan looked at him and as the music burst forth into its answering coda, the warmth of her gaze told him that all was forgiven.

While the coda continued to build toward its ending, Siobhan become Michael's daughter. She was looking down with perfect love at her son. She looked up and smiled, thanking Michael without words.

Michael drifted off, back up through the shifting, swirling colors to where they all combined into perfect white light. And finally to the plane where the final majestic chord of the fugue would echo on forever.

Epilogue
VALLEY OF DREAMS

What's past is prologue.

> William Shakespeare, *The Tempest*

You road I enter upon and look around,
I believe you are not all that is here,
I believe that much unseen is also here.

> Walt Whitman, "Song of the Open Road"

During Spencer Galloway's eight years as Chief Executive Officer of the Incorporated States of America, he initiated many changes. Among them was the fostering of greater competition among the corporations and initiating legislation to encourage smaller, startup companies.

He furthered the effort to ensure that all children had the same educational opportunities in starting out in life, and that their further education would be based on merit, not on the band level they were born into.

But most importantly, he moved the Bill of Rights into a position above the Corporate Mission in supremacy. He also made the court system independent of the Board of Directors, so the courts would guard people's rights, not just when economically convenient.

Galloway appointed a key ally to be the director in charge of law enforcement. In Galloway's years in office, he worked especially closely with this ally to restructure and retrain law enforcement with the goal of enforcing people's rights and well-being and not just guarding the goals of The Corporation. They specifically concentrated on reforming the infamous Corporate Bureau of Investigation, nicknamed "the corpos".

Galloway had observed talented people as he moved up the corporate and Corporate ladders, and had encouraged and sponsored them to run for the ISA Board. As a result, he had a number of similar-minded allies when he became CEO of the ISA. As the CEO, and eventually also Chairman of the Board and President, he only had to deal with a small number of directors. Changes were much easier to accomplish than would have been the case for a President of the United States dealing with a 2-house, dysfunctional congress.

People called him a second Kenneth Rechner. As with Rechner, he was widely popular which made his job much easier. Some called his tenure a "third revolution" after 1776 and the Corporate takeover. But Galloway preferred to think of his work as more of a natural evolution. After 75 years of iron-fisted Corporate rule, people, and even CEOs of corporations, were ready for change.

When Galloway left office, he felt that the ISA was starting to move down the right track, that his successor was a right-minded person who would continue in the direction he had set and would make additional improvements.

She had served well on the ISA Board of Directors for the past four years, so he had groomed her and supported her in her run for CEO.

He agreed to stay on as President, a largely ceremonial role, for some time. Not surprisingly, he wasn't out of office for long before he was tapped to help initiate his changes internationally, starting with the Incorporated States of Europe, the former European Union.

It was while he was doing this work that he suffered a heart attack and decided to bow out of public life. He had never devoted time to himself, and, he felt, not enough to his wife, his daughter and her husband, or to his grandson. He realized that this could be his last chance. He was mortal.

As he devoted more time to his family, as well as to his personal interests, Galloway began writing his memoirs. Written media had made a resurgence in popularity in recent years. He felt that writing, and even hard-copy print, was a valid and important means of communication, especially when it came to communicating important ideas.

In his memoir Galloway covered many of the key times in his life, starting with the all-important influence his mothers had had on his development, and on through his turbulent youth and the influence of his teachers and friends. He ended with what he felt he had accomplished as CEO of the ISA and why he believed the changes he had made were so important. He also wrote about what he felt was important in life.

The following is the epilogue to his memoirs, *Valley of Dreams*.

Not many know why I worked so hard to establish the Valley of Dreams National Monument which is dedicated to those who had disappeared during the Corporate Bureau of Investigation's years of excessive guardianship of The Corporation. So I thought it would be appropriate to cover this in an epilogue to my memoirs, especially since its title was borrowed from the National Monument.

The following is the story of my journey to the Valley of Dreams.

I've always been interested in all forms of religion. Though not tied to any one religion, I try to take the best from each, whether traditional ones like Christianity, Judaism, and Islam, or the more obscure Native American and Norse religions.

Hindus believe there are three stages in a person's life. The first stage is growing up and learning what is needed to function in life. The second stage is having a family and working to support them and accomplishing personal goals. And then as one's children become independent adults and goals have been accomplished, the second stage gives way to the third. This is where one becomes more circumspect and reflective and seeks to understand what life has meant personally, as well as what life is about in general. This is the way I see life progressing. I have entered this third, and final, stage of my life (with a little nudging from my heart attack).

Working on this memoir has given me the chance to slow down and reflect on my life, my family and so many dear friends I have had over the years. I've had a chance to reflect on all of the support and advantages I've had throughout my life, but especially when I was young. I have been truly blessed.

As I thought about my life, I became increasingly haunted by the disappearance of two people who had had an important, though short-lived, influence on me at a difficult and formative stage in my youth: Ian Vanderkill, my upper-form historical awareness teacher, and his friend, Siobhan Carlson, a counselor at an assessment camp I had attended. Ian was more than my teacher; he was my adult friend when I badly needed one. Siobhan was a mother figure. She fluttered around me and the others at the camp like a mother hen. She reminded me of my own mothers – a mother away from home.

I can still vividly recall the last (and only) time I saw the two of them together. We had met in a garden at my school, and as I took my leave, they waved, as if they were my proud parents, watching me go out into the wider world.

A few days later I was in the school office when a CBI detective came in and asked to see the director. He was there to talk to her about Ian Vanderkill.

I was stunned. What could the "corpos", as we called them, want with him? I stayed, milling around and eventually discretely followed him down the hall to Ian's office. He was there for a brief time, but I didn't dare get too close. I don't know what he did or found. After he left, I tried the door. It was locked.

When I went to my historical awareness class, Ian wasn't there, so we students started working in our debate teams. The director came in and announced that Ian Vanderkill would no longer be teaching at our school. We would have an interim teacher starting the next day. That was that. No explanations. The word had already gotten around that a corpo had spoken to the director about Ian, so we all knew better than to ask questions that couldn't be answered.

We just sat there stunned as the director left the room. We started discussing what Ian could have possibly done to get into trouble with the corpos. We tried 'sponding Ian and were shocked when the response came back, "unknown entity". Ian had been disappeared. I also tried 'sponding Siobhan and got the same response. We all left the room, too shaken to stay and discuss Ian any further. Most simply went home or to the dormitories.

I went to Ian's dom and hung around in the lobby for some time, hoping he would show up. I didn't dare go up to his apartment. In those days one distanced oneself as quickly as possible from a disappeared person, trying to remove the possibility of "contamination".

Finally, accepting the futility of what I was doing, I went home and waited for my mothers to come home from work. They were shocked when I told them about Ian and Siobhan.

I lashed out in my frustration, saying I'd find out what had happened to them. My mothers pled with me to be careful and not do anything rash. They were afraid for my safety, so I told them I'd calm down, get control of myself, and not do anything stupid.

A great help to me in dealing with my frustrations and feelings of helplessness was my physics teacher, and Ian's good friend, Walter Sherman. He was also distraught over Ian's disappearance, but he had the mature perspective that helped me through those times. Walter took me under his wing and became a friend and mentor that I continued to rely on until his death.

As time went on, I became ever more wrapped up in climbing the corporate ladder. Ian and Siobhan receded further into my past, though they always remained in a sad part of my heart.

After all these years, I now made it my mission to find out what had happened to them. Though the old CBI erased all recorded evidence of individuals they disappeared, they did keep track of their eventual remains, as if they were too afraid of totally making them disappear. I soon tracked down Ian's and Siobhan's remains at the Mid-Hudson Valley Interview Center, a large facility outside the City of Poughkeepsie. These facilities have always been well guarded and inaccessible. But when I arrived in Poughkeepsie, I had immediate access. I was happy to see that this facility was now little used – a good indication that our reforms were working.

I was led through the facility by the director and a guard to what was called "the great hall" in the back. We walked past numerous locked "chambers", which the director informed me were for storing evidence related to cases. We then approached a locked door. The guard opened the door and the director and I entered a cavernous, windowless hall, with rows of shelving reaching high up in the hall. All the shelves were filled with urns.

I drew back in horror. Seeing my response, the director said, "Right this way Mr. President," and quickly led me to, and down, an isle about a third of the way into the hall. He led me to a moveable stairway, which he mounted toward the top. He then brought down two urns which had been located next to each other. They had alpha-numeric writing on them. One was the remains of Ian and the other Siobhan. He then showed me a print out that indicated that the writing on the urns cross-footed to their names and security numbers. He also assured me that he had double- and triple-checked for accuracy.

I thanked him and told him I'd like to be alone. He looked at me, bewildered. But remembering who I was he said, "Yes sir, Mr. President."

As he turned to go, I said, "You said that the urns are stored chronologically. Would you please read me some of the names before and after these two?"

"Certainly," and he began slowly reading about twenty names leading up to Ian and Siobhan. I looked up at the shelf and tried to imagine the people behind these names. Then he began slowly reading the names after them, "Guy Fawkes Crawford, Carmela Blanca Ortiz, Paul Garbowsky, Michael Ma Chan, Jonathon Simpson Raston, Hiro Yamaguchi ..."

"Stop!" I said gasping out. "Did you say Michael Chan?" I could hardly believe I was hearing the name that I had hated for so many years, a name that had symbolized to me what was wrong with our law enforcement establishment.

"Why, yes. Did you know him too?"

"I might have. Can you tell me anything about him?"

"No sir," the director said. "You know, they typically did everything they could to erase all records of the existence of disappeared people."

"I understand. Would you please bring that urn down as well?"

Once I had that urn in my possession, I excused the director. He left and went back to where my secret service agent was waiting.

I sat on the steps in the dead silence for a long time, feeling guilty that I had waited so long to learn about the fate of my friends. I was overcome with grief as I asked them to forgive me. I tried to hold back the tears, but they came. I cried for Ian and Siobhan. And as I looked up from their urns that I held in my hands to the other urns, I cried for those countless others who had also met their fate.

I thought of the interrupted, uncompleted lives that lay gathering dust. Of the anguish and sorrow of their loved ones and friends who had never known for sure what had happened to them. I wondered how many had been our best people, like Ian and Siobhan. How much betterment had our country lost as a result of their disappearances? In the end, feeling sad, depressed and old, I slowly stood up, gathered the three urns and left that tomb of sorrow.

I took the urns back to my friend's home in Poughkeepsie where I was staying, resolved to force our government to release the names of the disappeared people so that relatives, if still living, could claim them and have closure. I am proud that I was successful in my efforts.

At my friend's home, I stared at Ian's and Siobhan's urns, thinking about what to do with them. They had been only-children, their parents were long dead, and they had no children of their own, so there were no immediate relatives. Any friends would probably be gone by now.

But as I stared at their urns, thinking about what to do, my eyes kept darting over to that third urn. Could that possibly be Detective Michael Chan, the CBI agent who showed up at our school when Ian disappeared? The Michael Chan that I'd hated all these years? I finally had my secret service agent 'spond a list of Chans in the Mid-Hudson Valley and contact them to see if any were related to Michael Ma Chan.

After several hours, my agent came to me and said that he had located a Caitlin Chan, Chan's daughter. She was living in the historic-homes section in South Poughkeepsie. I thought about whether I should make contact with her, and if so, what would I say?

Finally, I knew I couldn't *not* meet with her. I felt there had to be a connection between Chan's disappearance and Ian's and Siobhan's. So I had my agent set up a meeting with her.

Being back in Poughkeepsie brought back a flood of memories. On the way over to Ms. Chan's house I had my agent drive by the upper form school, which still looked very much the same, though somehow more historic than how I had remembered it. We drove by my boyhood home. It still looked great. The Corporation had wanted to turn it into a museum to honor Poughkeepsie's "great native son", but I asked them not to. I preferred seeing people's lives passing in and out of it. I'd like to have gone in and reminisced, but was reluctant to disturb the people who lived there now.

South Poughkeepsie was now designated an historic district, which gave residents tax incentives to restore and maintain these reminders of the past. After the dom district had expanded from the central part of Poughkeepsie and filled the north, The Corporation started planning to expand into the southern part. Surprisingly, people rose up and petitioned The Corporation to preserve that historic part of Poughkeepsie. And maybe even more surprisingly, The Corporation had consented. This was one of the earlier, subtle ways The Corporation had started loosening up, realizing that Thomas Hobbes had not had all the answers.

After driving through some of the winding streets, we pulled up to a large, old white Victorian house with a small, well-kept garden in the front. I instructed my secret service agent to stay in the car while I went in. He hated it when I wouldn't let him go in and checkout places first, and then wouldn't let him stay plastered at my side. I reminded him that Ms. Chan had checked out as an upstanding citizen and was probably ten years older than myself, so fears of physical violence to my person were probably unfounded.

I walked up to the front door and rang the old-fashioned door bell. I loved the way these old houses were so "physical". An older, attractive oriental woman came to the door, immediately recognized me, and invited me in. She peered out at the waiting car and at the secret service agent as if to convince herself that it was really me.

"Mr. President, this is such an honor. I was absolutely stunned when your agent 'sponded me." She led me into a Victorian parlor and had me take a seat on a large chair, while she sat down on a sofa, which made her look even more petite. "Would you care for some tea? The water's heated." When I indicated that I liked the rooibos tea from her selection, she asked me to make myself at home while she went into the kitchen.

While she was gone, I looked around the room. It was very nicely done in the Victorian style, but yet was also comfortable. There was a simple, yet stately, old grandfather clock slowly ticking in between two front windows. And three antique wall clocks hanging on the opposite wall. They all seemed to be working, so I walked over and studied them. I wasn't familiar with antique clocks, but these appeared to be some kind of calendar clocks. In addition to showing the time at the top, they showed the month, date and day at the bottom.

From the clocks, I moved on to the next wall which was an old-style collection of framed pictures, certainly of family members. I liked these much better than wall- or holoplays of family members, especially in older homes. There were a number of pictures of a Caucasian man, and one with him and what appeared to be a young, beautiful Ms. Chan in wedding garbs; Buddhist if I wasn't mistaken. There were many of a boy, showing him growing up into adulthood.

Then I froze in my steps. There before me was the face of the man who had come into our school those many years ago. In a flash I was transported back to that day.

Ms. Chan came back into the room and set a tray with a tea pot, cups and cookies down. She said, "Oh, my rogue's gallery, as my dad used to say. He was in police work. Sit down and let's have our tea." As she poured, she glanced up at me as I made my way back to the sofa. I think she noticed that I was upset, confirming that this wasn't a social visit.

"I love your house. Obviously Victorian. When was it built?"

"In the 1860's. It has a very interesting history. It was built by a famous music teacher who came to teach music to the young women at Vassar College when it first opened. But its real claim to fame was that Walt Whitman stayed here with the teacher for about a month while the two of them worked together setting some of Whitman's poetry to music."

"That's fascinating. So much history. It was unfortunate that much of it was lost when The Corporation tore down so many old houses to build the doms. But I'm glad they spared this area. My boyhood home was also spared. It's located on the other side of the upper-form school."

"It must be nice to come back and see it," Ms. Chan said, obviously noticing that I was gazing around the room again, especially at the pictures. "Mr. President, I'm honored to have you here, and to myself!" She said smiling with a hint of embarrassment. "But I know you're still a very busy man. So please feel free to proceed with the purpose of your visit. Your agent had asked if I was related to Michael Ma Chan. And when I said yes, he set up this meeting."

I appreciated her openness, and quickly went over in my mind how I would best get to the bottom of this mystery without insulting her or getting too emotional myself. Finally, I began. "Ms. Chan, when I was in my teens here in Poughkeepsie, I had two dear friends who disappeared – and I know your father disappeared too at that time. I believe somehow their fates were intertwined, and I'd like to know how."

Ms. Chan stared at me for a moment, then turned to the pictures on the wall. I continued, recounting my journey of discovery that had brought me here. When I told her I'd discovered the urn holding the remains of her father, she broke down crying. I went over to the sofa and sat down next to her, putting my arms around her shoulders.

When she had recovered, she asked me for his remains. I went and got the urn from the car. When I handed it to her, she looked at it for a long time, feeling it, and holding it close to herself. She finally said, "Thank you, Mr. President. This means so much to me. We knew the CBI had disappeared my father – but to finally have his remains – to know for sure what happened to him. I feel I can let him go now. I just wish my mother could have been here now."

Feeling a fondness for her I said, "'Mr. President' is too formal. Please just call me Spencer."

"OK. If you'll call me Caitlin," she said looking up, smiling again through her tears.

"Sure," I said. "But Caitlin, I'm afraid the connection I had with your father was that he came to our school to talk to our director about Ian Vanderkill on the day Ian disappeared. I have to admit that I had always carried a grudge against Michael Chan all these years – till yesterday. Now I'm confused. That's why I'm here. To see if you can help me, if we can help each other, better understand what had happened."

"You've already helped me," Caitlin said looking down at the urn. "I hope I can help you. You see, my husband, Bill, was a casual friend of Ian's. They lived in the same dom and would meet occasionally on the way in or out and have talks. I met Ian a few times too. And though neither of us had met Siobhan, we knew of her through Ian; that he had started seeing her."

After a reflective pause, Caitlin continued, "Do you recall the huge scandal that broke out over the CaringMother Corporation's handling of fetuses entrusted to them for wombcare? How they had been selling fetuses to other corporations, including LEPGen Technologies, for use in research?" Caitlin asked.

"Sure. It shook the foundations of the wombcare industry and exposed the human engineering that was being conducted by a number of corporations – sanctioned by The Corporation." I reflected on how the resulting loss in people's confidence in The Corporation led to many important changes, including the halt to insidious forms of human engineering as well as prompting the beginning of the women's international Natura movement. Personally, it had confirmed my feeling that there needed to be safeguards for individuals built into the structure of The Corporation.

"Well, my father could never tell us about the specifics of cases he was working on, but we knew he had been working out at the LEPGen labs on South Road with a Dr. Treadwell on a case of suspected sabotage.

"On the day that the first recordings of what was happening in the labs was 'sponded out, mentioning Treadwell, my father contacted Bill about Ian's friend's name. Bill was concerned about Ian, so he took the very brave step of going to Ian's apartment to warn him. He was convinced that Siobhan was in the apartment at the time as well.

"Later in the evening, after my mother and I had returned from the Buddhist temple service, Bill was heading over to my apartment when he saw my father and his two protégés walking into his dom. They were on a mission and hadn't seen Bill. He watched from the lobby as the elevator stopped on Ian's floor. Bill was very fearful for Ian and Siobhan and very upset with my father, and 'sponded me that he wasn't coming over. He went back to his apartment and stewed. He was ashamed of himself for being too afraid to check on Ian.

"The next day both Ian and Siobhan had disappeared, and Bill started thinking seriously about breaking up with me because of my father, even though we had recently received permission to get married and have a child. That would have been the day when you saw my father at your school.

"But then something happened that changed everything. First, that horrific holoplay of the CaringMother CEO cutting deals with other executives was released by CorpiLeaks. The release of the HAL labs scenes earlier by the

Phantom'ogger had been bad enough, but the CorpiLeaks release was huge, international. The two were like a softening "one" and then a powerful "two" punch right to the gut; or for women, more specifically to the womb.

"Then my father disappeared late that day. We were distraught. My mother nearly went crazy, first trying to find out what had happened to my father, then retreating into the safe agony of silence. Bill stuck by me through those times – God bless him and rest his soul. He told me what had happened the day before, but never told me till years later that he had been very close to calling things off till my father disappeared.

"It was obvious to us that my father had been wrapped up in the whole story including the CorpiLeaks release; but how? Was he disappeared because of failing to stop the leaks? No, they wouldn't have disappeared him for that. Was he responsible for the CorpiLeaks releases himself? We tried to make sense of everything, continually wracking our brains for clues.

"The one thing I kept thinking about was the evening Bill and I told my parents that we had received permission to get married and have a child. We excitedly talked about wedding plans, but then my father brought up the question of having a baby. He thought we should hold off for a while. He asked me if I had thought of getting pregnant naturally and carrying the baby in myself. I was shocked that he had even mentioned the idea. I pounced on him pretty hard, saying that no one now-a-days did that. It would most certainly hurt my career and be a financial, not to mention physical, hardship.

"He dropped the subject. But he was obviously preoccupied the rest of the evening. He knew at that point what was going on at LEPGen with CaringMother's involvement and probably knew what was going on at the other corporations. That knowledge must have conflicted terribly with our plans to have a baby using CaringMother."

Caitlin could tell I was working at putting all these pieces together and said, "Taking these events into account and considering that my father's personality often conflicted with authority, we finally summarized the events of that Tricentennial week. We believed Ian and Siobhan were somehow involved in the sabotage going on at LEPGen and in the Phantom'ogger's release of the recordings of the experiments going on at LEPGen. It was after this that they disappeared. Then somehow my father got ahold of the CaringMother

CEO holoplay and passed it on to CorpiLeaks. And that is why he disappeared. Because of the way things were handled by the CBI in those days, I'm afraid we'll never know. But we always believed the three of them had a profound effect on the course of events in our country after the Tricentennial."

I nodded, "I agree, the pieces do fit together. Our country owes a great deal to the three of them. And you never got any kind of indication of what had happened from the CBI?"

This was the one time Caitlin looked at me as if I were a naïve school boy and said, "Spencer, you know how the CBI operated in those days. We never got a word out of my father's boss at the CBI. She passed away many years ago. My father had said that she was always bucking for an executive position, but my understanding is that she never moved beyond director level.

"A few years ago, after you had restructured the CBI and I felt comfortable enough, I tried contacting the two agents who had been working under my father at the time. Both had been transferred out to other CBI offices immediately. After some time both resigned from the CBI to go into other areas of police work. By the time I tried contacting them, one had died in the line of duty and the other of natural causes. With the three of them gone, so was all direct knowledge of what had happened during that time."

I nodded and asked, "What impact did all this have on you?"

"Bill and I did a lot of soul searching after what had happened. We continued on with our wedding plans, but knew we would never trust CaringMother with our baby. So we decided to hold off on having a baby till later. In the meantime this house came up for sale very cheap, so we jumped on it. It turned out it had belonged to a disappeared person, since there was no record of who the previous owner had been. People were always reluctant to buy something that had belonged to a disappeared person; you know, bad luck, fear of connection, returning ghosts, whatever.

"But I liked it immediately; it felt so homey. And it came fully furnished. The clincher, though, was that I loved the nursery upstairs. It's almost like the house had anticipated our hopes and dreams and was just waiting for us to move in.

"Since we were holding off on having a baby, we were able to afford the house. We moved in and enjoyed it being just the two of us for some time. We introduced ourselves to the neighbors. They were polite but obviously didn't want to have regular contact with the people living in this ill-fated house. And when we did talk to them, like when everyone was out working in their gardens, the subject was always the gardens, or weather. If I ever brought up our house they'd clam up. The subject was taboo, and we eventually dropped it completely.

"But one day while I was working out in the garden, my next-door neighbor commented on what a lovely job I was doing in the garden, that Siobhan had always done such a beautiful job too. She immediately realized what she had said. When I pushed her, she admitted that Siobhan Carlson had been the previous owner. But she would never speak about the house, or Siobhan, again. She was an elderly widow and died a few years later."

For a moment I stared at her. Then, as I looked around, I said, "This is a surprise. I knew Siobhan had lived in Poughkeepsie, but I didn't know where."

"Just imagine how surprised Bill and I were. But we were comfortable in living here. If anything, it made us love the house more – made it more personal.

"But you said there was a nursery? As far as I know Siobhan had never been married, nor had a child," I said trying to figure out this new piece of the puzzle.

"Yes, that had us mystified as well. It could have been that she had bought the house with that room already set up as a nursery. But it was done so beautifully that it became my favorite "thinking" room. I would go in there during quiet hours on the weekend or at night and sit in the rocking chair and think – and dream."

"I've always been a type-A personality, driven by ambition, planning everything. You know, career first, then meeting the right guy, getting married, having a baby. I had it all planned out.

"But the CaringMother scandal had left me questioning things, maybe for the first time in my life. I had never really questioned The Corporate Way, and now I was full of questions. I could imagine other women sitting in that nursery with their babies. Or maybe Siobhan sitting there dreaming about having a child. I began to understand that if I did have a child, my career would lose its central focus. I didn't want to screw this up.

"Finally, one day, I walked down stairs and told Bill I wanted to have a baby, but to have it naturally. Bill wasn't surprised, given the CaringMother scandal and the developing Natura movement. But how could we afford it? I agreed with him that it'd probably affect my career, but there were things in life more important than careers. I then told him to wipe that sudden smirk off his face because he'd now have to fill in the financial gap by pursuing advancements in his work more aggressively.

"Like many other young women at that time, I was beginning to see men as part of the solution, and no longer the problem. You know, maybe seeing them as equals – as partners."

After some reflection, Caitlin continued, "Those events in the Tricentennial week did have a huge influence on attitudes. You could argue that they made it possible for you, a male, to be elected CEO of the ISA."

"I have to agree. You're right."

"Well, nine months later, our son Michael was born. He was diagnosed with male-pattern aggressiveness. Of course, MPA has been debunked since then and is no longer considered a defect. Michael did have his temper problems and displays of aggressiveness, as many kids do, especially boys. But Bill and I worked them through with him. And he turned out fine," Caitlin said with a whimsical smile on her face as she looked at the photos on the wall.

Then turning back to me she added, "Of course, if we had used wombcare, he would have been terminated. Looking back, I think my father would have been diagnosed with MPA as well, but he was born before all that. You know, the way he flirted with women, which drove my mother nuts. And he had problems with authority. He didn't automatically do what he was told by his superiors, which was definitely not good in the CBI. When push came to shove, he just followed his own path."

"That's why I think he was the one who released the CaringMother holo-play to CorpiLeaks – even though he knew it would cost him his life. And I really believe he was trying to stop me from making a big mistake; protecting me," Caitlin added looking sadly at the wall of pictures.

"Our little Michael kept my mother going. She appreciated us naming him after my father. We visited her as much as possible, which made her day. She always remarked at how much he reminded her of my father. Even from an early age he could be quite demanding but yet get his way with the women. Like every time we went to her apartment to eat, he'd insist on sitting between my mother and me. He always said that Grampa told him to sit between his two girls. My mother got such a kick out of that. He had her wrapped around his little finger.

"Also, like my dad, he took an early interest in antique clocks. He was fascinated with all the clocks at my mother's. On his tenth birthday, my mother gave him one of my father's old American clocks – a simple, robust shelf clock. When we got home, Michael took his clock to his room, and to my horror, took it apart to see how it worked. But then he put it together again and it started right up. When he became a teenager he joined the local clock collectors association, and was soon doing the maintenance on Grandma's clocks. When my mother passed away, she left Michael all the clocks from my father's collection except for the four in this room."

"Yes, I was admiring them. Why did she, then you, keep these four?"

"The grandfather clock is to be a family heirloom, to be passed down to each generation. My father had received it from another clock collector who had had it in his family for over 300 years, originally in England, and had a complete history of the clock, which is very rare. My dad called it his 'love clock' because one of the owners had followed his heart and married the girl he loved in spite of being disinherited by his rich uncle as a result. This clock was the one thing he inherited from his uncle.

"Other than the three calendar clocks, it was the only clock that wasn't running when my mother returned home on the day my father disappeared. It had always been so robust and my father had kept it running religiously. She tried to start it again, and even had a clock association member stop over to check it out. It would run for a day or two, but then stop again. It wasn't till many years later, when she trusted my Michael enough to work on it, that he got it going again. It's never stopped since," Caitlin said looking fondly at the old clock.

"And the other three? They're calendar clocks?" I asked.

"Yes. American. From the late 1800's. Like other mechanical clocks, they tell you the time but also the day and date, though not the year. They were popular in the heyday of mechanical clocks. My father was fond of calendar clocks so he had three of them. He usually had at least one of them running all the time.

"But on the day my father disappeared, my mother found all three of them stopped at about 9:20 and set to Saturday, July 4. That was a clear sign to my mother that he had been back to their apartment that day. It was almost as if he had been indicating *that* July 4. You know, July 4 was on a Saturday that year, and all three were stopped and set to that date; three, Tricentennial.

"My mother tended to read a lot into it, as if he had signaled that he was declaring his independence and releasing those holoplays to CorpiLeaks. I didn't disagree with her. That would have been like my father. But it was obvious that he had been there that day, and had set the clocks to let her know he had been there. Kind of a goodbye before he disappeared.

"The grandfather clock had stopped about ten minutes later."

After we talked more about her family, and then mine, Caitlin offered to show me around the house, which I was looking forward to. While upstairs she led me into the room that was still a nursery.

"You never changed it?"

"No, we have four bedrooms up here and we had remodeled another room for Michael when he outgrew the nursery, so we just left it as is. I still liked to use it as my thinking room – and to commune with mothers long gone," Caitlin said somewhat embarrassed looking up at me. "It's a woman thing."

"Yes," I said as I considered the room further. "I can imagine Siobhan, sitting in that rocking chair, dreaming of the child she hoped to have some day."

Caitlin seemed to sense that I would like to spend a few minutes alone in this room so she said, "I'm going to go downstairs. Spend as much time as you'd like to up here."

I thanked her as she left. I slowly looked around this room of long-departed children. The old-fashioned toys were too orderly on the shelves. The crib was too neatly made up. The mobile was too stationary. The room was too quiet with no laughter of children or singing of mothers' lullabies. I went over to the rocking chair and sat for a long time in the silence, thinking about what Caitlin had told me today.

After all these years, I now had a good idea of what had happened to my friends. After all these years, I now no longer hated that detective who had visited my school. In place of the sadness and hate in my heart I now had the warmth of tremendous respect for, and gratitude to, Ian, Siobhan and Michael for all they had done for our country; for me.

Even though I now had the comfort of this knowledge, I knew there was much more that I would never know. I wanted to punch through this wall of not knowing.

As I again looked back to that last time I saw Ian and Siobhan in the Shakespeare garden, and at their tentative waves that I felt I could now almost touch, I had the feeling that there was a greater connection between myself and them than I was aware of.

What was it? Could I ever know?

I found myself wishing that I could have gotten to know them better; that they could have continued to live and to be happy; that they could have married and had a child to fill this room with life and happiness.

But they had chosen a different path; like Michael Chan, they had chosen to expose an evil in our midst knowing it would cost them their lives. They had done what was right. Could I have been so strong?

I knew that I was now at a decision point. I could carry on trying to uncover what had happened back during that Tricentennial week, those many years ago. I could risk becoming obsessed with tracking down the actions of ghosts, never reaching an end in a world that had gone beyond human knowing. Or I could use the limited days I had left helping others. Starting with bringing peace to the families of victims of those dark days, and in so doing, maybe bring peace to those victims themselves.

It didn't take me long to decide. I stood up and looked one last time around this room of hopes and dreams, now at rest but ready to welcome future people with promises of happiness. Then I went downstairs and told Caitlin about my intention to push the government to release the remains of all the disappeared victims and to see a national monument established in their memory, finally acknowledging the great wrong that had been done.

Caitlin expressed how important it was to her to have her father's remains, so she could lay him to rest next to her mother. She agreed it was important to give the same opportunity to all victims' families, and would be happy to help me in my efforts.

As we stood in the front hallway to say goodbye, I again thanked her for helping me understand the circumstances around Ian's and Siobhan's disappearances, as well as her father's. I told her I wished I had known her father, and apologized again for having judged him wrongly for so many years.

And as we were saying our goodbyes, the old grandfather clock began tolling the hour. I turned and looked into the parlor at this old time piece that had been marking the passage of life for over four centuries. My God, what had all taken place around that clock! What a forward-marching witness to history!

I could understand Michael's fascination with these functioning works of art. Peering into their works as he must have peered into the workings of his soul in the end. I suddenly had a vision of him working on one of his clocks, listening to music as an accompaniment to his toil of love. Music? It would have to have been baroque; yes, Bach.

With the last toll of the bell I realized Caitlin and I had been standing at attention, listening to its reminder to us. Caitlin and I turned to each other, smiling knowingly as we hugged each other, promising to get together again. And we would.

Reaching the car, I turned and looked one more time up at that historic old house, and at Caitlin standing waiving in the doorway. I reflected that in another world that could have been Siobhan, and maybe Ian, waving to me. But I was in this world, and still had things to do. I waived back and got into the car.

When I returned to my friend's home, my daughter, her husband and my grandson had arrived from their home in Boston. I told them about what I had discovered over the past few days and my new mission. Michael's remains were now where they should be. But what should I do with Ian's and Siobhan's?

I finally 'sponded my wife, Allison, who was in Australia attending a working conference on improving the lives of the aboriginal peoples of the world. She recalled Ian talking about the early Dutch settlers to the Hudson Valley in our historical awareness class, and that his ancestors had landed and settled in a valley down by Bear Mountain. When we sync'sponded Bear Mountain Park, and saw the name Doodletown, I remembered its name in Dutch was *Dodendal*, or Valley of the Dead. Ian had said that he'd often go there for a hike and to think. To commune with his past. We decided that that would be an appropriate final resting place for Ian and Siobhan.

As we were concluding, Allison 'sponded, *Do you remember the night we went to the Walkway over the Hudson to watch the Tricentennial fireworks? And you and Juan were so drunk?*

Oh yeah! But I've always tried to forget it!

And Ian saved you from that cop and waited till your parents showed up to take you home.

Yeah.

I've always wondered. After that, you started becoming more focused in class – leading discussions on independence, leading debates. And taking a real interest in me. Did Ian have a "man-to-man" talk with you that week before he disappeared?

I thought back to that week and 'sponded back, *Yes, more than once.*

Well, that's when I started noticing you – thinking of you as more than just a shy kid in class who got drunk one night.

I let that sink in for several moments.

Are you still there? Allison 'sponded.

Yes. I am. Thanks for sharing that with me, Honey. I love you.

I rented a boat to go down the river to Bear Mountain Park. I wanted to spend more time with my grandson so I decided to take him with me.

I was sure Siobhan hadn't been to Doodletown in the short time she had known Ian. But I felt they had had a greater connection to each other than just being co-conspirators, so it would be appropriate to keep them together. Call me romantic, but I had sensed a strong bond between them when I had last seen them at the school garden.

When we docked at Bear Mountain, my secret service agent helped me locate the Doodletown historic marker and the largely overgrown path behind it that would lead me to the Valley of the Dead. He was concerned, as usual, when I said I'd go alone with my grandson. I insisted my grandson would know what to do if I had any problems. It was a beautiful, late autumn, "Indian summer" day with no inclement weather in the forecast, so I was quite comfortable.

I was surprised at how overgrown the path was, but somehow it seemed appropriate. After walking along the path for some time, we finally found what had been the main road up from the Hudson near Iona Island, which was now largely an overgrown path. As we walked we passed the occasional indication of a stone wall or even stone foundation peeking out of the undergrowth. I was concerned about finding our way, but then I saw the pond with a graveyard just beyond it that Ian had described, so I knew we weren't lost.

We walked beyond the pond and up along the path next to a stream. I was amazed at how peaceful and quiet the valley was. I looked around and explained to myself that it was indeed cut off from the outside world by the surrounding mountains, the river, and the highlands on the other side of the river.

But there was more to this Valley of the Dead than just being cut off. The very atmosphere felt different, and seemed to penetrate my being with such a feeling of peace and release that I almost felt as though I were floating along up the path. The warmth of the sun brought out a sweet, honeysuckle smell. But there was an even sweeter, more subtle fragrance underneath that humbled me. It was an ancient breath that spoke of a world beyond time.

After several minutes we came upon a large rock next to the stream, and I decided to rest on it. The flowing water induced me to 'spond up a number of piano barcarolles by Ravel, Faure, Bennett, Griffes and Schubert. As my grandson drifted back toward the pond, I told him to be careful.

After sitting on the rock for some time, staring at the moving water while I listened to the flowing music, I took the two urns out of the day pack, opened them and slowly sprinkled the ashes from both into the stream. As I watched the ashes fall and swirl together in the current, I said a prayer for Ian and Siobhan, and for all the others like them who still needed to find peace.

I don't know how long I sat there. I had switched to listening to the prayerful chants of Rachmaninoff's *Vespers* and at first I felt a deep sadness. But slowly that sadness flowed away with the stream and only a calm, timeless peace was left. I know I wasn't sleeping, but was also not awake. I felt like I was in a world between the two.

In my reverie, I heard a young boy laugh. I could feel a smile creeping over my face, thinking of my grandson playing by the pond, probably trying to catch a jumping frog. But then I realized that the laugh wasn't coming from the pond but from up the path in the other direction. I slowly looked up into the cool darkness under the towering trees and saw two figures looking back at me. In my dream-like state it seemed only normal that there would be other hikers here, so I smiled at them and they smiled back.

But something started nagging at me. Again, as one would sluggishly do in a dream, I realized that we hadn't encountered any other people since we started, and even though the two were standing in the dark shade of the giant trees, they were clearly visible – almost radiant. Was the sunshine making its way through the dense leaf cover and falling on them?

One was an older man and the other a boy. I smiled, thinking of myself and my grandson and of Ian's descriptions of when he used to come here with his grandfather. I looked into the man's eyes and we both smiled and nodded, understanding each other, not needing words to pass between us.

But then I noticed that he was wearing very old-fashioned clothes, like what one would expect an early European immigrant to be wearing. I also noticed that though the man had graying blondish hair and a tanned complexion, the boy had dark hair, almost black, that contrasted sharply with his pale, almost translucent skin, and incredibly light blue eyes. No, I didn't think they were grandfather and grandson after all.

As if prompted by my realizations, they looked at me, smiled again, and turned their gazes past me and down the path toward the Hudson, as if for one last time. Then they turned and walked up the path together and into the cool darkness of the trees and vanished.

Still in a state of peace and finding nothing strange about this encounter, I pondered who the two might have been. I believed the man was an early settler, who, straightening up from his back-breaking toils of survival, took a minute to dream about the future, wondering what life would be like in this new world, for himself, his wife, his children, his children's children, and on through time.

But the boy puzzled me. He had a much more ephemeral, elusive quality about him, as if he were less solid than the man. And that puzzlement stayed with me.

Since my visit to this valley, and in nights after I've had especially peaceful and contemplative days, he has sometimes visited me in my dreams. In those dreams I'm again about his age, three or four years old, and we play together. Sometimes we play with my favorite big-machine and muscle-car toys in the backyard of my boyhood home in Poughkeepsie. Sometimes we're back in this valley playing in open grassy fields or in the pools of the stream. And there are other children too, of varying ages, dressed in clothing from various times in history.

Whatever the place, we always have such fun playing together. The weather is always perfect with lush, green vegetation, perfectly blue skies and a brilliant sun that almost shines through the boy and the other children. Time doesn't exist there – it's as if we could go on playing forever.

But then my adult self starts scratching its way in. I begin asking him questions, like what his name is and where he's from. And this is always the beginning of the end of the dream. Finally the boy's mother calls him to come home, as do the other children's mothers.

As he and the others turn to go home, I realize who his mother is. But then I wake up and that knowledge is gone. I try to claw my way back into the dream to find out again who she was, but it's always too late.

I can't explain why, but I've come believe that that boy was someone's unrealized dream. That at some point in the past she had come to the Valley of the Dead, had reached into her deepest being and lifted him out. She had known that he'd never come into being in this world and hadn't been able to accept it. But here she found peace and acceptance, and was finally able to let him go.

With a start I looked up and stared down the path toward the pond, feeling a sudden wakeful sense of concern for my grandson. I hurried down the path and found him watching dragonflies by the water. I bent down, hugged him, and felt overcome by emotions. When he asked me what the matter was, I told him I felt so fortunate.

I did feel fortunate. But I felt terribly confused as well. In so many ways my life had followed a path that had seemed so understandable and natural to me. I had been brought up by two wonderful parents and had had so much support from so many good friends as I sought my way. I was fortunate to have had exceptional abilities which I felt I had made good use of by working hard over the years. I had seen my life as a simple, straight line leading down the path I had chosen.

But everything I had learned over the past several days made we wonder if I had really understood my life – life – at all. It left me wondering how much more there was that I would never know. And had I forged my own destiny as I had always assumed, or was I really a receptacle, and beneficiary, of the destinies – indeed of the dreams – of all who had ever touched my life? Had I come to *Dodendal*, or had I been brought here?

I gradually straightened up and gazed across the pond to the graveyard. I watched the long, thin branches of the weeping willows gently caress the tops of the tombstones, having received their movement from invisible breezes. I looked at the barely-visible, rolling waves on the pond and up toward the creek whose progress had delivered the waves to the pond. And finally I looked up the creek toward the rock I had sat upon and thought one more time about the man and the boy.

Slowly that same calmness and acceptance I had felt while on the rock seeped back into my being. And looking at where the stream flowed into the pond, and at the ash-flecked waves as they sought me out on the shore, I wished Ian and Siobhan peace one last time.

It was while my grandson and I were walking hand-in-hand down that narrow, dusty, dirt road toward the river, that I resolved to make this Valley of the Dead a national monument to the countless souls who, like Ian and Siobhan, and Michael too, had met untimely ends because they had had thoughts and dreams that conflicted with The Corporation.

But as I thought about the dreams that Ian, Siobhan and Michael must have had, and what I had experienced up on that rock by the stream, I began to think of this valley as a place where people could come and let their thoughts flourish and dreams soar.

It was the Valley of Dreams.

Appendix A

The Rise of the Corporation

Linda Xiaobo7
Historical Awareness
Ian Vanderkill
July 3, 2076

"For by art is created that great LEVIATHAN, called a COMMONWEALTH, or STATE, in Latin CIVITAS, which is but an artificial man; though of greater stature and strength than the natural, for whose protection and defence it was intended; and in which the *sovereignty* is an artificial *soul*..." Thomas Hobbes, *Leviathan*

The forerunners to corporations were the companies that were formed to exploit the riches of colonies being founded around the world in the age of world exploration. The king or queen of a country would grant a specific company a charter to found and populate a designated area in the new world. The company would explore that area and determine what resources were available to be exploited, and then set about exploiting these resources. The king normally did not have the resources to undertake such a venture – his resources were usually tied up in preparing for, or fighting, wars in Europe. But what he did have was the land in the new world that was claimed in his name.

The king recognized that these charters were mutually beneficial; that the companies would become wealthy by exploiting the resources of the colonies and would in turn be taxed by the king to increase his wealth. But the king had the ultimate power. If a company did not produce to his satisfaction, he could revoke their charter and give it to another company that would perform to his satisfaction.

When the United States became independent from Great Britain, the king was gone and in his place were the individual state governments, as well as the US government, representing the people who put them into their positions. In essence, or at least in theory, the people became the sovereign who would grant and revoke company charters. Of course, the people with say at that time were white men with property. As with the king, charters were granted to companies for specific purposes and for specific periods of time and could be revoked at the will of the people, especially if the company had exceeded its authority.

After the American Civil War, more and more companies incorporated in order to limit their liabilities. Also, the 14th amendment was written and passed ostensibly to help ex-slaves. This amendment included the important words: "...nor shall any state deprive any person of life, liberty, or property, without due process of law; nor deny to any person within its jurisdiction the equal protection of the laws".

Corporations recognized that it was imperative for them to attain "personhood", and worked on attaining this through the courts until the Supreme Court declared them legal persons in 1886. This led to a dramatic reduction in the abilities of states to structure and control corporations, as well as to revoke their charters. In the early 1900s the increasing trend was to grant corporations charters in perpetuity.

As corporations grew in size in the twentieth century, they increasingly worked at influencing politics. At the same time, states and the federal government worked on laws trying to restrict the influence corporations could have in the political process, especially through campaign contributions. However, in the *Citizens United* case in 2010, in a 5 to 4 ruling, the Supreme Court declared unconstitutional laws that restricted campaign contributions by corporations. After all, they were "persons" and therefore had the right to speak their minds. This opened the way for the vast resources of profitable corporations to influence the course of American politics.

Of course, some politicians, including the president, voiced concerns, but this soon faded as politicians increasingly accepted money from corporations and, with this, did their bidding. Unleashed spending by corporations, coupled with the already huge spending by those who had benefited from corporations, would increasingly determine the direction of American politics.

In 2005, there was a concerted effort by the president and his supporters in congress to "privatize" social security. Under "privatization", instead of contributing money to the social security fund for their retirement, Americans would invest that money in corporate stocks and bonds largely through mutual funds, with the idea that they would have more money for their retirement.

There was a great concern among the American public that the ups and downs of those markets would make their retirements more risky. This outcry, as well as firm resistance from a large faction in congress, put an end to this idea at the time. The Great Recession of 2007, in which the stock market lost almost half its value, only reinforced the perception that this was not a good idea.

It was not until 2024 when corporate spending in elections, coupled with that of the very rich, had increasingly dwarfed the contributions of individuals and other organizations, and when the ravages of the Great Recession had receded from the immediate memories of most people, that the president and congress finally fully "privatized" social security along with medicare for younger people. Massive corporate spending in the media, as well as "urban legends" spread through the media, had convinced most younger people that traditional social security and medicare would not be there for them when they retired.

The United States had always been a capitalist society, whose fortunes had been tied into the fortunes of private enterprise. But this privatization of social security and medicare solidly locked in the fortunes of Americans with those of corporations. Corporations were becoming the sovereigns and people their subjects.

Corporations increasingly put up their people to run for congress and for the presidency, quite often ex-CEOs, and poured billions into their elections. The candidates touted their abilities to run government economically like a business. This was also done at a state and local level, so all levels of American society were becoming more influenced by corporations.

With a progressively more corporate-friendly atmosphere, all levels of government were increasingly privatizing their agencies and services, including all levels of education, kindergarten through university. The armed services had become ever more dependent upon outside corporations, as had first become obvious in the Iraq and Afghanistan wars. But it wasn't till 2050 that the armed services were finally "privatized" and were then run by a consortium of prior private contractors to the armed services.

But no matter how pervasive corporations and their influence became in American society there was still always a level of unpredictability. Once in office, elected officials did not always do the corporations' biddings, or more often went off on tangents that often proved disastrous. Sometimes it was due to a lack of coordination on the corporations' parts. Like the mideastern oil wars of the 2030s as oil was increasingly scarce. The oil corporations and defense contractors supported going to war, and in fact largely engineered the United States getting dragged in to them.

But these wars were astronomically expensive and were devastating to the US's budget deficit. As in the earlier part of the century, to prevent the economic collapse of the US government, new and higher taxes, including on corporations, as well as drastic cuts in spending, had to be initiated. Beyond the oil corporations and defense contractors, most corporations did not support these wars, especially when the resultant higher taxes showed up.

In the 2040s the writings of the 17th century philosopher Thomas Hobbes became popular again. Hobbes said that humans as individuals were self-centered, anarchic and war-like, and were simply driven toward pleasure and away from pain. Their most fundamental drive was survival, and to that end they submitted to the power of a sovereign who would keep them all in line with reward and punishment; in essence, protecting them from other humans. People's submission to the sovereign lasted only as long as he was able to protect them. Hobbes further said that society could be and should be run with the efficiency of a machine, introducing the idea of social engineering.

It was at the 2042 meeting of the CEOs of the top 100 large international corporations where the need for a major change in direction was earnestly discussed. Like the United States, many other countries were again teetering on economic collapse and were riven by special-interests-driven civil strife. Given corporations' now paramount influence in most countries, these top CEOs realized that they were in the position to make major changes and now was the time to act.

Kenneth Rechner, CEO of LEPGen Technologies, the large, very influential multinational technologies corporation that was the developer of the transponder, handed out copies of Hobbes' *Leviathan* and recommended that each CEO not only read it but study it as a road map to where they needed to go. (Note: much of this and the following "insider" perspectives were sourced from Kenneth Rechner's memoirs first published in 2056, revised in 2061 and again in 2065.)

When they reconvened three months later, they decided that corporations needed a much more direct influence on the course of events. In fact corporations should become the sovereigns of countries and engineer those societies into efficient, well-oiled machines, eliminating the wearing friction of civil strife and war. They believed that if they approached things correctly they could convince the populations of their countries not only of the need, but desirability, of corporations taking over the running of their countries.

They realized that each country was different and at different stages of receptiveness, and that each country would be more receptive to corporations at least nominally "based" in their countries. So they decided that they would initiate this change in stages, with spheres of control based on where corporations were based. But in the end, all important matters and problems would be resolved by an international consortium of corporations, ultimately looking very similar to their top 100 corporations meetings.

After much discussion, they included the United States in the first tier of transformation. The US was a huge, complex, and diverse country which in itself would make one shy away from the undertaking. However, three important elements made it a good place to start. First, it truly was on the brink of financial collapse, and had been for many years, largely from the many wars which were causing it to drop ever further into a financial black hole. People were scared and realized that something drastic had to happen, but government was doing nothing to correct the problem.

Second, with the long history of corporate influence, much more so than most countries, Americans would be certainly receptive to the idea of having corporations run their country. In fact their very well-being, especially in old age with privatized social security and healthcare, was inextricably tied into the well-being of corporations.

And third, the long-celebrated "diversity" in the country was tearing it apart, because people chose to not just celebrate their supposed uniqueness, but to use it in a way that would serve them individually, and their own special-interest groups, best. They were very much like the humans described by Hobbes.

Fortunately, Rechner was not only very intelligent and visionary, but he was also very charismatic. So he took up the challenge to transform the United States and become its first corporate president. Taking a leave from LEPGen Technologies, and using billions in corporate contributions, and contributions from the wealthy who had benefited from corporate wealth, he ran a presidential campaign of promising to truly run the country like a business, leading it back from the brink of bankruptcy, and once and for all ending special treatment for special interests. He also had some of his best people take leaves as well and run for congress to further enhance the corporate-friendly atmosphere in congress.

Once in office, he did exactly what he said he would. As a strong leader, as he had been in LEPGen, he reviewed major areas of expenditures, and began wisely cutting spending in areas where he saw fat and least resistance to cuts. He also convinced congress to pass laws banning special treatment for special interests, whether race, sex, ethnicity, age, political or other. Civic-minded Americans of all ethnic backgrounds loved him and what he was doing. They were his base support.

When reelected to office by a landslide, Rechner announced that it was time to take the next step and form a more efficient corporate-style government structure, in which he would be the first CEO and chairman of the board.

Congress would now be disbanded and there would be special elections for the fifteen-member Board of Directors who would take their place. Anyone could run for The Board, though in the end result it was typically CEOs taking leaves from their corporations and running with billions in corporate backing who won the positions.

Of course, Rechner and "The 100" were astute business people and knew they had to sell these changes, so in advance of this announcement they tapped all large, medium and small corporations that they felt they could trust to donate large sums of money to finance an unprecedented media blitz. Also, knowing that Americans would overwhelmingly support "What's good for corporations is good for America", they gave these corporations a high-level briefing of what they would be proposing and got their advanced support for the new government to be included in the blitz.

Not surprisingly, once the corporations were contacted, word got out on what Rechner was intending to do, and many people, especially congresswomen and -men began to cry that the sky was falling. But Rechner and the corporations moved quickly and efficiently to launch their blitz. In the end, with constant, positive media coverage at all levels, and with the support of so many corporations representing so many jobs, the new changes were supported by the overwhelming majority of Americans. This was proven by polls taken by AmPoll, the most trusted polls-taking corporation in America.

With a straight line of financial support to corporations for on-leave CEO candidates, there was no longer a real need for the financial support of political parties, who had only represented special interests anyway. There was very little resistance to the disbanding of congress and the rapid demise of political parties since most people had come to believe that their two-party system only gave them "tweedledum/tweedledee" choices, and party-driven government was always locked into special-interest battles, never solving the real problems.

After the special elections, The Board's first order of business was to construct the corporate mission and bi-laws to replace the antiquated constitution. The old constitution itself merely stated how the government was structured, with president, congress and the supreme court, so that was easily replaced with the new structure described in the bi-laws.

The potentially touchy part was what to do about the "after-thought" amendments to the constitution, which contained the rights of individuals. This was resolved by first stating that the corporate government was supreme and then somewhat vaguely enumerating most of the same amendment rights as still being granted to individuals as long as they did not interfere with the efficient running of the government. So, for example, people had freedom of religion as long as their religion's teachings did not oppose the corporate government. People could also speak freely as long as it did not interfere with the running of the government.

The bi-laws were written so that each board member had hands-on responsibilities for specific areas of the government, somewhat like the president's cabinet under the old structure, but with more power. For example, one member would be responsible for all police and intelligence agencies, including the FBI (now CBI) and CIA. Another would be the head of the court system, including the Supreme Court. Any member, as well as the CEO, could propose a law or propose revoking a law and the proposal would pass with a majority of votes from The Board members. If the CEO vetoed the law, The Board members would have to muster 60% yea votes to override the CEO's veto. The Board could also remove the CEO or any member with a super majority of 60%.

Different from the old constitution, states' rights were deliberately not mentioned in the bi-laws, since the intention was to increasingly marginalize the states to the point where they could be done away with and replaced by efficient corporate divisions. At best, states were an unnecessary level of semi-independent government, and therefore uneconomical. They still often insisted on doing things their own way, which could make governing very messy. But the Second Mexican War had shown that states could be downright dangerous.

To set the stage for the direction they were going in, The Board voted to change the name of the country to the Incorporated States of America (ISA). In other words, they were no longer individual, though united, states. They were now incorporated – made into one indivisible entity. When the question of what to do with the national flag arose, most members wanted to retain the basics of the old flag, but change the 47 stars to equilateral triangles, to reflect the basic corporate structure. However, in the end, in keeping with the idea to deemphasize the states and emphasize incorporated unity, it was decided to go with just one large, white equilateral triangle on the field of blue, while retaining the quaint, and recognizable, red and white stripes of the original thirteen states.

Rechner was again ready with a coordinated blitz once The Board of Directors had completed their work and the new Corporate Mission and Bylaws were announced. The new structure of the government was supported by the large majority of Americans. Again, this was demonstrated by polls taken by AmPoll. ... And, as the saying goes, the rest is history.

If one looks back at the progression of America's history, especially since the Bicentennial, the progression towards becoming a corporate state was obvious and inevitable. Many consider the incorporating of the United States to have been a revolution. I think it was more of an inevitable evolution and fortunately a bloodless one at that. In the past quarter century since this transformation was first kicked off, the ISA has not only balanced its budget but has begun paying off the huge deficit left to us by the USA. This was largely due to running the country like a business; from eliminating pork and special-interest spending to restructuring government from the top on down; states and local governments were economically combined with others and transformed into efficient corporate divisions answering to headquarters.

By eliminating the need for political parties, and thereby the inroad to influence, special-interest groups largely shriveled into rather quaint reminders of the divisiveness they had created in our country. And as a result we have become a much more civil and respectful society.

And finally, with many more countries following our corporate model, there is less and less cause for war. When another country is also incorporated, we know that their interests are economically identical to ours and that our CEO and Board of Directors have direct access to theirs to iron out disagreements and other problems. This was the outcome of the Stockholm Accords of 2070, which also laid the groundwork for corporate officials from other countries to be allowed to run for office in the ISA, and vice versa, thus fostering ever greater international cooperation. Thomas Hobbes would indeed be proud.

Corporate Mission of the Incorporated States of America

Our mission as the Government of the Incorporated States of America (The Corporation) is to structure and run the Incorporated States of America as one would a corporation; that is, in a manner that is geared toward ever-increasing efficiencies; and in so doing, optimizing the "profit" of the country. "Profit", which is the excess of revenues to The Corporation over expenditures, will be used to pay down the deficit left to the ISA by the USA, or to return that excess to the citizenry or a portion of the citizenry, to be determined by the Board of Directors. Citizens will retain the rights as addressed in the first ten amendments to the Constitution of the United States, also known as the Bill of Rights, so long as these rights do not interfere with the above expressed mission. All other amendments are no longer necessary and are hereby abolished.

Appendix B

The Declaration of Independence

Spencer Galloway
Historical Awareness
Ian Vanderkill
July 3, 2076

What is the essence of being human and the purpose of the human life? I had thought about this question many times without being able to answer it. But one experience set me on the road to answering it. We have a schnauzer-mix dog named Timo who spends his days laying around, obviously bored. He gets excited when we come home, or when we take him out on his leash and he sees other people and dogs. But these are restrained, limited experiences and he is soon back in the confines of our house.

One day when we were out for a hike in the "wilds" of Fahnestock Park, I realized what Timo's essence as a schnauzer was. As usual, we released him from his leash and he went running off sniffing the ground, marking his spots, and peeking over the old stone walls, till he saw squirrels and chipmunks and proceeded to chase them. Of course, they would always get away from him, but that didn't matter. He was doing what schnauzer do – chase rodents.

As he went on to discover the next one – sniffing, looking, listening – I could tell that he was totally alive and happy to have the freedom to do what was in his nature. He was in his element, experiencing his essence. When we got home, he plopped down from exhaustion, not boredom, and in his sleep his legs would occasionally move rapidly; he was obviously chasing squirrels in his sleep.

So what of humans? Reading the Declaration of Independence started me on the path to answering that. It states, "... that all Men are created equal, that they are endowed by their Creator with certain unalienable Rights, that among these are Life, Liberty, and the Pursuit of Happiness." This last part is a chain of dependencies. First you need the basic right to life, to not have it taken away, in order to have liberty. And you must have liberty in order to pursue that great end of happiness.

But what is happiness? It has always seemed vague, and therefore disturbing, to me. Thomas Jefferson, the main author of the Declaration, as well as the other rebels present at the signing of the Declaration, were greatly influenced by the European philosophers of the enlightenment, who were in turn heavily influenced by the great Greek philosophers, primarily Aristotle.

Aristotle said that the one thing that defines humans, that distinguishes them from all other animals, is their mind and their unique use of their mind. He further said that to lead a meaningful, fulfilled life we must use our minds in a eudaemonic manner.

Many would translate the Greek *eudaimonia* as the "pursuit of happiness". But I believe this is too vague and misleading. A better translation is "flourishing". *Eudaimonia* does not mean to attain a vague *end* called happiness; it is a way of life in which one continues to develop one's essence as a human being, one's mind; to lead an intellectually flourishing life. A life of contemplation, but also a life of using one's mind to help others.

Interestingly, Aristotle believed the most eudaemonic life is one that is involved in the affairs of state, one seeking to perfect the state as he seeks to perfect himself. By this definition, Thomas Jefferson, and many of his fellow rebels, had certainly lead eudaemonic lives. I think Aristotle got it right, and Thomas Jefferson rightly captured the idea of leading a "flourishing life" as a basic right of all people.

The Declaration of Independence goes on to say that people found governments to secure these rights and "...that whenever any Form of Government becomes destructive of these Ends, it is the Right of the People to alter or abolish it, and to institute new Government...." When Americans won the War of Independence they accomplished the end of abolishing a government that did not meet their needs, but after trying an unsuccessful confederation of states for a number of years, they finally established a federation of states in 1787.

Although the objectives and wording of that Constitution were ideal, the reality was far from perfect. Without specifically stating it, the benefits of the new federation were for white men with property. Of course, their wives and children benefited as well, as long as they toed the line. Others, especially black slaves, did not. But by using the wording of the declaration and of the constitution, and making amendments to the constitution, other groups were eventually able to gain those same benefits.

When the young French aristocrat Alexis de Tocqueville visited the United States in 1831, he was extremely interested in and excited about the young democracy. He greatly admired the rugged individualism and confidence he found in most Americans and the profound freedoms they possessed, especially that of religion. He was impressed by the deeply religious beliefs of Americans. And was amazed at the religious diversity that flourished in America, as opposed to having only one state-sanctioned faith as in France.

But he was also concerned that this democracy's equalizing effect would produce a nation of materialists concerned only about their individual well being, losing sight of the greater good and loosing an interest in the future. This could be a new despotism that, "...does not break wills, but it softens them, bends them, and directs them; it rarely forces one to act, but it constantly opposes itself to one's acting; it does not destroy, it prevents things from being born." Of course, many of his contemporaries in the USA dismissed his negative concerns as the elitist comments of an old world aristocrat.

Unfortunately, if you look at the post-bicentennial history of the United States, you can see where his concerns eventually took full effect. Americans increasingly ignored the well-being of their country and concerned themselves largely with their individual material well being. Instead of getting involved in civic concerns, they cynically turned toward those special-interest groups that would help them get to the "top of the heap". And as we saw in the end, the United States became a failed state, bankrupt financially, bankrupt of people who cared, and locked into an ironclad gridlock of special-interest demands. It had become a country of squabbling groups whose elected leaders were not leading eudaemonic lives of trying to perfect the state, but were merely pandering to selected groups' demands to get elected.

As the United States was descending into financial and civil chaos, The Corporation stepped in to save the country. As the Declaration of Independence stated, if a government does not meet the needs of its people, they have the right to alter it or abolish it. So The Corporation formed a new "corporate-based" government, running the country like a business with financial responsibility. There is no question that The Corporation has been not only balancing the budget, but making a profit too (i.e. creating a surplus). They also seem to have gotten us beyond much of our past special-interest-induced civil strife. Plus, realizing how uneconomical and non-productive wars of the past century have been, they have avoided wars and have been building bridges of cooperation to other like-minded, corporate-based governments, which certainly helps in preventing wars.

However, The Corporation as a government has a number of structural deficiencies that must be rectified. Just as Thomas Jefferson finished the Declaration of Independence with a list of grievances the colonies had with the King of England, I will conclude my composition with a preliminary list of the grievances we Americans should have with our current government.

The purpose of government is to serve the people, not the other way around. This basic fact has been increasingly forgotten and ignored by the succeeding governments of the USA and ISA. Each individual should have certain basic rights including Life, Liberty and the Pursuit of Happiness. Each individual should be allowed, and encouraged, to lead a flourishing life, expanding her/his intellect and spirit in a direction that she/he sees fit without the fear of interference by the police. This includes freedom of religion, the freedom to speak one's mind in the open, and the freedom to act on one's ideas, without fear of reprisal from The Corporation.

The current government structure does not allow this and must be amended to address the following shortcomings.

The Bill of Rights that include freedom of religion and speech, are subordinate to the Corporate Mission Statement, and therefore only exercised when convenient, which in practice is never. *The Bill of Rights must be put on the same level of the CMS, or above it, and those rights must be protected. This will be done by moving the courts back to a position of independence from the rest of the government. The police structure must also be educated on these rights of individuals and made to enforce them.*

Gestations at wombcare centers are terminated for perceived health defects and for predicted aggressive personality without the consent of the parents. *Gestations should only be terminated for perceived health deficiencies with the consent of both parents. Terminations for predicted aggressive personality should never be performed. These predictors have never been proven to be accurate. And if a child does display aggressive tendencies, his parents, teachers and other adults should work with him in a humane manner to overcome them.*

By law, every individual must have a transponder implanted in her/his brain at the age of two. Due to complications related to the still-underdeveloped level of children's brains at the age of two, and the often unsanitary conditions in which transponders are implanted, especially in lower-band children, the mortality rate of two-year-olds is much higher than children of other ages. This is unacceptable. *The following steps must be taken:*

Implants must be performed at the earliest at the age of five. A number of studies, which The Corporation has attempted to suppress, indicate that this is a much safer age and allows the child's creativity to grow more fully.
Sanitary conditions and the child's mental development must take precedence over the convenience of The Corporation.

The inventor of the transponder, LEPGen Technologies Corporation, currently has a lock on all transponder implants. This monopoly has eliminated LEPGen Corporation's need to compete and thus improve their product. Other corporations must be encouraged to develop a superior product and allowed to bid their products to The Corporation.

Lower-band children are immediately put into learning factories where they are trained in skills to perform certain work that The Corporation projects it will need them for. Any education that might expand their thoughts and intellect is excluded from their training. *All children should receive the same education through the elementary years, which should also include fun and creative activities that will help develop their minds. They should all then have the opportunity to compete for placement in higher form schools based on their abilities, not on their parents' band levels.*

The Corporation says that it is running the country like a business, yet everywhere one turns one sees where specific corporations have a monopoly over their sphere of expertise. For example, LEPGen Technologies with transponder implants, Euthanesta with sleep palaces, and DomFab with domicile construction. It is a well-known and proven fact that with no competition, monopolies hike their prices and profits, reduce their spending on research and development, which depresses improvements to products, and they become lazy and arrogant in serving us, their customers. *To rectify this situation, The Corporation must institute a new policy that encourages competition from all sources, including with grants where necessary, and that all big C Corporation divisions and small c corporations must put requests for services and products out to bid to at least three competing corporations as well as to smaller start-up companies. Those who violate this policy must be investigated, including procurement agencies acting for The Corporation.*

Appendix C

Bill Of Rights
FIRST TEN AMENDMENTS TO THE CONSTITUTION OF THE UNITED STATES OF AMERICA

Amendment I
Congress shall make no law respecting an establishment of religion, or prohibiting the free exercise thereof; of abridging the freedom of speech, or of the press; or of the right of the people peaceably to assemble, and to petition the government for a redress of grievances.

Amendment II
A well regulated militia, being necessary to the security of a free state, the right of the people to keep and bear arms, shall not be infringed.

Amendment III
No soldier shall, in time of peace be quartered in any house, without the consent of the owner, nor in time of war, but in a manner to be prescribed by law.

Amendment IV
The right of the people to be secure in their persons, houses, papers, and effects, against unreasonable searches and seizures, shall not be violated,

and no warrants shall issue, but upon probable cause, supported by oath or affirmation, and particularly describing the place to be searched, and the persons of things to be seized.

Amendment V

No person shall be held to answer for a capital, or otherwise infamous crime, unless on a presentment or indictment of a grand jury, except that cases arising in the land or naval forces, or in the militia, when in actual service in time of war or public danger; nor shall any person be subject of the same offense to be twice put in jeopardy of life or limb; nor shall be compelled in any criminal case to be a witness against himself, nor be deprived of life, liberty, or property, without due process of law; nor shall private property be taken for public use, without just compensation.

Amendment VI

In all criminal prosecutions, the accused shall enjoy the right to a speedy and public trial, by an impartial jury of the state and district wherein the crime shall have been committed, which district shall have been previously ascertained by law, and to be informed of the nature and cause of the accusation; to be confronted with the witnesses against him; to have compulsory process for obtaining witnesses in his favor, and to have the assistance of counsel for his defense.

Amendment VII

In suits at common law, where the value in controversy shall exceed by twenty dollars, the right of trial by jury shall be preserved, and no fact tried by a jury, shall be otherwise reexamined in any court of the United States, than according to the rules of the common law.

Amendment VIII

Excessive bail shall not be required, nor excessive fines imposed, nor cruel and unusual punishments inflicted.

Amendment IX

The enumeration in the Constitution, of certain rights, shall not be construed to deny or disparage others retained by the people.

Amendment X

The powers not delegated to the United States by the Constitution, nor prohibited by it to the states, are reserved to the states respectively, or to the people.

Acknowledgements

My special thanks to my wife, Alste, for reading and editing the first draft of this book. To Eileen Charbonneau, author, teacher, and editor extraordinaire for her invaluable advice on improving this book. To John Ranger for his astute advice and help in copyediting the final version. To Tony Musso, author and advisor, for his insightful help during the publishing process.

I would like to acknowledge the influence Elizabeth Stalter's book *Doodletown* had in inspiring my imagination in developing the *Dodendal* setting.

In structuring the historical background of corporations in Linda Xiaobo's composition, I wish to acknowledge Richard Grossman's insightful "Revoking Corporate Charters".

And I would like to acknowledge Daniel Robinson's "Aristotle and the Perfect Life" from *The Great Ideas of Philosophy, 2nd Edition* for insight into the concept of *eudaimonia* used in Spencer Galloway's composition.

Non-public-domain quotations:
Excerpt from *Peeling the Onion* by Guenter Grass. Copyright 2006 by Steidl Verlag, Gottingen. English translation copyright 2007 by Houghton Mifflin Harcourt Publishing Company. Used by permission of Houghton Mifflin Harcourt Publishing Company. All rights reserved.

"If I Should Fall Behind" by Bruce Springsteen. Copyright 1992 Bruce Springsteen (ASCAP). Reprinted by permission. International copyright secured. All rights reserved.

Excerpt from *Alina* CD insert by Arvo Paert. Copyright 1999 by ECM Records/Verlag GmbH, Graefelfing. Used by permission of ECM Records/Verlag. All rights reserved.

Made in the USA
Lexington, KY
08 December 2013